THE
LAST

THE
LAST

A NOVEL

HANNA JAMESON

ATRIA BOOKS

New York London Toronto Sydney New Delhi

ATRIA
BOOKS

An Imprint of Simon & Schuster, Inc.
1230 Avenue of the Americas
New York, NY 10020

Originally published in Great Britain in 2019 by Viking

First Atria Books hardcover edition April 2019

ATRIA B O O K S and colophon are trademarks of Simon & Schuster, Inc.

For information about special discounts for bulk purchases, please contact Simon & Schuster Special Sales at 1-866-506-1949 or business@simonandschuster.com.

The Simon & Schuster Speakers Bureau can bring authors to your live event. For more information or to book an event, contact the Simon & Schuster Speakers Bureau at 1-866-248-3049 or visit our website at www.simonspeakers.com.

Interior design by Laura Levatino

Manufactured in the United States of America

10 9 8 7 6 5 4 3 2 1

Library of Congress Cataloging-in-Publication Data

Names: Jameson, Hanna, author.
Title: The last / Hanna Jameson.
Description: First Atria Books Hardcover edition. | New York : Atria Books, 2019.
Identifiers: LCCN 2018038274 (print) | LCCN 2018039163 (ebook) | ISBN 9781501198847 (ebook) | ISBN 9781501198823 (hardcover : alk. paper) | ISBN 9781501198830 (pbk. : alk. paper)
Subjects: | GSAFD: Suspense fiction.
Classification: LCC PR6110.A495 (ebook) | LCC PR6110.A495 L37 2019 (print) | DDC 823/.92—dc23
LC record available at https://lccn.loc.gov/2018038274

ISBN 978-1-5011-9882-3
ISBN 978-1-5011-9884-7 (ebook)

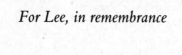

For Lee, in remembrance

New antagonists will forever rise and step into the arena, and piece after piece will crumble off our beautiful world, as though it were an ancient ruin through whose decaying walls the wind and rain whistle. Every day another piece will crumble off, until nothing but a heap of stones marks the place where it once stood, in better days. And we take part in the cruel game, under the illusion that we can bring it to a happy conclusion. It saddens me to think what the end will be.

—Hans Keilson, *The Death of the Adversary*

OBSERVATIONS FROM L'HÔTEL SIXIÈME, SWITZERLAND

sensitized to the imagery by too many movies. Watching a whole city be vaporized like that seemed too fast, and too quiet.

A plane crashed in the outskirts of Berlin, and we knew Berlin was gone only because someone in the plane had uploaded a video of their going down. Dust in the engines, maybe. I can't remember what she was saying; she was crying and wasn't speaking English. It was probably just good-bye.

Breaking: Nuclear Weapon Detonates over Washington, Hundreds of Thousands Feared Dead.

Breaking: Canadian Prime Minister Calls for Calm as Nuclear Attack Hits US.

Breaking: US without Government as Nuclear Bomb Devastates Washington.

Maybe I was lucky to be watching the end of the world online instead of living it, reacting to an explosion or a siren announcing one.

We're not gone yet. This is the third day, and the Internet is down. I've been sitting in my hotel room watching what I can see of the horizon from my window. If anything happens, I'll do my best to describe it. I can see for miles over the forest, so when it's our turn I imagine I'll have some warning. And it's not like I have anyone to say good-bye to here.

I can't believe I didn't reply to Nadia's text. I can't believe I thought I had time.

I figure I should keep writing things down. The clouds are a strange color, but I'm not sure if that's just me being in shock. They could be normal clouds.

I've also started checking off the days since we last had sunlight or rain. So far it's been five.

The likelihood of Armageddon appearing on our horizon seems smaller now, but with the Internet gone and our cell phones refusing to make any connections, we have no idea what's going on in the wider world. Either way, I'm not spending the majority of my time keeping watch at my window anymore. I need to eat.

I spoke to a few acquaintances down in the restaurant, where some of the staff are still providing food. They're going to leave on foot. I'm going to wait until someone comes for us or an official procedure for evacuation is announced. We have no way of knowing when that will be. But someone will come eventually.

you always know what to say when I'm feeling like this. I feel bad about how we left it. Love you."

I hadn't replied to her crisis of faith because I thought I could get away with the delay. She knew the time difference meant that I was probably asleep. I wanted to give it some thought and reply in the morning with something measured and reassuring. There was still a need for excellent journalism, she could still make a difference . . . something like that. An email might be better.

We all thought we had time. Now we can't send emails anymore.

A strange noise erupted from one of the tables, a shrill exclamation. The woman didn't say anything, just cried out.

I looked up to see her sitting with her partner—I assume—and staring at her phone.

Like everyone else in the room, I thought she had just become over-excited by a message or a photo and returned to my book, but within seconds she added, "They've bombed Washington!"

I hadn't even wanted to go to this damn conference.

I can't entirely remember what happened in the hours that followed, but as I started scrolling through my own phone, the push notifications and social media timelines, I realized that Nadia had been right. It played out exactly as she had feared it would. In fact, the headlines are almost all I can remember at the moment.

Breaking: Nuclear Attack on Washington in Progress. Story Developing.

Breaking: 200,000 Fatalities Estimated, Say Experts.

Breaking: Confirmed: President and Staff among Dead in Nuclear Explosion. Awaiting More Information.

Then there was some aerial video from London, and we all watched the buildings vanish into dust in real time, under the iconic pillar of cloud. That was the only footage available, so we watched it over and over. It didn't seem as real as the headlines. Maybe we had all been de-

Nadia once told me that she was kept awake at night by the idea that she would read about the end of the world on a phone alert. It wasn't exactly Kennedy's Sword of Damocles speech, but I remember that moment word for word.

For me, three days ago, it happened over a complimentary breakfast.

I was sitting by the window, looking out onto the encroaching forest and the cleared path around the building leading to the rear parking lot.

There was a hum of chatter from couples and one or two families checking out early. I was the first of the conference attendees to come down. We had all stayed up late drinking the night before, but I tried not to deviate from routine, even if it hurt.

We weren't supposed to be at this hotel. The conference had originally been situated slightly closer to Zurich, farther north, but there had been a fire at the intended venue eight months before. The move had been arranged without much fuss and the location changed to L'Hôtel Sixième, which we had joked was in the middle of nowhere. A pain in the ass to get to.

I was reading the opening chapter of *What We Talk about When We Talk about Photoreconnaissance: The Legal and Performance History of Aerial Espionage*, taking notes for an upcoming lecture series, and my phone was on silent.

A glass of orange juice to my left, and a black coffee. I'd spilled a little on the tablecloth in my eagerness to drink it and get a refill. I was waiting on eggs Benedict.

It's the banality that pains me.

The last text I received from Nadia was sent at eleven thirty the night before. It said: "I think everyone in my line of work is doing more harm than good. How can anyone love this job anymore? I miss you so much;

DAY 6 (2)

That was a lie, what I wrote before. I wanted to come to the conference. I was glad for the time away from Nadia and our children. I might die soon; there's no point in lying about it now.

I'm sorry, Nadia. If you ever read this, I'm so, so sorry.

I'm not sure anybody is coming.

Weather is unchanged.

I went for a walk around the hotel and found the bodies of two people who had hanged themselves in the stairwell. Two men. I don't know who they were. Dylan, the hotel's head of security, helped me bury them out front. A few other people came to stand with us, holding candles in an impromptu vigil.

On our way back from the burial, I asked Dylan if anyone was coming to evacuate us. He said no, probably not, but he didn't want to cause panic. In the meantime, at least we're all following a routine of sorts. We come down for breakfast and dinner, and the rest of the time we hide away in our rooms.

I wonder if the bombing is still going on, whether one will hit us soon. Maybe it would be for the best. It's the not knowing that I can't stand.

Today was the first day I realized that I'm probably never going to see Nadia, Ruth, or Marion again. Or my dad and his wife, my students, my friends. Even the people I knew at the conference have gone. They left.

I feel nauseated. I can't tell if it's radiation poisoning or not.

DAY 18

So far, no one has died of radiation poisoning.

No one is coming for us. There is definitely no evacuation.

Dylan and a couple of other men left the hotel this morning with hunting rifles and returned with deer. The assumption seems to be that we're going to be here for a while. I counted heads this morning in the restaurant and there are twenty-four of us. There are at least two young children, and an elderly couple, one of whom can't hear.

Is this it? I mean, for humanity. Am I the last person alive making notes on the end of the world? I'm not sure whether I would rather already be dead.

Weather unchanged.

We have a doctor in the hotel. I don't know her name yet.

I know that we have a doctor only because a Frenchwoman killed herself in the stairwell. She had tied her shoelaces together and thrown herself down the stairs while holding her baby daughter. Unfortunately, it was too late for the doctor to save the mother, but the baby survived, at least. The Japanese couple have been taking care of her.

I had another talk with Dylan. He was thinking of cutting the gas and electricity to the top floors at the end of the week. He doesn't know how long we have before we run out of either, so he would feel more comfortable saving the electricity to keep our food frozen over the coming months, and the gas for cooking.

Earlier, we had a brief vote on it while we were eating dinner. When Dylan explained the food situation, everyone voted in favor, and the electricity and gas in all our rooms were cut off. It's the beginning of July, but the first thing I noticed was how cold it is now.

DAY 21

Another two gone. The elderly couple stepped out of one of the top-floor windows. It's hard to judge them under the circumstances, but for the ordeal that we all went through cleaning them up and burying them.

I noticed that people have started chatting at mealtimes. No one had really been speaking to one another before now.

I think I recognize one of them, a blond girl. I'm not sure where from, as she wasn't attending the conference. She's the only other American left, as far as I can tell. But I haven't spoken to her. She seems to prefer being alone.

A man named Patrick is staying in a room a few doors down from mine. Sometimes he runs up and down the corridor right outside my door. It's a little disconcerting, hearing the footfalls at night.

The bartender said to me today, "This is nothing like how I thought dying in a nuclear war would be, but I'm glad there's an open bar."

I'm sure I heard guitar music last night. I went for a walk, which was terrifying even by candlelight, and tried to locate the room it was coming from. But I couldn't find it. In fact, I couldn't find anyone. Fourteen floors, almost a thousand rooms, and I didn't see or hear a single person. This place is much larger than I had realized. It makes me feel uneasy.

Dear Nadia,

It's been a month now, and I don't imagine you'll ever read this. I'm not sure you're even still alive. But while there's the slightest chance you could end up reading these notes, you should know, you deserved so much better than me. Maybe you came to realize that toward the end.

I'm sorry that even at the end of the world, I was absent. Late again! I never was any good at being in the right place at the right time. I'm sorry you had to endure so many of my failures. Everything I admire in our children came from you.

Please stay as safe as you can, for as long as you can.

I'm sorry for assuming I had more time.

I love you. I will never stop. I promise that, even if it's not in this life, I will find you again somehow.

Yours,
Jon

I haven't left my room in a while. I've been too depressed to write or see anyone. Today was the first time I went outside in over a week. I took a walk out front.

I asked the bartender, whose name is Nathan, about the sky, and he agreed with me that the clouds are a funny color.

"Rust colored," he said.

The doctor, whose name I now know is Tania, had gone for a run in the surrounding forest. She stopped near us and followed our gaze up to the sky. It's freezing. None of us brought enough winter clothes to adapt to the abrupt end of our summer, and of human civilization.

"Are you talking about the clouds?" she asked.

"Yeah; weird, aren't they?" Nathan said.

"They're orange." She shielded her eyes, even though there wasn't any sun. A habit from the time before.

"I'm glad it's not just me," I said. "I thought it was shock making me see things."

"Do you think it's . . . like, radiation?" Nathan asked.

"No," Tania said with certainty. "That color is probably dust and debris from the explosions. The same thing would happen if an asteroid hit us."

We all watched the orange clouds for a while in silence, before Tania appeared to cool down and start shivering.

"Creepy," she said as she headed inside. "All the trees will start dying soon."

Weather unchanged.

Keep it together.

I'm going to keep writing. I feel like if I don't keep writing, I'll lie down and die.

A NARRATIVE CHRONICLE OF
THE INITIAL POST-NUCLEAR
MONTHS BY POSSIBLY THE
LAST LIVING HISTORIAN,
DR. JON KELLER

The water has been running cloudy and tasted off, so Dylan, Nathan, and I went up to the roof to check the water tanks.

Dylan is one of the only members of staff who hasn't fled. A tall black man in his late forties with an infectious smile and cropped hair, he's become our default leader after the breakdown. He knows the hotel and the surrounding terrain better than anybody, and has worked here for over twenty years. When he speaks English it's in a rich baritone, with barely any trace of an accent. I can't tell where he's from. He may be Swiss.

"Dead birds, probably," he said as we scaled the thirteen flights of stairs. "They must be looking for water too."

I wish it had been dead birds.

I had to stop at the tenth-floor landing and sit on my box of tools to rest. Nathan followed suit.

Dylan shrugged. He didn't bother putting his toolbox down while he waited for us to catch our breath.

"How are you staying so ripped?" Nathan asked.

"Effort."

"That'll do it." He looked at me. "What about you, Jon?"

"Oh, I maintain this impressive lack of physique with absolutely no effort." I looked down at myself. "My job involved a lot of sitting. A lot of intense reading and thinking."

"I don't think I realized how useless we'd all be at this until I tried starting a fire without a lighter." Nathan snorted. "I couldn't believe no one here knew how to start a fire. I mean, I knew *I* couldn't, but I thought someone else might."

"I hated camping," Dylan said. "A vacation isn't a vacation if you can't sit in a robe and drink schnapps in peace."

"I hated camping too," I agreed.

"I hated schnapps," Nathan chimed in.

I smiled. "I think only children like camping. I have two, so I had to go more than I would've liked."

"How much would that have been?" Dylan asked.

"Never."

Nathan laughed. He's a skinny young Australian of mixed race who used to run the hotel bar. His eyes are heavy lidded and his voice strangely monotone, which initially makes him seem apathetic. But he's one of the most animated and upbeat members of the group. He can still make others laugh; a rare occurrence nowadays.

"Didn't know you had kids," Dylan said, finally putting his toolbox down. "I have a daughter."

"How old?" I asked.

"Thirty."

"Where . . . um, where is she?"

"She lived in Munich, with her husband." He didn't need to elaborate on what that meant. "What about yours?"

"They're back in San Francisco with their mom. Six and twelve."

"What were you doing out here? Were you attending the conference?"

"Yeah."

"I thought they all left."

"Yeah, most of the people who tried to get to the airport were my colleagues, acquaintances from other colleges."

"I thought more of them might have come back," Nathan said, standing again. "Once they realized . . . I always wondered, why go at all? We were told that planes weren't taking off and the roads were gonna be insane. Surely more would have come back."

Dylan picked up his toolbox. "No, I think once you're out, you're going to keep moving."

"I was surprised, that's all," said Nathan. "So many of them. Like, where did they think they were gonna catch a plane to?"

I got up and hoisted my box of tools onto my hip, and we started climbing again.

"A lot of people confuse movement with progress," Dylan said. "I knew it was a bad idea, but what were we gonna do, barricade them in? They weren't ready to face any kind of truth."

I leaned against the wall of the stairwell as Dylan got out his set of keys. The air in here was too thick, full of dust and last breaths. It stank. I hated the stairwell, but of course the elevators weren't working anymore; hadn't worked for two months, not since that first day.

"Confusing movement with progress. I wish more people had thought that way before," I said. "Might have avoided all this."

"Jon, you're not wrong. Where were you when people needed a sane guy to vote for?"

I didn't have an answer for him.

We spread out on the roof and took one water tank each. There were four towering cylinders with ladders running up the sides. I tucked a shovel into my belt and started climbing.

I had to take my gloves off to grip the rungs, and it was freezing. I thought I'd known cold before, but it was nothing compared with this. It was constant and invasive. It rearranged the structure of your body and you found yourself walking with your head bent, shoulders hunched, and back rounded all the time.

When I reached the top, I turned and looked out over the forest and down at the grounds. The air was clear but the cloud cover was low, and everything was dusk. On my first night here, I had been able to hear the whir of insect activity from the third floor. Now the trees were silent, browning and dying even though it was August. No birds; total stillness. It took over an hour to get to the nearest city, and the woods went on for miles after that.

I couldn't remember the last time I'd truly seen the sun. I saw it passing behind the clouds sometimes, as though it were dancing just out of reach, visible only as a dull, two-dimensional ornament behind a gray veil.

I wondered which of my colleagues had made it to the airport and what they might have found there. Not all of them had driven away immediately. The ones who had left later, alone or in groups of two or three, and on foot, had severely underestimated the depth of the forest and how cold it would be. I had tried to stop some of them, but people weren't as open to reason as before.

Actually, people hadn't been that open to reason before. That was part of the problem.

A balled fist of emotion rose up into my throat and took hold of it, cutting off my breath.

I pushed it back down.

"You okay with that?" Dylan shouted over to me.

I gripped the lid's handle and my fingers stung, starting to go numb. I couldn't feel my lips or my nose. "Yeah. It's pretty solid. Won't budge!"

"Wait there; I'll come over! This one's fine." Dylan started climbing down.

"No, I think I've got it!" I reached behind me for the shovel and jammed it into the space where the lid of the trapdoor met the tank. Metal clanged and screeched, making my teeth clench. Then the lid began giving way, and I leaned the shovel across the top of the tank to pry it open.

Darkness.

Shifting my weight on the ladder, trying not to think of the height and the cold, I lowered the shovel with my right hand and fished around. The water was so low that I could barely touch the surface, but from what I could see, there weren't any carcasses or debris floating below.

We were going to run out of water soon, I realized.

The dull flutter of panic that had settled permanently into my chest over the last two months intensified, making me light-headed. It happened every time I focused on anything outside the task immediately at hand. I had to lock myself into the present and refuse to acknowledge the past or the future as real. It was the only way to stay sane.

"This one's fine too!" I called, but my voice got lost in the wind.

I heard a sharp, gasped "Fuck!" and looked across the roof in time to see Nathan slip and plummet from the top of the ladder.

Instinct took over and I moved as if to catch him, stepping clean off the rung. I lost sight of Nathan as I fell, hooked my right arm over a rung, and took my whole weight in the crook of my elbow, slamming into the side of the water tank with a bang.

I thought I'd dislocated my shoulder as agony shot across my chest and collarbones. But I hadn't. It held. I pulled myself back to safety with bleeding fingers and saw that I had sent the shovel flying.

Nathan was on the ground but getting to his feet. He was okay. Dylan was next to him, also finding his footing.

I climbed down as fast as I could and jogged across the rooftop.

"What happened? Are you guys okay?"

"There's something in there. I'm not fucking joking." Nathan was inspecting his arms, rolling up his three layers of sleeves. "Tank's almost empty, but there's something in there."

Dylan looked like he had taken a beating. At second glance, it seemed like Nathan had probably landed on top of him.

"It looked like a body," he said.

"A human body?"

"Yeah, I thought it was . . . I don't know, an animal or something. I leaned in to try to hook it out." Nathan went quiet, put a hand to his mouth. "It was small, but it's not a fucking animal; it's got hair. *Girl* hair. Fuck. How would a kid even get up here?"

"A child," Dylan said. "Jesus."

I looked up at the tank. It was over twenty feet tall, easily. Maybe thirty. "Who has the keys to the roof?"

"There's a few, but only staff members have them." Dylan frowned.

Nathan sat on the roof, massaging his forearms and his right ankle. "We need to cut the tank off or get that thing out and clean it. Everyone's . . . shit, everyone's been drinking it. Fuck. Fuck! I'm gonna throw up. I can't believe we've all been drinking that."

I had to rest a hand against the water tank and steady myself. My stomach turned.

Even Dylan looked rattled, but he shook it off faster than me. He said, "We need to open the other tanks up, like way open, and saw the tops off so they can collect rainwater."

"Does it even rain anymore?" I asked.

We looked at one another, but none of us seemed sure. Truth be told, I couldn't remember if I'd seen any rain since day one. That day had been sunny. Nothing about the environment from then on stuck out in my memory. We lived under a constant blanket of cloud, and some days it was a lighter shade of gray than others. That was it.

"Well, it needs to be done. If we don't have weather, there's a lake nearby, and we've got other sources. But first we need to get that kid out of there. Nath, go get a tarp or a sheet of plastic. Get Tania as well. Jon, I'm gonna need the shovel."

I helped Nathan up and he left the roof, returning with a plastic tarp. From the pallid shine on his cheeks I could tell he had been crying.

Dylan took the shovel and scaled the tank with the tarp slung over his shoulder. I was glad he had offered and that we hadn't drawn straws or something. In all honesty, I don't think I could have done it.

As Dylan came slowly back down the ladder, the tiny body wrapped in plastic and tucked into the crook of his arm, another wave of sadness hit me, and this time it almost knocked me flat.

Nathan hung back.

"Girl? Looks about seven or eight, from the size of her. I don't know." Dylan laid the body on the ground. "Where's Tania?"

Nathan's voice didn't come out right the first time, and he had to clear his throat. "She's . . . She's seeing someone else but said we could bring the body down to her room."

"A little kid couldn't have gotten up here by herself," I said, unable to wrench my eyes away. "Someone put her there."

"She might have climbed in looking for—"

"She couldn't have climbed in herself," Dylan cut in. "We're three men, and we struggled to open those lids up."

"How long do you think she's been in there?" I asked.

"I don't know. What do you think?"

"I can't tell."

The body had bloated a little, but she still looked so human to me, the girl. Almost alive, preserved somehow. Her skin was mottled gray and yellow, some bits of green, but there hadn't been much rot. It made sense, given the drop in temperature. The only parts of her that had fallen away were her clothes.

"So she was killed." I said it because I could tell no one else wanted to. "She was murdered."

Nathan started shivering, and it was catching. I wrapped my arms around myself.

Dylan sighed. "Maybe. But let's face it: we don't have a way of finding out who she was. Her parents are going to be long gone. No one here's been talking about a missing girl. Whoever it was, they could have checked out even before all of this started."

"Checked out without their daughter?" I thought of my daughter Marion laughing and running away from the sea at Fort Funston. "That doesn't seem right."

To distract myself from the image, I stepped forward and bent down to gather up the girl, wrapping the crackling plastic tarp around her as though she were sleeping. I didn't notice until I was holding her that my hands were still bleeding. I hadn't been able to feel them for a while.

"I'll carry her down," I said.

She weighed almost nothing.

Tania's the only doctor in the hotel, and we're lucky she was staying here. With our deteriorating nutrition and constant requests for medication (unsurprisingly, most people have asked for antidepressants that we don't have), she's inundated. But you would never know it. She carries herself with a terse pride. Her skin is dark, and at the moment her hair is a purple-tinted Afro, though I've seen its style change from week to week.

During one of our first conversations she told me she had grown up a foster child in England and then Switzerland, but she also had family in Nigeria and Jamaica.

Her boyfriend ran on the first day, taking his chances on the roads against the advice of the public service announcements; he'd also taken their car. She chose not to go with him, and she continues to stand by her decision with a regal silence. She hasn't spoken a word about him since, which is why I can't recall his name.

She looked the child's body over in her makeshift examination room and confirmed that it was indeed a girl—nine years old but on the small side—and that she'd been dead for approximately two months.

I sat in a chair beside the bed—Tania's ersatz examination table—and rubbed my throbbing hands together.

Dylan and Nathan were off searching for heavier tools to carve open the water tanks. It would be a huge operation; likely to take a few days, maybe even a week. I was looking forward to it. Less time to think.

"How did she die?" I asked.

"I can't tell. I'd have to do an autopsy, and I've never done one before, only watched. It's never really been my job."

Unless she becomes animated, which is rare, her voice is quiet, soothing. It might just be professional.

"I can't see any marks."

"Could be deceiving. Water can do weird things to flesh, and you can see the skin has started to split and come away here, and here. But . . . no, I agree, I can't see any marks that would indicate a blow to the head or strangulation. It doesn't look like she's been sexually assaulted either, though that's much harder to tell."

"Are there ways to check that? Now?"

She met my eyes. "Yeah."

I took a breath. "So she died around the time—"

"A couple of months ago, definitely, so maybe just before everything happened, or just after. Bodies decompose more slowly in water—even slower when it's this cold—but there's no way to be certain about her time of death. I'm sure that it's not recent. I'd like to see if there's water in her lungs."

"Wouldn't that be the case anyway?"

She shook her head, speaking without looking at me. "Not unless she went into the tank still breathing."

Tania surveyed the tools she had lined up along the dressing table: a selection of all the hotel's first-aid items, plus some choice pieces of cutlery. I noticed a fish knife and wondered if she'd had to use it yet.

She sighed and rubbed her face. "I wish I had some of my things. That would make this so much easier."

"Make a list; we could look next week."

Dylan had arranged another food expedition: a real one, to the city, rather than a hunt through the forest. He'd estimated that we would start running out of supplies within the next three months. We also needed meds, more so than food. The nearest pharmacy was in a large supermarket that was a significant trek through the woods away, and we couldn't guarantee it hadn't already been looted.

Dylan was in charge, and Tania had volunteered but had been refused; she's too valuable. Patrick Bernardeaux, a fit and practical French dentist, was coming. He spent a lot of his time running. Adam, a serious but strong-looking young Englishman, had volunteered, and so had Rob, a much less serious young Englishman. Tomi, the only other American and a student of history and urban development, was also on board.

"You need to focus on finding everyone's medications."

"If you need scalpels and . . ."

She smirked. "And?"

"Whatever else doctors use." I smiled, then remembered we were sitting in the presence of a dead girl and quelled it. "Seriously—write a list, and I'll have a look. It's not like I'll be the most instrumental part of the team anyway. I'm better with my eyes than—"

"Yeah, we can tell you're not gonna be the muscle of the outfit." She looked me over. "Biked to work three or four times a week, maybe swam a bit, but otherwise spent most of your life bent over books?"

"How can you tell?"

"From how you sit and walk. Eighty percent of the patients I used to see came to me with chronic back and neck pain because of bad posture. You would have been one. A change in lifestyle will be good for your spine, though." She looked away from the table and gestured at me. "What's wrong with your hands?"

"Nothing. I had to take my gloves off to climb, and I'm not a great climber."

She carefully folded the plastic back over the girl, like a mother, and then pulled up a chair. "Let me see."

"They're fine."

"We can't wave things away anymore. We don't have enough antibiotics to risk an infection." She took my hands in hers, turned them over, and surveyed the torn knuckles and raw palms, the bitten nails. "You'll need to keep them clean. God knows what bacteria is lurking around those tanks. No wonder people have been getting sick."

I grimaced.

She went into the bathroom and hesitated. "We're not still getting water from that tank, are we?"

"No, Dylan went to cut it off."

"Good. Come here. I need to use alcohol, so it's going to hurt." She shrugged, leaning her hip against the sink and running a shallow pool of soap and water.

The water was ice-cold. It's hard to articulate how much it weighs on you when everything is always cold. I've known nothing but cold for two months. I washed my hands quickly and sat next to the dead girl again. Tania took my right hand and dabbed a cotton ball in clear alcohol.

"So you were here for the conference?" she said, lapsing into rehearsed small talk to distract me. "What did you do?"

"Historian. I taught at Stanford."

"So where is your accent from?"

"It's southern. I lived in San Francisco for a long time, so the edges wore off."

"What did your wife do?" She nodded at my wedding ring.

"She's . . . Nadia was a journalist. It was tough, especially with the kids. I had a long commute. But we both had to work; rents were so damn high." I smiled suddenly. "Talking about things like rent feels weird."

She laughed. "I think every other conversation I used to have was about rent."

"Or elections."

"Protests. I went to a lot of those."

"Yeah, me too, toward the end." My hand spasmed with a white, burning sensation, and I almost jerked it away. "You weren't kidding when you said it was going to hurt. Wow."

"Well, it was you guys who fucked everything up," she said, deadpan, as if this were my punishment. "We were fine here in Europe. We were just praying you wouldn't do anything stupid. Well, to be fair, the whole world was pretty stupid. We just hoped it wouldn't be *end-of-the-world* stupid."

I grimaced and withdrew my hand, and we both sat for a moment while the alcohol seeped into my knuckles. The world we were talking about seemed—and I apologize for the cliché—like a dream. This—the present—seemed more real than anything that had come before. I felt so awake now, painfully awake compared to how I had lived only two months ago.

"Give me your other hand," she said, beckoning it forth.

"I just need a second."

"Do you want to listen to some music?"

The word provoked a sharp intake of breath, as my own laptop had been dead for weeks and I hadn't been able to convince anyone to let me charge it downstairs. "You have music?"

"Yeah, I've been rationing my battery. I only listen to a song when I feel like . . . To be honest, I only listen to something when I feel like I might go crazy if I don't."

"Yes! I'd love to, if you're sure you want to waste the battery on me."

"It's not a waste."

The last time I had heard music was a week ago, when I caught Nathan sitting on the floor and out of sight behind the bar listening to something. He stopped as soon as I found him, ashamed to have been seen wasting his phone battery on something so frivolous. He let me listen to a song, though. I can't remember what it was, but it was country. I used to hate country, but any music is good now. My standards aren't so high anymore.

He shouldn't have felt guilty when I caught him; those of us who still have working phones know, however much we refuse to admit it out loud, that we're not going to reach anyone on them. I no longer have my phone, but that was only because of my own stupidity.

Tania returned to her chair with an MP3 player, one of those older models, heavy and rectangular, and gave me an earphone. I leaned forward, our heads less than a foot apart, while she took my other hand in her lap and went to work with the cotton balls.

It was the warmest I had felt in weeks. Embarrassingly, I felt like crying and tensed.

"I know," she said. "It creeps up on you. I won't tell if you need to have a moment."

"Doctor-patient confidentiality still stands?"

"Sure, why not?"

"It's beautiful, like a . . ." Pain again, sharp, but I was prepared for it. "Like a waltz. Is it old?"

"*You're* old. This is Rihanna."

"This is Rihanna?"

"Yeah."

"I didn't know Rihanna sounded like this."

"You ever listen to her?"

"Is it possible to give an answer that's less than never?" I managed not to retract my hand, and Tania started wrapping it in minimal bandages. "I turn thirty-eight soon. I might already be thirty-eight."

"I'm winking at forty. That's no excuse."

She finished bandaging my hands, and we waited for the song to end. A shiver ran across my shoulders, but it was nothing to do with the cold. It was pleasant. The track ended, and she took the earphone back.

"Let me know if you need any help with the autopsy," I offered.

"Really?"

"Yeah."

"Thanks; I might take you up on that. I'll try to get it done today. It'll become unhygienic now that she's out of water, so she should be buried fast." She stood up and lifted the edge of the plastic to take another look. "In fact, can we move her to another room, just for my morning appointments? This won't boost morale."

"Sure."

She looked directly at me, which was rare. "You're one of the most helpful people here, you know? You volunteer for everything. I wish everyone here were like that."

I shrugged. "What other purpose do we have?"

"There isn't anything else wrong with you, is there? Any symptoms?"

"No."

She looked me up and down but didn't press me.

I'd had a mild toothache for a day or two, in the back right-hand side of my mouth. But I didn't mention it. I didn't want to cause her any further hassle. I was also worried she'd suggest removing the tooth, and I didn't want to fast-forward to more pain.

I went to take a nap instead. At some point, I'll try to find out some more about the girl.

History is only the sum of its people, and, as far as I know, we could be the last ones.

I should tell you a bit about the hotel. L'Hôtel Sixième has fourteen stories. Two or three of the top floors are sealed off for a renovation that will now never be finished. Once, the outside had been gold, and the grand lettering just over the entrance had been gold too. It attracted a lot of wealthy visitors throughout the eighties and nineties, who made use of its conference rooms. But it wasn't gold anymore, and visitors had been sparse in the last decade. There's a fire escape, which was added during an attempted renovation a few years back. Half the rooms were modernized around the same time to use key cards. Others use old-fashioned keys.

When the electricity was cut from the upper floors, those of us who'd stayed—almost thirty at first, and now around twenty—migrated from the renovated rooms to the older rooms with keys and dead bolts for our safety. Doors that operated with key cards relied on electromagnets to stay locked, so no one has been able to shut them again.

As for the people who are still here, I noticed that Dylan has been keeping a register. It's so that he can keep track of everyone and note their presence every morning. I've copied his list down here for my own reference, along with all nationalities and occupations I know of. The only name not on there was, obviously, Dylan's. I've added him at the end.

> Nathan Chapman-Adler—Australian, bartender (staff)
> Tania Ikande—English-Swiss, doctor
> Lauren Bret—French, unknown occupation
> Alexa Travers—French, unknown occupation
> Peter Frehner—French, unknown occupation
> Nicholas van Schaik—Dutch, unknown occupation
> Yuka Yobari—Japanese, unknown occupation

Haru Yobari—Japanese, unknown occupation

Ryoko Yobari—Japanese, minor

Akio Yobari—Japanese, minor

Chloë Lavelle—French, minor

Patrick Bernardeaux—French, dentist

Coralie Bernardeaux—French, dentist

Jon Keller—American, historian

Tomisen Harkaway—American, postdoc student

Adam Warren—English, unknown occupation

Rob Carmier—English, student

Mia Markin—Russian-Swiss, receptionist (staff)

Sasha Markin—Russian-Swiss, waiter (staff)

Sophia Abelli—Swiss, chef (staff)

Dylan Wycke—Swiss, head of security (staff)

Tomi, the American student—who was based in Leiden—told me she was writing a thesis on the hotel. She had been living here for a month before the end, interviewing staff, taking photographs. She is tall, tanned, athletic, beautiful, but in an aggressive and hard-edged way that makes me uncomfortable. I think she deliberately tries to make people feel uncomfortable; that's how she keeps the upper hand.

Or I might simply be trying to validate my own reaction to her by implying that it's somehow universal. Don't take me at my word.

I went to ask her some questions about the hotel before we buried the child. She knows more about the history of this place than I do, and I want to give these records a sense of place. If anyone reads this, I want you to know we were here.

We talked in the bar for a while. I noticed that her teeth were still perfect.

"Noticed you're writing as well," Tomi said, holding her own folder of notes. "Makes you feel more normal, doesn't it?"

"It might be important."

"No one's going to read it," she countered.

"We don't know that."

"We do, though." She crossed her legs. "Where's your accent from, Mississippi?"

"I grew up in Mississippi, but I lived in San Francisco."

"That explains it. I'm from Ohio. I think I've heard of you. Did you give a guest lecture at UC Berkeley?"

She was right. I had.

"I worked at Stanford, so probably."

"I knew it! I did my undergrad at Berkeley."

"I might have done something on the—"

"The failed U-2 flight."

For some reason, I was irritated by the fact she remembered me. "Yes, that sounds right."

She laughed. "Hey, a lot of people were talking about how cute you were, but from what I can remember, you made some great points as well."

I didn't say anything.

She laughed again. "Oh, chill out. Come on, then, ask your questions. Don't just sit there radiating scholarly disapproval."

"What interested you about the history of the hotel?"

"Well, you know, this hotel has a pattern of suicides and unexplained deaths. Even a couple of murders in the eighties and nineties. The most recent owners are pretty shady, hard to pin down. The place has been sold and resold a lot due to the bad press. Also because a famous serial killer stayed here once. My work, well . . . I was planning to spend my time in the hotel mostly writing biographies of the people who died here."

"A serial killer stayed here?"

"He didn't actually kill anyone here. This was just where he was caught."

She spoke fluently, with a robotic amount of eye contact. She'd have made a great news anchor, or maybe a successful TV historian.

I reached for a drink that wasn't there and quickly retracted my bandaged hand.

"What happened?" she asked.

"I was helping Dylan with something."

"What, Fight Club?"

"Who's the hotel's current owner?"

She rolled her eyes. "There were two: Baloche Braun and Erik Grosjean. Braun bought Grosjean out after he'd been trying to sell for a while but no one wanted to buy. I couldn't find out much about Grosjean—or either of them, really—but Braun was from old oil money, son of a big deal. Most of his ventures quietly failed before he bought this place."

"The unexplained deaths and murders," I said. "What happened? I mean, how did they die?"

"There were a lot of drownings—people dying in their tubs or walking into the lake, never to be seen again. A lot of ODs—a surprising amount—and some hunting accidents. A lot of husbands and boyfriends snapping one day and killing their wives and girlfriends, though at the time it was barely considered newsworthy."

I reached for a drink again and found empty space. We were the only two people in the bar, sitting in plush green armchairs surrounded by mahogany and gold, the finery fraying at the edges. Most people stayed in their rooms during the day, for warmth. Only those of us still concerned with organization, with structure and company, were found wandering the hotel or congregating in the bar and restaurant. I badly wanted a drink, but Nathan was hoarding the alcohol stash.

"I might have what you're looking for." Tomi took out a hip flask and put it on the table between us.

"What is it?"

"Do you care?"

I unscrewed the cap and waved it under my nose. Whiskey.

"Did you steal this?"

"When everything went to hell, I knew I was going to be staying until the end. I'm not dumb, despite appearances." She gestured at her face and her long blond hair. "So while everyone was running around trying to contact loved ones and catch planes that were never going to take off, I collected things I knew I would need."

I realized she might have more antibiotics.

"That's an extremely calm response to the end of the world."

"It's shock that makes people stupid. I wasn't shocked. I also don't think it's the end of the world. We're being pretty civilized, don't you think?"

"You didn't try to contact anyone?"

She raised her eyebrows. "Like I said, I'm not dumb. I might need the battery life for survival at some point. If your loved ones were in or even near any of the major cities, they're already gone."

My breath caught, and I took a drink to avoid replying. I didn't even taste that first gulp.

I was prepared to bet that she had voted for him.

She recrossed her legs. "Sorry. I know some of you haven't come to terms with that yet."

I put the flask down, knowing she wasn't sorry.

"Did you and your wife have kids?" she asked, her eyes darting down toward my ring and up again to my face.

"Yes," I said.

"Sorry."

I wanted to flip the damn table and throttle her. It was a surge of rage like I hadn't experienced for months, and I hated the base part of myself it erupted from. She could see it as well. She watched it cross my face and stared me down with icy symmetry. Instead, I picked up the flask again and knocked back a good amount of whiskey.

The burn that fell down the back of my throat and into my empty stomach was soothing. I shut my eyes for a second, and it neutralized the anger.

I wanted to ask her if she got off on provoking people, or if the reason she hadn't tried to call anyone was because she didn't love anything, but I didn't want to give her confirmation that she'd rattled me.

"Whoever dies second," she said, "out of the two of us should combine the other's work into their project."

"Why would I do that?"

"Wow, you're confident I'm gonna go first!"

I hadn't thought about it like that. It had just come out.

"Between two unreliable narrators we might get one half-accurate account," she said.

"I'm not being unreliable. It's my duty to be as objective as possible."

"Men always think they're being objective and that everyone else has some kind of special interest. I'd love to read your work, to see how hard you're trying to convince your future readers you're a swell guy." She shrugged. "Anyway, it was just an idea."

I bit. "And you're not trying to do that?"

"What?"

"Convince your future readers you're a good person?"

"I'll care even less what people think of me when I'm dead. Let me guess: your description of me for this interaction will mention I'm blond, blue-eyed, and hot, because male writers have to do that by *law*. This will be followed by an acknowledgment of your irrational dislike of me, and how that makes me *unattractive* in your eyes, and then an attempt to dilute that reaction by universalizing it or by referencing your own bias. You think this will convey that you're enlightened and trustworthy. In reality, it'll betray that you're too self-conscious of your legacy. You have 'This is my moment' written all over you."

She did drag a smile out of me at that point, I admit.

I asked, "So, for comparison, how have you described me?"

Looking at her notes. " 'Stick up his ass. Young Harrison Ford–ish but way more of a dweeb. Vibe of someone who didn't get laid in high school because he was a nerd, and/or from a religious upbringing.' I'll write it into a paragraph later. Come on, how well have I nailed you?"

"Not even close," I lied.

I made an excuse to leave, because I wanted to help Tania with the autopsy. As I walked out, I looked back, and Tomi was sitting cross-legged in her chair, already scribbling away. It struck me that at some point we might run out of pens, and it was likely she had already thought of that. She probably had a stash of them.

———

I threw up less than a minute and a half into the autopsy and had to leave. It wasn't my proudest moment. I heard Tania laughing as I hunched over her sink, supporting myself on trembling arms.

In my defense, I can't even find the words to describe what the smell was like after Tania sawed down the middle of the girl's chest. She cut right down to the navel and then peeled two great flaps of skin back. I had never seen a human body look more like waste.

I sat on a chair outside the room, taking deep breaths. Dylan and Nathan were waiting downstairs to help bury the body when we were done.

After about an hour or so, Tania emerged, flushed. Her gloves were covered in grime and blackened blood. She seemed tired today.

"Okay, this isn't my area of expertise," she said, rubbing her forehead with the back of her wrist. "I can't work out exactly what killed her, but looking at her lungs—specifically the lack of water in her lungs—I think it seems unlikely that she drowned. I can't do a tox screen, so . . . it's possible she was drugged. Maybe it was a chemically induced cardiac arrest or something like that. I can't see any significant trauma to her head or throat. The only thing that's certain is that she can't have gotten onto the roof and into the tank on her own. Other than that, it's too hard to tell for sure. I can only tell you what's likely. Sorry."

"Don't be sorry. That tells us she was probably dead when she went into the tank."

She smiled, taking off the gloves. "You're not going to find out who did this. You know they're long gone."

"Maybe. Maybe not." I stood up. "Are we okay to take her?"

"Yeah, I've sewn her up."

"Thanks for this. You didn't have to do it. You've got the living to deal with."

"It's my job. Believe me, I'm not trying to be a hero." She took off the poncho she was wearing, looked at it, and went to stuff it into a trash bag.

I looked beyond her through the door at the body on the bed and tried to conjure a passage of Scripture, or any religious text, to make sense of the tiny lifeless hands that I wanted to take in my own because I couldn't stand the idea of how scared she must have been. A sentence from Graham Greene came to mind instead: "Why, after all, should we expect God to punish the innocent with more life?"

"Are you okay?" Tania had returned to the doorway and was eying me with concern. "You're grinding your teeth. Not getting any pains, are you?"

"No, I'm fine." My hand went to my jaw as I lied, circling the aching tooth. "Stress."

I knew I would have to ask Tomi where she was stashing her toothpaste. Mine was down to the last granules, and I was only using it every other day. It bothered me because it meant speaking to her again, and I had her pinned as a ruthless trader.

She had also been right on the money with her biographical assessment. That bothered me as well.

We took the girl downstairs and buried her out front, with the rest of them. Each grave is marked with a small wooden cross; just little pieces of wood chopped up and strung together. Nothing fancy. Names written across them in permanent marker.

The flowers left outside are fake, from our rooms. They're wrapped in white ribbons that say, "Enjoy your stay with us!"

I persuaded Dylan to give me the keys to the offices behind the front desk and set off on my investigation. Earlier today, he double-checked that the tank we found the body in was still cut off, so that's some small mercy. We're no longer drinking that water.

I shut the door behind me and pulled out every folder and ledger I could find, piled them on a desk, and sat down. It was quiet. This felt familiar.

First I searched for a list of reservations, starting around two weeks before everything ended—one week before our conference attendees would have started checking in. We accounted for a lot of bookings, and it had still been relatively early in the summer, not peak time for vacations. I highlighted the name of every reservation made with a child, removed the ones who had ordered a crib for the room, and ended up with a short list of six families.

Then came the hard part. I went back up to the roof, but this time I took Nathan, a length of rope, a change of clothes, and a flashlight.

"What do you think you're going to find?" Nathan asked as we climbed again.

"Maybe nothing. Mostly I just want to see if there's any evidence we missed the first time."

"Giving yourself a detective project—I like it."

"Don't you feel we should find out who she was? She was murdered. The person who did it could still be here."

"Really, though?"

I looked over my shoulder, and I could see he was skeptical. "Why not?"

"Most people cleared out right away. If you'd just committed a murder, would you really hang back in a small group and risk being found out?"

I unlocked the door to the roof. Luckily it was warmer today. No wind. I didn't have to squint or grimace against a chill.

"Think about it," I said as he helped me tie the rope around my waist. "Why wouldn't you? The world ended. The police aren't coming, probably not ever again. It's not like they have much reason to think the body would even be found. To them, they're in the clear. Doesn't that make you feel a bit . . . uneasy?"

He made a face. "No. Is that bad?"

"So what, right and wrong just aren't a thing anymore?"

"No, it's just . . . unless people start getting murdered now, I'm not gonna lose sleep over it."

"Someone *has* been murdered."

"Okay, okay, I'm here, aren't I!" He raised his hands. "Come on, let's get this over and done with. I've got some weed, and I think you need it."

I climbed up the side of the tank, and the trapdoor opened a little easier than last time. I looked down into the dark and checked that the rope around my waist was tight. I hadn't given much thought to how I would get down. The only method that had occurred to me was to somehow rappel in an amateur fashion, which was the only fashion I knew.

"Are you sure you can take my whole weight?" I called.

"Probably. Let's give it a shot."

Suddenly, I had no confidence in my plan. I had no idea how to get into that tank and then back out again. I took the flashlight and shined it around, but I couldn't see much in the water. If her clothes were down there, any form of ID or evidence, I would have to go down into the water to get them.

"Are you sure?" I called again.

"We can only try."

"You keep saying that, but it's, like, thirty feet, Nath. If I jump and you drop me, I might knock myself out!"

"If I fuck up, I promise I'll go get Dylan and his strong, manly arms will pull you out!"

I glanced down and Nathan shimmied at me, making me laugh.

"Okay," I said. "Just give me a sec, I need to . . ."

"It's cool; take all the time you want. It's not like I've got an appointment to get to."

I climbed onto the lid of the tank and placed my feet on either side of the trapdoor. Shining the flashlight in again, I noticed there was a maintenance ladder running down the inside wall, one that wasn't immediately apparent when you approached from the other side.

"Hey, Nath—it's okay, there's a ladder here!"

"That's great, mate, because I'll be honest, I can't hold an adult man in the air—you were always going down!"

"You're an asshole!"

"I am, yes."

Taking a few deep breaths, I lowered myself through the opening and felt for purchase on the first rung. I put the flashlight in my mouth, braced my hands against the rim of the tank, and walked my feet down until I could grip the top rung. I paused, took the flashlight in my right hand, and descended.

The rope around my waist went taut, then slackened as Nathan let it run through his hands.

"You're doing great!" I heard him shout.

I knocked on the side of the tank. It was surprisingly spacious. If the water was emptied out, it would make for a good bunker.

The black water was pungent, and it smelled worse the lower I got. I stopped just shy of the surface and tried to judge how far down I had come and how deep the water would be. The rope was too slack. I banged on the side of the tank twice, and Nathan pulled it tight.

"This is fine," I muttered to myself, looking at the contents of the tank, the surface totally still and undisturbed. "This is fine. You can do this. Everything's fine."

The rungs carried on down into the water. I stepped into it, and the freezing water filled my shoes instantly, making me grimace. It was so cold it hurt. Catching my breath, I took another step down, and another, the water rising until I was in up to my waist. I stifled the urge to vomit and stepped down again until I felt myself hit the bottom. In up to my chest, I held the flashlight over my head, teeth literally chattering from the cold.

Realizing I wasn't going to find much walking around one-handed, I balanced the flashlight on one of the metal rungs and swished my feet through the water, feeling for the sensation of fabric against my legs. Holding my breath, I ducked both my arms under and felt around the inside of the tank for the end of the pipe that funneled water into the hotel. It was hard to locate without the feel of the suction to guide me.

The stench was intense. It smelled like chicken stock left in the fridge for too long, with a sweet, tangy edge, like rotting apricots. I retched, but nothing came up.

My foot slipped sideways into an indentation, and I plunged both hands into the water again to feel around the end of the pipe. The water rushed up to my neck, making me gasp, and then I ducked my whole head under as I felt some sodden fabric caught in the opening. I wrenched it out and slung it over my shoulder. Exhilarated by the discovery, I went back under the water again to feel around for anything else. I grasped something soft, like a small animal, and involuntarily recoiled away from it.

Forcing myself to look, I pulled it out of the water and saw that it *was* an animal. Turning it over, horrified, I was relieved to find it was a stuffed one, a rabbit.

Weighed down by my clothes and with my feet completely numb, I returned to the ladder. Toy bunny under my arm and the piece of clothing over my shoulder, I climbed toward the light. I felt three times heavier on my way out.

"Shit, did you find something?" Nathan called as soon as I was visible.

I braced myself against the caustic air striking my soaking clothes and skin. Wordlessly, I dropped the piece of clothing and the toy and tried to focus on getting down without slipping. As I landed on the rooftop again, Nathan bundled a towel around me, saying, "Mate, you smell like a sewer. That was crazy."

I couldn't speak. I untied the rope with difficulty, stripped out of my wet clothes, and tried to get dry before pulling on the change of pants, shirt, and shoes I had brought with me. Three pairs of socks took a long time to feel like they were making any difference.

We gathered everything into a dripping pile, without taking much notice of what I had found, and went straight down to the basement level without talking. There, Nathan switched on the boilers for half an hour so I could sit near them and regain my sense of self. It was a kind gesture.

Most of the power remaining came from hydroelectrics, but we had no way of knowing when it might cut out. If it did, we still had some juice from the backup generator, but it was finite.

Wrapped in a fur throw he had brought from his bar stash, surrounded by boxes of glasses and kitchenware and some alcohol that had been locked away, I nodded at the piece of sodden fabric on the ground next to my drying clothes.

"Looks like a dress."

Nathan sat next to me, rolling us a couple of joints. "Pressure from the pipe would have kinda . . . sucked her out of it. We're lucky it didn't end up in the pipes. We'd never have found it."

I reached out and pushed my clothes farther to one side to get a better look at the girl's dress. It was yellow and white, checkered, with an old-fashioned white lace collar. It was the sort of thing you'd dress your daughters in if you wanted them to look like little dolls. I wouldn't have bought it for Marion. Ruth wouldn't have been caught dead in it.

Checking the label, I saw black marker that had been almost entirely washed out. It could have been a name beginning with an "H" or an "M" or an "N." I couldn't be certain.

I sat back against the wall near the boiler and kicked the dress away across the floor.

Nathan handed me a joint, and we smoked in silence for a while.

"And there weren't any marks on her when Tania looked?"

"Nothing." I thought back. "She said it didn't look as though she'd drowned. She said it was possible she was drugged or incapacitated in some way before going into the water."

He shuddered. "Gnarly."

"I can't believe you don't seem bothered that this guy could still be here."

"What makes you think it's a guy? And I am bothered, I'm just . . ." He exhaled. "My barometer for bothered is a bit skewed right now."

"We can't stop caring about right and wrong just because—"

"It's the end of the world?"

I countered. "We're still here."

The pot was starting to go to my head. It was pleasant.

Nathan's expression was sad. "I can't believe I'm probably gonna die here. Like, starving to death or something. It's fucked."

"We're going to be hungry after smoking these. We didn't factor that in."

He snorted. "Okay, that was actually funny."

"Am I not usually?"

"No, it's just that you're older than my mates."

"How did you end up working here?" I asked.

I had seen his reaction upon finding the body, so I didn't really think he had anything to do with the murder. All the same, I wanted to record as much biographical information about the people here with me as I could.

"I haven't even been here that long. Like, six months. But it's such a weird story, you wouldn't believe it if I told you."

"I bet I would. Everything is weird now."

"It's about my dad. Well, stepdad. But yeah, my dad. That's why I'm here."

"That doesn't sound weird."

"Oh, mate." He grinned. "You have no idea."

The boiler let out a bang, reminding Nathan that it was probably time to turn it off, but the cellar remained warm for a long time, so we sat there smoking for a few more hours while the clothes dried out.

So he told me, while we were both high. It was a remarkable and bizarre story, and I wouldn't do it justice if I tried to paraphrase it in my own words. I asked him to write it down himself, and he said he would. I'll attach it when I can.

This morning I asked Dylan if I could use his set of master keys to search the hotel. He was about to go for a run to the lake and back—a distance that he estimated to be about three miles—and he seemed more interested in stretching outside the entrance than entertaining my newfound sense of purpose.

"It'll take you days to go through the rooms alone, Jon."

"I know, but . . . if someone in the hotel took a girl up to the roof and—"

"You know they're gone."

"We don't know that!"

He pulled each of his arms across his chest, taking deep, measured breaths. "You could probably find a better way to spend your energy."

"Have you even searched this place yet?"

"For what?"

"I don't know. Anything useful."

"Not yet."

"Well, then, let me do it. Saves you the task of going into hundreds of rooms yourself, and I might find extra food, weapons, medicine . . ."

At that point, I suspected he mostly wanted me to go away.

He said, "You can't tell anyone you have the keys."

"The killer must have had a set. To get onto the roof. But you said only staff have them."

"If you think she died around that day—that first day—a bunch of keys wouldn't have been hard to steal." He sighed. "But you can't tell anyone you have master keys."

"I won't."

"I mean it—not any of them."

"Why?"

A look; stretching his hamstrings. "I don't know them."

I thought of Tomi and her collection of unknown items and understood what he meant.

I asked, "So why are you trusting me?"

He shot me a grim smile. "Because I need you to volunteer for the next food expedition."

Dylan handed me the heavy set of keys, eyed the forest—loud today, disturbed by the strong wind—and ran off, vanishing into the trees.

———————

I returned to my list of reservations. Only one family I'd circled, aside from the Yobaris, had requested a room made suitable for children. The Luffmans, in room 377.

There was a draft coming from somewhere, whipping through the hotel. I zipped up my coat and climbed the stairs. I rarely came to this floor, even when walking around. The Yobaris lived here, and Sophia, who had been the hotel's chef and still, miraculously, continued to make all our food.

I think a few of the young women lived on the same floor also, maybe comforted by the presence of the Yobaris' two children and the baby they had adopted from the late Florence Lavelle. The women were Mia, a Russian-Swiss girl who had formerly worked in housekeeping and more recently behind the front desk; Lex (Alexa), a French girl whom I have never spoken to; and Lauren, another French girl I have never spoken to.

Mia has a twin brother, Sasha, who was also a member of staff. To my knowledge, he still sleeps in staff quarters on the first floor, next door to Dylan. Aside from Patrick, I'm not sure where the rest of the men are. We're more scattered, whereas the women have grouped together.

I went to 377 and let myself in. The room smelled occupied, but not by death, thank God. There were a couple of huge suitcases on the floor at the foot of the bed. The closet doors were open, exposing bare hangers. There was a pack of cigarettes on one of the bedside tables, and, I'm embarrassed to admit, I pocketed those first.

It looked like the Luffmans had been packing, which begged the question: Why hadn't they taken all their stuff with them?

I thought back to my own actions on that day. I couldn't exactly claim some rational high ground; I had been a shocked mess. It was entirely plausible that the family had fled the hotel without all their luggage, swept up by the panic. They could have taken a lighter bag and left the heavy suitcases here.

I started and steadied myself against the dresser, as something like a myoclonic jerk spasmed through my body. It happens whenever I recall that day in any detail. The only sensation I could grasp at that moment was a memory of sitting against a wall on the floor of the hotel lobby, no vision, just clutching my phone to my chest.

I sat on the Luffmans' bed and thought I was going to cry, but I managed to keep it together. It had been a while—too long—and the urge to lose control scared me. I didn't know what else I might end up doing if I gave in to it.

Pulling myself together, I crouched by the half-packed cases and started going through them.

"What are you doing?"

"Fuck!" I stood up, losing my balance momentarily.

It was Sophia, the chef. She was a tall and very pale redhead in her mid-thirties, with an aquiline nose and a stern, proud demeanor. I think she used to speak Swiss French, but, like the rest of the hotel staff, mostly speaks English now, because that's what most of us speak. She made us feel suitably bad about it.

"How did you get in here?" she asked.

"Dylan gave me his keys," I said, immediately regretting it. "Though I'd appreciate it if you didn't mention that to anyone."

Her eyes narrowed. "Why?"

"I'm investigating something. Dylan didn't want too many other people to know. I'm sure he trusts you, though. He knows you."

I don't know why I began acting so guilty. I suppose Sophia made me nervous. Not surprisingly, she didn't look impressed with either of my answers, and I sighed.

"Look, can you shut the door?"

"Why?"

I spread my hands—*please*—and she did as I asked.

"You know about the body in the water tank?" I said.

"Yes, Dylan told me yesterday. I think he's telling everyone separately, to keep things quieter."

"Well, it was a little girl, a guest here. Tania did an autopsy on the body and the cause of death was inconclusive, but it looks like the girl might have been murdered before going into the water tank, maybe before . . . all of this happened."

"Who was she?"

"I'm not sure; I'll have to see if I can access the booking forms on the database. But that depends on whether the hotel stores its bookings on a system that doesn't need Internet access."

She paused, scrutinizing me. "So . . . what are you doing in here?"

"Oh, yeah. I worked out who she might have been by going through the hotel records. I think her name was Harriet Luffman. This is where they were staying. I thought I should at least try to find out what happened to her."

"You think the murderer is still in the hotel?"

"Maybe."

"They will not be."

"How do you know?"

"If you were a murderer, would you have stayed?"

I frowned. "I'd stay if I thought no one could ever find out who I was, yeah."

Another pause, then a shrug. "I see your point. What are you looking for?"

"I don't know yet."

"I'll help."

With a businesslike expression, she moved past me and fully unzipped the other case, which was full of adult clothes.

I returned to the case next to me, about to ask her a question, when she addressed me instead.

"I've noticed you're writing things down," she said. "Why is that? Are you keeping a diary?"

"It's not a diary; more of a historical account, written in real time."

"Was that your job before? You were with the conference?"

"Yeah, I was a historian."

"So are you interviewing people? Looking for stories?"

"Not just stories, I'm not a journalist—"

"You say 'journalist' like it's a bad thing."

I laughed. "Well . . ."

It was a good idea, though, interviewing people. Nathan had already offered me a story. Why not everyone else? It would give me a better sense of everyone who was still here, why they stayed when others didn't. Someone might even remember something that would provide me with a lead.

"I've worked at this hotel for four years," she said, taking some clothes out, sorting them into piles and checking pockets. "I wasn't here when any of the incidents happened, the murders and suicides."

"Why did you choose to work here?"

"There was a job, there was money. My husband was here."

"He's not here now?"

A look. "No."

She didn't elaborate.

I glanced at her hands and saw that she wasn't wearing a ring. But she had answered with such finality that I didn't ask her anything else about it.

"Did you see or meet this family?"

"I don't remember. I work in the kitchens so I don't have to speak to people."

"I can understand that." I picked up another dress, a child's size, and checked the label inside the collar: H. L.

My ankles were starting to strain from crouching, so I sat cross-legged on the floor.

"This doesn't make any sense," I said.

"Why?"

"We think she was in the water tank before everyone ran. Why didn't her parents alert anyone?"

"Maybe they didn't have time. When we got the news, survival was the only thing most of us were thinking about. Maybe they didn't have time to search for their daughter. Maybe they just had to take their chance."

"No, they wouldn't have left without her." I looked up from the dress. "Do you have kids?"

"No."

"If I knew one of my kids was missing, I'd sooner die looking for them than try to save myself by getting to an airport."

"Even if you thought the world had ended?"

"Especially if I thought the world had ended." My throat became tight, but I continued. "If one of my kids was missing and the world ended, then at least the last thing they'd see would be me trying to find them, protect them. They'd have to know I was at least *trying* to find them."

She tilted her head and joined me sitting on the floor. "Then why did you stay?"

A prickle of guilt again, but a different kind of guilt. "I listened to the announcements. There were no planes. I thought that someone would come eventually. The Red Cross or the army or something."

"Me too."

"Did your husband leave? If you don't mind my asking. Did he leave the hotel?"

She returned to sifting through the suitcase, found a toiletry kit, and said, "Huh; toothpaste."

"There two?"

"Yes. Let's not mention it to anyone. Need a razor?"

"Sure. You need hair products? Got some here."

We swapped a few items and zipped them into toiletry kits. I handed Sophia a makeup bag, and she tried on a new shade of lipstick in a hand mirror before eyeing me over the top of it.

"He owned the hotel," she said.

"Excuse me?"

"My husband. He left the hotel, yes. He owned it." She got up and gathered her things. "Let me know if you find anything else. I need to work."

"Hey, does Tomi know about your husband?" I asked as she opened the door. "She was writing a history of this place."

"Probably."

She seemed unbothered, and disappeared into the corridor. I got to my feet and shut the door behind her.

I'd been holding off on talking to some members of staff because I wasn't sure I would be able to make myself understood, and, truth be told, Sophia was an intimidating presence. I was glad I'd had the chance to meet her and get over that preconception. Maybe I'd thought that because I'd only heard her in the kitchen giving orders, and because she was tall.

She had seemed nonchalant about the dead child, especially for a woman. But then, everyone's perspectives were skewed now. Everything that had happened before—our past lives—barely mattered. We lived day to day and could no longer remember all the people we hated, the things that upset us, made us angry online, Facebook statuses that made us roll our eyes, cute animal videos that made us cry, vendettas against journalists, news anchors, politicians, celebrities, relatives . . . all gone. A girl was murdered, but it had happened before. Before didn't exist anymore. The giant slate of the world was clean. Consequences no longer existed.

I repacked and zipped up both suitcases and carried them back to my room, locking the door behind me. The Luffmans didn't seem to have left any obvious identification, which pointed to their having fled in the direction of the airport without their daughter. All the same, I wanted to take another look without feeling like I was being watched.

I need to write about day one, before too much time passes and my memories of it become too repressed. That's what the mind does with trauma; it erases it, making you relive it occasionally in flashbacks and dreams, sensations of vertigo, hyperventilation, and panic. But the memory itself becomes a work of fiction.

In a sense, I've devoted my whole life to time, even though none of us can be sure what time is. Is it a social construct? An illusion? Is it cyclical? Or parallel? Time feels linear to me, because I have to believe in progress to make sense of the things I study: people. But as I think about it now, time feels more elastic, like an attempt to reach out, to move farther, before an event abruptly snaps you back into place.

So I have to come back to it sometime. I have to get it down, in one shot, so that I never have to remember it again. We're all trying to move away from it, to give ourselves the illusion of progress to stay sane; but sanity isn't going to save us, and there is no distance to be found, not from that day, not until I force myself to write it all down.

It happened at breakfast. A scream. The woman looking at her phone. "They've bombed Washington!"

It would be easy to write that everything from that moment on became a blur, because it did. But this is my clearest memory of what happened next:

I stood up, because my first instinct was to go for that woman's phone. A couple of other people did the same.

The woman was crying, staring at her phone and crying.

I met their eyes across the restaurant—the other people who had stood up—and then I sat back down again, remembering my own phone on the table. One text had made it through.

I wondered if he ended up regretting what was likely the last text he ever got to send.

Someone yelled, "Oh my God!" but I didn't see who.

I left my seat, phone in hand, and sprinted to the lobby. There was a line at the desk, about three people deep. I looked at my phone, at the desk, and at the door. I don't know how long I just stood there, but it was a while. I had no idea what to do, whether I should leave, attempt to call someone, or get more information from the staff. So I just stood there until someone knocked into my shoulder, heading for the exit at full speed.

It startled me into movement. I tried calling Nadia, but the line was busy, or dead. It wasn't connecting, not even ringing. For some reason I tried calling the PhD student who had texted me—Luke—because he was at the top of my call log, but that didn't connect either.

I could feel myself panicking, but I told myself no. I kept telling myself no. It was probably a terrorist attack, yes, but we'd had those before. Selfishly, I told myself that I didn't have family or friends in DC anyway. It was bad, but everyone I knew was fine. It could be another 9/11, but everyone I knew was fine.

Backing away from the front desk, where people were arguing loudly in an incomprehensible mass of languages, I opened up the social media apps on my phone and leaned against the wall of the lobby, out of the way. I considered going back to my table. Then I saw a headline.

Breaking: Nuclear Attack on Washington in Progress. Story Developing.

It was like a cold hand had gripped my neck. My jaw went numb. A shiver racked my whole body, from my stomach up to my shoulders and along my back. My hands started shaking. I couldn't read. All I could see was the word "nuclear."

I caught myself. It couldn't actually be nuclear. Not in that way. Nuclear meant the end. They were probably just using the word for clickbait.

I regained control of my phone and scrolled down my timeline.

Breaking: Nuclear Bomb Detonates over Washington. Story Developing.

Breaking: Nuclear Attack on the US.

Breaking: 200,000 Fatalities Estimated, Say Experts.

Breaking: Confirmed: President and Staff among Dead in Nuclear
Explosion. Awaiting More Information.

There were other headlines too, about radio silence from the UK and another attack in Albuquerque.

I remembered there was a TV in my room.

But suddenly I couldn't see. My sight cut out, like a light. Everything went dark, and I dropped my phone. I think I vomited, but I can't be certain. I had to feel my way along the lobby back to the restaurant, but realized it was useless and sat on the floor with my back to the wall.

For a while I thought I was in a *Day of the Triffids* scenario. I thought I had actually gone blind. I could hear activity, people running and crying, and someone screamed once. No one stopped to talk to me.

My sight returned after what felt like hours but was probably only thirty minutes. I had felt my way back along the floor and found my phone, hugging it to my chest until I could see again.

Someone stopped as I blinked, trying to clear my vision, and I became aware of a woman standing over me. Looking back, I know now that it was Tania. I didn't know her then.

She said, "Are you okay? Do you need help?"

Someone else, a man, told her to hurry, they had to get to the car.

I didn't say anything, or I might have said I was fine. I don't know. I'm sorry I can't be clearer.

Then I found myself back at the restaurant. Or at least I remember being in the doorway, staring at my book and my coffee and my table. Two people were standing by the door to the bar, gripping each other's hands; Mia and Sasha, I think, sister and brother. Everyone else was gone.

I realized they were looking at a TV mounted in the top corner of the room, and I ran toward them. Of course I couldn't understand what was being said, but a short piece of footage was being played over and over again. The newscaster was tripping over his words, visibly sweating.

Someone had been filming something, one of their friends, before a blinding light enveloped the entire screen and the video cut. White noise.

"What is he saying?" I snapped at them.

The young man, Sasha, said, "It's just light. City is gone."

More footage, filmed from far away and lifted from Twitter, caught the lights of the New York skyline at the moment they blacked out; buildings vanished into darkness, or were obliterated by it, and to the left-hand side of the frame was a gigantic column of pulsating, rising cloud. That's all anyone could see. A blinding flash of light, the cloud—the biggest cloud I had ever seen—and the lights going out.

"How many American cities?" I asked.

"They're talking about three so far."

"Three?"

Mia said, crying, "Somewhere in Texas."

She started speaking frantically to Sasha in a language I didn't know.

My legs became weak and I staggered away, colliding with a woman and nearly knocking her clean off her feet.

"Sorry, sorry . . ." I muttered, still running.

She was shouting, but I don't think it was at me.

I went upstairs and then I was in my room, packing. I turned on the TV, but all the main US channels had cut out. Only the Swiss channels were working, and I almost lost my mind trying to work out how to add subtitles. I tried calling Nadia again from the landline in the room, wondering if it was just cell phones that weren't working, but I couldn't get through there either.

I wanted to smash the phone, but I didn't. Irrationally, I thought they would charge the damage to the room. I had lost my ability to see from the shock, yet I'd had the presence of mind to worry about my bill.

I didn't finish packing because, honestly, I didn't know what to do. I left my room and started wandering the corridors, looking for some of my colleagues from the conference. I imagined that one of them would be coping with the shock better and would tell me what to do. I wanted so desperately to be told what to do. It was like I was back at school, and all I wanted was for an adult to take charge.

Scrolling through my phone obsessively for headlines in English, I kept seeing the word "nuclear." I kept thinking I must be reading it wrong. Logically, there could not have been a nuclear attack on Washington, because it had never happened before. If there had been a nuclear attack, then this was the end, and the world we knew didn't just end. It didn't end because that had never happened before.

Breaking: Nuclear Weapon Detonates over Washington, Hundreds of Thousands Feared Dead.

Breaking: Canadian Prime Minister Calls for Calm as Nuclear Attack Hits US.

Breaking: US without Government as Nuclear Bomb Devastates Washington.

The only photo of Washington, DC, they had so far was from someone's phone camera. It showed darkness and cloud. That was it.

I wasn't equipped. I needed someone to give me direction. Doors opened and closed on my floor. I saw some people running for the stairs. A man left his room and turned to stare at me. I knew who he was but I had momentarily forgotten his name.

Joe Fisher, a professor from Penn State. I know who he was now. I'd known him for seven years.

He pushed his glasses up his nose and said, "Jon, we need to call a cab. Scotland's gone."

"Scotland's . . . gone?"

"Yeah, we need to call a cab. You got a number?"

It took a beat to understand what he had said. None of us had cars. We had all arrived from the train station by taxi.

I started laughing. It was like I'd lost my mind. He certainly thought so. He looked at me like I was crazy and just left me there. I couldn't stop laughing. I had to sit down, with my head in my hands, staring at my phone and the stories still rolling in. It was so absurd to me, that in that moment the only thing he could think to do was call a cab. Scotland was gone, so of course we should call a cab.

After a while the laughing stopped. It didn't mutate into tears or anything. It just faded, leaving me confounded by my own reactions.

I stood up, went to get my half-packed case, and took the elevator down to the lobby. It was swamped. Everyone was shouting, in so many different languages. One of the receptionists was trying to make herself heard, but no one was listening. Two of them climbed onto the front desk and stood above the crowd, and the woman yelled, "Shut up! Shut up! Shut up!"

The younger man stood next to her, trembling, and translated everything she said into English. Everyone went quiet for a second.

"There are no flights leaving from anywhere! It is very unlikely that other forms of public transport will be running today! Please, try to stay calm, and we will assist you! We would advise you not to leave by car at this time!"

But people were leaving, flooding out the entrance. I watched them, my back to the wall, partially hidden by a potted plant. It started to dawn on me that no one was going to tell me what to do. My country had no government. Scotland was gone. Hundreds of thousands of people were dead, and everyone was waiting for a government that no longer existed to talk them through the protocol for something that had never happened before.

I tried calling Nadia's cell again, but it wouldn't connect.

They would be at home. It was midnight there.

I thought of the flash of light, a gargantuan cloud creating an artificial daylight, then the lights of the city going out.

I tried calling the landline instead, and it did ring.

My heart—

No, I can't write it like that.

I thought if I could just speak to Nadia, if one of my kids picked up the phone, it was all going to be okay. Everything fell out of focus apart from the ringing. It rang, and I could see the phone in my mind, in the hallway in my house. I was about to hear Nadia's voice, and it was all going to be okay. She was going to tell me that she and the kids were okay, and then we were going to decide what to do. We could coordinate and talk each other through this.

It kept ringing, and no one picked up. The voice that broke me was the one on the answering machine. It wasn't Nadia's voice, or Marion's, or Ruth's. It was just me, my own voice, asking me to leave a message.

That's the moment that time stopped for me. It doesn't matter how many days have passed. Everything comes back to that moment. It ripped out my foundations.

I lost control and threw my phone, and it hit the wall to the left of the second elevator. I heard the screen break, and that was the end. I covered my face with my hands and cried, right there in the lobby in front of everybody—though no one was paying me any attention—and only a little time had passed when I became aware of people talking about more bombs exploding in China, and another near Munich or somewhere else in Germany. I can't quite remember.

Then it became harder to get news from anywhere but social media, because most of the TV channels were no longer broadcasting. I heard similar stories about bombing in Russia from someone later, and then in Jerusalem. I have a list somewhere, which I jotted down before the Internet cut out. I don't know why I'm trying to remember the precise order here. I don't know if it even matters. I heard, "They've bombed Washington!" and even now I'm unclear on who *they* were.

That was the real day one.

The couple in room 27 killed themselves this morning. Or, at least, it looked like they did.

I was awake early, because I now get up immediately upon waking. No sleeping late anymore. Sleeping late means downtime, and inevitably I would start thinking about Nadia, Ruth, and Marion. I would construct fantasy after fantasy of them driving along the coast, taking detours, maybe carpooling with friendly hitchhikers with kids of their own. I created visceral scenes where Nadia fought off entire gangs of carjackers.

It was excruciating. I hated myself for doing it. I hated even more that I enjoyed dwelling there, disassociating myself from my daily reality.

I noticed that the Bernardeaux weren't at breakfast, so I went back upstairs to check on them.

Dylan and Nathan were way ahead of me when I got to our floor, and I immediately knew what had happened. In the month after day one there had been a spate of suicides, and the stairwell—which was always dark and stank—was the easiest place to do it. No one else had killed themselves in the past few weeks. But the first three had made such an impression that every time I used the stairs I expected to find another body.

"J, don't come in here," Dylan warned. "It's not pretty."

"What is pretty now?" I replied, stepping into the room.

Nathan was staring into the bathroom, arms folded. He said, "It looks like he killed her, then killed himself."

He was right.

Patrick was slumped, face-first and shirtless, over the edge of their bathtub, his arms thrown forth into a shallow pool of blood. He was a muscular man in his late forties; kept himself in good shape. I used to pass him on my walks around the hotel. Sometimes he would run barefoot from the top floors to the first floor and back up again. Sometimes he would only run up and down our corridor. He ran barefoot—and never outside, like Tania or Dylan—because he didn't want to wear out his last pair of shoes.

Behind Patrick, on the floor, was his wife—her name was Coralie—her face turned toward the door, toward us, eyes swept open with shock and a black wreath of bruising around her neck. I couldn't tell whether it had been a consensual death for her. It could have been her idea, but she hadn't trusted herself to see it through.

"There's no sign of foul play, is there?" I asked, making sure that neither of them could see something in the scene that I couldn't.

"I can't see any," Dylan replied.

They had both been dentists, from Lyon. They kept to themselves, but Coralie had spoken to me a few times in the restaurant. Her English wasn't fantastic, but I could understand her. Patrick and I had never really spoken at length, save for one uncharacteristically frank conversation early on after he returned from the hunting expedition with Dylan. He told me about a summer he spent on his uncle's farm in Romania. He was fourteen at the time. His uncle had taken him out hunting, but not for food or recreation. They followed trails of blood to shoot dead the victims of a rabid bear, and spent seven hours in the woods putting mutilated deer and smaller bears out of their misery. Patrick said it was a memory that he had kept coming back to in the last couple of months.

I got the impression that he'd wanted to tell me because he knew I was keeping a record.

Patrick and Coralie had three grown-up children, and their eldest had kids of her own. Unfortunately, I don't remember any of their names.

"You noticed they weren't at breakfast too?" I asked.

Dylan nodded. "It's why I keep a register. Not just safety."

"Did you know them?" Nathan asked.

"They were dentists," I said, because that was the only thing I really knew.

"You know they have crazy high rates of suicide."

Dylan and I both stared at him.

He shrugged. "What? They do. They have, like, the highest rate of suicide of any profession. Google it."

"Google it?" Dylan raised his eyebrows.

"Well, I know you can't . . . You know what I mean. It's true, though."

"Google it," Dylan repeated, snorting.

"I use humor to cope with the abyss. So sue me!"

" 'When you stare into the abyss . . .' "

Nathan spread his hands. "I laugh. Ha ha."

I was amazed that they both managed to laugh.

During their exchange, my eyes kept being dragged back to Coralie Bernardeaux. I was frozen by the hopelessness and misery. It felt like the first day again, or the second, or the third.

I said, "Should we take them outside?"

"I'd rather not with everyone downstairs." Dylan met my eyes. "I'm worried it'll set off a domino effect."

He was right.

"Well, come find me. I'll help you take them out later."

Nathan and Dylan stepped out of the bathroom. Neither of them seemed rattled. Maybe they had seen too much. Maybe the reason I felt such despair was because I hadn't yet seen enough.

I crouched down to shut Coralie's eyes. She was cold. Whatever happened, it had happened during the night. I tried to remember if I had heard anything, a struggle, shouting. But to my knowledge, I'd slept the whole night through.

One time, Coralie had offered to check my teeth. I leaned back in my chair in the restaurant and she peered in, squinting in the limited light, rattling around with a toothpick, much more comfortable with her fingers in my mouth than she had been attempting conversation. Her hair kept falling over her eyes.

She said, "You drink too much coffee."

I'd sniffed back a laugh.

She paused and smiled fleetingly. "Not such a problem anymore, I suppose. The coffee here is terrible."

My teeth had been in good shape at that point, before we all started rationing toothpaste.

"Jon, you good?"

Dylan rapped his knuckles lightly on the door.

I stood up and said, "This sucks."

"I know, man."

"I mean it; this is bullshit."

"I know."

Nathan said, "Maybe they've got the better deal."

Shaking my head, I followed them out, and Dylan shut the bathroom door behind me.

In a building this big the Bernardeaux could have been left there forever. Their room would never need to be opened or occupied again. But ritual and humanity, or maybe just hygiene, kept us burying the bodies. Someone always had to say a few words, and no one aside from me was ever nominated. I was the only person left who could remember Scripture.

Left to our own devices, we seem to have so little control over what we remember. I'm forgetting names—the names of my children's schoolmates, their teachers, Nadia's colleagues—and I'm forgetting faces as well. Even the memory of my own father seems blurry. But I can still recite Scripture. Remembering long passages of text is more like muscle memory.

Nathan returned to the restaurant, but I loitered. I opened and closed a few of the drawers in the Bernardeaux' room, noticing that they didn't seem to have much in the way of possessions.

"Looking for something?" Dylan asked, waiting for me in the hallway.

"Yeah . . . Toothpaste, painkillers, whatever."

I looked in the closet and saw a suitcase. In the zipped compartment in the front, I found their passports. I flipped them open and confirmed their identities, trying not to act like I was making a big deal out of it.

The only other item of interest I found was a small packet of cig-
arillos, which was surprising. Then I finally left the room, and Dylan
locked up.

"You should eat something," Dylan said.

"I'm not feeling that hungry."

He nodded. "Understandable. I had to break up a fight just now.
Nicholas—you know, the Dutch guy—was getting in Nathan's face,
wanting to start something."

"Why?"

"Because he's angry and looking for a fight? I don't know. The men
here, Peter and Nicholas, I don't trust them. Adam and Rob, the English guys, seem okay. And Peter's been quiet, but . . . I don't trust him
or that Dutchman. I've been watching them a lot, but it takes energy,
you know."

"Adam's fine," I said. "Rob I've said hi to a few times. Peter and Van
Schaik . . . I've never talked to either of them."

"Well, they sure don't want to speak to any Americans." He smiled.
"I'm going to go work on the tanks and smoke. Want to come?"

I was already walking alongside him by the time he finished the
question.

Dylan and I were up on the roof most of today. In the morning a few of the other young men were helping us, but as the afternoon wore on and the temperature dropped we were left alone. Between us, we managed to partially remove the top of one water tank. Scrap metal was strewn everywhere. My hands were bleeding again, and so were Dylan's.

He suggested we smoke. I decided to take him up on it. Perhaps I could start my longer interviews with him.

He told me that the roof became tranquil in the evening, and he was right. It was freezing, but the view of the forest made it possible to pretend that we were at a real resort again, where the gentle rustle of the wind through the trees wasn't laden with the names of the dead, with lost relationships, with missing family members, friends. For a while, it made me feel like I was back at the conference.

Dylan told me about the years he had worked here, about the rooms that used to be rented out for drug-taking, and some of the more infamous residents.

"We usually had spare rooms. The guy who used to be in charge ran a small scheme, years before I was promoted. It helped sell drugs to split among the rest of the staff. Working here was mostly thankless, but we could do whatever we wanted back then, as long as the clientele was decent. Didn't matter that they were doing drugs, so long as they were expensive."

"Wasn't that risky?"

"There was a time when we had a spate of overdoses, and ambulances were here a little too often for management's liking. My former boss got fired, quietly. Then I became more cautious. That came with age as well, I think. I grew up and started to think long term, about my family, rather than just eating fine steaks and drinking nice beer. There are more important things in life. There were."

He handed our second joint back to me, and I took a long drag.

We were sitting side by side, legs hanging over the edge of the building. It wasn't as dangerous as it first appeared, with the serpentine iron fire escape not far below us. It would be incredible to watch a sunset from up here, but obviously there were no sunsets anymore.

I thought that the breeze was almost verging on warm, though it may have been my imagination. I was pretty stoned.

"Did you ever meet any of the murderers?" I asked. "Tomi said a famous one stayed here."

"Yes, Victor Roux . . . Well, you could say that he met me."

"How?"

"I got to know him much the same way I got to know you. He used to go wandering the corridors too, though mostly at night. I didn't think anything of it at the time. Lots of people who stay here find it helps them gather their thoughts, going for a walk when it's quiet, and you don't want to go into the forest. Victor and I even shared a blunt once, just as I'm doing with you now, outside the kitchens. He was a charming man, a hit with the ladies, but then I think you already know that if you're asking me about him."

"I don't know much. Tomi's the one writing the history of this place. Did you ever see him approach any women?"

"I'm not in the habit of drinking in the bar downstairs. But I know he used to go there, watch a band play, sometimes leave with different women. He told me a story once about how he entered a reality-TV dating thing when he was young. I forget which one . . . But the episode never aired."

"Really? Victor Roux was on a dating show?"

"You know the kind, a row of men compete for a date with a woman and no one talks how anyone talks on a real date. He won too, according to him. But the episode never made it on TV."

"Did he say why?"

"He said the woman made a fuss and complained, said he was creepy and refused to go on the date with him. The prize was a vacation to

Greece or something, so she *really* didn't want to go. Quite something, when you think about it. That woman's intuition probably stopped her from becoming one of his first victims."

"How young was he at the time? Would he have started killing by then?"

"No one knows when he started killing."

Goose bumps rose along my arms, and I handed the joint back. I thought I would pay almost anything to see the footage of that episode. Of course, we would likely never watch any entertainment on a screen again.

The realization was a harsh one and brought me more sorrow than I'd like to admit.

"Did you see him with Natalie du Morel?" I asked.

Dylan raised his eyebrows, and disgust clouded his face for a second. "Once. I liked her; she stood out. She was very small, a tiny lady, with short hair. She didn't stand a chance against him. He was tall, even taller than he looked in the papers. And strong, like he wasn't all human."

"Did you see him the night that . . . ?"

"I took him down."

"What?"

He nodded, inhaling ferociously. "You heard me. My manager arrived about three minutes after I did. Took the hit for me. This was another manager, not the guy who got fired. I saw a lot of them come and go before they promoted me."

"What do you mean, he took the hit? You mean he took the credit?"

"He was worried that if the papers here found out that a black man had beaten up this white man, all of it might be blamed on me somehow. All the murders—everything. No one would try to twist the story of a white man being a hero, but with me it might have turned bad. It was different back then. Not as different from now as you people might think, but enough for me to want to avoid being famous for almost murdering a man."

"Wow. So what happened?"

Another drag, and he waved a hand, indicating that he was regressing to the beginning of the story. The same hand then fell to his stomach with the sharpness of holding a reopened wound.

"She disappeared for a while, Natalie, the woman he tried to . . . But we thought she might have been staying with someone in the city, visiting a friend. Then someone heard screaming later, a day later, on the sixth floor where Victor was staying. I got a call on the radio and I ran up there. I wasn't scared. I didn't know what was going on. There were disturbances sometimes, fights breaking out, so that kinda thing didn't scare me right away. But then I ran into them."

A pair of birds shrieked at each other, passing close by our faces, and I started, heels knocking against the side of the building.

"Birds!" I exclaimed. "Holy shit!"

"Nice," he agreed, and we watched them circle each other until they descended into the trees somewhere.

"Sorry, you were saying?"

He passed the joint to me. "You know, I always think of a song when I think of that time now. I was coming back from a break when the call came in, and I'd been listening to Billy Ocean on my old tape player, a Walkman."

"Damn, a Walkman."

"Remember those?"

"Yeah; I went straight to CD player, though. My dad raised me on records. I was in my twenties before I listened to anything else."

The mention of my father stopped me in my tracks. The smile fell from my face, and my throat closed up. For some reason, I hadn't thought much about Dad, or his wife, Barbara. They might have escaped a blast radius. I tried to work out if Dad would have been working in Memphis that day, and whether that would have even mattered, but there was no way of knowing anything for certain.

It was too much to think about.

"So I was listening to 'Love Really Hurts Without You' just before, and it was still in my head as I was running. It was still stuck in my head days after. I can't listen to that song now without it making me want to throw up. Gives me the shakes. Anyway, I got to the sixth floor. Elevators were out, so I was taking the stairs, and I could hear the screaming even before I got near them, and I knew it was her. It hit me as soon as I heard her, that I hadn't seen her for an evening or two. Victor had chased her out of his room and he had this big blade, like a machete. Her hand was pretty much gone, just flaps of skin and blood everywhere. Sorry if I'm being too graphic."

"No, go on."

"He had her on the floor, hitting her with this foot-long evil-looking blade. If he wasn't so furious, he might have taken her head off, but his aim was bad. She had her hand up to stop him from hitting her face and it was just . . . mangled."

"What did you do?"

"I didn't realize what I had done until I was on him, and I remember thinking, *You fool, he's going to kill you now*. But I was on him, and I don't think he noticed until I was punching him. He swung at me, but he didn't have the space to get me good. I held him on the floor and started beating his face. Being a hero never crossed my mind. I didn't even think about the poor lady. All I could think was that this animal had to be killed, or he was going to kill me."

I passed the joint back. Clamping it between his teeth, Dylan untucked the beige shirt underneath his coat and exposed his stomach. Across his torso, just above his gut, was a deep scar. He rolled up his left sleeve, and there were another two on his upper bicep.

"Anyway, she survived that," he said. "She lived in Marseille, so she might have survived this. I don't know. We don't know what happened to France, do we? I heard something about Paris, but . . . I don't know."

"That's a remarkable story."

I wasn't sure what else to say. There was no reply that seemed substantial enough.

"It's probably why I was allowed to run my team the way I wanted to here, do as I pleased as long as I kept the hotel and the residents safe. I could make my money on the side, choose my hours, and all my staff. Once you get scarred for a job, management treats you with respect."

"Where did your boss go? Your old boss?"

"He died of pancreatic cancer. Must have been . . ." He shook his head. "You know, I can't remember. I went to the man's funeral, but I don't remember the year. I should. I feel like I should remember."

The joint had gone out. He tried to relight it, but it wouldn't catch. He flicked it away and started to roll another. He said, "Did you find out anything about the girl?"

"No. Just her name."

"You still set on searching this whole place?"

"Maybe. Can I hold on to the keys for now?"

He shrugged. "I guess. It's not like you're going to find anything."

DAY 55

I had an idea, but I needed an accomplice, maybe two, and I didn't know many people well enough to ask. At breakfast this morning I spent a lot of time looking around the restaurant sizing people up. There are people here I've still never even spoken to.

The only other person sitting on their own was Tomi. I had been waiting for Tania, but she hadn't come down. My first choice, before either of them, would have been Patrick, because he'd been physically strong and being part of a couple had made him more trustworthy than anyone staying here alone.

I stood up and approached Dylan.

"Is Tania okay?"

"I knocked. She took some food up to her room early, before everyone else." He smiled. "Don't miss a thing, do you?"

"Good to know," I said, weak with relief.

I returned to my table and drank the last of my coffee. We had been down to the instant kind for a while, and it was bitter and almost cold. I drank as much of the stuff as I was allowed, but that wasn't much.

Across the room, Tomi got up and left. I decided, in that moment, that I would ask her to help me first. I don't think she's likely to be involved with the murder—she's a young woman, and young women don't tend to commit violent crimes—and, given her penchant for stealing and psychoanalyzing, she could be a useful ally.

Not wanting to look too conspicuous, I followed her at a distance.

Dylan watched me go, and I stayed quiet until I reached the stairwell, where I called, "Hey! Tomi?"

The footsteps above me faltered, I looked up past the banisters, and I saw her head appear.

"Oh, it's you." She sounded amused.

"Can we talk?"

"Sure."

I heard her jog up another couple of flights and exit the stairwell. I followed, and when I reached the sixth floor I found her waiting for me in the corridor. She was still holding her mug of coffee.

"I hate that stuff," I said.

"It's gross, but I sometimes add a shot to it." She shifted. "So . . . do you want to go to my room or . . . ?"

"Yeah, in private."

"Oh, *private*."

"Trust me, it's nothing like that."

She laughed. "As if I'd invite you in if it was."

Tomi lived in room 505. It hadn't been her original room, I don't think. Like the others, she had moved from one of the temperamental key-card rooms to one of the manually lockable ones. I wondered whether she had picked this number for the symmetry, and why she hadn't chosen a floor lower down, with more female company.

It struck me that she must know Victor Roux's story; that a woman had almost been hacked to death mere feet from where we were standing. Yet she still chose to live on this floor, alone.

I suppose it wasn't that strange, if she wasn't superstitious. But I wouldn't live on the sixth floor.

"So what's so urgent you stalked me from breakfast to talk about it?" she asked.

I shut the door as she sat on the edge of her bed. "It's about the body in the water tank."

"The little kid?"

"Yeah." I pulled out the stool from her dresser and sat on that, and as I did so I scanned the room for items. "I don't know how much you've heard, or what rumors are going around."

"That she was murdered, but it was before."

"Looks like that."

She stood up, leaned down toward me, reached past and opened the drawers of the dresser. "If you want to see if I have anything you want, just ask. You don't have to make up a pretext just because I told you I have a stash of whiskey."

To my annoyance, I couldn't resist the urge to glance down, and I saw that she had several tubes of toothpaste, lots of miniature bathroom bottles, and some foldaway toothbrushes. She was standing way too close and I had to stand up.

"Look, don't get me wrong, I'm curious about the stuff you stole, but I'm not here about that. I'd actually like your help."

"With what?"

I noticed that the room smelled nice. No one's room smelled nice anymore.

"Investigating," I said, settling for sitting on the floor.

With a slight roll of the eyes, she sat on her bed again. "You want to find the killer?"

"I want to know what happened. What's weird is that no one else does."

"Why are you asking me?"

"Why not?"

"You don't even like me."

"That's not . . ." I sighed, glanced at her coffee. "Can I have some of that?"

Snorting, she passed me the mug, picked up a bottle of whiskey and poured a dash in. "You're kind of an asshole, coming into a girl's room, telling her you don't like her and then taking her free coffee and booze."

I knocked it back, and the whiskey made the coffee palatable. "Thank you. And I don't dislike you, I just don't know you. It's not like any of us know each other that well."

"It's so stifling, not knowing anyone. I thought it would be the opposite, it would feel really freeing, but it feels more like being stuck in a room alone." She gestured around us. "I mean, I like hanging out with myself. But it makes your thoughts feel real big."

"You're right."

"I used to take having friends for granted."

"I thought you didn't try to call anyone when it happened."

She snatched back the mug of coffee. "What do you want me to do?"

"I don't know whether it's just me, but the staff—Dylan, Sophia—whenever I mention the body they act weird."

"Everyone was drinking dead-body marinade and the world's gone nuclear. People are going to get weird." Averting her eyes, she lit a cigarette. "Shit's already pretty weird."

"No, but this is evasive. It's not that they don't want to talk about it, it's like they don't want me to even look. And there are four tanks up there. We weren't necessarily drinking . . . dead-body marinade."

"Maybe they just think it's pointless."

"No, it's something more, I'm sure of it. Do you think you could help me find out?" I reached into my pocket and showed her the keys, as a demonstration of trust. "I have the master keys. I'm allowed to search whatever rooms I want. I need this to look like a one-man operation, but I also need someone to keep an eye on everyone else, particularly the staff."

A tiny smile. "What am I watching them for?"

"I don't know yet. But will you do it?"

Picking up the bottle, she poured herself another shot. She didn't care that it was morning. As she replaced the bottle on the floor, her hair fell forward over her right shoulder and was caught in the rare, weak rays of struggling daylight coming through the window.

"Hey," she said, laughing. "It's the end of the world. Everyone needs a hobby, right?"

On the way back to my room I stopped by Tania's office and loitered outside for a long time. I wasn't sure what she did in there when she wasn't treating people. Everyone's routines were so fiercely private, especially hers.

Suddenly her door opened and she said, "Can I help you?"

I was unprepared and didn't think of an excuse fast enough.

She raised her eyebrows. "Is this about the tooth?"

I wasn't sure if she gave me the out to spare me embarrassment, but I took it. She sat me in a chair and put on a pair of plastic gloves with her back turned. She seemed distracted and tired.

"Sit with your head leaning on the back of the chair. I'm going to have to use a flashlight."

I did as she said. She pushed the curtains as far to the sides of the window as she could, but it didn't make much difference. As she leaned in to shine the light into my mouth, I noticed her lips were chapped, like she had been biting them.

The back of my neck started to pinch, but I didn't mention it.

She sighed and stepped away. "It looks like it's dying."

I struggled upright. "Why?"

"I'm not a dentist, but it's discolored. I don't know what's caused it; it could be loads of things. It'll probably need to be taken out, I'm afraid."

She noted the expression that crossed my face because she quickly added, "Not now. It could fall out on its own, or you could grind it out; you look like you grind your teeth. If it starts to look like it could get infected, though, or the area around it starts to hurt, then it'll have to come out."

"Do you even have anesthetic here?"

"No. We'll work something out." She took the gloves off and threw them neatly into the trash on the other side of the room. "I'm not saying it will be pleasant."

"Are you okay? I didn't see you at breakfast."

She sat heavily on the edge of the bed, which she had pushed against the far wall. "Sometimes I just think a bit too much about the day everything happened. I don't think it's healthy."

"Do you want to talk about it?"

"I don't particularly want to be interviewed for your project."

I smiled. "That's not why I asked."

"No, it's just why you're visiting."

There was a brief silence and I considered leaving, but I didn't really mind that she could see right through me. That someone could see me at all was oddly comforting.

"Maybe you're not the only one who needs to talk sometimes." I spread my hands. "It's not like I'd write anything that you didn't want included."

"It's probably decent therapy for you," she mused, crossing her legs and resting the side of her head in her hand. "Why did you stay? Everyone else at the conference left. Why not you?"

"You know what, I don't remember. That day has so many gaps in it. Why did you stay?"

It took a long time for her to answer. The memory seemed to be causing a great deal of pain.

Eventually, she said, "I was going to leave. I almost got to the car but then I just . . . didn't want to do it. I remember reading this story about a plane crash—I think it was a plane crash—and one of the girls who survived ran onto the runway and was hit by an emergency vehicle. She died. I don't know why that story occurred to me, but I just realized that leaving might not be the common-sense reaction. We could all just die on our way to the airport, or even at the train station, because that could be where the next bomb hit. But it seemed unlikely anyone would nuke the hotel, so . . ." She shrugged.

"It makes sense," I said.

"Does it?"

"It makes more sense than your boyfriend leaving." I decided to go for it and ask the questions. "How long were you together?"

To my surprise, she didn't shut me down. "Would have been three years about . . . two months ago. That's why we were here. Just a week away for our anniversary, pretty city nearby, a lake, you know."

"Three years?"

She nodded. "And he wasn't my boyfriend. He was my fiancé."

I was stricken. "And he left?"

Another nod.

I had no idea what to say. I felt terrible for bringing it up. There was no point in trying to catch her out like this. Of course Tania had nothing to do with Harriet Luffman's murder.

"I genuinely thought he might come back when he realized he wasn't going to make it anywhere. Or he might have come back anyway." A terse gesture at the room. "As you can see, that didn't occur to him as an option."

I felt a surge of fury, like I wanted to return to the hotel lobby and punch this guy in the face.

"I'm sorry."

Looking at her nails. "No, I'm sorry. Sorry I wasted the last three years. I could have spent them sleeping alone, going out whenever I wanted, eating more, having my own place, having sex with whoever."

For some reason, I said, "Maybe something happened to stop him getting back."

She looked right into my eyes, as if I had completely missed the point, and said, "I hope he's dead."

I missed a couple of days. I hate to fall out of routine, so allow me to explain the gap.

I have recently taken up smoking again. I haven't smoked since I was twenty-four. Of course it was Nadia who convinced me to stop. Maybe "convinced" is the wrong word. She asked me to, and I stopped. That was how our relationship worked.

I approached Adam at breakfast, as he seemed like a good person to talk to next. By that I mean he speaks English, and he's always seemed friendly to me, despite his serious tone and heavy brow. He's extremely pale, almost worryingly so, and has flecks of red in his dark beard.

He offered me some of his tobacco and I politely declined at first, but he insisted.

"What are you afraid of? Dying?" Lighting his own cigarette, he said, "I heard you're writing everything down so people in the future know that we were here."

"Aren't you afraid of no one remembering who you are?"

"Nah. I only came here to get off my face. Didn't have much to go back to."

"Parents? Girlfriend?"

"Nah," he said, as if he'd never had parents. "I had a brother but . . . eh, he never called me either."

He suggested we go outside, so people wouldn't smell the smoke and start hassling him for cigarettes. So we put on a few extra layers, hats and gloves, and went to sit in the grounds. We found a bench and, I confess, I am really enjoying smoking again. I had become so accustomed to the permanent rigid anxiety in my chest. The cigarettes caused my aching shoulders to relax.

We must have smoked three each in the time we sat there.

"How many more do you have?" I asked.

"Lots," he replied. "Stocked up at the airport on the way in."

"What were you doing at the hotel in the first place?" I asked, turning to face him so that he couldn't pay too much attention to my notes.

"Playing guitar and doing drugs. I was on tour, wasn't I." He avoided direct eye contact. "Nothing fancy, just a few venues around Europe. Fell out with my singer, and those raging uncontrollable sphincters took his side, so I stole all their drugs and left one night. Turned my phone off. Fuck them."

He snorted.

"Do you know if they made it?"

"No. Honestly, I know it sounds bad, but I don't care. I care about my friends back home. I don't care about drinking buddies. Don't even miss my parents, really. I miss my mates, though, the people who actually knew me."

"You said you stole all their drugs? You weren't going to get all that back to the UK."

He hesitated. "Yeah. I'm not sure I planned on going back."

I decided not to ask what that meant. He decided not to elaborate.

Across the grounds, I saw a group of men—Dylan, Sasha, Peter—dragging a newly killed deer into the parking lot on a tarpaulin. I hadn't volunteered, not because I can't shoot but because everyone else had seemed more eager to start killing things than me. Now that Patrick is no longer around, I should probably think about putting my name forward.

"I didn't know there were any deer left," Adam remarked.

"Me neither," I replied sadly.

Peter directed the others to tie the hooves and hang the deer from one of the lights that would have illuminated the parking lot. Its throat was already cut. Adam and I could see the ugly trail of blood leading back around the hotel.

The body was probably going to hang there for three or four days.

I steered the conversation toward Harriet Luffman.

"When you arrived, did you notice any kids in the hotel?"

"You mean that girl you guys found in the water tank? No." He then added, "I hate kids, actually. I stay away from them."

I laughed. "Why do you hate kids?"

"It's a weird story."

"How weird can it be?"

He took an exceptionally long drag and smirked. "When I was younger I did a Ouija board with some mates. We all thought we were faking it, then we ended up talking to some boy who had died in a car accident in Australia. Whoever he was, he said he didn't like me. Obviously, it was just my mates fucking with me. But ever since I've had this recurring nightmare that this creepy boy is standing in the corner of my room."

That wasn't the answer I had expected. I stopped taking notes for a moment.

"Really?"

"Yeah. Weirdest thing is, every girlfriend I've ever had refused to sleep over at my place because they'd wake up in the night freaking out that there was a creepy little boy in the corner." He glanced at me. "I had Tomi over the other day, think we were actually about to throw down, and then suddenly she sat up, and you know what she said?"

"What?"

"She asked if we could go to her room instead, because she thought she saw something in the corner of my room."

My pen hovered over the paper, but I had no idea what to scribble down. For some reason, I was angry with him, but only for a moment.

"I . . . I don't believe in ghosts," I said.

"Neither do I, mate. It bothers me, you know. Because I can't work out how these girls ended up seeing the same thing." He frowned. "Anyway, that's why I hate kids. I don't remember seeing that little girl you found. Funnily enough, I haven't had any nightmares about the ghost kid here either."

I wrote *Doesn't seem to know anything* next to Harriet's name.

Adam said, "Maybe this just isn't a good place for kids, eh? Living or dead."

I put next to it: *But hates children.*

We went inside when the cold became too much. We followed the blood back to the entrance, where I stopped and looked at where it pioneered down the deserted road and then took a sharp turn into the trees.

Adam mentioned that when he'd been in Geneva he'd picked up some cocaine and other stuff, and for some reason I thought: Why not? It's not as if I have to be an example to anyone anymore. It's not as if I have to worry about getting into a bar fight or a car accident, or even overdosing.

So we went back to his room, and on the way he asked if I minded if he invited Tomi.

I said that I didn't mind, but I did a little.

"She seemed like a bit of a bitch until we hung out, but she's funny, actually," he said.

"Whatever you say."

"She's also banging hot."

I laughed. Everything Adam says is in the same slightly sarcastic tone of voice. He's funny without realizing he is. Deadpan.

"If you say so," I said.

"Oh, come on," he scoffed. "You're a liar, mate. Didn't have you down for a liar."

I tried cocaine once when I was twenty-five, with Nadia. I never did it again, but I know she did a few times. It came with the job, with her colleagues, with just staying awake while covering a party conference or a rally or the release of a new declassified report they had to read by midday.

Adam rolled me another cigarette, and I sat cross-legged on the edge of his bed smoking while he went and knocked for Tomi. His room was in a state of disarray, like he'd considered leaving and decided against it. He hadn't tried to make it look like home.

Or maybe he had. If I'd had more time alone I would have been tempted to look through his possessions, as he didn't seem to have much. But then he returned with Tomi, who was wrapped in a couple of extra blankets.

"Can you make me one of those?" she asked, spotting my cigarette.

I gestured at Adam, who sat on the floor and started rolling. It crossed my mind that I wanted to invite Tania, but I wasn't sure if she would approve, or if it would be taking advantage of Adam's generosity.

"What have you two been doing to be snorting this early?" Tomi asked. "Emotional outpouring?"

"Adam told me a ghost story from his childhood," I said.

Tomi sat on the floor beneath me, and Adam lit her cigarette with a match.

"It wasn't a ghost story," he said.

"Do you believe in ghosts, then?" she asked.

Adam said no.

I said, "I don't think so. What about you?"

"I'm an atheist," she said, as if that explained it.

"And ghosts mean God to you?" I said over the top of Adam's head as he knelt over an upturned mirror he had brought from the en suite, crushing the tiny blocks of white powder he had poured out of a bag.

"Ghosts mean duality," she replied. "There's no scientific evidence to suggest the human body holds a separate intangible entity called a soul, so I don't believe there's an afterlife. I don't believe in God. I think, when we die, that's it. I'm guessing you disagree."

I wasn't sure where to start. I was distracted by the tapping of Adam's keys on the glass.

I said, "No, I don't believe that."

Tomi pointed at me and grinned. "Religious upbringing. I knew it."

"Yes, I was brought up in a religious family, but anyone could have told that. I'm the only one who speaks at funerals anymore."

It didn't seem to dent her self-satisfaction. "So you think people have souls?"

"I think science can explain how but not why."

"There doesn't have to be a why—why is for children."

"You were writing a thesis on urban folklore!"

"My undergrad was in history with anthropology, my masters was in urban development. I study things that happened in the past and how they affect the present, not abstract, unprovable concepts. And?"

Adam sat back, smiling to himself. I felt that he was enjoying listening to us debate more than anything. I admit, it was the closest thing to normality I'd felt since I'd been here. I felt like I was back in my office, students coming in and out to argue over an essay grade or ask for extensions. Sometimes they'd want to talk over something that had captured their imagination in a lecture. Those were always my favorite talks. Tomi would have been a pain in the ass as a student. But she probably taught her professors a few things.

I heard Adam snort a couple of lines, and he pushed the mirror toward Tomi, who held back her hair, swept forward and did the same. I asked for a clean banknote and Tomi laughed at me. I snorted two lines and marveled at how easy it was.

Tomi said she was going to fetch some of her stash, and while she was out of the room Adam stretched out on the floor and put his hands behind his head.

"You're blushing," he said.

I told him I was only blushing because the coke was getting my heart rate up.

"You could probably get laid if you want."

"She doesn't even like me."

He looked at me as if I had just said something unbelievably childish. "Mate. It's the end of the world."

Tomi came back with a bottle of Jack Daniel's and I thought, *Here we go, no turning back now*.

I don't remember everything about the conversations that followed but I'll write them as best as I can recall.

Adam didn't talk much, but he laughed a whole lot. I think that was what he wanted.

Tomi and I restarted the conversation about dualism. I drank a few shots in quick succession. I can't tell you how good they tasted. I couldn't even bring myself to savor them.

"Why devote any time to worrying about superstitions and speculation when there is *So. Much. Happening. Out. There.* That's *more* amazing, that actually blows your mind, things like other galaxies and black holes and space travel. *These* are the things we should have been wasting brain power on, not church!" She banged her fist against the carpet as she spoke.

"I don't think it's a waste of brain power to spend time speculating on why we're here! Whether there are such things as free will, whether we are more than just animals—"

"But we're not."

"Can you let me finish?"

"Fine!" She seemed to be enjoying herself.

I think I was too, because for minutes at a time I was able to forget where I was.

"It's important for people to feel like their lives have purpose," I said.

"And it doesn't have purpose if you don't believe you're getting a sticker and some candy at the end of it? Like this life doesn't have meaning unless you then live on somewhere else? That doesn't even make sense!"

"How can you be so atheist and so . . . so . . . right-wing libertarian?"

"What makes you think I'm a libertarian?"

I can't remember what I said to that, but I think she was offended. But she also admitted that she was a libertarian, and she had always voted in opposition to me. So, ultimately, her taking offense was the part that didn't make sense.

The cocaine started to wear off. We snorted another two lines each. Tomi shrugged the blankets off and I sat on the floor, leaning against the bed. The room had filled with smoke and it warmed the air.

"It makes things way more fun if you imagine everything being narrated by the *Arrested Development* guy," Tomi said.

I laughed. It felt so alien to actually laugh.

Adam started narrating, in a deadpan American accent, "*Adam has spent the day with two historians, snorting cocaine in the east wing.*"

Tomi's laugh was loud, showed a lot of teeth. *"Dylan likes to keep everyone out of the staff living quarters because he doesn't want them to find out about his huge armory of guns."*

"What?"

Tomi poured us both more whiskey. "It's true! This is a famous hunting spot. There are tons of guns here; people used to rent them."

"Gives me the creeps, people walking around with guns." Adam blew out his lips in amazement. "It's not cool."

"Oh, it's fine. They won't be able to use them for much longer anyway."

I asked, "Why?"

Tomi smiled conspiratorially and whispered, "I might have done a bad thing."

Adam said, "Oh, please say you did."

It shouldn't have been, but at the time it was funny. Adam flicked ash at the saucer and missed, so he brushed it into the carpet.

Tomi looked at me. "On the day it happened, I found a handgun in a desk drawer in a staff room and I mighta . . . kinda taken it. And the staff quarters were just left open and, for real, there were so many guns in there. Hunting rifles, you know, for renting out to guests."

"Shit," Adam murmured, glancing at the door, which was shut.

I frowned. "Did you steal them all?"

"Of course not—look at me! I put all the bullets I could stash in my pack and stole those instead. They don't have any more bullets after they get through the couple of boxes I left."

I waved the smoke away. "Wait, Tomi, wait. You have all the hotel's ammo, and a gun?"

She took a drag on Adam's cigarette, trying not to smirk. "Yep."

"Bloody hell, marry me." Adam got up and went into the en suite.

I was more interested in the weapons. My last hit hadn't yet worn off.

"And Dylan never said anything to you about it? I mean, that must be his gun, right?"

"He doesn't want to admit how many weapons they have lying around," she said. "He wants everyone to think there's only one or two hunting rifles. Not twenty. I'm guessing he assumed the ammo was looted when everyone left, that someone stole the gun out of his desk and took all the bullets with them. Why would he think it's still in the hotel?"

"But why would you do that?" I asked, concerned about the possible implications.

"Why would I *not*? All I knew was that everything had gone to hell and that at some point I was gonna need protection. It's better if other people are worrying about how they're gonna hunt for deer and don't have anything to come after me with."

"But no one's coming after anyone, Tomi."

"That's not what you implied when you asked me to spy for you."

I had nothing to say to that.

The idea of her being the only person in the building with excess ammunition made me uncomfortable. It made me feel like she was foreseeing a war.

"Hey, wanna do some crystal meth?" Adam asked, nonplussed by Tomi's revelation.

He had returned with an alarming plastic contraption that, after a second or two, I realized was just an improvised pipe. He flicked the lighter open and inhaled, lips pressed against the top of the pipe. Water bubbled.

"What does that stuff do?" I asked, extremely reticent.

Schedule II drugs weren't my area of expertise. Crystal meth was in the same mental box as things like crack and heroin, and marijuana and cocaine were the experimental drugs, the ones you tried a few times at college and never made a habit of unless you were planning to die.

Adam said, "It makes everything . . . sharper, brighter. It's like superspeed but lasts a bit longer."

Tomi shrugged. "Sure."

I gave it some thought, and then said yes. I accepted because I was having fun, and I didn't want to leave the room. So I smoked some crystal meth and it was surprisingly nice.

I remember snatches of conversation taking place over the next four hours, but they aren't worth writing down here. We talked about TV shows mostly, quoted films we loved. Tomi told a funny but gross story about one of her ex-boyfriends—at least I think it was funny; Adam and I laughed so much at one point that I couldn't breathe. Adam spent a long time telling us about Alan Partridge, then Tomi and I talked books for a while, side by side. Adam smoked more and fell asleep, hands behind his head, a small smile on his face.

Tomi's eyes were wide and slightly unfocused.

Crystal meth made alcohol taste even better, I noticed. It made my skin feel dry and everything tingle with an electric heat, like my nerve endings were being fried. My center of gravity felt high, as if it were in my neck, along with all my breath, and the mild irritation of stale smoke was making me swallow several times a minute.

Somehow we got on to politics. I don't remember how, but I remember her sighing and saying, "Can we *not* with Iraq? You're such a buzzkill."

"You voted for it."

"I only ever voted to make the country better!"

"And how'd that work out?"

I think I managed to annoy her, or touched a nerve.

"That's so *reductive* now," she said, putting an extra scornful emphasis onto the word "reductive."

I was struggling with multisyllabic words at that point so I was impressed she still had a decent command over her vocabulary. She looked for her cigarette and realized she had finished it. She leaned her head against Adam's mattress and exhaled for a long time. The air in the room was so dense it was like a summer night in Florida.

Tomi opened her eyes and said, "I want to have sex."

I don't remember what I said; it may have just been, "Um, sorry, what?" or something equally nonsensical.

"I'm not kidding," she said. "It's not a marriage proposal. I just want to have sex."

I still didn't know what to say. I couldn't even decide whether I liked her or not, as a person. Sex was another question entirely, separate from likes and dislikes. It was easy to compartmentalize, to the extent that, in that moment, I don't remember Nadia crossing my mind.

"What's the matter?" Tomi said. "Never banged a libertarian?"

"It's not that."

"Wow, you have? Now *that's* interesting! Though you did surprise me when you went for the meth as well. I thought you were gonna square out."

"So did I! Then I thought, *What the hell.*"

"Right on. What do we have to gain by denying ourselves anything anymore?"

"I'm just not sure it's a good idea." I reached for an excuse. "Adam likes you. I'd feel like an asshole."

"No need. Adam turned me down."

"What?" I said, like I hadn't already heard the story.

"Yeah, we were going to. But . . . it was weird. I got creeped out because I was drunk and I thought I saw something in the corner of his room. When I mentioned it and suggested we go to mine instead, he just weirded out and told me to leave."

"What did you see?"

She gave it some thought. "Nothing. I saw nothing. You know when you see normal objects in the dark but your mind turns them into a person? It was just that."

We both looked to the corner of the room for a moment, and then back to Adam.

Tomi laughed. "Anyway, guys who take that many drugs can't usually keep it up for long."

"So I'm your second choice, that's what you're saying?"

"Well, I asked Rob, but he's gay, so." She shrugged, and at the time I couldn't tell if she was joking or not, but she probably wasn't.

"So what do you say?" A raise of the eyebrows. "You just wanna go back to your room and, what, *write* or something?"

I looked at her, and it might have been the meth or the whiskey, but again I thought, *What the hell.*

The decision must have been visible in my expression, because she stood up suddenly and held out a hand. I let her pull me to my feet, and we both wavered, unbalanced, fingers interlocked, and I knocked over Tomi's glass with my heel. She laughed and rested her forehead against my cheek and we stayed like that for a while. I was unsure who was holding whom upright. The proximity after so long without any prolonged human contact sent a powerful oxytocin high straight to my brain, where it mixed with the crystal meth, and we hugged each other tight. Her hair smelled like smoke and her body against mine felt nothing like Nadia's—Nadia was shorter, smaller—but it felt too good to let go of. She reached up and stroked the back of my neck with the tips of her fingernails and I damn near cried.

I had no idea what she was feeling, if anything at all.

"Shall we go?" she said, pulling away after so long, my hands still grasped tightly in hers.

We left Adam asleep and peaceful on his floor. I left a glass of water for him next to his head. I was on the verge of coming down, but not quite. My high had gone from fluorescent to candlelit. I was still present in my mind, but my heart had slowed. It was the best imitation of contentment I had come across since my time here, and I was grateful to Adam for sharing it with us.

Tomi came back to my room and stayed for the rest of the day, and the night, which brings me up to date. Obviously I haven't written anything about that. It was nice not to sleep alone.

I didn't eat anything yesterday, so I feel dehydrated, empty, and lethargic. Nathan brought me up some food but I haven't yet touched it. I plan to sleep. I still haven't looked through the Luffmans' cases again, but I'll get to that when I'm more alert.

Dear Nadia,

If you ever end up reading this, I know this must be hard for you to know about. But it's the end of the world. I figured, of all the times to start being a decent husband, now would not be the time to make much difference. If it makes you feel any better, she's made it clear that her interest is more due to limited choice than anything else. Maybe mine is too.

You must think I'm a hypocrite, being so angry with Tania's fiancé for leaving. You think I don't remember the question you asked when I was leaving. I was listening. I heard you.

You must have suspected that I just pretended not to hear you, and you were right. I'm sorry. You were always right about me.

Yours,
Jon

It occurred to me during the night that I might be able to find security camera footage from around the hotel. I took a walk in the early hours, before anyone else was awake, and counted about a dozen cameras at strategic points. If there were cameras, and any of them were in regular use, there must be a room in the hotel where Dylan, or one of the other employees, used to keep an eye on things.

I took the master keys and did a speed-run of the upper floors, opening and closing doors without stepping inside. I found myself peering into cleaning cupboards, linen cupboards, storerooms, but nothing that looked like security until I reached the sixth floor and unlocked a room full of blank computer screens.

No electricity.

"Well, shit," I said out loud, shutting the door behind me.

I tapped a few of the keys, in case any of them were in an energy-saving hibernation state, but nothing happened. A few magazines had been left on the desk, and two half-empty mugs of coffee with contents that had turned to mold.

There was no way I could turn the electricity back on without alerting Dylan.

Leaving the computers, I turned my attention to the desk drawers and the filing cabinets. They weren't locked.

Inside one filing cabinet I found hundreds and hundreds of CDs, filed in order of date. I returned to the week preceding day one and realized that I'd have to take all of them. I had no idea what day Harriet Luffman actually went missing. I wasn't sure how I would even watch them, but I took two weeks' worth, just to be on the safe side.

Then I noticed a day was missing. I returned to the cabinet and searched through three months of CDs in case it had been misplaced. It hadn't. Only one CD was gone. Day one.

I searched the other filing cabinets for CDs linked to other camera feeds and quickly confirmed my hunch. Every other CD of that same date—the end date—was gone. At least I knew the date Harriet had disappeared, and that watching any of the other footage would be pointless.

I also knew now, for certain, that this was a cover-up. What's more, it could only have been covered up by someone who had access to this room, which narrowed my investigation down to staff. I can no longer trust any of them. Nathan is the only one I feel comfortable absolving, as no matter how hard I think about it, I can't imagine he'd have been able to fake his reaction on the day he found her.

Selecting the CDs dated immediately before and after the missing day, I left the room and locked it again behind me.

The hotel was deserted. Walking down the corridors alone when it was dark felt like being in the middle of an optical illusion. The mad pattern on the tiles bled into the patterned wallpaper and there were mirrors everywhere. Footsteps echoed. It reminded me of Patrick running on the floors above.

Aware that I was scaring myself, I paused and took a couple of deep breaths.

I heard footsteps again.

In the dark it was easy to think I was imagining them, but I wasn't. There were footsteps, uneven and heavy, like someone was having trouble walking farther down the corridor.

"Hello?" I called, like an idiot.

The footsteps halted.

I have no idea why I drew attention to myself.

I stared at the end of the corridor, where it split off into a fork. The stairs to the right, more rooms to the left. The elevators were somewhere behind me, but they were useless. I wondered if I could make a break for the stairs.

The footsteps started up again.

I backed up.

It crossed my mind that if I forced the doors, maybe I could hide in the elevators. For a crazy second, I thought that it might be the serial killer Victor Roux. His ghost. Still prowling the corridors of the sixth floor in the hotel where he had been taken down.

Then a person came into view: quite short, broad shoulders, leaning heavily against the wall.

"Sasha?" I called.

It was Sasha, Mia's twin brother.

The relief that I felt when I recognized him was short-lived. He responded to his name, but only by lurching forward. I couldn't tell what was wrong with him; maybe he was drunk. He fell from one wall into the other, then reached out to me and mumbled something.

"Sasha, are you okay?"

Then he started coming toward me at speed.

"Sasha, wait, hold on, are you okay? Do you need help?"

It was dark and I was scared, so my first instinct was to punch him. But I didn't want to hurt him.

"Sasha, wait!" I yelled as he reached both hands out for me.

I dodged sideways into the wall as his fingertips grazed the side of my head and I dropped the CDs with a clatter.

"Sasha!"

That shout came from Dylan, who had appeared at the end of the corridor.

Sasha turned at the sound of his voice, losing interest in me.

Dylan walked toward us and took Sasha by the shoulders, with barely a glance at me. "Sorry about this. I didn't realize he'd left his room."

"What?"

"He sleepwalks. I don't think anyone else has bumped into him before. Not many people go wandering around the hotel at this time." He looked pointedly at what I'd dropped, then started walking Sasha away. "You should probably get some sleep. You're going to need your energy in the morning."

I was too self-conscious to draw more attention to the CDs by picking them up, and annoyed that he had caught me.

I asked with some disbelief, "What, so he climbs stairs while he's asleep?"

Dylan glanced over his shoulder. "He set the kitchen on fire trying to make himself a stew while he was asleep. Sleepwalkers get around."

I bent down to gather the CDs as they neared the end of the corridor, my heart pounding from the odd disturbance. When I went to ask another question, both Dylan and Sasha were gone.

I was going to ask where else sleepwalkers had apparently got around.

Agitated and jumping at shadows, I returned to my room and locked and bolted myself in. I put the CDs on my desk, next to my papers and laptop, which had been out of battery for a long time. We're going on the food expedition in the morning. Maybe I can find another battery in the store, or charge it somewhere. It's worth a try.

I woke up twice more before some light started to creep through my window, convinced that someone was rattling the bolts on my door. Both times, my room was silent. But I don't think it was a nightmare. The sound had been too vivid. At one point I heard a child crying, distantly, and tried to tell myself that it was just Yuka Yobari walking the baby along the corridors.

I had never been so scared to leave a building before. We've spent almost two months in the same place; you'd think we'd have felt more inclined to reconnect with the outside world. But no one wanted to go. We weren't running low on food, not yet, but winter was creeping up on us, and Dylan wanted to have enough to comfortably get to spring.

The last time we sent anyone on a food expedition was when Dylan, Peter, and Sasha had returned from the woods with deer to freeze. We hadn't needed to.

It was only the image of the first English settlers, Jamestown, unable to grow crops and struck by famine over their first winter, digging up their own graveyards to eat their dead that filled me with any urgency. They had underestimated winter too. We couldn't afford to do the same. Like them, we couldn't rely on ourselves, the weather, or the soil to grow anything.

It was Adam, Tomi, Rob, Mia, and I. We met Dylan in the lobby. He asked us to bring whatever weapons we might have, as the hunting rifles were better at long range. Obviously I had nothing stashed away, so I was given a small knife from the kitchen like everyone else.

We were told to bring empty backpacks, and we were taking two cars. The women in the hotel had also instructed us to bring back as many tampons and sanitary pads as we could carry.

"Do you think anyone in the city is still alive?" Rob asked, because no one else would.

We all looked at each other.

"We didn't hear anything about Switzerland being in a blast zone, so maybe," Tomi said.

"We'd have seen it, surely," I added. "An explosion, I mean."

She shrugged. "At this stage it's being killed by other survivors you might wanna worry about."

"Who says we don't have sun anymore?" Rob laughed. "We have our own ray of sunshine right here."

"I'm just saying," she countered. "It's not radiation we should be worrying about. Radiation doesn't get hungry or go insane. You've all seen *The Road*, right?"

"If we get captured by cannibals, can someone promise to kill me?" Mia looked around the troop.

"Likewise," Tomi said.

"No one's getting eaten by cannibals!" I snapped.

Dylan nodded at me. "You heard the man. None of that talk. Let's go. I want us back before nightfall, and this shouldn't take more than a few hours. We're just going to the food store and back. That's it."

We made our way to the cars.

Dylan took his, with Tomi, Mia, and Adam, and I offered to drive the Volvo, with Rob in the passenger seat. I thought the familiar motions of driving would calm my nerves, but I hadn't driven in so long that, as Dylan pulled away in front, I thought I might have forgotten how. But muscle memory kicked in and I drove the Volvo around the hotel and down the woodland road.

The farther we drove away from the hotel, the lighter I felt.

"This feels trippy," Rob said, giving voice to my inner thoughts.

"I don't know what would be worse," I said, eyeing the gas dial. "If everything was deserted, or . . ."

"Or if people were still around."

"I know."

"Well, if people have been reduced to eating each other within a couple of months, we don't deserve to flourish as a species," he said with a wry smile.

I liked Rob. He was such a private person that you would assume he was shy, until you got to know him. He was quietly witty, with a brilliant smile and very bright, enthusiastic eyes. He spent a lot of his time in the woods, taking photos of what wildlife remained. His camera was one of the expensive ones. When I'd asked him about it, he said that he had been doing a degree in photography.

"We'll be fine," I said, more to myself than him.

"Did you see the sun this morning?"

"Yeah, actual sun."

"It made me think that maybe more than the cockroaches will come out the other side."

At the sight of sun this morning, a tiny break in the clouds after breakfast, several of us had rushed out to find a clear patch of ground. We stood there in total silence, gazing upward. It wasn't powerful. It wasn't the sort of sunshine where you could feel the heat on your face, but just knowing it was there, catching sight of it for a fleeting moment, was enough to fill me with hope. We stockpiled hope now, hoarded it within us and hoped it would be enough to tide us over until the next time there was a break in the cloud cover.

"How did you end up staying here?" I asked.

"I thought I'd spend a week here and photograph all the birds around the lakes. Black kites, barnacle geese, bean geese, warblers—it's such a rich area. I have a portable photo printer in my room so I'm hoping to print the series before we lose electricity completely."

"I'm trying not to think about that," I said.

"The electricity?"

"Yeah; it's coming. It's the not knowing that's the worst. Same with the Internet."

"Nothing more stressful than no Wi-Fi. Even before." Rob smiled.

I sped up a little as Dylan took a right, and Rob lowered his window to crane his neck out, looking down the other stretch of road heading toward the mountains. We hadn't seen another car yet, or another person. I thought about my colleagues who had left on foot that first day, how long it would have taken them to travel down these roads. I was worried that at any moment we were going to pass someone I recognized as roadkill.

"I feel sick," I said, becoming more and more agitated at the thought of other people. "What if we get held up?"

"Do you mean by bandits?"

"Yeah—the ratio of guns to people in Switzerland is huge."

"I'm surprised the hotel doesn't have more."

"We do; there's just no ammo."

He frowned, and I paused for only a second before taking the plunge. I had no allegiance to her.

"Tomi looted most of the ammo. After the first couple of hunting parties, we must be down to less than one box."

"Why would she do that?"

"She has a gun—just the one. She must have thought it best that no one else could shoot anyone."

"Um, who else knows?"

"Me, you, Adam, her."

"Dylan?"

"You don't think he would have staged a raid on her room by now if he knew?"

He looked perturbed. "Maybe we should say something."

"I don't know. She obviously told Adam and me in confidence. Maybe it's better if none of us has a gun."

"Yeah, but in situations like today?"

"Yeah, we could use them." I messed up a gear change and the car jolted. "Shit."

We both lapsed into silence, thinking about the same thing. On the one hand, Tomi undoubtedly had a point. A woman, in her room alone, would feel the need to be armed. Maybe she had to be. There was evidence that at some point there had been a murderer staying here, and there was a possibility the murderer could still be among us. Who were we to tell a young woman what she should and should not be afraid of? On the other hand, the calculated nature of it, removing the ability for the rest of us to arm ourselves and make that same call, was a problem.

"If we say something discreetly," I said, thinking out loud again, "I don't think Dylan would react too badly. He might take her to one side and have a quiet word. It wouldn't necessarily mean a full-on siege. We're not . . . savages."

"That's still a long way off," Rob agreed. "Though isolation does strange things to people."

"There's enough of us to stop this from turning into *The Shining*."

"*The Shining* only needed one man to go mad."

I thought of Harriet Luffman in the water tank.

Dylan took a right just before we reached the city, and I said, "Why did he do that?"

"Do what?"

"Turn off here."

"The big food shop isn't actually in the city. It's on the outskirts, barely any houses nearby. I think that's why Dylan suggested it. It might be safer."

I was relieved at the realization we were some way away from the city. It gave me a false sense of security, before the subsequent realization that nowhere is safe now.

The dying trees on either side of the road thinned a little and we emerged into the parking lot of a huge superstore. Dylan pulled up on the outskirts and I parked behind him. I saw him lean out his window and scan the area.

The place looked deserted. No cars had been abandoned here.

I got out.

Tomi had her backpack slung over one shoulder and had left it open just enough for her to reach inside at speed. She had definitely brought the handgun with her.

"What do you think?" I asked Dylan, who was sizing up the store, rifle in hand.

"I'd feel better if a couple of us stayed with the cars," he said. "In case we need to leave in a hurry."

"Shotgun staying with the car," Adam said.

Dylan nodded.

"I'll stay with the Volvo," Rob offered, and I handed him the keys.

"Don't come in after us," Dylan warned. "No matter what. Give us an hour, and if we don't come out, leave. If someone else comes out instead of us, leave. Understand?"

Adam and Rob exchanged a look.

The rest of us made our way across the parking lot. Mia had one hand on the knife she had brought, which was tucked into her belt. Tomi hung close to me, behind my left shoulder. I didn't mind. Seeing public spaces this devoid of activity was chilling. I felt like we were being watched, but I had no way of knowing.

"I'm really not digging how quiet it is," Tomi said.

"Me neither," Dylan agreed. "When we get inside, we split up. Mia, you come with me. Tomi, with J. We meet back at the entrance, but no one wanders around on their own. If anything happens, make noise."

"Like a signal?" From Mia.

I forced a smile. "My signal will just be yelling loudly."

"Is anyone else really fucking scared?" Mia asked.

"I'm shitting the bed, if that makes you feel any better," Dylan said.

"Okay, good. Not just me."

We approached the entrance and noticed the automatic doors were open. Dylan led the way in, very slowly. I thought we would be greeted by the smell of rotting food, but it wasn't as strong as I'd predicted. I knew then that there wasn't going to be much left. We approached the fresh-food aisle, and it was bare. A few rotten pieces of produce, some half eaten, were scattered about, but the majority of it had been plundered, probably weeks ago.

I looked up at the high ceilings and then at Dylan, who was shaking his head.

"I don't like this," he said.

I looked left toward the checkout lanes, then at the signs hanging above the aisles.

"We'll head for the pharmacy," I said.

Dylan nodded and took Mia off toward the canned-food aisle.

The sensation of being watched had gotten worse. I was glad Tomi was with me; she was the only one of us with the means to properly defend herself. We set off through the fresh-produce section, took a left at kitchenware, and headed toward the back of the store.

I said quietly, "Are you armed?"

"What do you think?" She raised her eyebrows, right hand hovering near the open zipper of her backpack.

"I think you should say something to Dylan about the bullets."

"Why?"

"Because the rest of us need to be able to defend ourselves too."

"And *my* ability to defend myself?"

"No one's out to get you, Tomi!"

"Have you *met* men?"

"What does that mean?"

"I mean it's not your decision to make for me!" she snapped.

"It's not your decision to make for everyone else either!"

We both froze. I thought I had heard something move. Tomi almost dropped her backpack, and all of a sudden the gun was in her hand. Her stance and grip were pretty solid; I had faith that if she needed to shoot something, she wouldn't miss.

"Can you even use one of these?" she asked, casting her eyes about.

"It's been a while." I paused. "Probably not well."

"Well, then."

She inclined her head in the direction of the pharmacy, and we resumed walking. She stopped and picked up a bottle of fabric softener, laughed, and put it back down.

I waited for her.

"It all seems so pointless now."

"I was thinking the other day about this collection of cactuses—cacti—that Nadia used to keep in the hallway. Ornaments, not real ones."

Tomi stared at me.

I spread my hands. "Why did we buy ornaments?"

She smiled. "Maybe we should find one for you. We'll swing by home and dining on the way back, make an adventure of it."

We reached the pharmacy and I jumped the counter. She did the same. There was nothing in the drawers, nothing behind the serving station itself. I took a piece of paper out of my pocket and scanned it. On it, Tania had written a hurried list of things she might need.

"Hey."

I turned and saw Tomi tapping a locked door with her foot. There was a metal lock with numbered keys on it that released the door, like a safe. I opened and closed a few of the drawers, but all the pills that had been readily available had already been taken.

"Doesn't look like anyone's gotten in here yet," she said.

I watched her give it some thought. If she shot the lock off, she would alert everyone not only to our presence but to the fact that she had a gun.

"Well?" I said.

"Just wait a second." She turned the handle, tried a few numbers, punched the button to cancel, and then tried again.

"You're not going to guess it," I said.

"Just let me try first."

"There might be more antibiotics in there," I said. "We don't have enough."

"I know! Stop *explaining* things to me."

I leaned out from behind the counter, looking left and right down the aisles. "Look, we can say we found the gun, if that's what you're worried about."

"You would do that?"

"Yeah, but only because it's for you to tell Dylan, not me. I don't like to make decisions for people."

"You're actually insufferable." She sighed and looked down at the gun. "I'll say I found it in the hotel. There's no way Dylan wouldn't recognize his own gun. I'll, um . . . I'll deal with the other thing in my own time."

I nodded.

She had just taken aim at the lock when someone else, from behind me, said, "Jon?"

I was glad I hadn't been holding a gun, because I would have shot blindly at the sound of a voice that wasn't Tomi's. My legs almost gave out and I ducked instinctively as Tomi swung around and aimed at the space over my head. To her credit, she didn't pull the trigger.

"Jon?"

"Who the fuck are you?" Tomi shouted.

I stopped shielding my head and turned around on my knees. It took me a moment to recognize the faces that were peering at us, terrified, from over the counter, but then it hit me. Their names took a while longer to come, but I recognized them. I knew them!

"Tomi, wait!" I said, standing. "Jessie? Al!"

They broke into smiles, and Jessie—Jessica Schrader—climbed over the counter to hug me. She was a warm-faced professor in her early sixties, from Detroit originally but taught at . . . UCL? She definitely taught somewhere in London.

As she threw her arms around me I could feel that she had become stronger. She almost lifted me clean off the ground.

Over her shoulder, Albert Polor, a professor of Latin American history in his late fifties, had lowered a hunting rifle.

"What are you doing here?" I let her go and Tomi stepped forward to stand at my shoulder, still wary. "Tomi, it's fine, I know them. They're from the conference."

"Where did you get that?" She nodded at Al's rifle.

He clutched it close to his chest in what looked like an involuntary gesture. "I found it."

"You left months ago. What happened?" I asked.

"We only made it so far," Jessie said. "I thought we were goners; we didn't realize how far away the city was. Then we found this place. It was chaos, being ransacked. We . . . found some weapons."

She glanced at Al, and I saw the look that passed between them. I knew then that they had killed someone for that gun. It sent a slight shudder through me and made me move closer to Tomi.

"We stayed here, for the shelter," she went on. "Stockpiled some food and drove a few of the mobs out. It's just Al and me now, has been for a while. You're not looking for food, are you?"

"We are, actually."

Jessie shook her head. "Ours is running low too."

"Weapons?" Tomi asked.

"We have a few of those." Al shifted. "Sometimes we still get groups coming in from the city. Well, we assume they're from the city. But it's nothing large or organized. They know pretty much all the food is gone, but they know we have some."

"It's gotten that bad?"

"Seems about as bad as expected," Al said.

"What's behind this door?" Tomi asked.

"More medication, we think," Jessie said. "We've been good for drugs so far, and lucky. We were saving the stash back there for emergencies."

There was a brief silence, and I heard activity farther down the store. Out of the corner of my eye I saw Dylan and Mia edging toward us. Dylan was holding his rifle, and it struck me that it might not be loaded.

"Dylan, it's okay!" I waved at them. "They're fine!"

"Who are you?" he called.

"They're from the conference! I know them!"

"Jesus." Dylan lowered his gun.

I noticed that he and Mia had managed to fill their packs. I saw Dylan take in the image of Tomi holding his gun. He eyeballed her but said nothing. I suspected he didn't want to have the discussion in front of strangers.

"You've been here the whole time?" he said, looking Al and Jessie up and down.

"We made one run toward the city, but it's dangerous," Al said.

"What's it like?"

"Not busy. People barricaded into their homes. Lots of shooting if you venture out into the road in plain view of any houses, or even appear on the outskirts. It's like a war zone. Though before our electricity went down we were able to get online for a while. Now our phones are dead."

"Was there news?" Mia instantly went for her phone, unsure whether to turn it on. "We don't have any Internet."

"You're still at the hotel?" Al seemed incredulous, and I resented him for it. "Why?"

"You're still here. Why?" Tomi replied.

"Back to the Internet," Mia interjected. "What's going on? Are people online?"

"Yeah, it's patchy. Not everywhere still has it, and obviously the major cities are wiped out, but people could still get on social media as late as a month ago. Some people were still using Messenger and Twitter, though it's mostly just trying to find family members."

An electric feeling—hope—soared in my chest. I said to Tomi, "Does your phone still work?"

"Yeah," she said.

"Please, could you check my wife's Facebook account? Her Twitter page?"

"Yeah."

"Please. Please, could I use your phone?" I actually clasped my hands together, overcome by this irrational, dizzying fear that she was going to say no. "Please, only for a minute."

"Buddy, relax." She handed over her phone. "It's fine."

I took the phone off to one side, barely aware of what anyone else was doing anymore, and jumped the counter again, turning the phone on with clammy hands. I don't know why I moved so far away from the group, but it felt like something I wanted to keep intensely private.

Behind me, I could hear a terse conversation taking place. It didn't become apparent until I returned, but it was about the locked door and medication.

The phone came to life and I turned on Tomi's data, praying for it to connect to something. There were two bars of signal. It was the most I'd seen on any cell since that first day.

It connected. I went straight to Twitter, which was what Nadia had used most.

Her last post was from the night before everything had started. Or ended. It had been a retweet of a headline from CNN, about a breakdown in communication between our president and the other representatives of the UN Security Council. It was bizarre seeing it now. I remembered feeling doom-laden about politics, but there had been no sense of urgency in me. I had never believed it would come to something like this. Even after all the marches I accompanied Nadia to, all the antinuclear protests that had made me feel like I was living in the sixties, the mounting hysteria, I had never believed it.

With no sign of new activity on Nadia's Twitter page, I logged in to my Facebook account.

There was nothing from Nadia, but I did have messages—three of them.

Heart beating wildly, unable to keep still for excitement and walking even farther away from the group, I scrolled through the messages. One was a public service announcement from Facebook to its users. The other two were from former students who had added me after graduation. I read those first. By the looks of it, they were sent to a long list of people.

The first, from Millie Santiago, said, "Can anyone see this message???"

The second, from Alice Reader, said, "Is anyone still alive? Pls answer me! I'm in St. Cloud!"

They had been sent over a month ago.

The message from Facebook was longer. It was an announcement that several nations had launched nuclear attacks in the last twenty-four hours, and that by checking the button below we could choose to let family members and friends know if we were safe. Going back to my timeline, only four people I knew had checked in as safe; none of my family, closest friends, or colleagues. Of those four, two of them had messaged me.

I returned to the messages and replied to both with "Jon here, I'm at L'Hôtel Sixième in Switzerland. I don't have access to the Internet all the time, but please let me know you're okay, and, if there's any way to do so, please try to contact my family, Nadia Keller in San Francisco, or Ian and Barbara Keller in Greenwood, MS. Stay safe. I'm not sure when I'll be online again, but if you can, stay in touch. J."

That seemed like enough.

I checked my email, on the slim chance that Nadia had sent something, but—tragically—my inbox was littered with automatic subscriptions from ticketing sites, stores, and weekly newsletters. That was it. Email wasn't immediate enough to turn to in an emergency.

If she had attempted to send me a message, it would have been by text or voice mail, and I had smashed my phone.

Before I logged off I sent a message to Nadia's Facebook and Twitter: "Please let me know you and the kids are okay. I'm alive and in Switzerland still. I love you all so much. Please be safe. J."

I stood for a while longer just out of earshot to deal with that tiny spark of hope having been extinguished. I switched off Tomi's cellular data and phone. I turned and saw that all were pointing guns at one another.

"Whoa! Hey! Hey, what's going on?"

"You stay there!" Jessie snapped at me, swinging a weapon around and pointing it at my face.

I'd never had a gun pointed at me before. I didn't hear Tomi shouting, or Dylan. All I could see and feel was the end of the gun. Then I met Jessie's eyes, and they were as dark and bottomless as the barrel I was staring down.

"What are you doing?"

"We're going to need those pills," Jessie said. "You need to go."

Behind her, Al had his rifle aimed at Tomi, and Dylan had his aimed at Al. Tomi also had her gun aimed at Al.

"You're not coming back with us?" I looked between them, and there was something ruthless in Al's face.

"Why would we go back?" he said, not taking his eyes off Tomi.

"It's safe!" I yelled.

"Nowhere is safe. At least here we have supplies and a good view of whoever comes to get them. We had our bags stolen the same day we got here. Then we knew . . . it's not the same anymore."

"Guys, this is crazy!" I took a step forward and Jessie jabbed the gun at me.

"Don't move!"

"Do you know how to use that, little girl?" Al's eyes darted toward Dylan, then back toward Tomi, who stood her ground.

"You'll find out soon if you don't put that down."

I couldn't believe what was happening.

"Jessie, Al, we're friends," I said.

Jessie laughed. "Are you serious? It's the end of the world, Jon. Grow up." And then the side of her head blew out in a shower of blood and skull. I threw myself to the floor, with my hands over my ears, and missed what happened next. Another two shots rang out, impossibly loud. I stared ahead at Jessie, a pool of blood expanding around her head, eyes half open and staring back at me, and behind her Al had fallen backward, the hunting rifle clattering to the floor and letting off a rogue bullet that missed Tomi by a couple of feet.

Tomi was crouching, having dropped after she fired the first shot. From there, she had fired twice into Al's chest.

The four of us were rooted to the spot as Al made rasping sounds, his lungs filling with blood.

Dylan was shielding Mia, rifle hanging by his side. It wasn't clear if he had fired or not.

After a minute I stood up and walked over to Al, who was dying with excruciating slowness.

"Can't you do something!" I looked back at Tomi, who had stood up again and was checking herself.

"I can't waste another bullet," she said.

"But he can't breathe!"

Tomi gave me a look, like the one Jessie had given me. *Grow up*. She coolly returned to the door behind the pharmacy counter and shot the lock to pieces. She kicked it open and disappeared inside.

Al choked, reached out with a grasping hand that found nothing.

"Guys, let's go!" Tomi called. "There's stuff here!"

Shaking his head, wanting to get away from the scene, Dylan followed her.

Mia was leaning against the nearest wall, trembling violently.

I didn't follow anyone. I sat on the ground behind Albert Polor, from NYU, and took his hand. He looked up at me and struggled to breathe, his grip on me getting weaker and weaker until he wasn't struggling anymore. Over my shoulder, Jessie Schrader from UCL had died instantly, and I realized I was sitting in her blood. Tomi's shot had been as good as her word.

We looked around for some more food but couldn't find much.

"At least no one will die of flu while we all starve to death," Adam remarked, looking at one of the boxes of pills we'd taken from the back room.

Dylan was slightly more optimistic and wanted us to venture farther into town, but the rest of us weren't keen on the idea and decided we'd done enough for one day.

I took some laptop batteries with me from the electronics aisle. It was hard to tell which ones were suited to my Mac, if any, so I took several, plus anything with an Apple logo on it. I also stole what I think is a portable charger.

I rode with Tomi and Dylan on the way back. Tomi was driving. I wanted to be there when Dylan started questioning her about his gun. I'm not sure whether I wanted to back Dylan up or defend Tomi. That was the problem with oxytocin: it had made me fond of her. Yes, she had saved us all, but she had also shot two of my colleagues, my friends. Despite all of this, the irritating urge to protect her persisted.

"Where did you get that?" Dylan asked as soon as we had pulled out of the parking lot and were back on the forest road.

"I don't remember," she said. "I found it the day it happened. I just saw it and thought I might need it. Didn't think to ask whose it was."

"Yes, but where?"

"I told you, I don't remember."

"You know that's mine."

"But you already have guns," Tomi said, artfully coy. "Why do you need this one?"

Dylan hesitated. On the one hand, he wanted his gun back. On the other hand, he was low on bullets and didn't want to give away just how big the hotel's arsenal was.

I chipped in from the back, "How many guns do we have at the hotel?"

"Some," he said. "Guests could rent them for hunting. I handed some out when we went looking for deer and collected them back at the end. I don't want too many people having rifles."

"Can we not distribute them?"

Tomi glanced back at me, surprised.

"I don't think that's a good idea," Dylan said, looking down at the rifle lying across his lap.

"Why?" I pressed.

"The more guns everyone has, the more likely accidents become."

"Well, you're not taking mine," Tomi said.

"Fine. But I don't think we should be distributing guns to the group. We don't know everyone here. Things could get nasty."

"Should that be your decision?" she countered, echoing my point from earlier.

"It has to be someone's. Do you trust everyone here to control themselves?" He paused, and then added, "Also, I don't want to create the opportunity for quick suicides. We don't know how many people are still hanging in there for fear of pain. I don't want to find out. I also don't want to find out if anyone's been holding a grudge, or feeling frustrated about rations."

"Bleak," I said.

"I'm realistic." Dylan sighed and appeared to come to a decision. "Okay, Tomi, keep it. You can clearly use it. How are you doing for bullets?"

"One bullet. Maybe two. Whatever was in the magazine."

"Okay."

I might have been mistaken, but a flicker of confirmation crossed Dylan's face and he went quiet.

Tomi met my eyes in the rearview mirror as she reached up to adjust it.

Dylan saw the look that passed between us but didn't draw attention to it.

I wiped my hands on my pants, but the blood had dried. My tooth had started hurting again, probably because I was grinding my teeth from the stress.

The car in front screeched to a halt, and Tomi slammed on the brakes.

I flew off my seat and smacked my face on the back of Dylan's headrest. I clutched my nose and my hands came away dripping with fresh blood. I hadn't thought to put on my seat belt. I shouted, "What the fuck!" and when I finally managed to open my eyes, Tomi and Dylan had left the car.

I grappled for the handle and almost fell out in my haste to follow them.

My nose was broken, I was certain.

"What the fuck?" Dylan yelled.

"Look!" Adam gestured at the trees at the side of the road.

I couldn't see anything until he pointed out the thin cross carved into one of them. I looked beyond it as the pain spread to my eyes and forehead, and saw another one, and another . . .

"Someone left the road and marked the trail," Adam said.

Mia: "It's a trap."

"Or they needed to remember the way out," Dylan countered.

"How long would it have taken them to get this far from the hotel on foot?" Tomi asked. "If they were from the hotel."

"I don't know, but more than a day. Takes us a while driving."

I snorted blood. "So how long to the city on foot from here?"

"I don't know, I've never done it."

"You can't guess?"

"I don't know; it's not a long drive, but on foot . . . this isn't flat terrain."

Everyone looked at one another, and Tomi exclaimed, "Jon, what's wrong with your face? Are you okay?"

"I wasn't wearing my seat belt."

Dylan touched my shoulder. "You need to sit down?"

"No, I'm fine! I'll come with you."

Mia grimaced. "So . . . we're going?"

"We have to check, right? Someone might be alive out here." Tomi slammed the car door. "You can stay with the cars if you want."

She walked off into the forest, and those of us who reckoned ourselves brave had to prove it by following her.

Mia and Adam stayed with the cars.

"Why would you leave the road?" Rob mused from behind me.

"It's cold. You'd rather camp with some cover." I glanced over my shoulder. "Or something scares you."

Rob reached into his pocket and handed me a tissue. "I think you need this."

I pressed it to my face, where it collected blood.

We must have walked in silence for about fifty yards before I saw Tomi stop up ahead, and then Dylan. I had fallen a little behind, lost in thought about Jessie, and how she had looked at me with no humanity in her eyes, like I was a stranger, an enemy looter.

Rob and I approached, and I said, "What? See anything?"

No one answered.

We started hurrying, worried by their lack of response, and came up alongside them. But Tomi's gun was hanging down by her side.

I took the tissue away from my nose and surveyed the small clearing with my aching eyes.

Whoever they were—the two young men, partially decomposed, with their arms around each other—they had tried to build a shelter out of branches and leaves and had lain among them in two sleeping bags. They didn't have anything else.

I noticed a pair of improvised crutches lying off to the right, next to their makeshift fort, and realized that, with a broken ankle or any other serious leg injury, they wouldn't have stood a chance. They would have frozen to death before they reached another building, let alone the city.

Dylan took a step into the remains of the camp and unzipped one of their bags.

"There's food in here," he said, holding up a box. "And these are prescription painkillers, photos, cooking equipment. They aren't from the hotel. It looks like they came from the city."

I don't know how that was all he said; those cool observations.

I looked at Tomi, because she usually had something to say, but she was just staring into space.

Dylan picked up both bags and slung them over his shoulder.

I said, "At least there's some food."

"Some canned salmon, vegetables, mackerel. Soda too." Dylan took another look through, trying to keep his eyes off the bodies and his voice light. "They even have some bags of gummy bears and chips. That's the good news."

Tomi said, "So people were fleeing the city."

In a way, she had said what we were all thinking but were too afraid to say out loud.

She nodded, as if confirming a harsh truth to herself, then turned around and left, leaving the rest of us to sit with the implications of that.

I offered to take one of the bags from Dylan, but he rebuffed me.

Then we all left that horrible scene.

Tomi drove us back to the hotel in silence. We had technically found what we were looking for, but it was hard to feel optimistic, given that we'd also seen such a damning loss of hope. Maybe we had all been afraid to consider what lay outside our stretch of land before, because it was too scary to think that the answer might be nothing.

The thought had occurred to me once or twice: Would killing myself really be that bad, considering? Did I want to see where we—and humanity as a whole—ended up? Did I want to see how much worse things got before they—*if* they—ever got better?

But the idea always repelled me. As long as I could continue to be useful, I would stay. I wouldn't voluntarily throw my life away. I'd never think badly of those who decided it was too much, because it was. It *is* too much. But I could have been in San Francisco when those bombs fell, I could have been in Mississippi with my parents, and I was in neither. I had ended up in one of the few places that escaped total devastation, and the idea of creating more by giving in to despair seemed ungrateful somehow.

I wanted to ask Tomi multiple times if she was okay, but I sensed she didn't want to hear anything from me. I couldn't get my head around the psychology of being more upset about the suicide of two people than the deaths of the two she had killed herself.

I watched her drive, still holding my throbbing nose, and thought about that nod. She had nodded to herself before leaving the clearing, and it was grim. Nod. *So that's it, then.* Nod. *There's nothing out there.* Nod. *There is definitely no help coming.* Nod. *We're totally on our own.*

Yesterday, when we got back, everything and everyone was disjointed. It felt like we were all avoiding one another. Even in the restaurant, few people were talking. The Yobaris, and some of the women who had formed a group, seemed normal. But not the people I was close to.

I went to bed as soon as we got back and slept through the night, after Tania confirmed that my nose wasn't actually broken. Tomi slept next to me, to keep an eye on me in case I had a concussion.

Today, I interviewed Peter, a single man in his forties who I had wrongly assumed was French but I now know is German. He would only be interviewed in his room, which is sparse and tidy. He has one of the palest and most weathered faces I have ever seen, like it was carved out of solid rock.

Tania agreed to be present to translate and also to transcribe his responses, as he refused to be interviewed in English (even though I know he can speak it).

I've edited Tania's notes, and the interview unfolded as follows:

> **Me:** So you were staying at the hotel alone?
> **Peter:** Yes. I don't think there's anything wrong with that.
> **Me:** No, of course not. Where did you live originally?
> **Peter:** Oranienburg.
> **Me:** Where is that?
> **Peter** (*rolling his eyes*): It's a small town outside Berlin, where I worked.
> **Me:** So what did you do?
> **Peter:** I was a children's counselor. I specialized in assisting attorneys in questioning child witnesses appropriately.

I hadn't expected this, so I hesitated. Tania stopped writing for a moment as she repeated the answer back to me in English.

Peter: What?

    Me: Nothing, sorry. It's just interesting to find out about people's lives before they came here. Why did you come and stay at the hotel?

Peter: I wanted time alone. I was going to hunt deer.

    Me: Any particular reason?

Peter: My wife said she wanted a divorce. I offered to leave the house for two weeks, to allow her to move out without my presence.

    Me: Did you manage to contact your wife, after . . . everything happened?

Peter: No.

    Me: I'm sorry.

Peter: I'm not.

    Me: Okay. So how long were you staying here before the morning of that day?

Peter: Two days, before it all ended.

    Me: What do you remember about that day?

Peter: I woke up late, just before midday, as I'd gotten a taxi back from the city at three in the morning the night before. By that point, most of the other guests had left, as you know.

    Me: You slept through the end of the world.

 Peter (*ignoring my comment*): I packed my bag—I didn't bring much, as you can see—and left on foot. I quickly realized that walking toward the city was going to be extremely pointless, especially as I then wouldn't be able to get further transport to the airport. I had only walked about a mile, so I turned and came back, let myself into my room, and waited to see if any help was going to come. (*spreads his hands*) We are all still waiting.

    Me: Do you remember seeing what anyone else was doing?

Peter: Who?

Me: Anyone still here. Do you remember them from that day at all? Dylan, Sophia, Nathan—any of them?

Peter: No, because I didn't know them then. I mind my own business. There are more important things to do than constantly observe strangers.

Me: Okay, I'll be more specific: Do you remember anyone acting suspiciously?

Peter (*a long pause*): No.

Me: Do you remember seeing any children during your stay?

Peter: The two Japanese children. There was a woman with a baby, who is now with the Japanese couple. Another girl, with red hair, strawberry blond.

Me: How old?

Peter: Excuse me?

Me: The girl.

Peter: I don't know. Eight? Ten at most.

Me: Where did you see her?

Peter: Getting breakfast the morning before the world ended.

Me: Did she attract your attention for any reason?

Peter: No. I just remember her existence.

Me: Do you remember anything about her parents?

Peter: Her father looked like a sad man.

Me: He seemed sad?

Peter: No. He looked like a sad person.

Me: Why would you notice that?

Peter: Why would I not?

Me: Do you remember anything about her mother?

Peter: I didn't see a mother.

Me: You said "parents."

Peter: You said "parents." I said "father."

Me: She was only with her father?

Peter: She was at breakfast with her father; the mother may have been elsewhere. I didn't feel the need to speculate.

Me: How much do you know about the history of the hotel?

Peter: I know a famous serial killer stayed here. Apart from that, all I know is that it is old.

Me: Has anything strange happened to you during your time here?

Peter: Apart from nuclear war?

Me: Yes, apart from that.

Peter: I sometimes feel that there might be more people in the hotel than we know about. It's such a huge place. It plays on my mind. And it's a very noisy building, a lot of bangs and bumps in the night. But I don't think that has much to do with anything but old pipes.

Me: You haven't seen anyone you don't know?

Peter: No. Not yet.

Me: Did you have any children?

Peter: No.

Me: Did you ever want children?

Peter: No. My wife did. I didn't.

Me: Why?

Peter: I've seen what happens when people think they're fit to be parents and they're not. People are so arrogant; they assume anyone is up to the job. They have kids in their twenties, or even earlier, before they know how to be an adult themselves. Anything you do not deal with through extensive introspection and therapy, you will pass on to your children. I would never assume that I was good enough to be a father. I doubt many people are.

I paused for a moment here. For some reason his answer got to me, and I reacted with annoyance.

Me: Do you like children?

Peter: It depends on the child. You can't say you dislike children, as a concept. Some children are great people, some are not. It's largely up to their parents.

Me: Why do you think someone would have murdered a girl
here and left her in the water tank?

Peter. I don't know, I'm not a criminal psychologist. But it's usually the parents.

Me: You think her parents did it?

Peter: If it's a dead woman, it's the boyfriend, or husband. Dead
child, usually the parents.

Me: Have you spoken to the Yobari children much?

Peter: No.

Me: Why?

Peter: I don't know the Yobari couple. And I haven't been required
to work.

Me: Do you think it might have been a mercy killing? The girl in
the water tank? World ends, parents kill her to spare her the
aftermath?

Peter (*shrugging*): It's a theory, but a very stupid form of reasoning.

Me: Why?

Peter: We are going to need all the children we can make. Or the
species dies out.

There was a pause in conversation as I checked my notes, to see if I
had prepared any further questions. Then Peter pointedly asked if we
were done, so Tania and I left the room. The interview was over.

She laughed. "He's a weird one. Can you believe he worked in mental health?"

I also laughed, and said, "No, I can't."

When I returned to my room I found Nathan waiting for me outside. He had written down the brief story of why he had come to work
at the hotel. It's surprisingly well written, and even stranger than I remember. I'll attach it here.

NATHAN

I love you all more than life.
I need to go. Don't try to find me.
I wish I could explain more.

Your Harold (Dad)

He was my stepdad, actually. But that was the note. Mum found it on Christmas Eve morning, a decade ago. She didn't mention it to either of my sisters. They were too young to understand. For some reason, at thirteen, I was considered adult enough to handle it.

I knew something was wrong from the moment I woke up. I sensed that leaving my bed would cause a horrific event, so I stayed in bed until almost two in the afternoon before going down.

The TV was on in the living room, and both my sisters were sitting on the floor.

Mum was at the dining table. The note was right there in front of her, but I didn't notice it right away. I noticed her expression first; staring a thousand miles into the future. Looking back, she'd probably been relieved.

"Are you okay?" I asked.

"Did your dad say anything to you last night?" she said, turning the note over so I couldn't read it. "I heard you two talking, but I didn't want to eavesdrop. I thought it was good for you to be talking again."

"No, nothing important. He was just asking about school and stuff."

"Anything in particular?"

"No," I lied.

"And he seemed normal?"

I forced a smile, kidding myself that it was a normal question. "As normal as Dad can be."

She'd been crying. I could see the traces of tears on her cheeks. Weirdly, they made her look younger. But I didn't ask about any of that because, more than anything, I just wanted the interaction to be over.

Blinking hard suddenly, she pushed the note away with two fingers. "He's gone away again."

Without reading the note, I knew he wasn't coming back. I'd known as soon as I woke up. To be honest, I'd known it since the night before. I knew something had gone wrong, and now it made sense. He was gone. He wasn't coming back. Fine. Good fucking riddance, thirteen-year-old me thought.

"So, sunny Switzerland like last time, then?" I said.

She frowned. "Switzerland?"

"Um . . ." I'd forgotten that I wasn't supposed to know that much. "I don't know. I just imagine that's where most guys having a midlife crisis go. Or Vegas."

"Oh."

Every time she believed one of my lies I lost more respect for her. I'm a great liar, but it didn't cause me to feel any sympathy, especially not towards my mum. Not knowing when your own kid was lying to you, that's just sad.

For the record, though, this story is true.

The Christmas tree lights in the living room were flashing red and blue on the floor.

I picked up the note.

"He'll be back," I said, and turned to go upstairs.

In my room, I replayed the nervous breakdown Dad had had in front of me the night before.

His breakdown had come not long after Mum had hers. My mum—the lifelong Christian—had stopped going to church and later stopped praying altogether when she realized God wasn't going to un-liquidate Dad's company. All those points she'd banked, giving money to our local church and the hours spent sitting in uncomfortable chairs listening to dudes talk. In her mind it made perfect sense for Him to give back in her hour of need because she'd never directly asked God for anything before. It didn't occur to her that He might have better things to do than cut deals with Australia's upper-middle class.

So there was no He, she decided.

On the night before the note, I was sitting at the dining table finishing an essay. The twins were at a clarinet recital. Mum was in the kitchen, and Dad was going crazy. He walked into the room like a ghost and sat next to me with this odd watery-eyed smile.

"Can I talk to you?"

"Don't know, can you?"

Silence.

"Yes. Obviously," I added. "What do you want?"

"Can you . . . leave that for a moment?"

I put my pen down and rotated exactly ninety degrees in my chair.

"There's something I wanted to tell you," Dad said, putting his hands on the table and then taking them off again.

I was glad we weren't actually related, only by marriage. Harold looked like a partially melted waxwork. He might have had a strong jaw once, but it had slouched into jowls very quickly. His once-blue eyes had become pale, like when water comes out of the taps cloudy.

"When I went away for that week—"

"Month," I corrected him.

"It wasn't a month."

"Yes, it was. I was here, remember?"

A flicker of impatience. "Okay, a month. I want to tell you where I was, what happened to me."

I raised my eyebrows but didn't encourage him.

"I went to Switzerland, to this hotel, the Sixième . . ."

Oh, here we go, I thought.

"I don't know why, I just picked anywhere. I had to get away and think. I was there for a couple of nights, not drinking or anything like that. I barely left my room. But after a few nights, something . . . happened."

I slouched a little, in preparation.

He's dying? I thought.

It was hard not to think so from the expression on his face. It was somewhere between rapture and grief.

Maybe him and Mum are getting divorced?

He had an affair?

He's too boring to have an affair.

After some deliberation, he said, "I found God."

I didn't allow him to see a visible reaction. I was blank, completely passive.

"I found God because one night, while I was lying there awake, I felt this terrible pain. It was agony, son, you can't imagine it. I thought I was having a heart attack, I couldn't even move to get to the phone, and I was certain I was going to die. Then I looked down . . ." He took a breath. "I saw something climb out of my chest. These long claws hooked into either side and this thing, this demon, hauled itself out. The pain was . . . the pain . . . Excruciating."

Goose bumps flew up along my arms. I covered my mouth, watching him over the top of it.

"And when it was out, it looked like a skeleton, or a lizard, somewhere between the two. It crawled across the room into the corner and looked back. He . . . it . . . had huge teeth, and it snarled at me and then disappeared."

I wasn't sure what I'd expected, but this level of insanity hadn't been it. In front of me had been a man who began every fucking discussion of my life with "And where is your evidence to support this?" He was an atheist, and not relaxed about it. He was the kind that told his kids we'd decompose into the dust and soil and that there was no God, no Easter bunny, no Father Christmas.

My dad, Harold Adler the atheist, said, "And that's when I knew there is a God. There must be. It was the most profound peace that washed over me. It was just . . . a knowing. All the worry and the doubt, and the pain, the evil. It all vanished along with that demon. I can't phrase it any better than that. It was peace. It was a knowing."

The silence had gone on for too long. I had no fucking idea what to do or say. I didn't believe in God; he'd made sure of that.

"A knowing," I repeated, because I was thirteen and I mostly wanted the selfish fuck to tell me what to say.

"It was important for me to tell you," he said, inclining his head.

"I get it." I nodded like I understood. "You've found God. Great."

"Are you okay with this?"

I hated him more than I had ever hated him before, or since. I hated him more than I even hated Mum. They'd both betrayed me, but this nonsense was so much more unexpected coming from him.

This was the guy who was in love with maths, formulas, science, and he couldn't just fuck a twenty-year-old or buy a stupid car or go on a bender like anyone else. No. Dad had to find God. Fucking God. Of all the rebellions he could have chosen, he chose the most offensive one.

You fuckhead, I thought, because that was the second-worst word I knew and I'd feel too guilty calling him the worst, even in my head.

"Don't you have any . . . questions for me?"

For the first time in my life, I wanted to punch him. I was never violent. I'd never done anything like that. I'd been angry, yeah, but I'd never felt the need to physically hurt anybody.

"Nope," I lied.

I should have asked if he'd said any of this to my sisters yet. They were eight. They might buy it. I should have asked if he'd considered that it was obviously fucking sleep paralysis or remind him of all the times he wouldn't entertain me or my sisters talking about nightmares or monsters at night because they don't exist, whether he'd ever considered how his kids might feel listening to this after growing up with the most hard-line of rationalists for a dad, who had poked holes in every childish fantasy we'd ever had and painstakingly explained the wonder out of everything we might have thought was magic. I should have asked how he'd somehow managed to humiliate us all even more. Disappoint us even more. I should have asked if it had occurred to him that killing himself might be the best fucking thing for the family at this fucking point.

But I didn't say any of that.

My cheeks were hot. I picked up my pen.

"No, I'm good."

Dad at least had the grace to look crushed, and in a way, that almost made up for not being able to punch him.

"Oh, well, I, uh . . . I'm glad we were able to talk about it."

I looked up, and my face said, *We haven't.*

Dad rose awkwardly from his chair and went to leave. Before he went through to the living room, he paused and said, "I do love you, you know."

I chose to nod. I hoped that somehow managed to convey the disdain I felt for how much of a fucking failure he'd been as a father.

As soon as Harold left the room I took my essay upstairs, alarmed at the thought of seeing either of my parents again that evening. Both of them, U-turns that could be seen from space, within a few months of each other. I couldn't remember hating them both more.

That turned out to be the last time I saw my stepdad.

I brought the note back up to my room, and Mum didn't try to stop me.

Don't try to find me.

I don't know why it took almost ten years for me to move my stuff out. I don't know what moved me to finally start making arrangements to come and work here. I checked job vacancies now and then. I'd even seen some come and go. But it took ten years for me to commit.

When I moved out, Mum made it clear that she didn't think I was coming back. I left her grieving two losses instead of one.

Well, three losses, if you counted God.

I'm not sure what to make of Nathan's story. It's got me thinking more about why we all came to be here. I can't imagine finding God here, like his father had. As far as I can see, He is conspicuously absent. If there is a God, and He isn't an interventionist, then I think He'd be feeling very disappointed by His failed experiment right about now.

There is always the possibility that Nathan could be lying, for the sake of a good story. But I can't see why he would do that. I wondered, fleetingly, whether mental illness was something that could be learned, inherited without being passed through a bloodline. But I'm going to keep that train of thought to myself. There is no evidence that Nathan is crazy.

After a quiet morning I spent most of this afternoon up on the roof with Dylan and Nathan, trying to fully remove the lid of the first water tank. Dylan, with a rope tied around his waist as a makeshift harness, was balancing on the far edge of the tank. I was at the top of the ladder, also with a rope tied around my waist, looped over a hook that Dylan had welded to the structure.

No one was sure if it would hold. We didn't have a way of testing it.

There was no wind today, and it wasn't cold either. The air felt heavy and dense. I was sweating for the first time in weeks. I shrugged my coat off and let it drop onto Nathan's head.

"Thanks!" he called.

I took hold of the saw with both hands and wrenched it left, right, then left again.

"You all right?" Dylan asked.

My face still hurt, but it wasn't hampering me.

"Yeah, almost!"

The metal began to slide and I dropped the saw, gripping the top of the tank so hard that the jagged edges left from our previous work cut into my hands. I thought the remaining part of the lid was going to fall onto me, dragging me off the side of the tank with it. It could likely have ripped me clean in half if the rope around my waist held. More likely pinned me dead to the rooftop.

"J, you good?"

I could barely see for the rush, but I gritted my teeth. "Yep."

"You think you can help me shift left?"

Nathan shouted, "Don't mind me, just dodging falling weapons!"

"Well, you need to pick up those tools and get out of the way. We're about to drop some iron on you!"

We gave one another the finger.

Dylan crouched on the small section of the lid that was still attached to the main tower and sawed the rest of it loose. The quarter circle threatened to fall into the tank, but Dylan and I shifted it onto the edge, let it rest there for a few seconds, and then tipped it into free fall.

It hit the deck with a clang that made my teeth rattle. Then I met Dylan's eyes. We'd accomplished the first of these four mammoth tasks.

Embarrassingly, I had never felt more like a man, in the basest sense of the word.

We both grinned, and the grim food expedition seemed further away.

Nathan whooped.

I started down the ladder, and as I did so I felt something cold hit the back of my neck. I had been staring down between my knees, checking that I had decent purchase on each rung, and as I looked up I found my glasses blurring with a flurry of drops.

"Holy shit, it's raining!" Nathan shouted. "Holy shit!"

I couldn't believe it. I scrambled the rest of the way down the ladder and stood on the rooftop with my hands outstretched, head tilted back, letting the freezing raindrops hit my face. Nathan was doing the same. I took off my glasses and put them in my pocket.

Dylan had climbed around the rim of the tank to the ladder and was making his way down.

We stood in the brief shower. It became heavier for about seven or eight seconds, enough so that I had to raise my forearm to shield my eyes. Then it slackened off and I was shivering, but I was so happy I didn't care.

"Never thought I'd be so stoked to see shitty weather!" Nathan exclaimed.

"I know!" I picked up my coat and slung it over my arm. "That was great. Maybe it's a good sign?"

"I think it's going to be rare," Dylan said, his tone loaded with sadness. "But I'm glad we got the top of that tank off."

"I need to get clean," I said.

"Actually, can you help me move that?" Dylan gestured at the scrap metal across the way.

"I'll do it. You go." Nathan waved at me. "You've done enough strongman-ing today."

He beat his chest, deadpan.

I laughed, knocking shoulders with him on my way past.

When I reached my room, I found it unlocked.

Before describing what I found I want to make one thing very clear: there is no way in hell I left my room unlocked. No one leaves doors unlocked anymore. I sometimes return to my door two or three times to check it.

Already knowing that something was wrong, I opened the door, took on a sideways stance and nudged it open the rest of the way with my foot.

"Is anyone there?" I called, terrified that I was about to be shot in the face in the doorway of my own room.

No reply or activity from inside.

The room looked exactly as it always did—except the Luffmans' suitcases had been taken. I did a quick circuit, checking to see if anything valuable was missing—not money, money was useless now, but toothpaste, shaving cream, razors. That was all there. All my stuff was there.

I sat on the edge of my bed and looked at the empty patch of carpet indented with grooves from the wheels of the two heavy cases. I followed them out into the hallway, but outside the floor was tiled. No marks.

I hadn't searched through the contents again, so I had no idea what I might have lost. It could be something crucial—actual evidence that had escaped me the first time Sophia and I had looked through them. I didn't know.

But of course I did.

I must have lost something crucial, or the cases wouldn't have been stolen in the first place.

Overcome with fury, I stormed back up to the rooftop, still wet, still shivering, and still holding my coat. Nathan and Dylan were in the stairwell, carrying the scrap metal between them. Dylan had floated the idea that he might use it to build something.

"You leave something up here?" Dylan asked when he saw me.

"My room's been broken into," I said, my voice shaking with cold.

"What?" they both said.

"Two cases, gone. My door was unlocked; it wasn't when I left. There's no chance any of the cameras are still working in this place, is there?"

Dylan shook his head.

Nathan seemed perplexed, and slowly they put the piece of metal down. "Your door was unlocked?"

"It wasn't when I left."

Dylan said, "But I have all the master keys. Apart from the set I gave you."

"Who else has a set of master keys?"

"No one. I collected them all from staff two or three days into this, and then I gave you one and told you to keep it quiet in case something like this happened. You didn't have yours stolen, did you? You didn't lose them?"

"No, they're in the pocket of my other coat. I checked." I realized everything was a little blurry because I'd ditched my glasses. "Two cases are gone. Someone just wheeled them out."

Nathan put his hands on his hips. "Sorry to say it, J-Dawg: I think you left your room unlocked."

"I did not!"

"Then how would someone get in there?" Dylan asked calmly, like I was a child.

"I never leave my room unlocked, Dylan. Ever."

"But you must have."

"I didn't. I'd bet my life on it!"

"Well . . ." Nathan spread his hands. "No forced entry, dude. No other explanation."

They didn't believe me.

Nathan said, "Hey, after this, I can help you look for your stuff, if you want."

"Can I search the rooms?" I asked, directing the question at Dylan.

"You were searching them anyway," he said, a little tersely. "You'll have to ask permission from people to search occupied rooms."

"Well, what reason would they have to refuse, unless they had the cases?"

Dylan shrugged.

Feeling unsupported and patronized, I turned and went back downstairs to my room, shaking all over. I changed my shirt, put on another coat, and left, making sure that I locked my door. I locked it, unlocked it, then locked it again, rattled the handle.

"I didn't leave it unlocked," I said out loud to myself.

I headed upstairs to Tomi's room, but she seemed off and didn't want to speak to me. When I knocked, she opened the door and said, "Can you come back later? I'm busy."

"Have you been crying?"

She sighed and shut the door in my face, so I assumed she would be sleeping in her own room tonight.

Tania was working, so I didn't want to bother her.

No one else I asked admitted to knowing anything about the suitcases. My best bet will likely be continuing the arduous search of rooms.

I returned to my room, locked the door, and took a nap.

———————

A few of us ended up sitting together at dinner. Lauren Bret and her girlfriend, Lex, stopped me to ask about the state of the Internet, and whether we'd seen anyone on the food run. I don't know either of them very well. The only facts I do know is that they're both French, they were not together before day one but they are together now, and they're both in their late twenties.

Lauren has long metallic-red hair that's grown out a little at the roots. She's very tall—taller than me—but has a round childlike face that always wears an expression of worry. Lex has shorter hair, blond, also growing out at the roots, and she's girlish, very small; I suppose stereotypically French. Her English isn't as good as Lauren's. Neither of them speaks very good English, to be honest.

"Did someone . . . ?" Lex mimed a punch, grimacing at my face.

"We were attacked, but . . . no, this was because I . . . um, didn't have my belt on."

They both looked a little disappointed.

"Wi-Fi?" Lauren asked, involuntarily turning her phone over on the table.

She pronounced it "wee-fee," which was endearing.

"I don't know about Wi-Fi, but Tomi's data was working at the store. I think the closer you get to the city, the better the signal is."

Lex said something in French and they gripped each other's hands.

Lauren added, "We might still be able to reach our parents."

"I wouldn't go without a car."

Lex said something else in French. As she and Lauren talked, Peter came and sat down opposite me and next to them. The Dutchman, Nicholas van Schaik, sat beside Peter. None of them seemed to particularly get along, but I supposed it was nice for them to not feel pressured into speaking English all the time. There was an obvious divide within the hotel, and it was between the English and non-English speakers.

Tomi took a look at us, hesitated, and sat off to the side, at another table.

The atmosphere became taut, and Lex muttered something. I saw both her and Lauren look at Tomi, and then at me.

"What?" I asked, trying to decide whether to get up for more coffee or water, just to get away from the table.

"She wants to know who you voted for," Lauren said.

"What?"

Peter coughed. "Who you voted for. Three years ago."

"Oh, *now* you speak English?" I snapped.

"I can speak English, and French. She wanted to know who you voted for in your last election."

"Who I . . . What?"

"Your *president*," Lex said, almost spitting the word at me. She pointed at Tomi. "She did. You?"

"Um . . ." I glanced over my shoulder at Tomi, and she was pretending to ignore us, face tilted completely downward toward her plate, hair hiding her eyes. "I . . . didn't vote for him. Neither did my wife."

Everyone nodded, like that made me okay.

I saw Dylan check the last few people off his register and disappear into the kitchens to get his own food off the hot plate. I wanted him to stay in the room.

Lex said something in French. It sounded angry.

"Are we okay here?" I asked.

"It was her fault," Lauren said, shrugging. "That's what she is saying. World is gone because of people like her."

"I don't think that's fair," I said.

"Why?" Van Schaik snapped, searching the room. "Where is the salt?"

"You can't blame one person for this just because—"

Lex slammed her cutlery down and shouted something that I didn't understand, and behind me I heard Tomi stand up. I stood up too, if only to put a body between them.

Peter glanced at Tomi and me, but seemed uninterested in the argument.

"Come on, this is stupid!" I looked between the French girls.

Tomi glared across me. "I'll leave, if you want."

"She is upset, you understand!" Lauren said with no hint of sympathy. "We lost everything because of you. Stupid fucking—"

She must have used a French curse word then, because I didn't recognize it.

"Fine. You got something to say as well?" Tomi folded her arms and raised her eyebrows at Van Schaik and Peter.

With an expression of total contempt, Van Schaik spat on the floor. "It's true."

"Oh, fuck you!" Tomi yelled, picking up her plate and striding out of the restaurant.

"Where is the salt?" Van Schaik asked again.

Lex sat down, her lip trembled, and a few moments later she got up and walked out. Lauren followed her.

Everyone was watching us.

Not wanting to sit alone with Van Schaik and Peter—who had said nothing and refused to look up from his food—I took my plate across the room to sit with Nathan and Tania, at my usual window table.

Tania's hair was in long braids, wrapped around her head.

"Hate to say it," she said, pushing some bean salad around her plate, "but she has a point."

I didn't have the energy to argue with her. I wasn't sure I even wanted to.

I wasn't going to write about what happened immediately after I left the restaurant, because it's hard to write about without sounding self-serving. But it is relevant, and after the argument over dinner I feel it's important to accurately convey what the atmosphere is like in the hotel at this time. Things are tense and melancholic between those of us who went on the food run, and my trust with the group is fractured by the theft of the suitcases. Everyone is now a potential suspect.

I've also come to realize that the non-Americans are stockpiling resentment. They blame us, Tomi and me, for what happened. They look at us and see one person who voted for this to happen and another who hadn't done enough to stop it.

Maybe I hadn't. Actually, there's no maybe about it. None of us did enough to stop it.

Van Schaik must have followed me out of the restaurant and into the stairwell.

My tooth was hurting, and so was my nose. I wasn't in the mood for company, so when he called, "Hey!" my first instinct was to snap, "What do you want?"

He caught up with me on the stairs, and he already looked like he wanted to fight. It wasn't hard to see why. Some people react to a crisis by shrinking into themselves. Others lash out. To be honest, the gender divide between these responses is obvious. Van Schaik had been locked into a state of fight or flight since day one, and so, to a lesser extent, had Peter. There was always aggression rumbling beneath the surface. None of us could fight the end of the world, so Van Schaik was going to fight everyone and everything else just to retain the illusion of control and power.

It was tiresome.

He didn't take kindly to my reply and said, "You think you're better than us, is that it?"

"No, Nicholas, I don't think that." I continued upstairs, and he followed me onto my floor.

"You think we're not seeing what you're doing."

I turned, refusing to allow him to get near my room, and faced him. "What? What am I doing?"

"You just stay away from Lauren and Lex, Sophia—all of them."

I frowned. "Excuse me?"

"Excuse *me*." He took a step toward me. "We see you. You mind your own business."

"Look, Nicholas, I don't know what you think I've done—"

"Stop saying my name like I'm a fucking kid." He thrust his chin out. "You're with Tania, you're fucking that Tomi girl. Now you're trying to get with everyone else like you're the only man here!"

I finally understood what he was getting at. It was the wrong move, but I laughed. Maybe it was the Dutch accent, but I had never taken him for a valid threat.

"Are you serious?"

"You're laughing at me now?" He shoved me in the chest, hard.

"Jesus, what?"

"We're the last people, and you think you can just have all the women for yourself."

"*Have* all the women? Are you crazy?"

I shouldn't have talked to him like that. I should have taken him seriously. But the idea that he was upset by the prospect of my starting some sort of harem was almost too funny for me to deal with. I even forgot about my toothache momentarily.

He put his hands on his hips. "Where do you think this is going? We're the last people."

"We don't know that."

"And what happens when we need to make kids, eh?"

I suddenly realized the gravity of what he was saying and backed off. "Is this really what you've been thinking about? You have this idea we're going to have to repopulate society and I'm some sort of threat to you?"

"We all need things," he said, like this was totally normal. "You make it clear all the women can just come to you."

"I'm not even thinking about that."

"You lie. I'm watching you, I just want you to know. I'm watching you."

"Honestly, Nicholas, I don't give a damn what you do."

He grabbed me by the front of my shirt and punched me in the face.

My nose may not have been broken but it was already hurt enough for that relatively weak blow to make my head spin. I raised my fists to defend myself, but instead of punching me again he threw me into the wall, and I stumbled and ended up backing away into the stairwell. Instantly, this struck me as a mistake. He could throw me down the stairs and claim it was an accident.

He was dragging me around by the collar and I was grappling with his shirt, and suddenly we were in a full brawl. We zigzagged across the landing—me desperately trying to steer us away from the stairs—until I tripped him and we both fell to the floor. I came out on top, and didn't want to punch him.

"Stay down!" I shouted.

"Hey! Hey, guys, what the fuck!"

Looking down the concrete stairs, I saw Adam and Nathan and exhaled with relief.

I got up and dusted myself off, checked my face. Thankfully, I wasn't bleeding.

Van Schaik did the same.

"I feel like we've interrupted something weird," Nathan said, to break the tension.

"Just a misunderstanding," I said, glaring at the Dutchman.

He grunted something and stalked off upstairs as if nothing had happened.

Nathan made a questioning face at me, and I shook my head. "Don't even ask."

"He's such a wanker," Adam said. "Wankers are gonna wanker, it's a rule."

"You know, I thought he was just a . . . a *wanker*, like you say, but he's got some crazy ideas." I held my nose again. "Maybe I should tell Dylan to keep an eye on him."

"Mate, Dylan wouldn't even let him go hunting for deer with them." Adam raised his eyebrows. "He knows."

"What was he saying?" Nathan asked as they came up to the landing. "It's too weird."

"Well, now you *have* to share." Nathan pushed open the exit door. "I have some painkillers in my room, if you want."

"No, I'm fine; he didn't hit me that hard."

The two of them followed me to my room, where I sat on my bed next to Nathan and Adam sat cross-legged on the floor. I didn't appreciate Nathan smoking in my room, but I didn't call him out on it. Adam filled a glass and I held it against my face, glad for once that the water was never anything other than freezing.

"Who started it?" Nathan asked. "I guess it's unlikely it was you, but they do say it's always the quiet ones . . ."

"He's gotten it into his head that we're all eventually going to re-populate the planet and I'm sleeping with too many women, which is absurd, because I'm only sleeping with one."

They both stared.

"Repopulate the planet?" Adam repeated.

"Yeah, he started going on about us being the last-ever people."

"Mate, that's so dark." Adam gestured for the cigarette. "Fuck me. That's so dark."

Nathan had gone quiet.

I looked at him.

He sighed. "I know no one wants to say it."

"What?" Adam and I said simultaneously.

"Well, what if we are?"

"We're not," I said, rolling the glass along my cheek. "I had messages from my students. There are still people out there."

"And how many are going to die of radiation poisoning? Probably most of us. Then . . . what if we do have to start thinking about kids, keeping humanity going?"

"Dude, are you high?" Adam exclaimed.

"No, I'm serious. I know we don't want to think about it because . . . But we're a species that almost went extinct. At some point we're going to have to think about it."

I couldn't believe what I was hearing. "I don't think many of the women here are going to want to bring kids into this."

Nathan shrugged.

Adam glanced at me.

I looked at Nathan. "What?"

"What?"

"What did *this* mean?" I imitated his shrug.

"It meant—" And he shrugged again, beckoning for the cigarette back. "Nothing. I don't know. It's a shrug."

I started to feel uncomfortable.

Nathan spread his hands. "I'm just saying, is it always going to be about what we want, or is it going to be about the right thing to do?"

"Seriously, what exactly are you suggesting?" Adam asked.

"I'm not suggesting anything. Nicholas is a Grade A dick; he just wants to get laid. And it's so obvious he wants to get laid that he's never gonna get laid! But the whole future-of-the-planet thing, that's a real question. Hypothetically, what do we do if the human race is gonna die out and none of the women want to have babies? It's a question! I'm just asking the question out loud!"

"Well, maybe keep it to yourself," Adam said quietly. "Sounds really rapey."

"It's not. Jesus, I didn't mean that. I mean . . ." He took a drag. "I don't know what I mean. I mean we should think about the future."

We all went quiet.

Adam looked deep in thought. "Hypothetically, what do we do if someone here gets pregnant and they want to get rid of it?"

"That hasn't happened," I said.

"I know, I said 'hypothetically.' People are having sex, right." He looked at me. "I mean, what if Tomi gets pregnant?"

"She won't," I said way too quickly, because the idea was terrifying. "She has six months of pills; she's not running out anytime soon. And, guys, are you really suggesting it'd be right to force women here to have kids they don't want? Who would bring a child into this?"

They both shrugged. I was mortified at the thought that any of the women here might find out about this; three men in a room discussing their reproductive rights like they weren't even people now that civilization was gone.

Then Adam said, "Mia has pills too."

"You're banging Mia," Nathan said, surprised.

"Just occasionally. She never wants to sleep over. I like that about her."

"Wow."

"What about you?"

Nathan, deadpan, said, "Lauren and I got drunk one night and did some stuff, before she got with Lex. But I think it was more being wasted than anything else. I think Dylan and Sophia are doing it. They're always having secret talks."

I put the glass down. "Really?"

"Yeah. I mean, even before all this they were tight. This was an incestuous place to work. Everyone's banged everyone else at some point."

"Sophia was married, though," I said.

Nathan shrugged. "So?"

I stood up. "That reminds me, I said I'd speak to Sophia. I need to go."

"What about?"

"She wanted to share a story, said I could talk to her after dinner."

Adam nodded at my desk. "For your diary?"

"It's not a *diary*. It's a record."

He smirked. "Okay."

Nathan stood up and patted me on the shoulder. "Dude, you're writing a memoir. Don't worry, no one's gonna review it."

I walked them both to the door and waved them down the corridor, and a slight shiver ran up my spine. Looking at the two of them—

Nathan with his lost father and Adam with his weird little boy in the corner—it was hard not to feel a sneaking suspicion that we were all supposed to be here. I know this is just one way in which the mind seeks to reestablish control, searching for meaning in a largely random and uncaring universe. All the same, this was a strange place. Those of us who had stayed were only here due to accidents, superstitions, because we had wandered off our usual paths. It was as if the building itself had drawn us to it from the most far-flung corners of the world. And when we arrived, the world had ended.

I don't know what I'm trying to suggest. It's just a feeling I have.

After Nathan and Adam had left, I interviewed Sophia, which I've wanted to do for a while.

Sophia insisted on working while she talked to me, preparing food in bulk to freeze for the next few days. It was distracting for me, taking notes like that, but it was better for her if she kept moving, forgot about what she was doing. She warned me that she didn't feel comfortable sharing personal stories.

She said, "But if we don't share them now, before we die, they really will be lost."

I was sitting in front of the stainless-steel work counter, writing under the hot plate, while Sophia prepped food alone. The kitchen was huge, made for a vast team of people. It stretched back behind Sophia in rows and rows of refrigerators and cupboards, stove tops and ovens.

She had tied her hair back and her sleeves were rolled up to her elbows. She didn't look at me when she talked.

"You asked me why I became a chef, and I thought you would appreciate the long story." She took a bag filled with individually wrapped hard candies from under the counter and held it out. "Don't tell anyone."

Looking around hastily, grinning against my will, I took one. She didn't move.

"Take more. You're not going to see them again."

I took a handful and put them in my pocket. I put one in my mouth as I started taking notes, and it was the nicest thing I'd tasted in weeks. The explosion of sugar almost made me light-headed. At the same time it made me think of my daughters, and I felt suddenly, desperately sad.

"My parents were in the army, so we moved a lot. I was about seven years old when my parents were stationed in Kosovo, briefly. It's a very beautiful place, but it was, um . . . how do you say it . . . sometimes it was violent."

"Volatile?"

"Yes, *volatile*, I think. It wasn't peaceful. My father was attacked by a gang of men on his way home one night, and they asked for his wallet. He was a proud man, or he was stupid, but he said no."

"What was your father's name?"

"Samuel Abelli. The name is Italian, like his parents. He would have been about thirty-five years old at the time. They had me late, seven years after my sister."

I wrote down the name, and Sophia continued with her story. She was making soup, mostly out of canned vegetables. She was severely rationing our meat, which left me feeling hungry most of the time but which made sense for winter.

"With this group of men was a child, and he looked only about sixteen, my father said. He was holding a shotgun, and the group with him started cheering, saying, 'Shoot him, shoot him.' My father turned to run and tripped on the curb. He fell and this boy shot him in the back of the leg. Around here." She arched her back and pointed to her thigh.

I hesitated and looked up. "Wait. This is the story about how you got into catering?"

"If you listen, yes."

I hid a smile, and when I met her eyes again she had raised her eyebrows at me.

"Sorry. I'm listening."

"I shouldn't have given you sweets," she said. "Now you are just going to get overexcited."

I realized she was joking. She just didn't smile when she did it.

Laughing, I remembered the candy in my pocket and ate another. They weren't going to do my tooth any good. Biting down so the outer shell cracked, my mouth flooded with the sourness of artificial apple.

"My father ran about half a mile; he said it was like a survival instinct came over him. He didn't even feel the pain in his leg. He ran into a hotel and begged the reception girl not to give him up, and he hid. The girl didn't give him up, and the group moved on. My father went home instead of to the hospital because . . . actually, I don't know why he didn't go to the hospital. It might have been because he was proud, or embarrassed. I don't know."

"He didn't call the police?"

"It was pointless then. Also, I don't think he wanted to have children arrested, and a lot of those criminals were children. Maybe that is why he didn't go to the hospital, because then his fellow soldiers would have insisted on revenge."

"What was going on in Kosovo at the time?"

"I was seven. I knew nothing about the state of Kosovo."

I made a note to look it up—*Search Kosovo*—and then remembered I couldn't. I had no journals, no library, no resources. The era of instant information was over. I looked at "Search Kosovo" and slowly put a line through it.

"So what happened after?"

"Nothing for a few days. But my father's leg became infected. He didn't want to tell my mother how bad it was, and she was out working most of the time. He had wrapped it in a bandage and refused to show anyone. But I caught him in the kitchen one day cleaning the wound in his leg, trying to see it with a mirror. It was up on the table and he was balancing. When he saw me come in he lost his balance, but he couldn't hide his leg. I asked him what had happened and he said he'd been shot and couldn't get the bullet out."

I began to see where she was going, so I stopped writing and just listened.

She said, "I offered to look. He said I was too young, but I didn't mind. The sight of blood didn't scare me. I picked up a kitchen knife and asked him what a bullet looked like, and he took a huge drink of something. I can't remember what it was."

The next candy was black currant or something. It reminded me of beach trips. I zoned out, thinking about the smell of warmth and unrolling beach towels, grains of sand under my feet, and when I zoned back in Sophia had said, "kitchen knife."

"He described a bullet to you?" I repeated the last thing I remembered hearing.

"He said it was a small metal ball. I would recognize it because it wasn't part of his leg."

"And you were seven?"

"Maybe eight, maybe even nine, but definitely not older. My father lay facedown on the table biting on a belt, and I took a kitchen knife and used it to dig into the wound, looking for this bullet. He was making a horrible noise but he told me to carry on no matter what. I don't re-member being upset by the blood. I knew it was something my father needed me to do."

She fine-chopped the vegetables into a pot and added stock and what looked like bulgur wheat.

"Did you find the bullet?" I asked.

"No, I found a nail."

"What?"

"Some of the people fighting in the streets had stopped using buck-shot and were cramming their guns full of nails and small pieces of metal instead. The reason my father's leg became infected was because there was a nail in there, not a bullet. Once it was out, he did go to the hospital."

"Was he okay?"

"He should have gone earlier. It healed, but it hurt him a lot during the rest of his life. I kept the nail. I still have it, upstairs."

"Is your father still alive?"

"You mean *was* he, before this?"

I hadn't wanted to phrase it like that, but I nodded.

"No, he died about four years ago."

The kitchen began to fill with the smell of food. The gas was on. It smelled so much like before, just having a smell in the air that wasn't disinfectant, that I wasn't prepared for the eruption of nostalgia it pro-voked in me.

I welled up. Sophia looked at me, and I said, "It's the smoke."

There was no smoke.

"It was a heart attack," she said. "He found it funny that I kept the nail, though. I still think, in a way, that that is why I ended up working in kitchens. It was the first place I felt like an adult. I did something for my father that he couldn't do for himself." She sighed. "I'm glad he didn't live to meet my ex-husband, or see any of this."

"You said your husband owned the hotel?"

"Try this," she said. "Come here."

I got up, skirted the hot plate, and went over to the stove. Sophia handed me a spoon. It tasted like another life.

"More pepper?" I said.

She nodded. "Yes, I thought so."

I went and sat down again.

"That's why I worked here," Sophia said.

"And he wasn't here when war broke out?"

A tiny hesitation. "No."

"So was he your ex-husband before or after day one?"

"You don't need to know that. Now you're being nosy." She turned away and directed most of her attention to the soup. "I think I have told you enough for today."

"You don't want to tell me a story about your mother?"

"No."

"Okay, that's fine. Thanks for talking to me."

She fixed me with a hard stare. "Did you find anything new about the girl?"

"Not yet. Why?"

"I'm just curious. I'm not sure why you're wasting so much energy on it."

"I'm not wasting that much energy on it."

She shrugged. "People see you around."

"A girl was murdered here."

"You know what we think of as right and wrong don't exist anymore. Everything that happened before, it has no meaning now."

"I don't believe that," I said, maybe too aggressively.

"No one is coming to enforce law. Even if you did find her killer, which you won't, no one is coming to take him away. What will you do? Do you think you're the law now?"

I frowned. "No. I just feel that human life still means something. It means something more than just . . . surviving by any means necessary."

Without looking at me, she said, "You're the only person who thinks that."

"I don't think so."

She smiled, but it seemed to be more to herself than at me. "I don't know whether it is sweet that you think that. Or just naive."

I asked, "What were you doing on that day?"

"I thought about driving away, but then I realized there was nowhere I could go."

"Did you see anything strange?"

"Strange . . ." I couldn't tell if she was mocking the thought or not. "No. I was happy after most of the people had left, when it went quiet."

"Do you like children?" I asked, unsure of the phrasing even as I said it.

"I can't have children," she replied, as if answering another question entirely.

I don't know whether she was saying that just to make me leave, because it made me uncomfortable. Either way, I gathered my things and went upstairs to write up my notes. It took a while for me to shake the coldness of her tone. I immediately wrote *Do you think you're the law now?*, and it looked just as hostile on paper as it had felt in person. I wondered what the implications were, of someone thinking like that.

I wrote down another comment she made too, so I would remember it, in case it became relevant later: *Even if you did find her killer, which you won't.* I pondered that one for a long time.

Even if you did find her killer, which you won't.

The next evening I went to check on Tomi, but she wouldn't answer her door. She might have been out. Either way, she didn't want to see me.

I returned to my room to retrieve the set of master keys and pondered resuming my search of the hotel, but the stolen cases had punctured my morale and I couldn't face an awkward search of everyone's rooms right now.

Now that Sophia had mentioned him, however, the hotel's owner interested me. Maybe I should try to find some more information about him.

I tested all the batteries I had grabbed from the superstore on my laptop, and none of them worked. I plugged the portable charger in but didn't see any sign of life, so I left it on my bed. Even though I knew I couldn't connect to the Internet, I desperately wanted to see some photos of my family.

As I was about to leave there was a knock on my door.

It was Tomi, accompanied by the Yobari kids. The girl is Ryoko, and she's seven years old. The boy is Akio, and he's six. Truth be told, I had been avoiding even looking at the Yobari children. Every time I caught sight of them or listened to snatches of their conversation I had to fight the urge to cry. They had so little idea of what was going on. I wondered whether, when they reached adulthood, they would remember anything of what our world used to be.

"Wanna take the kids out to play?" Tomi asked, as if I hadn't been trying to get ahold of her.

"Where are their parents?"

"They wanted an evening off, and the French bitches are busy. It's fine; I've looked after them before."

"Jesus, Tomi, they're kids, you can't say 'bitches.'" I tried to lower my voice.

"They don't know what 'bitches' means. Chill out."

"*Bisha!*" Ryoko piped up joyfully.

I couldn't help but laugh. "Okay, I'll get my coat."

It had occurred to me that perhaps Tomi could answer some of my questions about the hotel's owner.

As I locked my door I felt a tiny hand take hold of three of my fingers. It was Ryoko. I almost snatched my hand away. It was as if the floor had dropped from under me. My heart actually skipped a beat, and tears sprang to my eyes.

I looked up at Tomi, who was waiting with Akio nearer the entrance to the stairwell. She smiled.

Pulling myself together, I took Ryoko's hand and the four of us went out front. The kids didn't speak much English, but, to my surprise, Tomi spoke a little Japanese. Tomi and I sat on the grass by the edge of the woods and watched Ryoko and Akio chasing each other.

"I didn't know you liked kids," I remarked.

"I like them better than adults," Tomi replied.

Ryoko had strange features, I noticed. Something about her face wasn't entirely symmetrical, and I couldn't work out what it was.

I wasn't able to relax until the kids appeared to find something interesting on the ground and started digging a hole. It kept them in one place.

"I've been meaning to ask . . ." I began tentatively. "When you were researching your project—the history of this place—you said you couldn't find much information on the owners."

"There's so little public information available. Even when this place was taken over by companies, I'd do some digging and find that the companies didn't exist, or they went bankrupt. Such a weird lack of a paper trail, you know? I was obsessed. That's why I started the project." A sideways glance. "You must understand."

I nodded. A reluctant paper trail was sometimes the only thing that drove me when I was alone in a hotel room that looked like every other hotel room, no matter what state or country I was in, when I was starting the day with the same packet of cheap instant coffee and the miniature coffeepot.

"Do you ever think about all the empty libraries?" she asked with an expectant smile.

"My God. I hadn't."

"Can you imagine? Worth trying to get back to the States for that alone. The idea actually kinda turns me on."

I laughed, then remembered. "Balach Braun?"

"*Baloche*. I found a few articles about him taking this place over. It was a big deal, apparently, because of all the bad press in the nineties—you know, the murders, the ghost stories. Seems he had an asshole reputation."

"What do you mean?"

"Criminal record, hard partier who inherited all his money, a minor celebrity in Europe. That was why he was the only owner I could find anything on."

"You know he and Sophia were married?"

She grabbed my arm. "No way!"

"Way!" I was elated by her excitement. "*Were* married, *are* married, I'm not sure. I couldn't get it out of her."

"Is that why she works here?"

I nodded.

"You're good. Damn . . . I mean, it doesn't matter now, it's not like I'm ever going to finish the thing. But . . . that's interesting."

We watched the kids play awhile.

"I don't mean to be voyeuristic," Tomi said, choosing her words carefully. "Actually, I'm a social scientist—of course I'm voyeuristic. But you left your Facebook logged in."

"Jesus, Tomi—"

"Calm down, I didn't read your messages." She snorted. "I just wanted to say your kids are really cute. Your younger daughter looks freakishly like you. The older one doesn't; she looks like her mom."

"I'm not her biological father. She is her mom's."

"Nadia?"

"Yeah, Nadia."

"She looks like Tania."

I couldn't tell if she meant it in a pointed way or not. Either way, it made me feel uncomfortable. But she didn't seem interested in discussing it further.

"What were their names?" she asked.

I gritted my teeth. "Their names *are* Ruth and Marion. Marion is younger."

"I'm sorry, I didn't mean to look." A pause. "No, I did mean to. I'm just curious and have boundary issues. Lack-of-boundary . . . issues."

"It's not a big deal, it's just . . ." I didn't know what to say.

"Hard?"

I nodded, and we watched the kids play some more.

"I'm sorry about what happened," I said. "I don't know why they're suddenly blaming you. People are getting cabin fever."

"It's not sudden; they've been making comments like that since day one. Not just them." She shrugged. "I don't care. What are they gonna do? I'm not scared of them."

I ran my palm over the dry grass, still hanging in there. "I don't know why anyone would bother bringing this up now. It's done. *Voting*, it's done."

"You're not going to say something like 'It's not your fault'?"

"Well . . ." I wasn't sure what I wanted to say. "You can't lay fault with an individual. It was a collective fault."

"So you're saying this is *partially* my fault?" She made a vague gesture at everything.

I thought for a moment. "Partially."

"Jesus. I can't believe you."

"Well, whose fault do you think it is?"

"It's not *my* fault!"

"I didn't say it was, I said it was a *collective* fault!"

"So everyone who voted my way wanted nuclear war and the end of the world? Right, that sounds plausible. You're such a self-righteous asshole; that's why no one wanted to vote with you."

"People did."

She went quiet.

I felt like I had won the argument, but, at the same time, I wasn't sure if I was being unfair. We were talking about a world that was gone. What was the point in us trying to assign blame now?

The kids screamed and I almost leapt out of my skin, but I realized they were laughing too. Akio appeared to have found a bug, and he ran up to us with a thin wriggling worm dangling from his fingers.

Tomi said something to him in Japanese, maybe telling him to put it back, and he went away and placed it carefully in the soil.

"Good to know bugs are still alive," I said.

She didn't reply.

"I'm sorry, okay? It's not your fault."

"I can't believe everyone is so fucking simple that they look at me and think I'm the reason we're all here. The world didn't go to shit because I voted for it. The world had long gone to shit; it took years. We all watched it happen." She wrenched up a handful of grass and let it scatter. "We were all cowards, none of us did what needed to be done, so I don't know why you're all lining up to blame it on me."

I said, "To play devil's advocate—"

"Fuck off."

"Everyone knew how stupid and dangerous it was to vote for that kind of man, and those religious zealots!"

"It wasn't us who launched the nukes, was it?"

"No one knows who launched first! It's not like we can set up a committee now."

She shook her head. "I don't get it. What do you want me to say?"

For a moment, I just stared at her. I felt cruel. I realized that I was unreasonably angry with her. There was a rage in me that I spent most days trying to distract myself from, and it rose to the surface whenever I spoke to or looked at Tomi. It had only worsened since we started sleeping together. I did blame her. I did think it was her fault. On some level, I wanted to convince myself she had planned this somehow, must have wanted it to vote for the lunatics who had helped put us here, who had separated me from my wife and children, probably forever. I wanted to believe that her motive had been some spiteful urge to kill the world. It gave me someone to blame.

"Seriously, what do you want me to say?"

The better part of myself didn't win out, and I said, " 'Sorry' would be nice."

She got up. "Go to hell."

"We're already here!" I called after her, and grimaced.

I knew immediately that I was the asshole, but I was too proud to go after her. The Yobari kids watched her go but didn't seem perturbed by her absence. They just carried on playing. Ryoko yelled something to me in Japanese. I didn't understand but I gave her my biggest smile, and she laughed, apparently satisfied, and ducked behind a tree.

Kids didn't need to understand everything you said. Kids just knew if you were happy to be around them or not.

Every time one of the Yobari kids looked over I smiled, until I became choked up and couldn't smile anymore. They seemed so happy. They *are* so happy, because they have no idea. I'm envious that they have no idea they have even lost anything. I'm so sad that they will never know the world as it once was.

Sometimes I think of what I might be doing in my former life at this particular time of day, and today I'd probably be at work, sitting in my office waiting for students to come talk to me about assignments. I'd be reading, but now it was almost impossible to find any books that were in English. I'd have music on, but the last time I'd heard a song was when Tania let me listen to one. I can't go and get a sandwich from anywhere. Sometimes I get emotional if I dwell too long on what pizza tasted like.

Ryoko came and sat next to me.

"Hey," I said. "What have you got there?"

She didn't have anything. She reached out and put a hand on my arm, patting me like I was another child. She gestured at herself and said something. By her tone it sounded like "It's not so bad," and she beamed at me. Then she got up and went back to Akio.

Someone else sat down next to me and I started, but it was just Tania.

"Sorry, I saw you were having a moment there. Didn't want to interrupt you."

I sighed. "Kids are so pure, you know. It's painful."

"I know. I'm actually quite jealous of them."

"Me too. God, I feel like such a jerk."

"Don't worry, I won't tell anyone."

"Hey." I remembered the candy in my pocket. "You want one? Sophia gave me some. She has a secret stash."

"Awesome." She took one and gestured at the kids. "Though you should probably share with these guys too."

"That's how I was planning to lure them inside. I don't speak Japanese."

"Good idea." She rattled the candy around her mouth. "I saw there was some drama."

The sun was starting to go down, but it wasn't too cold. The white noise of the leaves rubbing against other leaves was hypnotic.

"Yeah, I maybe could have handled that better."

"You and Thomas are a thing, right?"

"Thomas?"

"Sorry, *Tomi*. I don't like her. She's Thomas."

I laughed. "That's mean."

"But you are a thing?"

I didn't answer fast enough, and I didn't deny it fast enough, so I just said, "It's . . ."

"Don't worry, everyone knows."

"*Don't worry, everyone knows*? Thanks, that makes me feel better." I went red; I could feel it. "We're not even friends; it's just . . . I don't know."

I don't know why I felt the urge to apologize to her.

"You don't need to explain yourself. Everyone needs to blow off some steam, and she's pretty, I guess, if you like that kind of thing. I imagine she's even quite nice, when she isn't talking. What do you do, gag her?"

I laughed again. I couldn't help myself.

She smirked. "Sorry. Now I *am* being mean."

"I was probably too hard on her," I admitted. "One moment I was trying to apologize, and the next I was blaming her for nuclear war. It wasn't my proudest moment."

"Do you think it's her fault?"

I had to think. "No. Rationally, no. But when I'm looking at her and talking about it, I just can't hold it all back."

"So you *do* think it's her fault."

"No, I don't think it is. That would be crazy, to think it was this one girl's fault. Do you think it is?"

"No. It feels nice to blame someone, though."

I said, "You think that's it, I'm just lashing out?"

"I think, in my *medical* opinion," and she rolled her eyes a little, as if "medical" were an exaggeration, "you're grieving."

For some reason the word shocked me.

I frowned. "I don't know for sure that Nadia and the kids didn't make it."

"I don't mean grieving for specific people, though not knowing is going to take a psychological toll. I mean grieving for the loss of your life, the whole world. Everyone here is grieving, and no one's dealing with it."

I thought about the symptoms of grief—blame, anger, despair, lethargy—and suddenly my irrational reactions didn't seem so irrational. I also felt more certain that I had been a jerk to Tomi, who, in her own way, must be grieving too.

Tania said, "I spend so much time wishing my life was back the way it was, that I was at home with . . . with my partner, and we were just watching TV. You know what I really miss?"

"What?"

"Pizza."

The laughter that burst out of me was borderline hysterical. It attracted the attention of the Yobari kids, who also laughed, like I'd told them a joke.

"Oh my God," I said, barely able to catch my breath. "Same! I was just thinking about it."

"It seems like such a small thing, but . . ." She put a hand over her lips and took a steadying breath. "It was nothing I thought of as special. Sometimes we would just order a pizza, and now we can't anymore. Can't ever do it again. Am I even going to taste food I like again? Like, a burger or something. God, even broccoli."

I reached out and put a hand on her back, but she shrugged it off.

"Sorry."

Tania rubbed her eyes, didn't look at me. "I'll watch them. Go and see if she's all right."

I said, "I'd rather be sure you're all right."

She didn't answer me. I pulled up another couple of handfuls of grass and let the breeze take them.

Ryoko came over and started talking to me, scratching the side of her face as if it itched.

"What is it?" I asked, hoping she'd be able to explain some other way.

She took my hand, reached up to her face, and took out her right eye.

I was so shocked, as she placed it in my palm, that I stopped breathing.

The light brown eye looking up at me was made of glass. I looked up at Ryoko's face and she blinked back expectantly, a pink sunken hole where her right eye had been, and her left eye radiating happiness.

"I, um . . ." I searched for the words but couldn't find any.

Tania took the eye from me and smiled. "She had retinoblastoma. Her eye needs cleaning sometimes. That's what she was trying to tell you."

"Right." I nodded, still reeling from the shock of suddenly holding her eye in my hand.

"I'll clean it. You go inside."

Ryoko looked between us, and I felt guilty for displaying any fear. I reached out and stroked her cheek, and she seemed nonplussed.

"I'm sorry if I didn't react well," I said. "You have beautiful eyes."

Ryoko said something that sounded happy, rubbing the skin under her eye socket. I think I managed to make myself understood.

Tania chuckled under her breath.

The carpets were filthy in the lobby, scuffed with deeper and darker shades of brown. I should organize a couple of people to help me clean it up. For some reason I find the accumulating dirt menacing and depressing to look at.

I heard a *psst* sound, like someone hissing at me, and I looked up from my feet and tried to locate the source. No one behind the front desk, or in the restaurant or the stairwell. It was starting to get dark, so I expected most people to be in their rooms.

"*Psst!* J!"

The whisper came from the bar. I could see two figures standing at the far end of the room, behind the bar itself.

I went to the doorway and squinted. "Tomi?"

"*Shh!* Come here."

I crossed the room. "What are you doing?"

Tomi. And Mia.

"What are you doing?" I asked again, confused by Tomi's beckoning and whispering and by how uncomfortable Mia looked.

"Tell him," Tomi said, hand on hip. "Tell him what we just heard."

"What *I* heard."

"What?"

Tomi said, her voice low and urgent, "Well, I came in here to have some time alone after you just blamed me for the end of the world, you remember?"

"I—"

"And I heard Dylan and Sophia talking in the kitchen. It sounded secretive so I stood right here by the door, but I didn't understand anything, so I grabbed Mia because I saw her going for a walk, and she translated for me."

"Translated what?"

Mia shrank against the shelves. "I don't want to be a part of this."

"Too late. Tell him what you heard, right now!" Tomi was fierce, and when Mia wouldn't say anything she turned to me. "Mia heard Dylan and Sophia talking about some kind of incident, something they don't want you to find out about."

"Are they still in there?" I gestured incredulously at the door to the kitchen.

"What? No, of course not. They left and we hid on the floor."

"Can I go?" Mia asked. "You can just tell him what I told you."

"Fine, then. Go! But wait—" Tomi grasped Mia's arm and made a threatening amount of eye contact. "You tell anyone about this, we're going to have a problem."

"Who would I tell? Fuck, you're crazy." Mia snatched her arm away and walked out.

Tomi leaned on the bar. "So, she said—"

"Can we not do this here in the dark like a Philip Marlowe novel?"

We went upstairs to her room instead and she poured me a drink. She must have bottles and bottles of the stuff. To my surprise she also had a bar of cooking chocolate that she ripped open and jammed into her mouth, taking off the top two rows.

"Don't get jealous," she said past a mouthful of chocolate. "Cooking chocolate is gross."

"Where did you get that?"

She had to take a moment to swallow. "They have tons of stuff in the freezers, you know. There are whole rooms of food. I bribed Nathan. You want some?"

"What did you bribe him with?"

She smirked. "Do you want some or not?"

"Well, I'm not going to say no."

It's a weird feeling to taste chocolate that you're aware is awful while simultaneously being aware that it's the best and only chocolate you're likely to ever taste again. We ate the whole bar between us.

"Mia said they were talking about how you were going to find out about something. Sophia was concerned, and Dylan told her not to worry. They said they'd have to keep an eye on the situation, or how things went. I'm not sure how she phrased it."

I'd known it. I'd known all along. There had always been something off about their reactions.

I asked, "Did they say anything about the suitcases?"

"No. I mean, I wouldn't know either way, but Mia would have mentioned it if they had."

"So the cases are still somewhere in the hotel."

A mischievous smile. "And you still have the master keys. At this point, it'll look too suspicious if he confiscates them."

I was exhilarated. "Should we start looking?"

"It's going to get dark, and I don't want to be feeling my way around. Especially with all the fucked-up stories about this place."

"Okay, in the morning, then?"

"What makes you so sure I'll just continue being your sidekick and spying on people?" she asked, taking her boots off and pulling her feet up onto the bed. "You're a prick. I only told you about this because it's the right thing to do, to help you find whoever killed that girl. But I'm not your Scully. You can leave now."

I was still holding my glass, and I put it down slowly on the dresser. I hadn't drunk anything. "Look, I'm sorry about what I said."

"I'm sure you are, but you can still leave."

I noticed that next to my glass was a cactus. "Where did you get that?"

She looked in the direction I was pointing. "Oh. It's nothing."

"That wasn't in here before. I don't remember seeing it."

"Can you go, please?"

"Did you pick it up from the store?"

Sighing. "Yes, I picked it up from the store, because we had that stupid discussion about ornaments. But you can't have it."

She'd blushed, and she was picking at the edges of her fingernails.

I felt awful, so guilty that I almost resented her for it.

"It's not your fault," I said.

"I know that!"

"No, I mean, I don't think it's your fault."

"Please go."

"No." I sat down on the edge of her bed, and saw her steel herself. "What I said was out of line."

"I know."

"I want you to know that I don't think that. I said it out of anger, I guess. But I'm not angry at you, it's just a directionless anger at . . . everything! I'm angry at *everything*, okay!"

A small frown sat upon her brow, and she rubbed her eyes. "I'm not interested in why you said it. I'm not your *thing* to lash out at."

"I know."

"Then why are you still here? I told you to get out, like, five times. Take the damn cactus if you want it."

"I'm not here for the damn cactus."

"Well, you're not here for me, you're here to make yourself feel better and you're worried you're not gonna get laid anymore. I'm sick of you talking to me like I'm trash. You have issues to work out, go work them out on someone else!"

She reached out and pushed me—physically pushed me—off the bed.

I had no idea what else I could say. I realized in that moment that I'd had a friend here and might have irreparably messed things up, for no good reason.

She crossed her arms, looking at the floor, her expression rigid and her eyes glassy.

I was about to say sorry again but decided against it, so I said, "Thank you so much for your help. I really appreciate it. I hope you know that."

Obviously, she didn't answer, and I didn't expect her to. I figured I'd said enough, so, feeling uncomfortable and unbearably sad, I finally let myself out.

The sun was going down fast now, and in the corridor it was so dark that in an hour I wouldn't be able to find my way back to my room without a candle, or at least a match. On my way to the stairwell I passed Tania returning the Yobari children to their parents' room. Akio yelled something at me, so I waved. He and Ryoko waved back.

Tania didn't say anything to me.

I can't stop thinking about the cactus. Every time it crosses my mind my chest feels tight. I realize now that perhaps my idea of usefulness had been limited. The only meaning we might have left as a species— indeed, the only thing left that might matter, that might keep us motivated to get up in the morning—is in the small acts of human kindness we show one another, and in my compulsion to be helpful, useful, to keep things moving forward, I've mostly forgotten to be kind.

Maybe I wasn't all that kind before. Nadia, I know you certainly didn't think so. Maybe we forgot how to be kind a long time ago. Maybe that was our problem. What are any of us working toward without that?

I moved my laptop off my bed to take a nap and opened it out of curiosity. To my shock, it glowed into life. The portable charger had worked. Out of habit, I immediately tried to connect to the Wi-Fi, but it failed for perhaps the fiftieth time.

The pile of CDs was on my desk, but I went through all my photos first. I read about a study once that claimed that after a breakup, loss, separation, the sight of your loved one's face had a similar effect on your brain to cocaine's. It was like that. I went through every photo I had and I still ached for a new one, one I hadn't seen before. I was worried that I couldn't remember them from every angle. None of these images captured just how much Ruth laughed like Nadia. Nadia laughs like a kid; I used to make fun of her for it. Marion loves singing. But there's no laughter or singing in these files.

Looking at the pictures, I didn't think Tomi's observation was accurate. Aside from them both being black, there weren't many similarities between Tania and Nadia that I could see.

I heard footsteps overhead, in the direction of the stairwell.

Without thinking, I stood up and went to bolt the door.

I had hundreds of photos of my daughters, hundreds of Nadia, a few of my parents: old ones of my mom, more recent ones of my father and his wife. There were photos of me with my students, holiday photos from countries and cities that didn't exist anymore. Rome—I wonder what happened to that? Scotland was one of the first to go. I knew people at Edinburgh University who had probably died of radiation poisoning by now.

I wanted to get hard copies of these photos, at least one of Nadia, but no one was going to let me waste electricity on using the printers. I had limited time with them, again.

I set a photo of the four of us—me, Nadia, Ruth, Marion—as my desktop background and started working my way through the hours and hours of security footage. This was good. It reminded me of real work. In my line of work, you have to go through everything, not just the parts you think are relevant. It was in a footnote, a margin, something scribbled by hand and attached as an afterthought, that you occasionally found something pivotal.

For hours, I watched random people enter and exit the elevators. I watched Nathan serve dozens of people behind the bar, and Mia and Sasha leaving the building for dozens of cigarette breaks. I watched the Luffmans arrive in the main lobby to check in, and paused the footage.

Her parents seemed normal. I don't know what I'd been expecting, but they looked like your average white European family. Harriet seemed smaller than I remembered, but not remarkably so. Her hair looked blond and she had a lot of freckles. I let it play on, and just before they left the front desk the guy behind it gave them a piece of paper along with their keys.

Pause.

I didn't recall being given anything extra along with my key.

Zooming in, I tried to make out what it was. It wasn't a room-service menu; I knew what those looked like. It wasn't a tourist leaflet either; those were still lying around. This was a folded piece of white legal paper.

Play.

Mr. Luffman took the piece of paper, and the family headed to the elevators.

Helpfully, the CDs containing footage from the elevators were labeled "Lift."

I followed them across the hotel, fast-forwarding to the same date and time. While in the elevator, Mr. Luffman didn't look at the piece of paper again, just held it in his right hand until they exited.

Had I missed it somehow? It was fairly innocuous. A piece of paper could have been dropped anywhere. Or had it been in one of the suitcases? I had to check.

With a renewed sense of purpose, I put on a coat and returned to room 377.

The hotel was quiet. It was always quiet unless there was a reason for us to be on the move, like breakfast. Even if we were all out of our rooms, in a hotel this big it's easy to move around without bumping into anybody.

Room 377 was empty, as I had left it.

Nothing in the closet, and, as I opened the dresser, I remembered that I hadn't searched the rest of the room. I thought I had, but it was a false memory. I had been interrupted by Sophia; we had searched the cases, and then I had left.

There were still clothes in the drawers: a couple of shirts, a bra, several pairs of socks, and a pair of men's jeans. I went through the pockets of the jeans and found a piece of paper, folded into eighths.

Footsteps outside. Someone coming out of their room. I edged over to the door and pushed it to, without quite shutting it. I clenched the paper in my fist until the steps had passed, then unfolded it.

The only thing written on it was a phone number.

I turned it over. Nothing. Just the phone number.

It didn't matter. It was glorious. I had a phone number!

I returned the clothes to the drawers and checked the bedside tables. There was a Bible—not in English—brochures about room service, the hotel, and nearby attractions. That was it.

But I had a phone number!

I took the piece of paper back to my room and bolted the door, resisting the urge to physically jump with excitement. Taking out my own collection of brochures, I searched the hotel's directory of numbers. It was clearly a hotel number, but it wasn't readily available to guests. I picked up my own room phone, remembered everything was dead, and put it down.

Putting the piece of paper in my pocket, I headed for the door again, with the intention of going downstairs to the offices behind the front desk. Surely they would have a staff directory somewhere that I could access without talking to the staff.

I slid the bolt to one side, went to open the door, and something stopped me. As I put my hand on the handle I was seized by a sudden feeling of utter dread, that someone was waiting for me on the other side. I can't remember if I heard anything specific; maybe I heard footsteps, but I heard them overhead all the time. Maybe I heard breathing, a shuffle, a scuff against the tile outside. But I knew someone was standing right outside my door.

Unable to move my hand, I tilted my head forward, trying to catch a sound.

Nothing. I think. I was listening so intently I couldn't be sure if I was creating a kind of white noise. Maybe it was the wind outside. Maybe it was my own heartbeat, my own blood rushing.

I considered calling out, but I stopped myself.

They would already know I was here.

I told myself not to be stupid, because there were only around twenty people in the building, and I knew all of them.

I moved my other hand to the bolt and slowly slid it home, fraction by fraction. Then I took a couple of steps back and waited.

Nothing happened, but I couldn't shake the feeling that there was someone out there waiting for me. I thought back to what Peter had said: *I sometimes feel that there might be more people in the hotel than we know about.*

I stayed in my room for the rest of that evening, and kept waking up in the night, thinking I could hear the bolts being rattled on my door.

At one point I yelled, "Who's out there?"

Of course, I didn't get an answer back.

I thought that maybe the isolation was doing strange things to my mind.

However, when I woke up for the third time, someone *was* hammering on my door.

Unsure if I was awake or not, almost delirious with fear, I shouted, "Who are you? Go away!"

"Jon? Jon, open the fucking door!"

It sounded like Nathan. But I couldn't be sure.

I scrambled around for some matches and candles, disoriented. I opened the door with a knife in one hand and a candle in the other and saw that it was Nathan. He was holding a flashlight, and my first thought was that it must be something urgent if he was wasting batteries.

"Adam's fucking OD'd!" he said, grabbing me by the front of my shirt as if he were going to drag me out of my doorway.

"Shit." Without pausing for anything, not even to lock my door, I ran with him toward the stairwell. "On what?"

"I don't know. Heroin? Whatever goes in your arm through a needle—I don't fucking know! I didn't even know he *had* heroin!"

We hurried down a flight of stairs, and then I remembered: "Where's Tania? Why didn't you get her?"

"I tried. She's not in her room!"

"What?"

He spread his hands wildly, sending the beam of light everywhere. "I don't know, she's not in her room!"

"Did you go to the right one?"

"I know what fucking room she's in, dickhead. She's not there!"

"Shit."

"We need to get into her office."

Nathan clutched both sides of his head, as if his thoughts were all bottlenecking and fighting for space, and then sprinted the rest of the way toward her office, which was locked.

I put the candle down and tried the door. I tried ramming my left shoulder into it, like that was going to make a difference. It stood firm, and I hurt my shoulder.

He exclaimed, "Oh, *you're* gonna knock down the door?!"

"Well, do you have any ideas?"

"Oh my God, he's gonna die," he said, ashen. "He's gonna die."

"Wait . . ." I tried to think.

"We don't have time, J!"

"Wait! Get Tomi!"

"Why?"

"She has a gun! We can shoot the lock!"

"She has a gun?"

"Just go!"

He did as I said, and I sized up the door again. I wasn't the sort of man who was likely to be able to kick doors down, but I gave it another try. It didn't do much. I hurt my foot kicking it three or four times, but it didn't do anything. It looks so easy in the movies. Maybe it *was* easy, for other men.

Nathan came back with Tomi, who snapped at me, "You told him I have a gun?"

"Tomi, just . . . I didn't have a choice!"

"Jesus." She took aim at Tania's door and blew the lock clean through.

Nathan and I had covered our ears, but the sound still shook the inside of my head. I felt it reverberate down the corridor. We pushed our way in, and I think we simultaneously realized that we had no idea what to do in the event of a heroin overdose. I picked the candle up off the floor but I could barely see anything with that feeble light.

"Nath, what do we need?"

"I've seen *Pulp Fiction*—it's adrenaline."

"We're not gonna have that, are we?"

"Narcan," Tomi said quietly.

"What?"

"It's Narcan you need, or it's called . . . Naloxone! You inject it!"

"What is it, like adrenaline?"

She snapped, "It's a nasal spray. You get it in stores, for fuck's sake!"

We looked. As Nathan had the flashlight, he found it first. I picked up a syringe that hadn't yet been opened and the three of us ran upstairs. It wasn't like Adam was my best friend, but he had given me some moments that made this lonely hellscape feel bearable for a while.

Plus, if another one of us died now, it would have felt like hope died too. Not just our personal reserves of hope, which fluctuated, but the abstract concept. We couldn't allow one another to give up like this, not when we knew one another's names and worked together and kept one another warm. We couldn't let Adam just check out.

That's what I was thinking.

"There was still a heartbeat, but it was barely there, man," Nathan said as we ran toward Adam's room.

It was deathly quiet. I was surprised we hadn't woken more people up with the gunshot. Maybe we had, but they were too scared to leave their rooms and see what was happening. I would have been.

"Are you sure it was heroin?" Tomi asked.

"It looked like heroin."

We ran into room 414 and there was Adam, with savage loops of saliva hanging from the sides of his mouth. He had been rolled into the recovery position. Nathan may have saved his life by doing that. If he hadn't, Adam might have choked to death on his own vomit before we'd even arrived.

Nathan slammed the door shut and shoved the Narcan at me.

I tried to press the syringe back onto him.

"I can't do it!" I shouted.

"Please, I won't! I can't!" Nathan was almost in tears.

I couldn't make him do it.

I had never given someone an injection in my life. I looked to Tomi, but she shook her head.

"I can't . . . needles."

"Oh my God." I ripped open the syringe packet with shaking hands. "I can't believe you're making me do this. Fuck!"

"I can't do it," Nathan kept saying. "I'm sorry, I can't."

Tomi snatched the flashlight from Nathan, handed him the gun instead, and checked Adam's arms. His murals of roses and mermaids— full sleeves—were blocking our lines of sight to any veins. I had no clue where I was supposed to go.

"What do you think?" Tomi asked, her eyes wide.

I shook my head, struggling to process the question. I might be a Dr. but I'm not a *doctor*. My job never meant life or death for anybody. I was a historian; it was words and books and people who were long dead, not someone dying right in front of me.

Of all the nights Tania could have chosen to go AWOL, this was the worst.

"Jon, what do you think? Can you do it?"

Tomi's voice snapped me out of it.

I said, "I'll try."

Nathan had backed against the wall, holding Tomi's gun to his chest like it was a stuffed animal. I took the Narcan. She helped me examine Adam's arms while I stuck the syringe into the container and drew some of the liquid up into it.

Adam's veins barely reacted to the belt wrapped around his bicep or the harsh slaps that Tomi dealt to the underside of his forearm. He gurgled and leaked more drool into his beard, but at least that meant he was still breathing. That was something.

My hands were just about steady. My breathing was not.

"Flick it!" Tomi said.

"What?"

"I don't know, check that there's no air in it, squirt some out. It's what they do on TV!"

I did as she said. I had no clue whether it made a difference.

There was nothing showing on Adam's arms. I didn't trust myself to look for the same vein that he had injected into. The IV access was virtually destroyed. I would be jabbing a needle into unresponsive flesh.

"Christ." Tomi looked for a pulse and shook her head. "I can't tell if it's just *my* pulse. If he's still alive, it's barely."

"Help me turn him over!"

She and I rolled Adam, deadweight, onto his back. I pushed him flat against the mattress and straddled him. A bead of sweat ran into my eye and stung. I blinked it away, my entire body went cold with shock, and I said, "I could kill him."

I looked at Tomi and repeated, "I could kill him."

She grasped my arm. "Jon. He's dying anyway."

"I don't know where to put this thing! Back of his hand?"

"I can't see anything with his tattoos." Tomi frowned, then said, "Open his mouth."

"What?"

"I saw it on TV. If you can't find a vein in the arms or the hands, you stick it under their tongue. You can always see huge veins there."

Tomi placed the flashlight on the bed, linked her fingers around Adam's forehead, and pulled back. Grimacing, sure I was about to pass out, overwhelmed by my own heartbeat, I opened the slack jaw as wide as I could and resisted the very real urge to vomit. I poked the tongue to one side, and it was shockingly resistant; so I jammed two more fingers into his mouth and slid the needle into a bulging blue-green vein underneath. I did it almost without thinking. I didn't hesitate. I just put the needle in, and a little blood pooled beneath my fingers as I emptied the syringe.

"Jesus, I don't remember if I measured it," I said, sitting back onto Adam's legs.

I heard Nathan quietly crying. He had slid down the wall.

Tomi let go of Adam's forehead, and I was shocked to see a couple of tears run from her eyes. She sat on the floor, taking deep breaths.

We looked at each other.

No ambulance was coming. No doctor. We couldn't call 911. We were it.

When I had been sitting back for about twenty seconds, I noticed that Adam had urinated on himself.

"Oh shit." I swiveled, trying to get off. "Shit!"

Adam jerked suddenly, sat bolt upright and screamed a mouthful of spit and blood into my face.

Tomi and Nathan were screaming.

I think I was also screaming.

I hurled myself off the bed.

Tomi leapt to her feet and grabbed Adam around the chest to stop him flailing, locking her arms tight.

While the two of them struggled, I was lying on the floor, my vision white with shock. The carpet smelled of old rot. I levered myself into a seated position and hung my head between my knees, gasping for air.

On the bed, Adam groaned, rolled onto his side, and shut his eyes, shivering. A hint of gray was still tainting his skin, but he was undoubtedly alive. Much more alive than he had been when we arrived. Alive enough to sit up and scare us all half to death.

I looked around for the syringe, worried that I had landed on it, but I had dropped it off the end of the bed and it was lying, empty, on the floor.

Tomi crouched and took my shoulder. "Are you okay?"

"Yeah, I think. No, I'm not sure. Is he okay?"

"Well, he's alive."

We looked around and saw the drug paraphernalia scattered everywhere. We hadn't been back to Adam's room since the day we all got high. If we had, we might have noticed that it was in more disarray than usual. It wasn't a happy room.

"Are you okay?" Tomi asked again, directing the question at Nathan. "Nathan, it's okay. He's going to be okay, I think."

"Yeah, I just . . . I thought he was gonna die." Nathan tried to get to his feet but thought better of it and sat on the floor again with his back to the door.

"You did good," Tomi said, letting out the sigh she had been holding in and rubbing my shoulders.

I said, "No, *you* did good. A sublingual injection? I'd never have thought of that."

Nathan added, "Yeah, that was smart."

She shrugged, and I realized I had absently taken her hand. I let go of it quickly, and said, "It's probably best we don't leave any drugs here. We might not be around next time."

Nathan got up. "Yeah, gimme the light. I'll take a look around."

I wiped some of the blood off my cheeks and found that I was covered in sweat, huge droplets of it running down my face.

"Where's Tania?" Tomi asked.

"Don't know. Nathan said she's not in her room."

"Who's not in their room at night?" She paused for a while, and then added, "You just saved a life. How many people can say that?"

"Probably not many. I imagine that might change the longer we're here."

Nathan had found a pack of cigarettes and offered me one.

I waved them away, getting to my feet. "No, thanks; I need water."

I looked down at the man breathing in unsteady shallow gasps on the bed.

The syringe was still on the floor.

I picked it up as Tomi covered him with a blanket. He was unaware of our presence, but he was breathing. It hit me again that I could have killed him, with another overdose or an air bubble injected into his vein. But I can't think like that. Accidents are going to happen sooner or later. We aren't always going to be around to stop the suicides; we aren't always going to be able to claw them back to life. We can't allow one another to carry the weight of so much fault.

"I think I've got most of it," Nathan said, slinging a shoulder bag across his chest. "How did you know it was Narcan?"

Tomi made a face. "Back in freshman year a friend dropped out, and . , . She was going through some stuff, so I did a bit of research, just in case."

"Did you know he was going to sit up and scream like that?"

"No, I didn't know they actually did that in real life."

"Scared the living shit out of me," he said, smoking furiously.

"Scared the shit out of *you*!" I laughed. "Do you think we should stay with him for a few hours?"

"I think we should take his razors too." Nathan started pacing again, picking things up off the floor and then searching drawers. "We can't let him keep them, for now."

"Isn't that going a bit far?" Tomi asked.

I gestured at Adam. "We just saved his life. Least we can do is make sure he stays alive long enough to know about it."

"Yeah, and did it occur to either of you he might wake up and not thank us?"

Neither I nor Nathan had anything to say to that.

Nathan offered to spend the rest of the night with Adam, so Tomi and I went to bed, in our own rooms. We didn't say anything else to each other aside from good night. I slept for about three hours and woke just as it was getting light. Instead of going back to sleep, I got dressed and went straight out into the hotel.

The cases were still around somewhere, and I planned to spend all day looking for them.

I made two calls beforehand, however, and the first was to Tania's room. I knocked gently and wondered whether Nathan might have just tried the wrong room while in a state of panic. But no one came to the door. I knocked once more, then left, satisfied that she wasn't there but also a little worried.

I stopped by Adam's room too, and found Nathan still awake, sitting on the floor by the side of his bed. Adam was still alive. According to Nathan, he'd woken up and eaten some chocolate before going back to sleep.

I continued on my walk around the hotel. I hadn't been awake this early in weeks. The light throughout the lower floors was dim, giving the impression of a light gray mist hanging in the air inside the building. To my surprise, I heard children's laughter coming from the lobby, and as I emerged from the stairwell I ran into Mrs. Yobari and her kids.

"Good morning," she said, and looked pointedly at Ryoko and Akio.

Akio made a face and said, "Hello."

"Hello!" Ryoko yelled louder.

"Hello," I replied, stopping in front of them. "I didn't know . . . Sorry, I didn't know your children spoke English."

"Not a lot," Mrs. Yobari said, unwrapping and rewrapping an olive-green scarf. "We weren't raising them to speak English, but they are going to need it now. They are a good age to learn. I learned too late, and mine is not so good."

"Yours is fantastic," I reassured her.

She shrugged away the compliment. I had never spoken to her at length before, but she is a very petite and lithe woman in her mid-forties. Her manner is refined and all her movements deliberate and precise, like she used to practice yoga or a form of dance. When she speaks, her tone and rhythm of speech remind me of a therapist's. Maybe because her voice is so calm.

"Do you usually come down this early?"

"They can play. I can meditate, stretch. I am teaching them as well. I'll also teach Gen when she is old enough."

"You renamed the baby?" For some reason, I was surprised.

"She won't remember her old name, and French names like Chloë are not so easy for us to say."

There was a pause, but I decided not to ask her any more about it. Since her mother's suicide, the baby girl was now theirs, after all. They had the right to call her whatever they liked.

I said, "Meditation and children never went together for me."

"You had children?"

"Two. They're six and twelve, a bit older than yours."

She'd used the past tense. I don't know whether it was the exhaustion catching up with me, or just the emotional punch of missing my kids, but I found myself unable to say any more.

Mrs. Yobari adjusted her scarves and said, "I am going to take them upstairs to sleep before breakfast. Would you like company?"

"I'm going to be looking through a few of the rooms. I'm looking for . . . Actually, yes, I'd love some company."

She nodded, as if it was no bother, and took the children upstairs.

"Bye-bye!" Ryoko called from the stairwell.

"G'bye!" Akio corrected her.

I waved them off and waited for Mrs. Yobari to come back down. When she did, I said, "Sorry, I don't think I've ever asked you your name."

Instead of wearing thick coats like the rest of us, she wore several layers of scarves and open-toed sandals with black tights. Her hair was pulled back and arranged neatly. Of all of us, she was maintaining her normality the best.

"It's Yuka." She surveyed the state of the lobby. "We need to clean this place."

"Thank you!"

"It's not civilized."

"Yeah, it really gets to me. I was thinking about it yesterday."

"We should. But first, you said you wanted to look for something?"

"Yes, I did."

"What are you looking for?"

"I had a couple of cases stolen from my room."

"That's terrible. Do you know who took them?"

"I have an idea, but no proof, of course."

I wasn't sure where to start looking for more information about the hotel's elusive owner, or matching the phone number I had found in the Luffmans' room to anyone in the hotel, so I returned to the offices behind the front desk. I thought that maybe I could also find staff disciplinary records, anything detailing a history of theft or other predatory behavior.

Yuka opened a couple of desk drawers across the room, then asked, "But why are we looking here for suitcases? You are not telling me everything."

I sat in a swivel chair, eyeing a pile of forms completed in French with no idea what they were for or what they said. There was almost no chance that Yuka Yobari had had anything to do with the girl's death. At that point, I almost didn't care. I was so tired of it.

So I told her about my investigation into the body we found in the water tank, and she listened with barely any change of expression.

"So," she said slowly, "you are not just looking for suitcases. We are really looking for who killed this poor girl."

"Yes. The suitcases had evidence in them, I'm sure of it. But it's not just the cases. I have this too." I held out the piece of paper with the phone number on it. "If you could help me find something in a staff directory that matches this number, that would be helpful right now."

"Okay. Then we will find it." With new resolve, she shut the drawers she had been sifting through and went into the neighboring office.

I followed. "Not many people care, you know."

The offices smelled damp, but they were mostly undisturbed. There wasn't much here that could be looted in the name of survival. I noticed that on a corkboard against the far wall there hung some postcards, as if colleagues had gone on vacation and sent souvenirs back. There was a photo of Hawaii. Below it, a photo of someone on a water ride with their family.

"They think we have other things to worry about." She found some keys to the filing cabinets and started opening them. "They think we don't have to act like we are human anymore. We do."

"I agree. If you see anything about the owner, keep it. Whoever owns the hotel, I'm interested."

"Do you know his name?"

"Baloche Braun, according to Tomi. He used to be married to Sophia—you know, the chef? Or they were still married when it happened. I'm not sure."

"You think he had something to do with the girl?"

"I'm not sure. I have a feeling he might have something to do with it, but that's only because of how Sophia and Dylan are acting. I'm sorry I can't tell you more."

"Is this what you're looking for?" She handed me a green binder.

Inside it were several clear sleeves with handwritten lists of phone numbers for different heads of staff within the hotel: technology, security, restaurant, housekeeping, etc. I placed the phone number next to it and searched the list.

"It's here!" I exclaimed. "*Suite présidentielle.*"

"There's a presidential suite here?" She folded her arms. "If I had known, I would have moved into it."

"I didn't see it in the ledger. The Luffmans weren't staying in the presidential suite, so who was?" I scrambled out of the office and re-trieved the book of reservations from the lobby again.

Yuka and I scoured it.

There was no trace of a presidential suite among the official reserva-tions. There was only a yellow sticky note, stuck to the page above the dates in question. On it was written *Suite présidentielle* and the specific dates of occupation: eight days.

"The owner you were talking about?" Yuka said.

"Who else wouldn't have to book using any details but some dates written on a Post-it?" I rubbed my eyes. "But why would the Luffmans have been given Baloche Braun's contact number? And why isn't the presidential suite in the ledger, like every other room?"

She smiled. "You will find out. I will see if there is anything else in here."

Yuka seemed more motivated to finish the search than I was. We searched all the offices from top to bottom within an hour and a half, and then she suggested we take a short break to walk outside before we visited the staff quarters to conduct a room-by-room search. I had a feeling I'd be better received if Yuka was with me. She wouldn't seem threatening to anybody.

We strolled down the forest road for a spell, and I saw that the mist I thought I had seen earlier actually *had* been mist. The air was thick with humidity. We could see only a few feet in front of us. No wind. It was the quietest the trees had ever been.

"How are your kids so happy?" I asked. "I don't think I'd have been able to pretend to my kids that everything was all right, if they were here. But yours are so happy."

"Your children are older, you said. When they get older, they start to look at you like you are human. You can't lie to them anymore. When they are younger, it's easy. They don't know any better. They are used to change. They're not attached to anything, apart from us."

"Do you have older kids?"

"Haru, my husband, we are both second marriage. We both have other children." She didn't elaborate.

"You're right," I said, dragging my hand along wet leaves, dying but not yet dead. "My wife and I . . . Things weren't great, and we tried to hide it from them, but sometimes Ruth—she was the oldest—she'd look at me like she hated me, and I knew that she knew we were lying to her. I don't think they made it."

It was the first time I'd said it out loud.

"Were they in a city?"

"Yeah. I don't know if it was hit, but . . . I looked online when we went on the food run. There were no messages. If any of them were alive, they'd have contacted me somehow; it's been too long." I took off my glasses to pinch the bridge of my nose. "How are you staying so positive?"

A matter-of-fact shrug. "We grow up very differently from Americans. My parents grew up under occupation. After the Second World War, Tokyo was in ruins. There was nothing left. You could sometimes only buy food from gangs, and there were soldiers everywhere. When my parents were children, they saw people die in the street, shot by Chinese, for stealing rice. Our history teaches us that we have built a civilization out of nothing before. So I believe we will do it again."

It took me a while to reply, but her words made me smile. "It never occurred to me before that in America we're all taught this idea that we're descended from rugged, self-reliant cowboys."

"Cowboys did not build anything," she said.

I laughed, because she had a point, and she gave me a look like I was an errant child.

She stopped and turned decisively. "Let's go back inside. We can find some justice for this girl."

We circled around the hotel, approaching the staff quarters from their separate entrance.

Yuka said, "I need their English to get better. They need to grow up able to communicate like you. If you would like to look after Ryoko and Akio, it would be very helpful to me."

"Yeah, I'd love that."

"It is sad there are not other children here. They need friends. They liked talking to other children."

I went to unlock the back door when it opened from the inside and we found ourselves face-to-face with Tania.

"Oh. I didn't expect to see you here," she said, as if Yuka and I were the ones out of place.

"Where were you?" I snapped, maybe too abruptly. "We were looking for you last night!"

"One of the . . . Sasha had a turn during the night so Mia wanted me to sit with him. He's fine, but . . . what happened?"

"Adam OD'd! He almost died. We had to break into your office and inject him with Narcan."

"Jesus, and you didn't look for me?"

"There's, like, a thousand rooms here. What were we gonna do, go door-to-door while he was dying?"

She glared at me and sighed, like this was somehow my fault and Adam OD'ing had been part of some elaborate plot to inconvenience her. I noticed that she wasn't carrying any of her supplies, but didn't say anything.

"I'll go see him now," she said. "Sorry. I didn't think we'd have two medical emergencies in the same night."

Sidestepping between us, she zipped up her jacket and walked away toward the main entrance.

"Hey!" I called after her. "I can help fix the lock on your door. We had to break in!"

"I'll deal with it!"

I turned the master keys over in my hands, and Yuka said, "Why was she leaving through the back?"

Yuka and I searched for the location of the presidential suite for most of the morning, paused for breakfast, and resumed until mid-afternoon, when I took the opportunity to ask her a few questions, and then she left to take over child care.

We hadn't found any rooms that seemed like they could be a presidential suite, but that didn't matter. I had my lead. It was unexplainable, almost impossible to follow up on, but it was something.

We also searched the staff quarters for the suitcases, but didn't see any sign of them. Sasha was a little hostile to the idea of having his room searched, so we mostly just walked in, scanned the obvious places for any sign of the suitcases, and then hastily left.

The idea of repeating this process with every room in the hotel left me lethargic, but I knew I couldn't stop. The overheard conversation between Dylan and Sophia was enough to tell me that I was on the right track, or at least *a* track.

In the restaurant, Sophia allowed us two mugs of hot water, and Yuka and I shared a green-tea bag while other people came and went with their lunch rations. I didn't think Yuka had done it. But she might have seen something on day one, so I questioned her anyway.

"How did you end up staying at the hotel?"

"We had a reservation in the city, but we were double booked and canceled. They paid for us to move."

"So you weren't supposed to be here?"

"No."

I paused, and the odd feeling that had been gathering weight in my chest intensified. The feeling that we were all guided here by a larger, unseen force.

"What did you do before?"

"I was a project manager for American Express. It's where I met Haru."

"And this was in Japan?"

"No." She stared at me. "In Frankfurt."

"Oh, right. Sorry." I wrote something down to distract myself from the embarrassing misstep. "So your children are bilingual?"

"Yes, they also speak German."

"Do you remember much about the day everything happened?"

She went quiet, swirled the tea bag around her mug exactly three times before removing it, and placed it on a saucer.

"We packed and went to reception, where we waited for instructions. They were telling us to wait, remember."

"Yeah, I remember. I think."

"Sometimes I think my memory of it is wrong."

"I get that."

She warmed her hands around the mug. "Then we decided it was safer not to leave. We could not take the children out there with no planes, no cars, no way of getting home. We do not even know if Frankfurt is still there. So we stayed."

I sat back and took a sip of tea. She was deciding not to tell me something. I could see it in her face.

"That's all you remember?"

"It's not easy to remember a day like that."

She had a point there.

I checked my notes and asked, "Do you remember seeing Dylan or Sophia at any point?"

"No."

"Do you remember seeing Nathan, Mia, or Sasha?"

"I remember seeing Mia and Sasha holding each other's hands in the bar, watching the TV in there." She pointed at the bar. "I do not remember seeing Nathan."

I wrote myself a short note to remind myself to interview Nathan properly, and Sasha and Mia, if either of them would speak to me.

"Do you remember anything suspicious?" I asked. "Did anything strange happen?"

"Apart from the bombs, no." She averted her gaze and finished her tea. "Nothing strange."

After lunch, when I had become bored with going through the largely empty rooms on the second floor of the hotel, I decided to stop by and see Adam. We hadn't spoken since last night, when we hadn't really spoken so much as screamed. I know Nathan had been spending a lot of time with him, but I didn't want him to feel isolated, or like the OD was anything to be embarrassed about.

The temptation to avoid him had been quite strong, but I think that was my own issue more than anything else. Attempting death by suicide was a cry for help. It was an outburst of extreme pain, and none of us wanted to deal with someone else's pain when we could barely deal with our own.

It's also occurred to me that attempting suicide could have been a manifestation of guilt, but I don't feel comfortable speculating as to what Adam had to feel so guilty about, if anything. It wouldn't be fair of me, to project motive onto him like that.

I pilfered some more candy from Sophia, then went and knocked on Adam's door.

He opened it, and I thrust my hand out, feeling like a Girl Scout.

"I thought you might like these."

He smirked, took them, and walked back into his room, indicating with his head for me to follow.

The place was cleaner, I noticed. Or at least everything had been shoved into the corners. I hadn't noticed that he'd had an electric guitar before.

"Can you play?" he asked when he saw where I was looking.

"A little." I was worried that he might ask me to prove it, but he didn't.

"I haven't got anything stashed, by the way," he said, sitting on his bed and slinging the guitar across his lap to lean on. "Nath took everything. He's making me ration my weed now. He's such a cunt."

"I'm not here for that, I just wanted to see how you are." I sat on the edge of the bed.

He shrugged. "Still here, aren't I?"

It hit me that the reason he might have shared those personal stories with me was because he was already planning on killing himself.

I found myself staring at the corners of his room, thinking about the Ouija board and the little boy.

"Stop looking for him," Adam snapped. "It sketches me out."

"Sorry!" I exclaimed, not realizing I had been so obvious.

"I'm not going to try it again, if that's what you're here to ask."

"I was mostly just checking that you're feeling okay."

"Just a bit knackered. Stupid time to try, to be honest. I knew Nath was gonna come by at some point, expecting to be hooked up."

"Did it hurt?"

He met my eyes then, clearly surprised I had asked the question.

"No," he said almost wistfully, tuning the guitar. "Didn't hurt at all. It felt like going to sleep. Waking up, now *that* hurt."

"I'm sorry. We didn't know what else to do."

"Don't be sorry, mate." He rubbed the gray circles under his eyes. "Really, you didn't do anything wrong. How fucking ungrateful would I have to be to give you shit about it? You saved my life. And Tomi too, but I haven't seen her. What's going on with you?"

Putting the guitar to one side, he leaned across me and took a piece of candy.

"I think I upset her," I said.

"Shit, what did you say?"

"In a roundabout way, I kinda blamed her for the nuclear war."

He chewed at his lip. "Yeah. That'll do it. Guaranteed upset there."

Even though I desperately want to speak to her again, I haven't tried to approach Tomi, and she hasn't tried to approach me. Even during mealtimes, she's taken to eating in her room. If she ever does decide to speak to me again, it will have to be in her own time.

"Yeah, I don't *think* I upset her, I *did* upset her," I said, leaning against the headboard.

"Holy shit!" Adam interrupted. "These sweets are fucking brilliant. Where'd you get them?"

"I know, right? Sophia has some."

"Sneaky."

"Perks of actually being useful, I guess. She *is* feeding us every day."

"Crazy how many people are still just working."

"Normal."

He picked up the guitar again, like a security blanket. "Why'd you blame Tomi for the nuclear war?"

"Because she . . . was ideologically aligned with the people who caused it."

"Long words there. Sounds like you really want to be pissed off with her, if you're using words like 'ideologically.'"

"Well, she was."

"I don't think Tomi wanted a nuclear war, mate. Just throwing it out there. I know shit about politics, but I don't think anyone's manifesto was 'Nuclear war on Tuesday.'"

His tone riled me. "Everyone else saw it coming!"

"Nah, they didn't."

I conceded, "No. No, we didn't."

"You should probably say you're sorry, if you ever wanna get laid again."

"I have said sorry. I think it's going to take a bit more than that." I glanced into the corner again and quickly dragged my eyes back to neutral. "Tania has a theory that we're all grieving, repressing stuff, like during a grieving process."

"Makes sense with most of the world dead, I suppose."

"She meant for society. We're all grieving for how we used to live."

"Nath reckons I should talk to her, like, about my problems or whatever. But she's a doctor, not a counselor. Doesn't seem fair. She already has so much to do."

"We should all be talking to therapists."

He nodded, then said, "Dude, I'm gonna take a shower. I'll catch up with you later."

"Oh yeah, of course."

I stood up to leave. Hesitated.

"How do you know you're not going to try it again?" I asked, unsure if I was crossing a line.

He frowned, strummed a few chords, and a string snapped. "Fuck!"

As he tried to repair it, I wasn't sure what to say, but he did answer me eventually.

"I must have been technically dead for a bit. Like I said, it was like going to sleep. I didn't feel anything, I didn't see anything."

"Yeah?"

"That's just it. I didn't see *anything*. I must have been dead, right, for a minute or so, and there was nothing. It was just black. Didn't feel like any time passed; it wasn't like being me but sitting in the dark. It was just nothing. There was nothing." A flicker of pure devastation crossed his face, but he recovered himself as he fiddled with the string. "It freaked me out. I'm not trying again."

I wished I hadn't asked. I'd expected an answer based in hope.

"For some reason I thought I'd finally get to speak to that fucker in the corner." And Adam nodded toward the corner of the room, nearest to the window, where a guitar case was leaning against the wall. "I always had the feeling he was waiting for me to die, just waiting . . . and I thought he'd finally tell me what the fuck's been going on."

It was the first time he had talked about the boy like a real entity. I wasn't sure what to say.

Adam laughed to himself, and said, "But nah, he wasn't there."

"Maybe you're not going to the same place," I suggested.

"I don't think I'm going anyplace." He stood up and searched for a towel. "You know, I've tried to off myself twice since I've been here. I tried the night before the world ended, and I woke up like I'd just shut my eyes to go to sleep."

He shook his head with irritation, throwing the towel around his shoulders. "Maybe I'm already dead, mate. Maybe this *is* the other place, and that's why I can't die."

———————

About half an hour ago, just before I stopped writing to go to sleep, there was a knock at my door.

"Who is it?" I yelled, having frozen in my seat.

"Yuka."

I had never seen or heard from her this late. I got up and answered the door, and the first thing I noticed was that she had let her hair down. It was longer than I had expected, and suddenly she looked a lot younger. She looked lovely.

"Something did happen that day," she said. "I just didn't want to tell you."

"Do you want to come in?" I asked, wondering if Haru knew where she was.

She shook her head, remaining a step or two back from my door.

I waited for her to speak.

Taking a breath, she said with her eyes downcast, "I lost Ryoko."

"What?"

"It wasn't for long, about twenty minutes. We were downstairs, waiting for news. There were so many people. She was upset suddenly, and she wouldn't stop crying. I snapped at her and told her to sit on the floor and be quiet. When I looked down again, she was gone."

If I wasn't mistaken, she seemed on the verge of tears.

"Why didn't you tell me before?" I asked.

"I was ashamed. Have you ever lost your children?"

I had, and the memory of it made me grimace and physically flinch every time it crept back into my head. When Marion was four, I lost her in a supermarket. I had to be called over the PA system to collect her, as she had, luckily, wandered into a security guard and not anyone else. I remember running from aisle to aisle, fighting the urge to vomit, imagining a thousand different nightmare scenarios as my hands and heart grew cold with terror.

I nodded.

"So you know what it feels like." She exhaled. "It was scarier than the bombs. I searched everywhere. After some time I returned to our room, and I found her outside. She was trying to open the door. She was crying, very scared, but she was all right."

"Do you know what happened to her?"

"Nothing happened to her. She just got lost when she ran away, after I snapped at her."

"What scared her?"

"She is seven. She was lost. Everybody was lost that day." She looked toward the stairwell. "I should go." And as I saw her face in profile, with her hair falling forward over her shoulders like that, I remembered something.

"I saw you," I said.

"Excuse me?"

"I ran into you, that day."

My memory had returned, in full color. I was running for the stairwell, to get to my room, and I collided with a woman who was shouting at someone, but it wasn't at me. I collided with a woman, almost knocking her clean off her feet, and I saw now that it was Yuka, with her hair falling out of its pins, falling across her face and forward over her shoulders, and she barely acknowledged me. She must've been calling for Ryoko.

"You were coming out of the stairwell, and you were calling for Ryoko. I ran into you."

She squinted at me. "I . . . think I remember that."

I remembered finding Marion that day, standing with the security guard, but she hadn't seemed scared. She hadn't even known she was lost. I was the one who cried. I picked her up and cried in the supermarket and she looked at me in bewilderment.

I leaned against the door frame.

Yuka asked, "Are you okay?"

I said, "I used to call Marion Beeps. My daughter, I called her Beep-bop, but mostly it was just Beeps."

Then I was crying once again, and it was Yuka who was holding me.

Either very late last night or very early this morning—it's hard to tell the time before it gets light—I went down to the bar because I couldn't sleep. I felt both empty and heavy, as if I couldn't lift my limbs but also at the same time like I was hollow. There was no more emotion left in me. I was spent. Yuka had her arms around me for what felt like hours, and she was so small, but it was as if she were the only thing holding me upright. She might have been weeping too, or I might have imagined that to make myself feel better.

Then I had apologized, and she had left.

When I got down to the lobby I saw that I wasn't the only one who couldn't sleep.

Nathan had brought down some of his alcohol and was trying to discreetly make a cocktail without any mixers. He had surrounded himself with a semicircle of candles and looked as though he were enacting an occult ritual with his cocktail shaker.

He had his earphones in and the volume turned up so loud I could hear the crackle and beat of his music in the silence.

"Shit," he said when he saw me, pulling his earphones out and pausing the music.

"Make one for me and I didn't see anything," I said, sitting in one of the armchairs.

"If you saw nothing . . ." Nathan considered my proposal, shrugged, and set another highball glass on the bar, "I guess I'll let you in on my secret recipe."

"Recipe for what?"

"Getting drunk exceptionally quickly."

"I'm glad there's someone down here," I said, putting my feet up on one of the low tables. "Creeps me out in the dark."

"You need to barter for more candles, mate."

"I have nothing to barter with, *mate.*"

"Sell your body, mate." He added something from an unmarked bottle and winked. "You must be doing something right if Tomi was getting on."

I snorted. "Well, first of all, Tomi's not speaking to me, and second, she made it clear I wasn't her first choice."

"Well, now I'm hurt. Where was I on her list?"

He poured out our drinks and came to sit opposite me, and the candles lit up the colored bottles behind the bar in a way that was almost festive.

I sipped the drink, which was excellent.

"What's in that?" I asked.

"Cheap Scotch and tequila, dash of tabasco, and the last of the tomato juice, because no one wanted to drink that shit."

I laughed, because I could imagine Nadia laughing at me.

"Hey, um, I heard a rumor. Does this place have a presidential suite?" I asked.

He looked at me strangely and said, "We don't have one. Dude, if there was a presidential suite here, you don't think we'd have all drawn straws for it by now?"

"Right. Yes, of course."

"I mean, I've only been here about six months, so what do I know? But I've never heard of one."

I watched him over the rim of my glass, but I didn't sense a lie.

"Do you remember anything about that day?" I tried to make it sound as if I was just making conversation. I found myself unable to take my eyes off the mirror above the bar, which gave me a view of the dark lobby behind me. "I've forgotten so much of it, you know. There are these huge gaps where it's like I blacked out."

"Yeah, I get that."

"How much of it do you remember?"

He swished his drink around his mouth, like a professional whisky taster. "Not much. I overslept for my shift. I came down and everyone was just . . . well, it was crazy, you remember that. Then I lose track of what I did. Everything gets fuzzy."

"I went blind for a while. My sight was gone."

"No shit?" He frowned. "Makes me feel better. I thought I was hallucinating."

"Hallucinating what? The nuclear stuff?"

"No, *that* I knew was real. No, I . . ." He gulped down the rest of his drink. "For a second, I thought I saw my dad."

That stopped me in my tracks, and suddenly I felt the chill. Suddenly, the candles on the bar didn't look like Christmas lights anymore.

Nathan shook his head. "In the crowd in reception, I thought I saw him. But it's been ten years, you know. It was just someone else's dad."

". . . Right."

"What was that?" Nathan sat up straight and peered over my shoulder. As he did so, I heard footsteps.

I turned in my chair, gripping my glass so tight I was surprised I didn't smash it.

"You hear that, right?" Nathan whispered.

"Yeah."

"Who's there?" he called.

Out in the lobby, a disoriented Sasha wandered into view, wearing nothing but a pair of boxer shorts. He was clearly asleep, and walking in the direction of the lights. He didn't respond to Nathan's voice.

Nathan let out the breath he had been holding and stood up. "Jesus, it's you. The fucking resident ghost. Let's turn you around."

I finished my drink, hoping it would calm my frayed nerves, and announced that I needed to try to get some sleep as well. Call me paranoid, but I couldn't help noting that this was the second time Sasha had followed me in his sleep. I kept a close watch on his face—the slack mouth, his eyes half closed and shielded by his long lashes—but there was no expression, no sign of consciousness. Nothing to suggest that he might have been faking.

Nathan had approached and gently linked arms with him.

"Come on, mate. We haven't got all night. Let's stroll all the way back to your own room, where you won't scare the shit out of any more people. That'll be awesome."

He wasn't acting as though he had told me anything of great consequence.

Maybe he hadn't. We had all been rendered useless and unreliable with shock that day.

But I had a bad feeling.

"Wait!" I called after them suddenly.

"Shh, you're not supposed to startle them," Nathan hissed.

"Wait, one moment."

I jogged up to them, holding my weak candle in one hand, and peered right into Sasha's vacant face.

His gaze didn't focus on me.

Nathan rolled his eyes. "What are you doing?"

I clicked my fingers a couple of times in front of Sasha's eyes, and then a couple more, holding the candle right up to him, illuminating every contour, looking for the smallest indication that he wasn't asleep.

But there was no response, so I backed off.

"Nothing. I'm sorry; it's nothing."

Nathan gave me a concerned look that made me doubt myself. Then he guided Sasha away through the staff door, and I blew out all the candles in the bar, feeling embarrassed for the second time that night.

I don't know if I'm just feeling pessimistic but, right now, I don't feel as though my investigation is making much headway. Talking to people isn't helping as much as I thought it would, because everyone's memories are too fractured to be trusted. Aside from the occasional flashbacks, the dreams that I lose my grip on as soon as I wake up, I'm not even sure how far I can trust my own memory.

We first heard about the incident from Dylan. Naturally, the woman concerned had gone to him first. He called us all for a meeting in the bar. Seeing the group gathered in one room was rare; it brought home just how few of us were left, and how vulnerable we were.

I was tired. I hadn't been able to force any sleep.

Dylan stood by the bar while everyone settled in, sitting on the floor or leaning against the walls. A few people brought extra chairs from the restaurant. Mia was standing to the side of Dylan, and she looked upset.

I stood next to Tania. "You know what this is about?"

"No. Food?"

"Maybe."

Tomi came in and stood on my other side, but didn't say anything.

When everyone had gathered, Dylan raised his voice a little, addressing us all.

"There was an incident this morning. Mr. Nicholas van Schaik attempted to assault a woman here. Luckily, she managed to fight him off, and he's locked in a room upstairs until we can decide what to do with him. I thought it was best to tell everyone, to stop rumors spreading. My instinct is that we should decide what to do as a group, rather than leaving this to one or two people. So . . . I think we should talk."

No one seemed to want to take the floor, and then Tomi asked, "Was it Mia? Are you okay?"

Mia smiled. "I'm fine; I carry a knife, so . . ."

Yuka asked, "He should be made to leave. No?"

Dylan countered, "If we make him leave, then it's exile, which is as good as a death sentence. Also, he might come back and cause more trouble. We can't assume he'll go quietly."

Tomi: "What, so we're gonna let him stay here and waste resources?"

Sasha, from out of sight: "He's still a human being."

"He tried to rape somebody," Tomi snapped. "Your sister!"

Silence.

Dylan took control of the room again. "Let's make this easier. We need some sort of trial, or . . . tribunal. Anyone who has no interest in being a part of that, raise your hand."

Most people put their hands up.

"But wait," Tomi said, "it won't be a democratic process if people can just opt out. We might need a vote."

"It won't be democratic if we force people to make decisions they don't want to make," I said quietly.

"What, Jon?" Dylan craned his neck in my direction.

"I said, it won't be democratic if we force people to take part."

Tomi made a noise of derision. "It won't be a fair representation if a vote doesn't come from everyone."

"How about a compromise," Tania suggested. "Everyone votes, but there's an option to abstain."

Dylan: "I like that idea. Is everyone good with that?"

The room was mostly quiet, but people nodded.

Adam raised his hand. "Um, don't know if anyone's gonna agree with this, but why don't we let Mia decide? Like, it was her who was attacked by this dude. Shouldn't we ask her what she wants to do with him?"

Everyone looked at Mia, who shifted from one foot to the other and shrugged. "I don't know."

Lex said something fast and angry that I didn't understand, and Lauren translated.

"She says, why? If he is a danger to all women, I don't want one woman to decide whether I am safe or not."

"Seconded!" Tomi said.

Tania: "Yeah, I'm with that."

"Okay, cool." Adam didn't seem bothered. "Just checking."

"So we all decide," Dylan said. "We'll put it to a vote. But we need to talk about options. I'm sorry to say this, but one of them is going to be execution."

I admired that he'd had the guts to say it. No one else wanted to, though it had been hanging over the room since we started talking. As soon as we knew a crime had been committed, the first thought was *Do we kill him?* because with resources scarce and getting scarcer, it was the only pragmatic course of action.

"If we decide to kill him," Rob said slowly, from somewhere near the front, "who would do it?"

"I would," Tomi said without hesitation. "Next question."

I glanced at her. She looked at me as if to say, *Yes, and?*

I wasn't sure whether I admired her or not. I was glad, in a way, that she had let everyone else off the hook so quickly. I volunteered for everything. I'm not sure whether I could have volunteered for that.

Dylan also seemed relieved. It would have been him or me, after all.

"Okay, so the options are one, kill him, or two, imprison him. Should there be an option to exile?"

Haru Yobari: "No. You are right. He will only come back."

"I second that," Tania said.

"Raise your hands if you think we should have an exile option," Dylan said.

Surprisingly, no one did.

"Are we missing anything, then?" Dylan asked.

Peter raised his hand. "So, we are assuming he did do this, then? No trial, like you said?"

Mia glared at him. "We're not assuming anything. He attacked me!"

Peter shrugged. "Did anyone else see this?"

No one.

My stomach turned. The atmosphere in the room grew tense. I felt Tomi bristle next to me, and Tania had also turned to eye Peter with disdain. The gender divide was painfully apparent.

"Are you fucking kidding me?" Tomi said. "You want her to prove to you that he tried to rape her?"

"I am saying it is a dangerous situation, when a woman can accuse anyone and then we decide whether to kill him or not."

"I can't believe this." Tomi shook her head.

"I got him in the ankle with a knife," Mia said. "What other proof do you want?"

"Then we only have proof you attacked him," Peter replied. "Forgive me, but you look fine. You do not look like someone tried to force himself on you. What does he have to say?"

"He confessed," Dylan cut in. "When I locked him in he kept saying, 'She stabbed me.' He was calling her a lot of names, saying she'd wanted it. He'd been caught. There was no doubt in my mind."

"That's not a confession," Peter said, doubling down.

"Are you saying I'm lying?" Mia folded her arms.

Peter snapped, "Anyone can lie just because they do not like someone."

A ripple of disgust moved throughout the room. Even Yuka, usually impassive, shook her head. I thought Tomi was going to explode. I glanced at her again and her lip was curling with contempt.

"Enough!" Dylan took a step forward. "Let's not disrespect the women here by assuming they would lie about something this important. We're better than that. If someone is called out as being a danger to the group, we have to deal with it, unless there is clear evidence to the contrary. *Clear* evidence. Everyone understand?"

"Thank you!" Tomi snapped.

"That goes for everyone here," Dylan said. "We don't have the time or resources to set up a full trial. I'm not going to waste days listening to what he says and what she says. So unless there's a witness willing to provide a different claim, we're gonna believe people. We're not going to assume people are lying for stupid reasons. We're a small group, so we need to treat one another with respect. Does anyone else here have a problem with that?"

Everyone nodded their agreement.

Tomi glowered at Peter. "Well, it's good to know who here thinks women are just waiting for an excuse to lie about rape."

"People do lie," Peter said. "For many reasons."

"Say we're liars one more fucking time!" Tomi took a few steps forward, and Peter averted his eyes.

"Come on," I said, reaching out and taking her arm.

"Yeah, it's decided. Unless anyone has another ethical point to bring up, I think we should vote." Dylan scanned the room. "Take the opportunity to speak now. No one is going to shout you down if you make any point with respect for your fellow people. Take your time, give it some thought."

Tomi returned to my side, still glaring, and I let go of her arm.

I glanced at Tania, but she looked away quickly.

I considered making a point about utilitarianism; that any vote that came out in favor of imprisonment was too flawed to be taken seriously, because the interests of the group dictated that to waste resources on a criminal would be an act of collective self-harm. But I argued myself down before I said anything. If we discounted any alternative, then we became a society—albeit a small one—that punished people for any kind of wrongdoing with death. Even if it was necessary, I wasn't sure I wanted us to become that.

In another life, I'd been against the death penalty.

So I stayed quiet, and so did everyone else.

"Okay, let's move on, then," Dylan continued. "Can we vote by a show of hands, or does anyone want the vote to be anonymous?"

No one made a call for anonymity.

Dylan said, "In that case, who here would see Nicholas van Schaik punished for attempted rape by being indefinitely incarcerated?"

Peter raised his hand. A few others did too, including Rob, Sophia, and Sasha, surprisingly.

"Who here would see him punished for attempted rape by being put to death?"

Every other woman raised their hand. Dylan also raised his hand, and Adam. I thought about abstaining, but decided it was a weak move, and that it was better to show solidarity with the women even if I would rather avoid committing either way.

I raised my hand.

For the first time in my life, I voted for the death penalty.

I couldn't work out how many had abstained.

"And the rest of you are abstaining," Dylan said with finality. "So it's decided. Tomi, are you still willing to carry out the sentence?"

"Absolutely," she said.

"Right. So, thank you, everyone. Is there anything else anyone would like to say?"

I suppose I might have underestimated the extent to which people are averse to conflict, even during a crisis, but I had expected more people to protest the result. No one did. The entire debate and vote had taken about twenty minutes. I wasn't sure if that was a good thing or not. Maybe, because there were so few of us, it was simply easier to make decisions like this. After all, direct democracy only works in small groups, and here we are.

It crossed my mind that I would have loved to tell my colleagues in the political science department about this. We had all written essays about democracy on our respective career paths, and I was now witnessing it in practice: the ultimate case study.

The room began to disperse, and I looked to my right and found that Tania was no longer there.

Tomi said, "That was quick."

"I knew some political theorists who would have paid good money to see this," I said quietly, in case I came off as insensitive.

She smiled. "I thought that too."

Dylan and Mia approached us. He said, "Should we just do this now?"

I watched Tomi's face, but she seemed unperturbed.

"Might as well," she said.

"You're okay?" I asked.

"With killing an aspiring rapist? I won't lose much sleep."

I couldn't tell if it was just bravado, or whether she truly didn't care.

Mia said, "Thanks. And thanks for, you know, doing all this."

Dylan was stoic. "We don't want people scared to report crimes. That's important."

As Adam left the bar, he stopped by the door and said, "Gimme a shout if you need help with anything."

Those of us who stayed behind looked at one another, unsure how to proceed. There was no protocol for killing a man, but we were about to invent one. I found myself thinking, almost like a mantra, that my vote, ultimately, had not mattered. Even though I had voted in favor, something that I would never have done under ordinary circumstances, my vote hadn't been a decider.

Even now, I don't know whether my need for that fact pointed to us having made the wrong decision.

DAY 66 (2)

After Tomi and Dylan went upstairs, I sat in the bar alone for a while, still deciding whether to accompany them to the execution or not. I had no desire to watch a man be murdered, no matter what he had done. But I felt it was my duty to record these things. Tomi had taken on the role of executioner, so an impartial account of the event was needed.

Nadia, if you ever read this, I know you might be disappointed in my stance here. I want you to know that it didn't feel normal, sentencing someone to death. It's not like human life has been cheapened because of the abrupt loss of most of our species; if anything, it's even more important, so threats to it have to be taken even more seriously. But then . . . that argument doesn't stand up. If human life is so precious that we have to neutralize existential threats to the group, then that same logic could have applied before.

Maybe I'm not as against the death penalty as I thought. Maybe killing Van Schaik was an act of humanity. I don't know.

This isn't a philosophy text. It's not my place to decide either way. But it was easier to argue these points before, when most abstract ideas about life and death hadn't affected me.

I got up and waited in the lobby until Tomi and Dylan returned with a hunting rifle, and Nicholas van Schaik between them. At the sight of him I felt a wave of deep sickness; not physical sickness but a pain in the soul.

Van Schaik was white and trembling. He could barely walk, due to the nasty gash in his calf caused when Mia had fought him off. I noticed that they had let him wear a warm coat for the walk, even though he wouldn't be returning.

It pains me to admit that, aside from our altercation in the stairwell, I had never before spoken to Van Schaik. He mostly sat with Peter, and sometimes Lauren and Lex. The divide between the English and non-English speakers manifested once again.

He said, "Please," and he said it while looking straight at me. He had obviously tried pleading with Tomi and Dylan, and now he was appealing to me.

I didn't know what to say, so I looked away.

"No, please! Please! I don't want to die!"

He said something else, but this time in Dutch. Probably the same thing.

"You don't have to come," Tomi said to me.

"I feel like I should."

"Wait."

We turned, and Peter had approached us, with his hands in his pockets and wearing his black outdoor coat.

"You want to say good-bye?" Dylan asked.

Tomi rolled her eyes.

Peter looked between Dylan and me.

"I should do it," he said with his coal-rolling voice.

Van Schaik said something in Dutch, or German, but Peter cut him off.

"I should do it," he said again, in English. "I know him. I should do it."

Dylan shifted. "Do you want to do it?"

"I said I *should*. You should not kill a man impersonally."

I wasn't sure that I trusted him, but Dylan did, and handed Peter the rifle. Maybe he saw it as a gesture of goodwill, or compromise, after the heated bar debate.

"Tomi, are you fine with this?" he asked.

She shrugged. "I don't care either way, so long as he doesn't miss."

So, with Peter now taking responsibility for the act itself, we all went outside and walked a little way into the forest. Probably not far enough that the people back at the hotel wouldn't hear the gunshot.

Van Schaik started crying, a desolate, strangled sound. At least they couldn't hear that.

I wondered what Peter was feeling. I found it hard to identify the emotions in his expression, even with him walking right beside me.

Dylan and Tomi walked a little ahead of us, with Van Schaik between them, and I heard the two of them talking.

"While we're all out here," Dylan said, "we're going to need to talk about your gun."

"Why?"

"You seem to have unlimited ammunition."

A brief silence.

"I have a few extra bullets," Tomi said.

"No, you don't. And I know my own gun. It's not right to hold the rest of the hotel hostage."

"I'm not holding anyone hostage," she retorted.

"Tomi." Dylan's voice was low. "You can't be the only one of us armed."

She gestured at Van Schaik. "If that piece of shit had gotten his hands on a loaded rifle, he would've been able to hold Mia at gunpoint."

"Do you trust me?"

She hesitated. "What does that have to do with anything?"

"If I had a loaded gun, do you think I'd use it to commit a crime?"

"No . . . of course not. But I don't know everyone here."

"I'm not talking about everyone here, I'm talking about me. I seem to have been appointed some sort of leader, or if not leader, an organizer maybe. Do you trust me, as someone who's made some tough decisions for this group, to have a working gun?"

I admired how he went about it. He could have laid into her, made threats, but he was calm. It made me doubt what I thought I knew about him. How could he have anything to do with the dead girl? I thought back to that day on the rooftop and his shock, the expression on his face as he carried the tiny body down the ladder. If he had known the body was there, why did he allow us onto the roof in the first place? Why did he instigate all the projects involving the tanks? It didn't make any sense. What's more, he had saved a woman in this hotel from Victor Roux, fought—literally tooth and nail—for her life, as he had for ours.

I had no concrete proof that anything he had told me was true, but, still, something didn't add up.

I want to trust him. That's the crux of it. I so badly want to trust him, because without that trust we're lost.

Tomi said, "You? As in *just* you?"

"Yes, just me."

Slowly, she nodded. "Okay. You can take whatever ammo you want."

"Do you want to give me my gun back?"

"I'll think about it. I want to be carrying something."

To my surprise, Peter didn't seem interested in their discussion, though he must have also heard it.

"What did you mean when you said you shouldn't kill a man impersonally?" I asked him.

"Exactly what I said."

"But why?"

He shot me a look like I was a child. "Would you rather be shot by someone who is going to care that they shot you? Or someone who doesn't care?"

"The former, I guess."

"Then you know what I mean."

A bird cried out, somewhere in the distance, and we both looked to the canopy. It felt as though I hadn't seen or heard any wildlife for weeks. The idea of seeing a bird again in the wild filled me with such excitement that it took me a few seconds to realize that I'd taken Peter's arm. I was smiling. I was actually smiling, and it wasn't forced or tight.

We didn't hear the bird again.

"Damn," I said to myself. "Damn. Come on, where did you go?"

The trees became dense, though they were mostly dying for lack of rain and sun. I touched one of the trunks and it was bone dry, crumbling from the outside in. I wondered whether the insects really would be the only things to survive this. I wondered how well we were really doing at avoiding the worst of the radiation poisoning. I wasn't even sure how radiation worked.

"Here," Dylan said, halting suddenly as soon as we reached another clearing.

"Please!" Van Schaik tried again.

"This is going to go a lot easier if you don't do that." Dylan took him firmly by the shoulders and stared into the sobbing man's eyes. "This is going to happen. It'll be quick. The longer you drag this out, the more pain it means for you. Don't make us wrestle with you. Have some dignity, and you'll die a good death."

Tomi and I exchanged a look. Even she seemed a little uncomfortable.

"Nick." Peter led Van Schaik off to the side, when Dylan's speech did nothing to lessen his convulsions, and gave him a talking-to in German.

I was impressed that Peter managed to speak to him, with the rifle in his hand like that.

"What's he saying?" I asked Dylan.

"I don't speak German."

Van Schaik trembled but nodded, and Peter helped him walk about ten paces farther. He stood at the edge of the trees, resting his weight on his uninjured leg. He faced us for a few seconds, before turning around and staring in the opposite direction.

I'd have done the same. If I had to die, I'd rather die facing the trees than my executioners.

Peter joined us, and his expression toward us was one of contempt. Then he turned on his heel and raised the rifle to his shoulder.

I saw him do the mental countdown. Five, four, three, two—

And Van Schaik fell onto his injured leg and made a break for it.

"Get him!" Tomi screamed, at the same time as the gunshot that cut Van Schaik down.

We all flinched, covering our ears as Van Schaik collapsed lifeless into the foliage.

Peter turned back to us and thrust the rifle into my arms. He reached into his pocket, took out a pack of cigarettes, and lit one.

He said, "Of course he was going to run."

Then he walked off.

Tomi took a few steps toward Van Schaik and crouched by the body.

Looking over her shoulder, she said, "It was a head shot."

There was a long silence while we watched Tomi maneuver Van Schaik out of his thick coat and try it on for size.

"Should we bury him?" Dylan asked.

"I'm not going to be digging any graves for rapists." Tomi looked between us, and followed Peter.

"Should we?" This time, Dylan directed the question at me.

"It wouldn't feel right leaving him out here."

"You a superstitious man, Jon?"

"No." I checked myself. "A little."

"You can still quote the Bible. I don't know anyone else here who can do that."

"It sticks with you."

"You go to Catholic school?"

I looked at Van Schaik's body and was surprised I didn't feel more disgusted. Now that it was over, his death wasn't nearly so confrontational. It was easier for me to think that we had definitely made the right call. The ease of it scared me. I wondered if I would be able to do the same if I ever found out who had killed Harriet Luffman. It would be the only sensible decision—the only justice available—but could I do it?

"Jon?"

"Huh? Oh, no, I went to a Christian school, but it wasn't Catholic. I wanted to work in the church until I was about nineteen, mostly because my parents wanted me to. Then I went to college instead."

"You're an interesting guy." He sighed at Van Schaik. "My instinct is we should bury him."

"Mine too."

"I don't think I have it in me to do it now, though."

"We can come back later. I'll help. Maybe Rob or Adam or someone can join us." I gestured at the trees and added, "I thought I heard a bird before. Been so long since I've heard one."

"Damn, we could use more birds. We could hunt them."

That hadn't been my immediate thought. The idea of hunting down the remaining wildlife to slaughter made me a little sad, but I kept that to myself. Dylan seemed in a reflective mood, though, and as we made our way back toward the hotel he frowned and turned to me.

"Can I confess something?"

I smiled. "I never qualified, you know. I can't save your soul."

"Funny. No, I . . . You know, I envied him for a moment."

"Who?"

"Van Schaik. Clean shot to the head and he's gone. He doesn't have to worry about food anymore, about the group, or fighting, or staying alive, or getting up in a snappy blond girl's face to get bullets. He wasn't even facing us. Must have been like flicking out a light."

I wasn't sure what to say.

He added, "Don't worry, I'm not thinking of checking out. I just thought . . . maybe he has gone to a better place. For a moment, I was jealous of that."

"You believe in Heaven?"

"I'm not sure."

"Well, that's a sensible answer."

"You must have at one point. What changed? You lose your faith? You an atheist now?"

"Not an atheist. More an agnostic. I realized that I'm never going to know, so I might as well focus on this life."

He nodded. "So you wanted to get laid, right?"

"Oh, so bad."

We both laughed.

"If anything is enough to turn a young man against God, it's that," he said.

Dylan eyed me for a moment, as if he wanted to ask something else, maybe something about Tomi and I, or maybe something about my investigation. But he seemed to think better of it and we continued walking.

Suddenly I asked, "Where's the presidential suite?"

He hesitated for a beat and I saw him miss a step, like the question had physically obstructed his rhythm. "We don't have one. We've got some nicer rooms, bigger, but not a presidential suite. Why?"

"No reason. My room feels small. I was thinking about moving."

"Right."

When we got back to the hotel people were starting to drift down into the restaurant for lunch. A couple of them gave us grave nods and glances.

Tomi had gone upstairs, I presumed, and Dylan left my side to go get bullets.

Rob spotted me in the lobby and approached me, handing me a cigarette.

"You're all turning me into an addict," I said, but accepted the lighter.

"How was it?"

"I thought I heard a bird," I replied.

His face lit up. "What kind?"

"I don't know, sorry. I couldn't see it, and it just sounded like a bird. I can't tell them apart."

"Well . . . did it sound like a *coo* or a *caaw*, or an *aair*?"

I smiled. "Kinda like a *peep*."

Our laughing attracted a few looks from people, and I realized it might have come across as tasteless. We'd just had to kill one of our own. I can't yet predict how that might end up changing us.

I'm running a day behind. First, I'll finish writing about the day when Nicholas van Schaik was executed.

Events moved fast from lunchtime onward, when Dylan, Adam, and I returned to the woodland clearing with shovels to bury Van Schaik. Rob came too, but ducked away from the group as soon as we hit the forest, in search of the bird I had mentioned earlier. He had a half smile on his face, holding his camera with two hands with his eyes to the upper branches. I didn't watch him go.

As we approached the place where we had left the body, I listened for any birdsong, any wildlife, but there was nothing this time. The wind had whipped up in the last couple of hours, and the rattle of withered leaves was abrasively loud.

Dylan said, "It was here."

We looked around but there was nothing. No body.

"Must all look the same," Adam said.

"No. No, this is the same place." I was certain. "It was here, right?"

I waved my hand over a patch of leaves and Dylan nodded.

"Yeah, Tomi and I were standing back by that tree. Peter was here. Van Schaik was there."

"So . . ." Adam leaned on his shovel, frowning. "Must be a mistake?"

"We're not mistaken." I met Dylan's eyes. "I'm sure we're not."

"It was here," he said. "Look! Blood."

And there was blood, right where we'd left it.

"So he's gone? How?" Adam started jumping up and down on the spot, teeth chattering in the wind. "How many times did she shoot him? Did he crawl off?"

"Peter shot him, in the head." Dylan pushed leaves around with his foot, searching for a trail of blood. "Trust me, he wasn't crawling anywhere."

"He was dead," I said, and then lost confidence. "He was dead, right?"

"He was dead. Peter shoots well. We all saw."

Adam: "Then what happened?"

I was suddenly overcome with an urge to run as fast as I could back to the hotel. It must have shown on my face, because Dylan reached out to grasp my shoulder, keeping his voice low and steady.

"Look, keep calm. We've still got animals alive in these woods. Any of them could have dragged the body away."

Adam didn't seem convinced. "What, like wolves? Bears? What animal would drag a whole human body away?"

"Other people?" I said, light-headed. "There aren't any wolves out here. I've never heard them."

"There might be." Dylan sighed. "Radiation could have pushed them farther north. We've almost never had bears, though. We had one back in 2013, but it was shot."

"So . . . there *aren't* any animals in these woods that could drag a body off?" I reiterated.

"No." He relented. "It's unlikely."

"Holy shit." Adam put a hand behind his head, wide-eyed. "Fuck. Fuck."

"Stay calm. We're going to go back to the hotel." Dylan's voice had dropped to almost a whisper. "We can make sure all our entrances are secure and talk about this."

"Come on, the hotel is so massive someone could already be in there hiding out and we wouldn't even know!"

"For fuck's sake, Adam!" I threw my shovel down. "Fuck you!"

"I'm just saying!"

"I know, I'm sorry, it's just . . . Did you have to say that? Jesus!"

Dylan shook me. "Keep it together, man. We've got weapons, so we can search the place top to bottom, military formation. But we can't panic."

I don't know how he stayed calm. This was the most scared I had been since day one. I was more scared than I had been even in the superstore, watching my colleagues get shot. This was a whole different kind of fear. It was the fear of something we haven't yet seen; the worst-case scenario we had only envisioned in our minds.

The atmosphere was solemn. We picked up the shovels and left the clearing. I glanced back once, as if we might have been wrong, but the body was definitely gone. Then it hit me:

"We can't go," I said.

Adam: "Seriously, why?"

"Rob's out here. He's looking for birds. We can't just leave him here when . . ."

I didn't want to say the words out loud.

"Have you got a gun on you?" Adam asked Dylan.

"No, I didn't bring anything."

"Then we can't stay out here looking for him."

"Guys." I spread my hands. "Come on, it's Rob. He doesn't know, he has no warning!"

"We'll be no use to him walking around unarmed and getting ambushed," Dylan said, taking a deep breath. "I know it feels bad, but we can come back when we're prepared. I don't like being out here right now. I don't know about you guys, but I want to get back and get armed."

I looked out into the forest and, for some reason, some stupid reason, I shouted, "Rob!"

Adam shoved me in the chest. "Shut the fuck up, what are you doing!"

"If he's nearby, he'll come!"

"No, *idiot*, you've just warned anyone listening that there's one of us out here alone!"

I stared into the gap between Dylan and Adam and felt weak with alarm. "Oh . . . I didn't . . . I didn't think."

"Come on!" Dylan took the lead, dragging me again by the arm. "Let's move. We can argue about this inside."

I didn't say anything else. I kept glancing back into the trees, hoping I'd see Rob, but he didn't answer my call, and I didn't see anyone else. Overcome with guilt, I sat in the bar as soon as we got back to the hotel. Dylan and Adam went upstairs to convene with Tomi and discuss weapons and a search of the building. I leaned my shovel against the side of my chair, and after a while Sophia walked past and asked me if I was all right.

"You didn't see Rob come back earlier, did you?" I asked. "Before us?"

She shook her head. "No, but I haven't been here the whole time. Maybe check his room?"

"Yeah, that would make sense."

But Rob wasn't in his room either. Dylan had checked. For the first time in a while, I started praying. I prayed that I hadn't gotten him killed.

We locked all the entrances and started to talk about organizing small groups to search every room in the hotel. Everyone was able to lock themselves in, so no one was too worried about being surprised in their rooms. It was everywhere else that now felt like the wilderness.

———————

Dylan announced to the bar, where all of us were gathered once again, that a couple of small groups were going to search the hotel from floor to floor, room to room, due to a possible breach from someone outside. He didn't mention that the body had disappeared.

Everyone looked tired, already stressed by how the day had started, and Haru asked, "Why do you think someone else is here?"

"We're not sure yet," Dylan said with remarkable composure. "A few of us noticed some suspicious-looking activity in the forest this morning. It's been a while since we did a search of this place. It's worth doing periodically, for safety."

That seemed to satisfy Mr. Yobari.

Less so Peter, who raised a hand. "What exactly was suspicious?"

"I don't want to get into that."

"I want to know."

Dylan glared. "I don't want to get into that, because it could be nothing, and I don't want to start a panic. Do you?"

No one else chimed in, so Peter ended up shaking his head.

I took a moment to scan the bar again, but there was definitely no sign of Rob. He hadn't made it back yet, and he had been gone for almost two hours. I met Adam's eyes, because he was doing the same.

Rob was the most gentle and good-natured of us all. I hoped he was all right, because his loss would be one we'd feel deeply.

"Can we talk about something else while we're all here?" Lauren asked from the far corner of the bar, holding hands with Lex. "Can we talk about rations?"

A few people nodded, including Mia and Sophia.

"What's the problem?" Dylan asked.

"We've noticed rations are smaller. You said we're well supplied. Why do we have to start starving ourselves now?"

"I agree," Sophia said. "I don't see any reason. We're all hungry most of the time."

"Winter is gonna creep up on us, and we don't wanna find ourselves with only a few tins each when that happens," Adam cut in.

"But we have time to find more food by then. I don't understand why we have to panic . . . what's the word?"

"Prematurely?" I said.

"Yes, I don't understand why we have to panic prematurely."

I had never heard Sophia take the floor before.

Dylan paused, giving it some thought. "Any more excursions for food are gonna have to go farther, into the towns. It's going to be more dangerous, and we can't . . . We can't guarantee we'd make it back alive. On the last trip we did come across people, people from this hotel, and they attacked us, and we had to kill them in self-defense. We need to keep in mind that we might not always be the ones doing the killing."

"You didn't say people died," Yuka said.

"I'm saying it now. That's why I decided it might be wise to cut rations, but . . . if you feel it's wrong, why don't we vote?" He shrugged. "I don't wanna see us starve. I also don't wanna put the men and women who volunteer to find food for us in more danger than necessary. I don't wanna put that kind of pressure on them."

Silence.

"Well," Dylan said, "do you want a vote?"

A lot of people looked at me, Mia, Adam, and Tomi. I could tell they were trying to work out whether the threat to our lives was worth being a little hungrier every day. No one had yet asked where Rob was. I hoped we could get through the meeting without the question coming up.

"How often would we have to go looking for food if we didn't change rations?" Sophia asked.

"I'm not sure. I would say at least four times in the next couple of months, assuming they're all as successful as our first."

Adam seemed startled.

This was news to me as well.

Tomi looked at me from across the bar.

Dylan added, "I know no one wants to do it, but we're gonna need to increase rations during the winter, remember. We don't know how much colder it's going to get. We might not even be able to leave. We need to have more than enough food."

Sophia nodded. "Then let's vote. It's only fair we vote."

"Okay. On one condition." Dylan folded his arms. "This condition is for fairness. Anyone who votes for an increase in rations needs to volunteer their name to me, and we'll do future food runs on a fair rotation."

"You can't force people to go," Sasha muttered, hidden from my sight behind his twin sister.

"It's not fair to put this danger on only five or six brave people. If you're willing to vote to put them at further risk, you have to be willing to take a share of it." Dylan held his ground, jaw thrust out.

Adam said, "It's unfair anyway! We should already be doing a rotation. If you think I'm gonna keep going out and risking my arse for people who are just hiding here wanting to eat more, you can fuck off, mate."

"I get you, Adam," Tomi said. "I agree."

"What about those of us with children?" Yuka asked.

"Hey, you think just because you spawned that gives you more of a right to not die than us?" Tomi snapped. "Sit down!"

"But who would look after our children if something happened to us?"

"The group, obviously," Dylan said. "We're not monsters."

"That's not acceptable," Yuka shot back.

"And us dying is?" Tomi raised her eyebrows. "We're expendable because we're not parents, is that it?"

Silence.

"Is that it?"

"Without getting sidetracked," I cut in, before things got nastier, "I think Dylan's suggestion is fair. It can't be down to the same people every time. It's dangerous and it takes a lot of energy."

"You said Tania didn't have to go," Sophia pointed out.

Tania leaned back against the wall, but her expression was firm. "I volunteered to go, remember."

"Maybe if more of you had gone to medical school rather than had kids, you'd be valuable too," Tomi muttered.

"So some people *are* more valuable than others," Peter said.

"I can't deal with sanctimonious bullshit right now," Tomi hurled back. "Being a parent doesn't make you valuable. Being able to save lives does! I'm a great shot and I brought your ungrateful asses back extra food, so, sorry, I'm more valuable than someone who just didn't buy Plan B one time!"

This time the dissent was louder. The atmosphere felt bad. The group had started to separate slowly into two opposing factions. On one side stood Dylan, Adam, Tania, Tomi, Mia, me, and some of the staff. On the other were the other young women, the Yobaris, and Peter.

Tomi had one hand behind her back, and I could tell from her stance that she had her gun with her. She was glaring at Peter with open hatred.

"If everyone could just stop for two seconds!" Adam shouted. "Dylan made a fair suggestion. We vote. Either we all do food runs, and more of them, or we do less and some people get to stay behind."

"Some cowards get to leech off the others, you mean," Tomi said.

"What did you say?" Peter snarled, stepping forward.

"You heard me."

"Where were you when we were out in the cold hunting deer?"

"Shut up! Both of you!" Dylan stood between them, taking the floor.

Without realizing, I had also taken a step toward Tomi, and I felt as though everyone in the room noticed. I have no idea why I did it. She clearly didn't need me in a fight. It was in moments like this that it became easy to see how animal instinct could take over, how groups could descend into tribal warring over resources and territory.

Dylan said, "We're voting. If you want to kill each other in a duel, do it in your spare time, and do it away from here. But don't forget, if anyone here hurts another person in cold blood, justice has to win out. We saw that today."

I nodded. "Come on, guys, he's right. Let's do this fairly."

"Tania has to be included," Peter said. "If it's going to be fair."

"It's like you *want* to die of infection," Tomi laughed. "Not that I'd care if it was you."

Tania got in there before Peter did. "Look, I've been offering basic medical training to people. Maybe before the next run, I can take a group and spend a few weeks teaching them. That way, if I die, it doesn't have to mean it's—"

"—game over for everyone," Tomi finished. "Unlike, say, if someone who happened to breed dies."

"We get it!" I snapped when Yuka looked ready to get back into the argument. "Tania, that would be great. If we started doing that and the rotation included everyone, would people be happy?"

Everyone looked at one another.

"Maybe not happy," Dylan said. "But do you think it would be fair?"

A few people nodded.

Tomi looked at Peter as if to say, *Well?* and so did Dylan.

Eventually, he sighed. "That would be fair. If it was all of us."

"Is everyone good with this?" Dylan asked, taking in the bar.

No one said anything.

"Okay. Option one, we make more food runs and increase rations to normal, on the condition we create a rotation that includes everyone. Everyone in favor, raise your hand."

The entire left-hand side of the room raised their hands. In fact, the only people who didn't were me, Adam, and Tomi.

"There you have it," Dylan said. "Democracy in action. Isn't it a beautiful thing?"

Then he left the room.

I paced the lobby for the rest of the afternoon. I couldn't bring myself to leave in case Rob came back. I took only one break to run around the hotel, up and down the stairwell, to keep up some basic level of fitness and take my mind off things. I ran into Dylan and a group of staff a couple of times, who were checking the first three floors for any intruders.

On my way back down, I paused by Tomi's room and knocked.

"Yeah?"

"It's me."

Locks clanged, dead bolts slammed, door opened. "What's up?"

She looked like she had been taking a nap. Her hair was messed up and her eyes were slightly red and heavy lidded. I was surprised by how pretty she was when she was caught off guard.

"Rob's still not back."

"I didn't realize he was gone."

I glanced down the corridor. "He came out with us when we went to bury Nicholas. He was going to look for the bird I heard this morning. He hasn't come back."

"He probably just lost track of time. Plus, he's actually doing something fun, so . . ."

"No." Another glance down the corridor. "The body was gone. We didn't bury him."

"What do you mean, gone?"

"I mean *gone*! Van Schaik wasn't where we left him. Someone or something took the body."

She made a face. "I don't know much about the animals around here, but . . . wolves?"

"No wolves in these parts, and no bears. Dylan was certain."

She leaned in. "Who else knows?"

"Just me, Dylan, and Adam."

Taking my arm, she pulled me inside and bolted the door. "So you think there are actually people out there?"

"There have to be. Can't be anything else."

"Shit."

"I know."

"And if it's people, the only reason they'd take a dead body is—"

"I know. I can't think about it."

Sitting on the edge of her bed, she rubbed her face to wake herself up. "How long has he been gone?"

"About four hours."

She glanced over her shoulder at the window. It was getting dark. "What did Dylan suggest?"

"He said we need to secure the hotel first before we send a party out."

"Might be too late by then."

"That's what I was thinking."

She smiled. "You came to me because I'm the only other person here with a backbone."

"In short, yes. Maybe." I nervously smiled back. "I know this doesn't make us okay. It's just not right that we leave him out there when he has no idea he's in danger."

"Well, cometh the hour and stuff." She stood up. "You can handle a gun, right?"

"I think, *cometh the hour*, I could still hit a target as long as it wasn't . . . moving."

"Cool. Here's the one I stole from your friends in the store." She opened a drawer and handed me the gun Jessie had pointed at me the week before.

I took it. I always forget how heavy they are.

"Do you want to tell Dylan we're going?" she asked.

"I don't think he'd let us go."

"It would be smart to let at least one person know."

"Adam, then." I cast my eyes around the room. "Do you think we need to take anything else?"

She threw me a look that made me feel three inches tall. "Knives, obviously."

———————

Adam wanted to come with us, but Tomi wouldn't hear of it. Someone who knew where we were needed to be back at the hotel, and it had to be someone who knew the gravity of the situation. Reluctantly, he agreed, but said he'd give us only two hours before sending Dylan after us.

"If we're not back in two hours, assume we won't be coming back," Tomi said, making me feel nauseated.

We left the hotel just as the sun disappeared behind the trees. I had a small knapsack with extra bullets and a bottle of water. There was a knife tucked into my belt. Tomi had brought some masking tape, a roll of wire, and a flashlight, as well as knives and more ammo.

She's going to outlive all of us. I realize that now. She gets it, in a way that the rest of us still don't. We're playing catch-up, dealing with the new world that has been thrust upon us. Tomi has become it.

Going out this time, our footsteps on the dead leaves seemed much louder. The quieter I tried to be, the more noise I made.

"Surely there's still enough food in the city that no one would resort to this," I whispered.

"Can't account for people hoarding," she replied. "Think about it. In the days after, everyone runs to the nearest store and takes as much as they can carry. Anyone without shelter, or who doesn't want to be caught out in a city, isn't gonna have much left to scavenge."

"You think that's going to happen to us?"

"I think Dylan's trying to keep morale up; can't blame him. But yeah, I don't think there's much food left to find. Sooner or later we're either gonna have to start plundering others or move on."

I stopped in my tracks. The thought of leaving the hotel made me irrationally upset. For better or worse, it's been safe for us. Compared to the rest of the world, we've been lucky. We have rooms and resources and even some luxuries. It's home now.

Tomi saw my expression and paused. "I don't want to leave either."

"Do you think the group will stay together?"

"Maybe not. Some people aren't going to want to follow Dylan. Then again, there's safety in numbers, and people stick with what's familiar. Why do you think we hang out?"

"What?"

"I'm the only other American. You seriously think we'd have been friends if not for this?"

I started walking again, shocked out of stillness. "I suppose not."

"It's weird, the stuff you find out about yourself when everything goes to hell."

"I guess."

She looked at me. "Before this, did you even know you were brave?"

"I got punched by a cop once. He was shouting at my wife at one of those marches. But no, I've never had to do anything . . . heroic. I never jumped into a frozen lake or anything like that."

"There's still time."

I steered us to the left, away from the clearing where we had left Van Schaik. "I think Rob went off this way. I wasn't paying much attention."

"Did he say where he was planning to go?"

"No. He mentioned the lake to me once, when he was talking about the birds he was here to photograph. I think it's this way. Can't believe I haven't been yet, just to visit."

"I wouldn't worry about it. It's not like we've been on vacation."

There was no wind, which made the leaves crunch louder underfoot. I kept my hands in front of my face, brushing branches and twigs out of the way.

"We shouldn't stay out here if it gets really dark," I said.

"It would be harder for anyone out here to see us then," she countered.

"Yeah, but we might shoot Rob."

I thought I heard something move far away and stopped, waiting to see if I heard it again. Tomi stopped too. Instinctively, we stood back to back, and the physical contact was reassuring.

"How have you been so okay with all this?" I asked quietly.

"What makes you think I'm okay?" I felt her shrug, tucked up against my shoulder blades. "Honestly, I didn't like people or . . . society that much anyway. I liked learning, and I enjoyed doing things. People, not so much."

"You didn't have a boyfriend or . . . ?"

"No. I didn't really do long-term relationships."

"That's surprising."

"Why, because I'm hot?"

"No, because you're . . . It's surprising, that's all."

"I just never felt the need to forge those kinds of romantic relationships. Maybe I'm aromantic, I don't know. I've never looked at someone and thought, *I want to be in a relationship with you.* I have looked at people and thought, *I want to bang you, but then I want you to go away.*"

"Don't you think that sounds like an illness?"

She snorted. "Presumptuous, much? If it's not a problem for me, who's it a problem for?"

"Fair point. But you just said yourself, that attitude might be one of the reasons you're okay with all this, like killing people and—"

"I'm not okay with killing people—how dare you!"

"Shh!" I ducked a little, and she did too.

The forest was rustling with a light breeze, but there was no movement that I could discern. The trees were getting denser, and less light was making it through. I stood up straight again and started walking, wanting to get to the lake and back before it became pitch-black.

"That was a shitty thing to say."

"I didn't mean it quite like it came out."

"I'm not a sociopath just because I don't like relationships. I still care about the people here. I'm just not going to waste energy crying over something that had to be done in a them-or-me situation. And I'm sure as hell not gonna cry over some rapist."

"It's fine. I'm sorry, I know you're not a bad person."

"Then maybe stop being an asshole. Obviously, I do take relationships a little seriously."

"What do you mean?"

"I still talk to you, don't I? God knows why."

We walked in silence for a while, without seeing anything or anyone. Then, suddenly, Tomi dropped into a crouch.

I looked over my shoulder, and she had picked something off the ground.

"What? Anything of Rob's?"

She said, "It's five francs."

"Could have been from any time."

"I know, it's just . . ." She laughed. "Everyone died for this, huh?"

I frowned, while she turned the coin over as if she had never seen one before.

"Everyone died for this!" she repeated, waving it at me. "Doesn't that seem so insane now?"

I haven't really reminisced in these accounts about why this happened as much as I thought I would at the beginning. Survival takes up so much space. The rest of the time, when I'm not surviving or writing, I deliberately occupy my mind with other tasks, like trying to find out more about the girl in the water tank, or making lists of practical skills I need to learn. Why this happened doesn't seem to matter. I haven't been dwelling on the whys, just the hows.

That being said, I still feel like I'm letting down Harriet Luffman. I haven't got any closer to finding her killer. But we always seem so short on time.

"It's like we all woke up from the same nightmare." Tomi took aim at the trees ahead and threw the coin as far as she could.

I followed it with my eyes and spotted movement at the exact moment I became aware that the white noise of the forest had intensified.

"Whoa," she said. "Lake's right there."

We fought our way out of the woods. The lake was glittering and royal blue, surrounded by struggling grass. It's about a mile long, maybe two, and it snaked off and to the left. There was no sign of Rob. There was no sign of anybody.

I was glad we had made it to the lake before the light disappeared. It was one of the most beautiful things I had seen in months, maybe the most since this had all happened. I wanted to come here every day and run around it. If we could be sure it was safe, maybe I could.

"Should we follow it around? Do we have time?" She was staring at the cloud cover, and a few rays of dying sun made it through, casting an ethereal glow over the surface of the lake that illuminated us for a minute or so before disappearing.

The trees at the water's edge were turning black.

"We should go," I said.

"Did you see the sun?"

"Yeah, sometimes it gets through for a second."

Her expression was sad, distracted. "You're right; let's go. We're not going to be able to see anything soon."

We turned back, and as we pushed our way into the forest again I found myself panicking that we wouldn't be able to retrace our steps.

"You don't think we got turned around at any point?" I asked.

"Shut up, you loser, you're scaring me!"

She kept hold of my arm with her left hand. In the other was her gun. Thankfully, the return trip turned out to be uneventful, and we made it back to the hotel unharmed.

As we entered the lobby I saw Dylan and Adam standing to one side, waiting for us. Dylan was glaring, and before I could say anything he had stormed up to Tomi and me and punched me in the shoulder.

"You fucking fool!"

Tomi yelled at Adam, "Thanks, snitch!"

"It was dark, okay? I didn't know if you could even find your way back!"

Rubbing my arm, I said, "We had to at least try to find Rob."

"Well, you weren't going to. He made it back just after you left." Dylan jabbed his finger in the direction of the bar, where I presumed Rob was.

"Shit, is he okay?" Tomi asked.

"He's fine. But we're not. We have a big fucking problem."

Dylan, Adam, Rob, Tomi, and I were in the bar. Adam stood by the door, making sure that no one could overhear us. Tomi went to her room and brought back some vodka. We each had a few glasses. Damn near finished a bottle. I've been drunk for the last three hours. That's how bad it was.

"I'm almost out of this, by the way," Tomi said, tapping the bottle.

Rob had come back with a series of photos; not of birds but of people. None of us recognized them, but there were about eight or nine different figures. Their faces were difficult to make out, but they looked mostly male. One or two of them maybe could have been women.

"Did you see the body? Did you see . . . what they did with it?" Tomi asked.

"I couldn't get close enough to know if they had a body, but they were definitely carrying something. It could have been a deer, or . . . I don't know. I followed them for a bit but, as you can imagine, I kept as far away as I could."

"Are there any houses out here?" I asked Dylan. "They can't be sleeping out in this cold."

"There are some houses, about six miles away. Everything is miles away."

"So they must have been watching us," Tomi said. "It's unlikely they stumbled across us today just when we were leaving a body."

"We don't know they have the body," Dylan said.

Tomi shrugged. "They do, though. They weren't carrying deer. When was the last time any of us saw a deer?"

"There's a lot of them," Adam commented. "People, I mean."

"There are more of us," I said, reaching for the vodka again. "That must be why they haven't made contact, or attacked."

"We can't tell anyone about this. I mean it. Not until we decide what to do." Dylan looked at us all.

"That's fucked up," Adam said.

I agreed with him. "Tania goes running every day, Yuka goes for walks—"

"Who's Yuka?" Tomi asked.

"Mrs. Yobari. Anyway, a lot of people go for walks. They need to know what's out there."

Dylan was swirling liquid around in his glass. "But if we tell them, everyone will panic."

Tomi made a weighing gesture with her hands. "Maybe they won't. We had to execute a guy this morning, and it went about as smoothly as it could have. No one panicked, we didn't go all *Lord of the Flies.* It could be fine."

"No one's gonna be fine if you keep a secret, though," Adam said. "Like, they're gonna be pissed off. I'd be pissed off."

Dylan inhaled and held the breath for a few seconds. "Dealing with things as a group is one thing. Telling everyone we're being watched by a group of men who took the body . . . who've started eating people. Or keeping the meat somehow."

"It's only been two months," I said quietly.

Tomi shivered. "We saw those people who killed themselves in the woods. It's obviously dangerous in the city. And if we didn't have guns, we'd have been shot in that store, by your friends."

"Acquaintances," I said.

She raised her eyebrows. "I always knew academics were waiting for an excuse to shoot one another in the face."

I stifled a laugh. We were hysterical with fear and alcohol.

Dylan added, "And there wasn't any food left at the store anyway, outside of what they had."

He rubbed his face and beckoned for the bottle. Tomi handed it to him.

I could tell Dylan was tired. He was tired of having to make decisions. He was tired of having to lead. I think we're all getting tired of our roles now. Tania was getting tired of the endless list of ailments and the lack of medication and equipment. Tomi was getting tired of shouting others down when they were wrong. Adam had already made it clear that he didn't want to stay. I was tired of volunteering when, with each passing day, the idea of simply giving up seemed more attractive.

That isn't to say I'm looking for pity. None of us are. But I could see that Dylan was exhausted.

"I'll be back," I said, standing up.

"Where are you going?" Tomi asked.

Adam squinted at me, his eyes bloodshot with alcohol. "You're not gonna do anything stupid, are you?"

"No," I said. "I just need a moment."

I left the lobby and went upstairs to my room, where I wrote this and did some thinking, mostly about the state of the hotel but also about whether it even made sense to keep going. What were any of us searching for anymore? We had always been propelled by this illusion of progress toward a utopian ideal, whether that ideal came from religion or democracy. But that was all gone now. The propellers themselves had blown.

Sitting on my bed, surrounded by paper, none of it seems to matter. I'm recording this because it's all I can think of to do, because it was my job. But it doesn't mean anything. It's unlikely anyone will ever read this.

It would be easier if Nadia were here. If the bombs had hit when I'd been in San Francisco, and we had—by some miracle—survived, we would have found purpose in each other, in our children.

What a pointless hypothetical—

I suppose what I'm trying to say is, I don't know why any of us are still here. I don't know what I'm doing, and I'm not sure I want to do it.

I don't know what I'm doing.

I stayed up in my room for a while. When I went back down they were all still there, exactly as I'd left them, only now they were wearing coats. It was obvious they had continued drinking. When I entered the room, Tomi and Rob were laughing about something. Nathan had joined them at some point and he, Dylan, and Adam were deep in discussion.

"I've got an idea," I said to no one in particular.

Tomi stopped laughing abruptly. "Hey, where did you go?"

"I was thinking." I glanced at Nathan, but Dylan gestured for me to continue, so I assumed they had filled him in. "We should leave."

Adam: "You're crazy, mate."

Tomi: "Um, how about no?"

Nathan: "Suicide."

Dylan: "Why?"

I sat down, unsure of how to proceed. "So this group, we don't know how many there are, but there are enough of them to send nine men out in a hunting party. That's people they can afford to lose. That's worrying."

"Unless they do everything together and there really are only nine of them?" Tomi interjected.

"Maybe. But that seems unlikely."

"I had to stop following them as soon as it started to get dark," Rob said. "But they were still moving when I left."

I nodded. "If they've been watching us for a while, which we can assume they have been, then they'll know how many of us there are, and they'll know we're mostly women and children. I don't want to sound pessimistic, but I don't like our chances against a group of men if they decide to attack."

"They probably don't have guns, though," Tomi said, more to the room than to me. "If they did, they'd have used them. So either they don't have any, or they might have had them at one point but ran out of bullets."

"Which gives them another reason to be watching us. They want what we have." Dylan shook the empty bottle.

I said, "So, either way, I don't think we can afford a fight. I don't think we'd win."

"Why? Too many women?" Tomi raised her eyebrows.

"No, Tomi, we're just . . . Some of us can shoot, but we're not all fighters."

"And even though some of us can fight, I don't want to," Dylan said.

"You're really on his side?" Adam gestured at me. "Seriously, you think we stand a chance out there?"

"It was always going to come to that," Dylan countered, looking at me. "Jon's right. Either we risk dying out there one by one looking for food, or we all die looking for food, meaning everyone back here starves to death. Or we try moving as a group and looking for somewhere safer."

"This has been pretty safe so far." Nathan gripped the arms of his chair.

Rob said, "Maybe there are still places that have clung to civilization. There might be whole cities, or at least towns out there, waiting to take us in."

"This is deluded," Tomi snapped. "It's freezing already, and it's just gonna get colder. And how much would we be able to carry on foot?"

"We've got cars," I said.

"We've got three. That's not enough for all of us plus cases and food."

Silence.

Dylan reached down beside his armchair for another bottle—I had no idea where he'd gotten it, but it wasn't from Tomi's stash—and refilled his glass, then mine. "We could send out two or three people in a car, find a place, do a sweep of the terrain, go into the city, go as far as we can. If we find somewhere, then we come back and move everyone."

Tomi: "*If* we find somewhere? That's a big if."

"Surviving at all was always a big if, though, wasn't it?" Rob said in a surprisingly lighthearted tone.

Tomi swiped the bottle from Dylan, shaking her head. "I can't believe this. You're all crazy."

"People must be living somewhere," Dylan said, as Tomi drank some more. "Somewhere, the army might have survived. Government might still be going. It's easy for us to forget because the Internet cut out here so early, but Jon, you said even students back in their hometowns were alive."

"Well, maybe that is worth doing," Tomi said. "We need to get back to where we have a cell phone signal. Give us enough time online, I bet we could find something. If civilization has survived somewhere, it's probably gonna be on the Internet."

I laughed involuntarily. So did Rob.

"Did you see the Internet toward the end?" Rob said, smiling.

"You know what I mean." She frowned at me. "Didn't you look at any sites the last time you were online?"

"I did—Facebook, Twitter, everything. But I was . . . I was only looking at messages."

"You didn't read any new content?"

I felt stupid. "No. Did you?"

She shifted. "No. I didn't check anything."

It was hard to believe that we'd somehow become so comfortable here that, when given the chance to observe the state of the outside world, so many of us had decided not to, or simply forgot. In our defense, we had been more focused on food and survival, but our indifference to the Internet after living without it for a couple of months was surprising.

"No one here with a working phone checked the fucking news?" Adam said slowly.

Everyone looked at one another, and most of us started laughing again.

"Okay, so that's what we do next. At least that's obvious," Tomi said. "We see if a PSA was put out."

Dylan: "A PSA?"

"A public service announcement. Anything from a government, or just—"

"An adult," Nathan said wistfully.

"Who wants to go?" Dylan asked.

Silence.

"Okay, easier question: Who *can* go? Who has a phone?"

Nathan and Tomi raised their hands. Adam shook his head, mumbled something about the battery being empty for a while.

"Adam, if we turn the power on for a while, you can charge it," Dylan said. "Tomi, you can stay here and defend people. I think Adam, Nathan, and I should go."

But Tomi wouldn't hear of it. "I'm going. Jon and Peter can both shoot."

"Are you saying I can't stay here and defend people?" Nathan said, jokingly affronted.

"With all due respect . . ." Dylan looked at him but didn't finish the sentence.

Everyone laughed.

"Wait!" I interrupted, unable to stomach the idea of them going on an expedition without me. "If you're going back to the store, I want to come and find another cell phone."

"There's no point putting yourself in danger over a new phone." Dylan seemed uneasy. "It might be better if you stay behind. We can pick you up whatever you want, if you write it down. We'll leave tomorrow morning, as soon as it's light."

I couldn't stand the idea. I was shocked by how angry it made me. I wanted to throw my glass across the room but couldn't bring myself to waste the alcohol. Instead, I took a breath, and a drink, and said, "Okay, if you think that's best."

"We'll find you one, don't worry." Nathan nodded at me. "Get you a nice rose-gold case. Maybe a SpongeBob one."

"Not good at staying behind, are you?" Dylan smiled.

I wasn't.

But that was the end of that conversation.

On my way back to my room, Tomi walked close to me and said, "Can I stay in your room tonight?"

"Are you sure you want to?"

"Well, I don't want to talk."

I wasn't sure it was fine, but I said it was.

I slept hard that night, woken up only once by Tomi, who was clutching her abdomen and vomiting in the bathroom. Her skin was shining, almost translucent, and she was shivering violently.

Blinking sleep out of my eyes, I sat on the floor next to her and brushed her hair back from her face.

"It's just a hangover," I said. "I don't feel great either."

For the first time since I'd known her, she looked at me with fear, and said, "What if it's an infection?"

"It's not," I said with no real clue. "It's probably just a stomach thing."

"Stomach things can kill us now," she said.

We went to see Tania, who told her in no uncertain terms that there was no way she could go on the expedition now.

With Dylan gone, the hotel has no one at its helm. We all played out our separate routines this morning as though nothing had changed, but there were empty spaces. There was the space where Dylan stood with his register while we ate breakfast, checking names off. There was the space behind the bar, where Nathan lurked to listen to his music in peace. There were spaces on either side of me, where Adam and Nathan sat to eat and smoke and chat, because they were part of "my" group. They were my friends.

More time elapsed, and with each passing hour my breath became shorter; an oil slick of dread settled on my calm surface, and I retreated to my room, thinking, *What if they don't come back?* I sat at my desk by the window and waited for my hands to stop shaking, but they wouldn't, because Dylan was our foundation, and if he didn't come back, I didn't know what we were going to do—or what the larger, more terrible implications were.

I went downstairs and knocked on Tania's door to check on Tomi.

"Yeah?"

I opened and asked quietly, "Is it all right to come in?"

Tania looked up from where she was sitting by Tomi's bedside. "Oh, I thought it was someone looking for another appointment. Got to make sure this madam doesn't dehydrate."

Tomi was asleep.

I asked, "Is she going to be okay?"

"Don't worry, your girlfriend will probably make it."

I stopped short of sitting down. "I didn't mean it like that."

She smiled. "I know, I'm just giving you shit. I'm tired."

"Do you think . . . ?"

"What?"

"Do you think that it could be something . . . other than an illness?"

A smirk. "She's not pregnant, if that's what you mean."

"Christ." That threw me off for a second. "She's . . . not, is she?"

"No, it's not morning sickness. It's sickness."

"But you don't think anyone did this to her, do you?"

"No." She looked at me a little warily. "I don't think it looks like that."

We were both tense, and, after I sat down, she waited almost a full minute before asking, "Are they back yet?"

I shook my head.

"Maybe you should call a meeting, so we can talk about what we're going to do. If they don't come back."

I swallowed. "Why me?"

"Well, you're . . ." She searched for a word. "Sensible? Everyone is probably going to want you to take the lead over someone like Peter or Yobari. Peter's not approachable, and I don't see anyone else getting involved, and I don't blame them."

"They might look to you."

"I'm not interested in leading. No, thanks."

"I don't want to either!"

She raised her eyebrows. "You're already leading. Don't pretend you haven't noticed. You don't volunteer for everything just to be helpful."

"No, I do it to stay busy. What am I going to do otherwise, sit and just . . . think?"

A shrug. "Okay."

Tomi grimaced in her sleep and turned over so that her back was to me. Instinctively, I went to adjust her hair, where it had become caught up in the cover, but I was too aware of Tania watching and halted my hand in midair, drawing it back to fiddle with the cuffs of my shirt.

"What are you avoiding thinking about?" she asked. "Cannibals?"

"My wife and children, mostly." I tripped over the words, like they were a punch to the throat.

"It's not your fault you were at a conference," she said.

"It was my fault," I said.

She looked at me without judgment, and I didn't deserve it. I had to make her understand.

"You know, Nadia and I, we didn't leave it on good terms," I blurted out. "I wasn't a good husband to her, because I was away so much and working so much, and she was tired because she was looking after the kids all the time. I didn't want it to be that way . . . like that makes it better. But we never had sex—we were both too tired all the time—and I assumed she must have been finding that elsewhere or she'd have been going crazy. There was never any proof of that. I never noticed anything that made me think she was having an affair. I just assumed she must have been because I found it so hard to be faithful to her . . . so fucking hard. I'm sorry. I'm so sorry, I don't know why I'm telling you this. I've never told anyone. Who'd want to know? It's boring. It's so predictable."

"How long were you married?" she asked, totally unfazed but un-doubtedly disgusted, as disgusted with me as I was.

"Eleven years. It's not like she stopped being attractive; if anything, I thought she was more beautiful. She just . . . No, it wasn't her. It was me. I felt like her roommate sometimes, after we had Marion. I still found her attractive, but I didn't feel like she felt the same about me. Or maybe she stopped thinking that part of her life was important when she had two kids to look after." I backtracked. "No, I know that's arrogant. Maybe it was me."

"Did you ever speak to her about it?"

"It always turned unpleasant. She said it would pass, she was just going through a phase where the idea of anyone touching her made her feel sick, and I stopped asking about it. I'm so sorry I'm telling you all this."

Tania reached out and felt Tomi's forehead. "I'm a doctor, I'm used to it. That's a lot for you to avoid thinking about."

I felt like her blasé manner was masking something.

She looked at me. "Are you waiting for me to tell you whether you're a bad guy or not, because you weren't happily married?"

I was holding half of my face in my hand, elbow resting on the arm of the chair and slumped sideways. The monologue had physically bent me out of shape.

"Am I?"

She laughed. "I'm not falling into that trap."

I thought, *She'll never look twice at you now. If you stood a chance before, you sure as hell don't after that.* I sat up, folded my arms, and pushed the thoughts away, because they were irrelevant and I knew I shouldn't be thinking things like that.

Suddenly, it hit me. I don't know why it took so long for me to notice. But it hit me.

"Are you . . . ?" I said.

"What?"

"You and Dylan."

Her expression tightened, her shoulders went up, and she leaned back in her chair, away from me.

I'd had no idea.

Tomi turned over again in the space between us.

I left shortly after, and fell asleep after lying on my bed for two hours, trying to control my breathing.

———————

"Help me."

I woke up and heard the voice right against my ear.

"Who's there? Who's there?" I grappled under my pillow for the knife I'd been sleeping with and stumbled out of bed. "I can hear you!"

The room was dark—it was early evening—but not pitch-black. There was no one there.

Sweat ran down the back of my neck, every hair along my arms standing on end. I was certain I had heard it. It was so clear. Not a vivid dream but a human voice—a girl's voice. It hadn't been shouted; she had been too close for that.

Help me.

I put the knife down, feeling stupid for waving it around. I couldn't stop shaking and felt feverish. As ever, I worried that I might be experiencing radiation poisoning. It was more likely another panic attack. I don't think I can cope with another round of losses. I can't lose my life, my family, the world, and now lose the only people I'd found who could make me feel like a person.

And I still haven't found out what happened to Harriet Luffman.

I thought I was going to cry for a moment, but I shook it off and went downstairs without putting on a sweater or a coat. I planned to grab a handful of ice from the freezers and cool myself down.

The corridors were quiet, as was the lobby. I stood for a while and watched the entrance. We had started locking the main doors at night, so people weren't as free to come and go as before. Until this point, we had been more scared of the environment than we were of people, but nuclear fallout wasn't going to sneak in, slit our throats, and loot our supplies at night.

I went into the restaurant and found Mia sitting at one of the tables, smoking. It was my table actually, by the window. She nodded at me as I came in but didn't instigate conversation.

I'd almost reached the kitchens when I stopped.

"Mia, do you mind if I ask you something?"

"I don't really want to talk about it, if that's okay."

I faltered. "What?"

"I know you're writing down stories for your diary, but I don't want to talk about what happened with Nicholas, if that's okay."

"It's not a diary, it's a . . ." I grimaced. "Never mind. I wanted to ask if you know where the presidential suite is. You worked behind the front desk. I thought you'd know."

She stubbed the cigarette out in her ashtray and sighed. "Are you still obsessing about Dylan and Sophia talking?"

"No, I heard there was a presidential suite, and I wanted to know where it was." I came forward and leaned on the back of the chair opposite her. "Why is everyone so secretive about it? Is there more vodka stashed there or something?"

"Don't act stupid."

"Goddammit, Mia." I swiped the chair to the side, and it flipped over with a bang that made her start. "Just tell me what it is!"

"It's just a room, it's a big room!" She stood up, trembling. "It's not a presidential suite. We don't have one!"

"Then why is it in your reservations ledger?"

"Because it's a joke!" A few tears worked their way out, and I realized she was terrified of me. "If either of the owners were here, we put a room aside for them and called it the presidential suite. It's just bigger, that's all!"

"Why would someone be given a phone number for that room?"

"What do you mean?"

"Why would a guest be given the phone number to that room?"

She shook her head, her voice strained. "I don't know. Sometimes if people had a bad stay they would be invited back, on the house. Baloche would give them his number, so they could phone him with any problems. Maybe that's why."

"You mean"—I hesitated, suddenly feeling incredibly stupid—"a guest would be given that number if they had had a bad customer-service experience?"

She nodded. "Yes! That's all I can think of! Now will you let me go?"

"I . . ." I backed off, holding my hands up. "I'm sorry, of course you can go. You could always go."

She pushed past me, and I looked at my reflection in the window. I wondered if I was losing my mind.

"Which room is it?" I called, before she was out of the restaurant.

She stopped and glared at me as though I were garbage. It looked like it took a lot of self-control not to come over and slap me. It struck me that it was probably fear that stopped her, though it would have been nothing less than I deserved.

"Room 909, asshole." She almost spat the words at me, then stormed out.

I didn't want to go up to the top floors and search a room in the dark with a box of matches, so I delayed it. It wasn't as if the room was going anywhere, and I couldn't face the idea of bumping into Mia again.

A night has gone by, and they still aren't back. No one at the helm. I barely slept because I was worried I would wake up and hear voices in the dark again. So I fell asleep when it began to get light and woke up later in the day.

I was tired of being paralyzed by indecision, so a few hours ago I knocked on some doors and called a bar meeting with the group.

Everyone turned up. They were all scared, and tired of being scared. Everyone looked to the spaces for Dylan, Nathan, and Adam, and saw that they weren't there. Everyone looked at me to say something, and I thought about how Dylan stood there, time and time again, taking the weight of their expectation onto his shoulders without showing any fear.

"I wanted to speak to you all because the guys haven't come back yet. As you know, they went out to find Internet access. I think they only would have gone as far as there was a signal, maybe back to the store. I wanted everyone to know they haven't come back yet and that we should talk about what we're going to do if they . . . don't return at all."

"Shouldn't we look for them?" Rob asked.

"And lose more people?" Sophia countered. "That's three men gone. I don't want to lose any more, especially not the ones who can shoot."

Peter asked, "Where's Tomi?"

"She's sick," I replied.

"Is she going to die?"

"We don't think so."

He nodded. I couldn't tell whether he was satisfied or disappointed. I couldn't help thinking, in that moment, that maybe Tomi's sickness wasn't due to natural causes. Maybe someone here had tried to take her out. My main suspects would be Peter or Sophia. Mia didn't like Tomi either, and Sasha I still couldn't work out.

Lauren raised a hand, and I pointed at her.

"Should we elect a new leader?" she asked.

Peter: "We didn't elect a leader before. Dylan put himself in charge."

"Well . . . maybe we should now?" Again, she looked at me.

The atmosphere was uneasy, and I hated feeling like I was at the center of it. I glanced at Tania, who was leaning against the far wall. At first she avoided my eyes, but then she unfolded her arms and stepped forward.

"Is anyone else here interested in leading?"

Peter shifted from one foot to the other and scanned the room, but Tania beat him to it by throwing out another question.

"Is there anyone here who wouldn't vote for Jon?"

Everyone looked at one another and then at me. I didn't have the heart to say I didn't want to do it, because I couldn't let them know there was no one at the helm, that I couldn't stand the weight in the same quiet, dignified way Dylan had been able to stand it.

Mia wouldn't look at me but said nothing.

In the absence of dissent, Tania gestured at me. "Well, then."

Peter glared at me but didn't have the courage or the energy to sustain it, so he looked away and cleared his throat instead.

"I have a suggestion," I said, unable to keep myself from looking at Tania, who seemed angry. "I don't think you're all gonna like it, but hear me out."

They were listening.

"I think we should leave. Not all at once, and not without a plan. But we're coming to the end of our time here. We're running low on food, expeditions are getting more dangerous, and . . . we have reason to believe that there's another group of people nearby who might cause trouble. Only Rob has seen them, but they look mean and they know we're here."

The room erupted in noise. Everyone started talking at once; a lot of it was directed at Rob, but some of it was at me.

"Jesus save us—"

"Are they dangerous?"

"Mean?"

"Where did you see them?"

"How many are there?"

"How do you know they're not friendly?"

"They could be just like us—"

"We don't have enough guns."

"Do they have Dylan and Nathan and—"

"It would be suicide."

"Guys!" I raised my voice. "Hear me out. We have guns, and we have ammunition. They're locked in staff quarters. The reason nothing has happened is because it's likely we have more in our arsenal than they do."

I noticed people glancing at the door, and it freaked me out.

"If we make our way toward the city, taking supplies with us, we stand a better chance of survival than if we try to last the winter here. In my opinion. We're about to hit fall, right? If it gets to winter, we're stuck here and there's no chance of moving anywhere. They know that."

"But if winter hits and they're still out there, they die," Peter said. "No more problem."

"Yeah, so they have more to lose. Do you want to fight desperate men? I don't."

Yuka said, "I agree with Jon."

I stared at her, shocked, and I wasn't the only one. Even her husband gave her a look, and she raised her chin haughtily.

"I agree with Jon," she said again, tightening her arms around her son.

"You think it's safe to leave?" Haru asked incredulously.

"It is not safe anywhere. If we die, we die as a family. But I will not starve here, I will not be hunted like an animal. If Jon thinks we should leave, I think he is right. We don't know what is left, or what the city is like now."

"That's right, we don't know," Peter snapped.

"So are we going to die not knowing, like cowards? Or do we find out?" She seemed to grow taller as she spoke, larger across the shoulders. "I hate this place; I don't want to stay here another day. This is no life. We cannot stay here just because we are scared."

Yuka had never said this much in front of the group before. She was right.

It seems bizarre to admit, given the circumstances, but I had been trying to sideline fear. We all had. Fear was embarrassing. It felt better to claim we were doings things out of hunger, or rage, or—like me— simple necessity. We wanted to be motivated by anything else but fear. In reality, fear was all we had left.

Her words had shocked everyone into silence.

Eventually, I said, "She's right. We can't stay just because we're scared."

"Being scared has nothing to do with anything," Peter said, thrusting his chin out. "It's safe here."

"Not anymore."

Lauren shrugged and said, "We were always going to have to go. Might as well do it when it's not freezing."

Lex said something in French that sounded like an agreement.

"How long before we give up on the others?" Tania asked, fixing me with a stare that made me feel like the worst person in the world. "Are you planning on leaving before they come back?"

"We're not planning anything right now," I said. "We're just talking."

Sophia interjected, "We should put a limit on it. It's not pleasant, but we should. We can't wait for them forever."

"A week?" I proposed.

A few uneasy glances, and Yuka said, "That's too long."

"Dylan kept this place going all this time! He kept us safe!" Tania snapped. "Show some respect."

"And if we die waiting?" Sophia raised her eyebrows.

"Three days?" I suggested.

No one wanted to commit to a number.

I added, "It's going to take at least that long to prepare everyone for leaving. We only have two cars now, so we'll have to leave in even smaller groups."

Rob said quietly, "Do we have a van, or . . . ? It seems like the sort of thing a hotel might have, for deliveries. If we had a van, we could all go, or take it in shifts."

"The men would take it in shifts," I said.

"We're not made of rose petals." Sophia glared. "We can take shifts sitting in the van."

"Okay, sorry. We can all take shifts in the van, then."

"We don't know if we have a fucking van," Peter said.

"So we give the others as long as it takes us to be ready to leave." I nodded. "That's going to take a few days, so that's how long they have. Is that okay with everyone?"

"And at no point do we send anyone out to look for them?" Tania asked. "We don't try to find them, is that what you're saying?"

I didn't know what to say, to be honest.

Yuka said the right thing for me. "Why do we not send only one or two people out, just to drive around? If it gets to the third day and we are going to leave, what is the harm to look for a few hours?"

I looked at Tania and spread my hands. "That sounds doable. Would that be okay with you?"

Tania walked out.

The rest of them murmured their agreement.

I regretted everything I had told her about my marriage; she didn't deserve to have me off-load on her like that, just because I was tired of feeling like no one here knew me, and the only people who did know me—even a little—were gone.

I suggested we should start gathering our things, and the meeting dispersed.

A couple of us went to see if there was indeed a van out back. There wasn't.

I returned to my room to document the meeting and had what I believe was another panic attack.

———————

Tania came upstairs to tell me that she needed a break, so I watched Tomi while she went for a run around the corridors. She wasn't running around the hotel grounds anymore. I'll be surprised if anyone leaves the premises alone again.

I sat in one of the chairs next to the bed, and for the first time in a while I was keenly aware of how much my tooth hurt. I think I'm going to have to bother Tania with it now. I was so sure that it would go away on its own, but it hasn't.

Tomi had been asleep, but when I came in she opened her eyes slightly and turned onto her side, shining with fever sweat. One of the curtains was drawn to keep the room from getting too bright; redundant given the weather, but maybe Tania had done it out of habit. Or maybe she was just worried about being watched from outside.

"Is there any water?" Tomi asked.

I handed her the glass that Tania had left on the side, and she took a few sips before handing it back.

"I'm gonna be so pissed if I die," she said weakly.

"You're not gonna die."

"Well . . . I'll be pissed if I do."

"And we'd be screwed," I added. "You're the best shot we have. I'd rather you be default leader if Dylan doesn't come back."

"Damn . . . straight." She rolled onto her back and wiped the back of her hand across her forehead. "But the others . . . think I'm a bitch."

"No one thinks that."

"You do."

"I can't believe you're going to lie there giving me shit when you've got a fever of 102. You're impossible." I leaned forward and took her hand, pressing it to my cheek. "I don't think you're a bitch, I think you're just . . . a pain in the ass."

She laughed but stopped abruptly, taking a deep breath. "Ow. God, that hurts."

I couldn't say it to her face, but I was worried about her. It was unbearable. Her hand against my cheek was scorching, yet she was shivering. I combed some of her hair back from her forehead and it was damp, and then suddenly I could barely look at her because I thought I might have another panic attack.

"Hey." Tomi squeezed my hand suddenly.

"What?"

"While Dylan's gone . . . and I'm not saying he's not coming back, but you should . . . search his room."

The suggestion caught me off guard, and I smiled. "You never switch off."

"You should, though, while everyone's . . . distracted. And I had a thought . . . you should speak to the kids. You know, the Yobari kids. Maybe they noticed something about the other kids here."

The idea had been playing on my mind, but I knew that neither Yuka nor Haru would let me interview their children. I have a suspicion that Yuka might be avoiding me for some reason. The last couple of times I asked about babysitting the kids, it seemed like she was thinking of an excuse to say no. It's possible she just feels awkward about my emotional outburst. That would be understandable.

"I'll wait until Tania gets back."

"I'll be fine, just . . . leave some water."

"No. Absolutely not."

"I'm fine."

"Stop complaining, or I'll start reading to you or something."

"God, please don't. Urgh."

"I will. Don't provoke me."

"Why are you like this? It's like you took your doctorate in being a dweeb."

"At least I finished mine."

"I think the end of the world counts as mitigating circumstances." She sighed dramatically and made as if to turn away, but she kept hold of my hand. "You're so annoying. If you're the last person I speak to before I die, I'll be so pissed."

I've been having a recurring nightmare. Every time I'm in a different setting. I'm in our garden back in San Francisco or in my friend's house, where my mom died. But they always end the same way, with an explosion. I die at the moment I wake up.

I wasn't going to mention it here, because dreams are mostly uninteresting. But my nightmares have forced me to think more about day one.

My laptop is running out of battery again, so I haven't been able to watch more footage to jog my memory. But some memories have started to come back, maybe prompted by the nightmares. Maybe they're shaking things loose. Just now I remembered something new, which I think might be significant.

The hotel emptied. Every person I stopped, pleading with them to let me look at their phone, was in the process of fleeing. I returned to my room, turned on my laptop, and got hooked on the news and social media for at least a couple of hours before the signal became sporadic. I turned the Wi-Fi off and on again a few times, but the Internet kept giving me a time-out error.

Social media was a mess. I was shocked by the number of people who attempted to live-tweet their experience of the end of the world, but there was no news about San Francisco, or even LA. To my knowledge, before the signal cut out, California was okay. London was gone, and had taken the south of England with it; so was Glasgow, and subsequently Scotland. There was nothing about Switzerland either.

I sent an email to my dad, starting to panic about the battery left in my laptop. It said, "I hope you're both all right; please contact me if you can. I'm in Switzerland for work and can't reach Nadia. Love, Jon."

It wasn't emotional. It wasn't a good-bye. I didn't do good-byes, and my father and I had never had that kind of relationship. At the time I wrote that email, I wasn't worried about him. He was a practical, if sad, man. He would take care of Barbara. They would probably head south and try to get over the Mexican border.

Horror-movie images were racing through my mind. Millions of people were dead. Millions. I couldn't process the number. How long before we were vaporized? How much time did I have left?

I went to the window and opened it, inhaling fresh air. That was the last time I saw the sun clearly, completely unobstructed. I didn't take nearly enough notice of it. I should have taken it in, memorized the colors and the warmth. Instead I looked down over the grounds and saw more people leaving.

Two people were arguing. They looked like staff. This is what I want to document here—even though I'm not certain if it's a memory, an invented memory, or a dream. I definitely saw two people arguing. It was a black man and a white woman with red hair. I remember her hair so vividly. Thinking back now, it must have been Dylan and Sophia.

I remember thinking at the time that they must have been fighting over whether to leave or not. I created the scene in my head. They were a couple, and one of them wanted to go and the other wanted to stay. The woman, Sophia, was crying, which didn't seem odd at the time, because crying, hysteria, sobbing—they were the only reactions that made sense.

It was weirder that I just stood in my room, leaning on the window frame, numb. I remember thinking that I should go, jump in someone else's car or—fuck, who cared anymore?—steal a car. I could get to the city, get a train, and find a plane. There must still be planes taking off somewhere . . .

The man was hugging the woman, and she had just about stopped crying.

If they left, I thought, *I could go with them*. If I ran downstairs fast enough.

But they both went inside, and I didn't see either of them reappear. They had clearly decided to stay.

At some point I left the room. The elevators weren't working so I took the stairs, feeling irrationally inconvenienced by this.

The lobby was quiet and deserted.

Devastatingly calm music was playing. It must have always been playing in the background, but I'd never noticed it before. It was eerie now.

A few people were huddled in the bar, but no one I recognized. As I stood in the doorway of the restaurant, paralyzed by indecision, my things still unpacked, I noticed I was holding a package of two cookies in my hand, the ones that came free with the packets of coffee and herbal tea bags in the rooms.

"Jon!"

I turned. I knew these people. Their names escape me now.

That worries me.

A man and two women; the women were from New York, the man from . . . I want to say DC. I can't remember. I can't even remember their faces now, only the events that unfolded. They were leaving. They had bags.

The man said, "Come with us, we're going."

"You coming?" one of the women asked.

I said okay and went outside with them. One of them had a rental car parked to the side of the hotel. It was fenced off and hidden from the gardens. I got into the back of their car. I had none of my things, but at that point I went along with it because I knew I had to go. It was the sensible thing to do. Someone was finally telling me what to do.

"I can't believe it," I remember hearing.

"Still nothing."

They were trying to make calls.

I snapped out of my daze and became fixated on the idea that I couldn't leave without my laptop. I got out of the car. I was still in shock. The magnitude of our new reality hadn't yet sunk in.

"Where are you going?"

"I don't have my stuff!" I called.

"But we're going!"

"I need to go back."

"You can't!"

I'd spent the whole morning searching for someone to tell me what to do, and when someone finally did I immediately resented them for it and wanted to do the opposite. Like a teenager.

"I can," I replied.

"We're *going!*" The woman enunciated the word at me like I was stupid, dragging it out until it seemed to have more than two syllables.

I stared at them. "Then go."

The three of them looked at me like I was crazy. Maybe I was. The car drove away, and I didn't regret not being in it. Deep down, I knew there were no planes, not really. I also knew I couldn't leave without my laptop, my clothes, my . . . stuff. I didn't know how to be, without stuff. I couldn't be caught adrift with nothing. What if someone official stopped me and asked for ID? What if I needed my passport?

I was still holding the complimentary cookies.

Instinctively, I reached into my pocket to check my phone, but found nothing. I opened the cookies, ate one, and slowly began to walk back toward the entrance. An insidious despair was threatening to engulf me. I wanted to be near my laptop, even though I knew the Internet was gone.

I was cut off. I'd destroyed my phone.

Leaning against the wall of the parking lot, I broke the other cookie in the pack in half and ate that too. I don't remember what it tasted like. It didn't taste of anything. Outside, it was quiet. Everyone had left. I found it surreal, impossible to imagine that in countless places on the planet, at this very moment, millions were dying. Nuclear weapons were falling onto the cities and buildings and statues and bridges that had, in some cases, stood for centuries. We had looked at them every day and thought they were permanent, and now they were turning to dust. *They wouldn't even find bones*, I thought. There probably wouldn't even be a *they* to look for bones.

History had ended, and I was standing here in the middle of nowhere, surrounded by strangers, eating free cookies, because I had no idea whether to stay or go. With the benefit of hindsight, it was fear that kept me here. The idea of driving into chaos, into explosions and

screaming and human ashes in the air mingling with poison: these were
the images that kept me here.

Was I just waiting here to die?

I tried to project myself into Nadia's head. I knew her so well. If
they had survived, she would have packed quickly, put the kids in the
car and then probably tried to drive up the coast to her parents, all the
way to Portland. From there they might have headed over the border
into Canada. It's what I would have done. I hadn't read anything about
Canada getting hit, and the farther north they went, the less likely they
were to suffer from radiation exposure.

Even if they did make it, I'll probably never hear from them again.

If the roads on the coast were clear enough for Nadia to somehow
make it to Portland, they wouldn't stay. If Canada was accepting refugees, American refugees—what a thought!—they would keep moving
north. Communication was going to be fragmented, and the Internet
could be down across the whole of North America. If that was the case,
they were gone.

I retraced my fictional steps and realized that millions of people on
the California coast would be heading north. Some south, heading for
South America. But enough would head north. If that was the case, the
coast would be a disaster area. People might have to abandon their cars.
People would be carjacking, looting, running out of fuel, out of food,
fighting one another for resources and water, making their way to the
border in gangs. It would be anarchy.

But Nadia was smart. She was good in a crisis. She might not even
take the coastal roads. She might go inland, take a slightly longer route
for the sake of safety.

But what if everyone had the same idea?

And that was why, eventually, after a few days, I had to stop thinking
about Nadia and the kids altogether. I was driving myself insane. They
couldn't be what preoccupied my mind. They weren't here. It was only
myself I had to keep alive. I could save them or witness their deaths in
a thousand hypothetical scenes. It wouldn't bring me any closer to the
truth, or to them.

I don't know how long I stood there.

My chest hurt; sharp, urgent pains that made me worry I might be having a heart attack.

I noticed a car arrive in front of the hotel, not making it as far as the parking lot and instead braking right at the main doors. I remember thinking that someone must have forgotten something important. Most people left that day, but this was the only car I saw arrive.

At that moment, I looked to my right and saw the black man and the woman with the red hair again. They were carrying something between them, but they were too far away for me to identify exactly what. Then they disappeared from view into the surrounding trees.

I squinted after them, and when I looked back at the only car that had arrived against the tide, it was empty.

I spent the rest of the day alone, and tried over and over to connect my laptop to the Internet. Every so often I left the room to look around, and found the hotel even emptier than before. Then I would return and try again to connect my laptop to the Internet. I didn't sleep, even when it started to get dark. I watched the horizon from the window and waited. That was when I first met Dylan, who went around knocking on doors, asking everyone to gather downstairs.

That was the first day.

I waited until everyone was at dinner and headed for the internal entrance to the staff quarters, which were on the first floor to the right of the stairwell. I followed a long corridor and took a left, walking quickly and quietly.

I had been to Dylan's room only a couple of times, and even then I'd only stood in the doorway and let him saddle me with tools before we went up to the roof. It was smaller than mine. All the staff rooms were, and some of them had bunk beds, but nonetheless Dylan and Sasha had stayed where they were. I thought they might have taken the opportunity to move into the more spacious parts of the hotel, but familiarity had obviously won out.

When I got to Dylan's room I knocked, just in case, and then let myself in and shut the door behind me. As soon as I entered, I knew the cases weren't here. If they were, I'd have spotted them from the doorway. I felt guilty. Just the act of being here was a betrayal; it was an admission that I didn't trust him, didn't trust any of them.

The suitcases weren't there, but I was, so I decided to search the place anyway. If I didn't find anything, no one had to know.

The corridor outside was silent.

Dylan had a great view from his window; his room overlooked the gardens, mostly obscured now by the browning hedges, and behind them the dense trees. I had a dim recollection of what it had all looked like in sunlight, when everything had been green.

The bed was a large single, impeccably made. There was a photo on his bedside table of an older black woman and a younger woman in her mid-twenties who looked enough like Dylan for me to identify as his daughter. She had the same smile and short braids. The other woman must have been his wife.

He barely had any stuff. I opened his closet and found three clean white shirts, a few pairs of black pants, a khaki jacket, and a spare pair of sneakers. There were several packets of tobacco tucked into the corner of the top shelf, and his box of tools on the floor next to his shoes.

I felt like a piece of shit for doubting him.

I spun the master keys around my fingers and opened and shut all the drawers in the small chest off to the right, but there was nothing in them aside from socks and underwear, a pair of gloves, and a black beanie hat. I pushed everything to the sides, in case anything was hidden, but it wasn't. He was hiding nothing.

I heard footsteps approaching in the hallway and looked around.

There was nowhere to hide. I hoped it was just another member of staff headed for a different bedroom. No one else had any reason to be in here.

I thought for a split second about getting into the closet. I crouched instead and quickly looked under the bed, trying to judge if I could fit into the space, but instead I saw a dark suitcase—

Someone inserted a key into the lock and found the door already open.

I turned at the exact moment Tania let herself in.

"Jesus!" She started, dropping her key. "Jesus Christ, what are you doing here?"

As she bent down to pick it up, I noticed that she was holding a single room key, not a bunch of master keys like Dylan had given me. I also noticed for the first time that there were a few faded gray scuff marks in the carpet, like someone had dragged a suitcase through and hadn't been able to get the wheel imprints out.

"What are *you* doing here?" I asked in turn. "Who's with Tomi?"

"I . . ." She blushed. "I lost something. It's none of your business. Anyway, I'm allowed to be in here. What are you doing?"

"I lost something as well, actually. I think I just found it." I crouched, grabbed the handle, and dragged the suitcase out onto the carpet.

There was no doubt in my mind that it was one of the Luffmans' cases.

"That's not yours!"

"It was stolen from my room."

She folded her arms as I unzipped it. "I find that hard to believe."

"Well . . ." I threw open the lid and found it full of disassembled rifles. "This . . . isn't right."

"Why would he steal something from you?"

"Because he knows something about that girl in the water tank, him and Sophia, and God knows who else." I pushed a few of the pieces to the side, as if I might uncover the case's previous contents, but of course there was nothing. "He must have tipped everything out, kept the case for storage."

"Or that's just his suitcase."

"You don't know!" I snapped. "Tomi heard him and Sophia discussing it. There's something going on, and I didn't imagine these cases going missing from my room."

I zipped it closed and dragged it around. The Luffmans' baggage labels had been on here, but he must have taken them off. I was certain. I was certain this was one of the cases.

I said, "Look, he's just taken the labels off."

"Jon, I've seen that case every time I've been in this room. It's Dylan's."

"No, it's not! It can't be!"

"More to the point, you had your girlfriend spy on people, on your friends, because you think someone here killed that girl?"

I sighed. "I know how it sounds."

"I think you should leave."

I pushed the suitcase back under the bed. I'd gotten what I came for. I didn't have to stay and argue with her when the second suitcase and the contents of the first might still be in the hotel somewhere. It crossed my mind that maybe he'd taken them into the woods and burned them.

Tania raised her eyebrows. "Well?"

"Sorry. Yeah, I'll go."

"Maybe you should give back those keys as well."

There was no way to say it without sounding hostile. "No."

"I know what paranoia looks like," she said.

"I'm not crazy."

"You've created a conspiracy theory out of nothing—that is textbook paranoia."

"It's not nothing! That's not his suitcase!"

"Yet, shockingly, it's full of his things."

I took my glasses off to rub my eyes. "I'm not crazy. Those cases were in my room for days! And you don't know everything else I've found, like the security footage of when the Luffmans arrived. They were given a piece of paper with a phone number on it to contact the owner in the presidential suite. Baloche Braun would have been staying there—Sophia's husband!"

"What are you talking about? What presidential suite?"

"It's room 909; the girl's parents were—"

"Show me, then."

I caught my breath. "What?"

She talked very slowly. "If you have proof that there's something going on in this hotel, show me. Show me this secret room—you've got the keys."

"I haven't been up there yet. I only found out about it yesterday."

"Well, show me now. Let's go."

She was serious. After being this emphatic, there was no way I could refuse. I steeled myself and nodded. The two of us went upstairs, climbing nine floors until we ended up in the upper east wing of the hotel. It was near the entrance to the roof. From the location, this side of the building probably had the best views of the forest, unobscured by the fire escape.

Out of breath from the climb, I fumbled with the keys before noticing that it was a key-carded room. I then realized that I had probably been here before, when I was checking these rooms at speed on my initial search. I remembered craning my head inside, ascertaining that it wasn't occupied, and moving on.

Tania was silent, her arms folded. I nudged open the door and we both walked in.

I had been here before. There was no "probably" about it.

Mia was right—it wasn't a presidential suite. It was a slightly larger room than mine, with a nicer bathroom and a nicer bed. There wasn't any luggage, but I checked the closet and the chest of drawers and found there were still a few clothes. They were all suits. In the drawers were some folded shirts—nothing in the pockets—socks, and boxer shorts.

Maybe Mia had also been right about the phone number. Maybe it really had just been customer service. But at the same time, I can't trust Mia. She could be lying. Any of them could be lying to cover themselves.

"So the owner stayed in this room," Tania said, unmoving.

"Owners. Though only Baloche was here at the time, according to the records."

"Right."

Avoiding her eyes, I went through the drawers in the bedside table and found that the Bible was dog-eared, scattered with bookmarks. I grabbed it and held it up.

"This must have been his Bible!"

She nodded. "And?"

"He's bookmarked parts of it—look." It was all in French. "I'm not sure which, it's hard to make out. He's underlined a lot of stuff in Matthew . . ."

And she finally snapped.

"Jon, you're exhausted. Just drop it, okay, and get some rest. Look around! There's nothing here! We have enough to deal with without you making things up." She held out her hand for the keys with the air of someone trying to coax a gun away from a maniac on a rampage. "Come on, give me the keys. Let's go."

"You still don't believe me?"

"What do you mean, *still*? You've shown me a guy's room. Big deal." She took a steadying breath. "Look, I know it's not the best course of action to tell someone in the midst of a . . . psychotic break that they're having a psychotic break. But I've got some medication that will calm you down a bit."

"What?"

She spread her hands. "Just so you can function."

I couldn't believe it. "Seriously, you think I'm psychotic?"

"I think you need help, Jon. That's all." She held out her hand again. "Give me the keys. Let me help you."

I took a step back and felt myself flush red.

"Who's watching Tomi?" I asked, evading the demand.

"She's doing better. She's been awake for a while."

Ignoring her answer, I walked out, taking the keys and Baloche's Bible with me. I was angry with her and didn't want to say anything I'd later regret.

"Jon, give me the keys!" she shouted after me.

I ignored her and kept walking.

After I left Tania in the presidential suite, I returned to Dylan's room and found a shovel. Then I went out to the grounds. I passed within sight of the parking lot where I had been standing on day one, and the wall I had been leaning against.

I was right. I knew that I was right. Something had happened that day that only Dylan and Sophia knew about, and it had something to do with Harriet Luffman and Baloche Braun. Maybe the rest of the staff also knew. I couldn't trust any of them.

It was darker than usual. The low clouds were an angry gray. If I didn't know any better, I'd have thought it was going to rain.

I walked across the yellow lawn to the edge of the trees and started zigzagging through the outskirts of the woods. I wasn't sure what I was looking for, but I remembered what I'd seen.

Withered leaves crunched under my feet. The branches just above my head were gaunt, and all the foliage was hanging dead.

I'm so disappointed in Tania. I thought she, of all people, might have believed me, might have had the moral fortitude to see the importance of this. I suppose Dylan might have told her something. Maybe she did see the importance but had already taken his side.

I walked back and forth around the edge of the trees, stamping hard on the ground, feeling for any change in texture. I knew they couldn't have carried the body far, not on that day. Even between them, they would have carried it only to where they were out of sight.

After maybe twenty minutes of stamping and weaving through the trees I came across a strange patch of earth that didn't match the rest. I looked around and saw a forest floor covered in plants that had keeled over, but nothing had grown here. Of course, we hadn't had much rain or sun since that day. Nothing new was going to grow on disturbed ground.

Taking the shovel in both hands, I began digging.

I threw off a layer of clothing and dumped it on the ground. I'd gained some muscle from the work I'd been doing. I broke a sweat but didn't stop shoveling earth until I was four feet deep. I leaned the shovel against the edge of the hole, gasping for breath. I was covered in dirt, and my hands were black.

I looked back toward the hotel, and my view was mostly obstructed by trees. I couldn't be seen. It would have made sense for them to dispose of something here.

Picking up the shovel again, I continued digging.

At some point, I started laughing. What was I looking for? I'd stumbled upon a funny patch of earth, and there I was, digging for over an hour, because I had to believe I was right. But what else was there now, other than being right? If I stayed out there digging holes the next day, the next week, month, what did it matter? Everyone who would have missed me, been at all affected by my absence, was already gone.

I stopped digging again until I stopped laughing. I took my glasses off and threw them on top of my coat. I removed my sweater and shirt and began again.

My arms were shaking. I didn't know how long it had been.

I rammed the shovel into the soil, leaned on it, and met resistance. Standing up straight, I hurled the clod of earth out of the hole and saw some brown fabric. Throwing the shovel down, I dug the rest of the soil away with my bare hands. There was more fabric—an old sheet, maybe—and when I'd scraped enough of the earth away to grab a handful of it, I started pulling.

"Come on!" I snarled, dragging it farther and farther out of the ground.

The top of the sheet came free suddenly, and I stumbled and fell backward, landing heavily on my lower back.

Startled by the impact, I struggled to sit up and realized I was now facing a corpse.

I was too exhausted to exclaim, or cry out.

There was silence.

I'd dragged the upper half of the body out of its shroud, and it was now at a forty-five-degree angle, almost sitting upright. It was a man. He was badly decomposed inside his suit. What remained of his face was a rotting, gaping mess. No maggots, though, like one might have expected. It smelled bad, but not as bad as the body we had fished out of the water. This was dry rot. It was harsh, but bearable.

It was hard to tell how he had died. All I knew was that he had been murdered. What would he be doing out here otherwise? If he had killed himself, surely he would have been buried out front with the other residents. We would know about him if his death had been self-inflicted.

I thought I'd feel accomplished, vindicated even. I had just discovered a monumental piece of evidence that could all but confirm Sophia's guilt, and maybe Dylan's. But instead I just felt sad.

I sat there, trying to regain my breath, toe to toe with the body, in the hole I had dug for the both of us. I was numb. I thought I would find some answers. But now there were only more questions, and Dylan was gone. Nathan and Adam, the people who might have helped me, were gone.

Are Tomi and I even safe here anymore? Had someone really tried to poison her?

I reached forward, exerting minimal effort, and checked the pockets of his jacket. They were empty.

After a long time, I took a deep breath and got to my feet.

I carefully laid the body back down in the hole. As I did so, I noticed that his suit was ripped in several places. He might have been stabbed, but it was difficult to be certain. As I examined the tears in the fabric I noticed that his suit was expensive. Tom Ford. It was then that it hit me: this might be Baloche Braun.

Is he what Sophia had been hiding in the trees? What I'd seen Dylan helping her carry on that day? A Tom Ford suit; it had to be Baloche. But even if it was, I realized, he had only the most tenuous link to Harriet's murder. Even if this was Baloche, he couldn't help me.

I covered his face again with the sheet, picked up the shovel, and threw it out of the hole. Summoning the last of my strength, I climbed out after it. Then I started to fill the hole in, slowly; not in the same frenzied state I had been working in before. All the breath, all the motivation, had been knocked out of me.

It was getting dark by the time I finished. I put my glasses on and looked down at myself. I was filthy. There was no point putting my clothes back on. I couldn't feel the cold anyway.

Slinging my shirt, sweater, and coat over my forearm, I started walking back to the hotel.

My legs were aching. My shoulders were quivering from the overexertion.

I crossed the lawn and looked up toward the hotel. I couldn't see anyone moving on the upper floors, but as I lowered my gaze to the restaurant I saw Sophia staring out at me from the window.

I paused, and for a beat or two we stood facing each other through the glass, ten yards separating us. Even from this distance, I could see her expression wasn't right. Her arms were folded and her hair was pulled back from her face. For a moment, I thought she might have been crying, or at the very least holding back tears.

Without saying anything, without the energy to even summon an expression to my face, I turned and walked around the hotel to the main entrance. Luckily, I didn't see anyone else. My appearance was probably alarming.

By the time I got back to my room I was already on the verge of another panic attack. I slumped and supported myself on the edge of my bed, trying to slow my breathing. My neck and head were too hot. My mind was clouding over, and I was worried that I might pass out. But I counted my inhales and exhales, breathing through the attack. I sat on the floor and rested my forehead on my knees until the worst of the nausea and light-headedness had passed.

Then I had a cold shower, which I think helped.

I'm so hungry, but I don't want to go down into the hotel and see anyone.

I don't know what to do now. I thought it would become apparent what I needed to do. I thought it would be enough to know that I was right. But it's starting to become clear to me, despite all my newfound convictions and sense of purpose in this post-civilized world, that what I'm doing might not matter. Baloche is dead. So what? The dead man could tell me nothing.

———————

I haven't told you much about myself. That's the first thing academia strips your writing of: any trace of you. I don't particularly care if no one remembers me, but I want to make sure my parents are written about, at least briefly. I also want to write this in case I don't come back.

My mother, Marion Keller, died when I was thirteen. She and my father had already been divorced for three years by then, and he had met his new girlfriend and soon-to-be wife—Barbara—less than a year into that. My mother always had too much grace to say it out loud, but it was heavily implied that my father had met Barbara long before he and my mother were through.

I never really stopped hating my father for that. I spent so much of my own marriage trying not to be like him that it took me a long time to realize that I had transformed into him.

My mother died of a brain hemorrhage while I was at a friend's house. She arrived to pick me up and chatted to his mom for a while in the kitchen. I wasn't paying much attention to what they were saying— Landis and I were playing Sega in the living room—but I heard her say, "Do you have any aspirin?" and I knew immediately that something was wrong.

I don't know how I knew. I just did. It was bad.

I left the game, went to the kitchen, and found my mom leaning against the counter with her forehead in her hands, and Landis's mom said, "Jon, run to the store and get some aspirin. We don't have any."

She managed to keep her voice calm.

"Mom, are you okay?" I asked, knowing that she wasn't.

Without meeting my eyes, speaking downward into the hands holding her forehead, she said, "Yes, honey, I'm fine; just run to the store. I'll be fine."

I didn't want to leave her, but I grabbed my bag from by the front door and ran two blocks. I wasn't much of a runner and it made my lungs hurt, and I thought I was going to throw up from the panic and exertion when I reached the store. I bought some aspirin, and the man behind the counter looked at me with concern because at that point I somehow already knew that it was too late, and I think it showed on my face.

But I still ran all the way back, even though my shins stung and my feet were in agony and I was sweating so much I could barely see.

I got back and the front door was still open and I thought, *They didn't think to close it behind me because she's gone*, and I was right.

I think it was Stephen King who said that the sum of all human fear is just a door left slightly ajar.

Help me.

That's what I was sitting awake thinking about all night, before coming to the conclusion that of course no ghost girl was attempting to speak to me. There are no ghosts in this hotel, just the ones we've created for ourselves.

I left my door unlocked and didn't slide any of the bolts home. It was a dare of sorts, but it didn't work. Nothing rattled during the night. No one cried out to me.

Maybe the voice that I thought I'd heard had been mine. Maybe Tania was right. Maybe I need help. Or maybe I just need an explanation as to why we're all still here. Maybe "Why me?" is the question I need answered more than anything else.

It was dark outside, even darker than yesterday.

I left my room and went upstairs to knock on Peter's door.

It sounded as though I had woken him up, and when he answered the door, shirtless, he looked me up and down with bemusement.

"You look terrible," he said.

"I need your help."

He crossed his arms. "Oh, the new leader of the group needs my help."

"I didn't want to be leader."

"Sure, sure, things just happen to you." Leaning against the door frame. "And what if I say no?"

"Nothing bad will happen, but it's the right thing to do."

"This is about your investigation? Your little project?" He smirked. "What is it that you want me to do?"

I took a breath. "Your job."

Yuka and Haru agreed to a half-hour session in their room. Yuka transcribed, as the interview took place entirely in German, and, even though I had provided Peter with some of the questions, I couldn't understand anything. These are Yuka's notes, verbatim:

P: Where did you get this?

R: It was a present, to keep us quiet on the train.

P: Can you show me how to build one?

R: Yes! It's easy, look.

P: You both like trains?

A: I like planes.

R: Yes!

P: Do you like it here?

R: I did, but I want to go home soon.

A: I don't want to go back to school.

R: I miss school.

P: You miss school?

R: I don't miss school.

A: I miss my friends.

R: Did the world blow up?

P: Do you think the world has blown up?

R: (*laughs*) No!

A: You're doing that wrong!

P: I'm sorry, can you build it for me?

R: What's your name?

P: Peter. What's yours?

R: Ryoko. This is Akio. His name is Jon.

P: I know him.

R: He's your friend?

P: Sure. What made you think the world had blown up?

R: Everyone shouting about bombs.

P: You know what bombs are?

R: They blow things up.

P: We're not blown up, though. We're fine.

R: So we'll be able to go home soon?

P: We might all have to find new homes. Would that be okay with you?

R: Hmm.

P: You miss your old home.

R: My friends. And snacks.

P: I miss snacks too.

R: We have a new sister, but I still miss snacks.

P: Did you make any new friends here?

R: Tomi! She's very pretty and she lets us say funny words.

P: What words?

R: I can't tell you, my mom's here. I'll tell you another time. It's not very polite.

P: Who were your other friends here?

R: I know Jon. My other friends left.

P: Which friends were they?

R: Harry and Sam. Sam was here with his dad; he was going to learn to shoot deer. I never want to do that. I think only boys like it.

P: So Harry and Sam left with their dad?

R: Sam left with his dad before everyone else left. Harry left with her mom and dad when everyone was shouting. She said bye to me.

P: Harry was a girl?

R: Yeah. She said bye and she didn't want to go because she was scared.

P: Did you know Harry for very long?

R: No. She gave me a hug when I was crying. I was shouted at, and everyone else was shouting, so she gave me a hug.

P: And then she left with her parents?

R: (*nods*)

P: Is that why you ran off? Your mom said she lost you for a while. Did you run off somewhere? Did you go say good-bye to Harry?

R: No. I was following the other girl.

P: The other girl?

A: I made it for you!

P: Thank you, Akio. Do you put it on the foldout tracks here?

A: Yeah.

R: No, you're doing it wrong!

A: You break it like that.

R: No, I don't! It's mine anyway.

(*Discussion about how best to construct and play with the portable train set, which Peter resolves by making it all fly and creating midair collisions*)

P: Who was that other girl you mentioned?

R: Who?

P: The one you followed when your mom couldn't find you. Had you seen her at the hotel before?

R: No. She came in with her dad.

P: Her dad?

R: I don't know, but I hid. I didn't get to talk to her.

P: You hid?

R: Yeah, I hid, and then Mom found me.

P: Why did you hide? Was it a game?

R: (*shakes her head*)

P: I promise, Ryoko, you're not going to get into any trouble.

R: I got into trouble for running away.

P: You won't get into trouble now. You haven't done anything wrong. Was the man being scary? Was the girl okay? Were you making sure she was okay?

R: I was scared, so I hid, and then Mom found me.

P: Have you ever seen this man again?

R: (*shakes her head*) I have bad dreams a lot.

P: You know you're safe here, don't you? We're all here to look after you.

R: Who looks after you when you're grown up?

P: (*laughs and points at Jon*) Him.

R: (*laughs*)

J: What?

On the third day we decided to send a search party out for the others. It would be for an afternoon; we wouldn't leave the hotel for longer than that.

In her condition, Tomi had to stay behind. I wouldn't have let her come anyway. She was sitting up, talking, and made it downstairs for some food toward the end of the third day. Even in a weakened state, I knew I could rely on her, and also Peter, to protect the group.

I volunteered to go because it didn't matter so much if I didn't make it back. At that point, I almost didn't care if I didn't come back. I didn't write anything else after Peter's interview with Ryoko. I was too demoralized.

I hadn't told anyone else about the body buried in the trees, or the revelation that the girl in the water tank hadn't been who I'd thought she was. I hadn't even told Tomi. Part of me was embarrassed that my lead had come to nothing. But she also has enough to worry about, and the less she knows, the less likely it is that she'll come to any harm.

It was colder than usual when we left, and I was wearing an extra sweater under my coat that made my arms stiff and cumbersome to move around. My shoulders and calves were already stiff, already painful, and my tooth hurt. I was tired because I had stayed awake worrying about the recon mission, and worrying in general.

Peter had volunteered to come with me, but he was the only decent shot left in the hotel who wasn't weakened by illness. In a surprising turn of events, Yuka also volunteered. I think she felt attacked by Tomi's insinuation that she wasn't pulling her weight. But that wasn't going to work out, because she isn't built to hold one of those rifles, let alone run with one or shoot under pressure.

In the end, it was Rob who accompanied me.

As we pulled away from the hotel, Rob said, "Did you ask me instead of Peter because I seem less likely to kill you and make it look like an accident?"

I laughed. "Exactly that. I know it's probably unfair, but I don't trust him."

"I'm glad I don't give you that impression."

"Maybe that's your secret."

"Maybe I've always been the most dangerous person here."

I laughed so much that I forgot to watch the road for a moment. It made me miss the others even more. My support network was out there somewhere. I hadn't appreciated how much I relied on them.

"We might find them," Rob said.

"That's not a great thought."

"I'd rather know either way, even if it's bad."

"I'm not sure."

"Has nuclear war been as bad as you thought it would be?"

I paused. "Huh. No, I guess it hasn't been as bad as I imagined."

"Did you always envision something more like the opening of *The Terminator*? I did."

"It was like that for some people."

He nodded, and I knew we were both thinking of the people we had lost. At least it would have been quick for them. Or would it have been, when it was just as likely they had all died slowly from radiation poisoning?

It was hard to tell if anyone was suffering from radiation sickness here. I've become accustomed to feeling sick all the time.

"While we're out here, we could look for a phone," Rob suggested.

"You have yours?"

He flashed the screen from his pocket.

"We can pull over at some point if you notice you have a signal," I said, eyeing the dying forest with trepidation. "When we're out of the woods. But not at the store. I've got a bad feeling about it."

"Me too. I've got a bad feeling about this."

Grinning, I replied, " 'You always say that, Frost. You always say, I got a bad feeling about this drop.' "

We were about fifteen minutes away.

I asked, "Should we do a drive-by of the store, just in case they stopped there?"

"If you want."

"No, I'm asking you. Do you think it's a good idea?"

He sighed. "We could be ambushed."

"But we could get attacked at any time along this road."

We both thought about it for a while, and Rob broke the silence.

He said, "We should do it for the others. Imagine if you were Dylan or Nathan and your car had broken down and you were stuck at the store, scared to death, and none of us ever came looking for you because we were too scared. It wouldn't be fair."

"Okay, decided. I'll do a drive-around."

The atmosphere in the car became tense. My heart sped up. I felt like we were driving into a trap, but he had a point: How could we live with ourselves if Dylan, Nathan, or Adam were still alive and we had never properly tried to find or rescue them?

"One drive-around," I said firmly as I took a left turn toward the store. "If anything seems out of the ordinary or we see anyone, we drive on. Anything gets near the car, shoot it."

"That would be my first instinct," he replied, reaching into the back for one of the rifles we had brought with us. "Though I've never shot one of these before. It's quite heavy, isn't it?"

"Are you going to be okay with it?"

"Point it in the vague direction and pray?"

"That's about it. Brace yourself for the recoil against your shoulder. Hold your cheek to it, if it helps you keep it steady. Try to hit your target the first time."

"That part goes without saying, surely."

"You've never shot a gun before—the first shot will send a load of adrenaline through your system. Your hands will start shaking. You probably won't be able to shoot again for a few minutes."

"Oh." He took a breath. "I didn't know that."

Something heavy dropped onto the roof of the car with a metallic smack, and we both started. Probably a branch. Rob put a hand to his head and blew out his cheeks. I gripped the wheel a little tighter, flushing red. We looked at each other and grinned with the mutual acknowledgment of our fear.

Approaching the store, I slowed.

"Don't slow down," Rob said, checking that his door was locked. "Do it really fast."

"You sure we won't miss anything?"

"A Land Rover isn't going to be easy to miss."

I put my foot on the gas and braced myself, taking a hard left into the parking lot.

Rob had his face up against the window, taking in the empty expanse of gray, while I kept my eyes fixed on the limited stretch in front of us. I was checking for upturned nails, trips, signals—anything that looked as if it had been laid by human hands.

"There!"

I jumped, swerved to the right, and took my eyes off the road. "What?"

"There." Hand flat on the window. "That's Dylan's car."

"Fuck. Fuck, what do we do?"

"Stop!"

"Stop?" I was already driving out of the lot. "We can't!"

"That's his car!"

"Do you see anything else?"

Two pairs of eyes frantically searched the space for danger.

"No, nothing. Stop!"

"I don't think we should stop!"

"They might be in there!"

"Fuck! Fuck!" I slammed on the brakes and the car skidded to a halt, throwing us both forward. "Fuck."

We waited for something, for an attack, for movement, but there was only quiet.

Neither of us made a move to get out of the car.

I put the thing in reverse and took us back slowly.

"Rob, tell me if you see anything!"

"I don't see anything."

"Is that definitely Dylan's car?"

We pulled up alongside it and both stared. It was his car all right.

"Fuck," I said again, because I knew one of us was going to have to get out.

"Fuck," Rob said, because he knew it was going to be him.

"I'll keep the engine running," I said, trying to disguise the tremor in my voice. "Take the gun with you. You'll be okay."

"Please don't drive off without me."

"I won't."

"No, I mean it, please don't drive off."

"I won't, I promise."

With shaking hands, he unlocked his door and slipped out. I looked around again, but nothing was moving. No one was advancing on us. Rob left the door ajar as he advanced toward the Land Rover, pressed his shoulder against the back, and rose on his toes to look in the window. He didn't appear to see anything shocking and glanced back to shake his head at me.

Hurrying back to the safety of our vehicle, he asked, "Should we go into the store?"

"They're not going to be camped out here," I said.

"So why is his car still here?"

"I know literally as much as you do!" I swallowed, and my mouth was sand-dry. "There are only two of us. If we get jumped, I don't like our chances if they're the sort of people who can overpower Dylan, Adam, and Nathan."

"We can't just leave this here."

"Go and check if the key is in there."

"What? Oh, yeah."

This time he was quicker, a little more assured, as he opened the door of the Land Rover. He put the rifle across the seat and rummaged around the footwell, the glove compartment, the floor, and I kept watch on the stillness, my heart beating frantically and my stomach heaving.

I have never known fear like that. It's like, every time I think I've reached the zenith of my capacity, I find a situation that surpasses it. This was the feeling of being part of the food chain.

Rob returned and locked the door. "No key."

"Figures; otherwise it'd be gone. You can't hot-wire a car, can you?"

"I'm flattered that you think I look like the sort of man who can hot-wire a car."

"I'll take that as a no."

"No. I mean, *no*, I can't."

I wondered if I might be able to do it, if we googled how. I decided it was worth a try.

"Try to get on the Internet," I suggested. "If you can find some sort of online tutorial, I can probably hot-wire a car. Maybe. Also, if we have another car, it won't take us as long to get everyone out of the hotel."

"I thought you couldn't hot-wire modern cars."

"Not a clue. We might as well try to take it with us, though, right?"

Chuckling at the absurdity of it all, Rob turned on his phone and his remaining data. "I can probably do it with a tutorial."

"Bumblebee!" I exclaimed.

"What?"

"The yellow and black wires go together when you hot-wire a car. I read it somewhere. Bumblebee, for the yellow and black, and . . . there's another word to remember the other two colors, but I can't remember it."

The screen glowed, and it connected. He searched YouTube. I wanted to snatch it out of his hands and check my messages.

"Can I . . . use that when you're done?" I asked as he got out of the car.

"Yes, of course." He left the door slightly open. "Please don't drive off."

"I won't! Hurry, I've got a bad feeling."

"What do you mean?"

"Nothing, it's . . . Nothing. Go. Go!"

Keeping hunched, as if expecting a shot, Rob returned to the Land Rover. I could hear the tutorial playing, some guy in his driveway talking him through the process. I reversed a little to bring the entrance of the store into sight. I couldn't see any movement, but the longer we loitered in one place, the worse the pit in my stomach became.

I noticed that he hadn't taken the gun with him and glanced over my right shoulder. I saw something—someone—retreat from the edge of the lot, back into the trees.

I didn't have time to doubt my own eyes.

"Rob! Rob, move!"

He was out of Dylan's car in a flash, and I was putting ours in gear by the time he flung himself into the passenger side. Watching the trees, I heard Rob lock his door, and barely a second later something hit our right fender.

"Fuck!" Rob looked back. "Fuck!"

I stepped on the gas and was going forty by the time we hit the exit. I felt us run over something, and the air went out of our tires with a bang. The whole car became almost uncontrollable. I slammed on the brakes and put us in reverse, backing up toward the Land Rover, hearing the ragged slap of burst tires.

"What are you doing?"

"We ran over nails or something!"

"Fuck, fuck, fuck—"

"Move!"

I grabbed my own rifle from the back, got out of the car, and pointed it toward two figures—two men. They had slowed to a jog when they saw the rifle, and put their hands in the air.

I heard a shot, and the men hit the ground, covering their faces and the backs of their necks.

I ducked and swung my gun rapidly toward the store, where a man was lying bleeding near the entrance. He was grasping his thigh and screaming. I could already tell by the amount of blood that he was going to bleed to death.

Rob had shot him.

I couldn't see the man's face. He was blocked by the cars behind me.

Barely able to see, or think, or recall how many bullets I had, I aimed my gun toward the men on the ground.

"Who are you?" I yelled, sounding much braver than I felt.

They didn't answer. I could see that one of them was holding a large blade, but Rob and I were the only ones with guns.

"Who are you?" I asked again.

"Don't shoot!" One of them looked up. I didn't recognize him, but his accent was Swiss, or French. "We are looking for food!"

I had to wipe sweat out of my eyes, despite the chill. "And you took our car out?"

"We are just looking for food!"

I looked over my shoulder at the store again. Rob was shifting from foot to foot, gun pointed at the other man on the ground. My hands and arms were shaking, and I struggled to regain some composure in case they sensed weakness and decided to rush me.

"Are we the food?" I asked. "Where are our friends?"

"We don't know your friends!"

"They were in that car!"

They hesitated. I made a decision and shot the man who wasn't talking. It sounds so quick, writing it here, like I didn't think anything of it. But I did. I've never killed a man before. I hadn't shot a gun in over ten years. His body jerked and a spatter of blood hit his companion, who cried out. I shot him in the chest, but I'd been aiming for his head.

The gunshot had shaken me. I couldn't catch my breath.

"Fuck! Are you okay?" Rob called.

"I'm fine, I just . . . I'm fine." I addressed the other man, feeling nothing but fear. "Where are the men who were in that car?"

He didn't say anything. He had dropped the blade the moment the blood hit him, and now his eyes were knitted shut and he was muttering under his breath, maybe praying, maybe cursing me out.

"Talk!"

He opened his eyes. I noticed that his face was dirty and his back teeth were gone. He was wearing several sweaters, a hoodie, and fingerless gloves. His jeans looked covered in dirt. Or old blood.

"Please don't shoot," he said.

"Tell me what happened to our friends!"

"We were looking for food. There's no food left out here."

The man on the ground writhed a little, and I realized he was still alive, and jumped. But they seemed to be his final movements. His arms and hands spasmed before going still. The blood kept gliding outward.

"Are you eating people?"

He shook his head. "There's no food left out here."

The shake of the head wasn't a denial. It was disgust with himself.

"What about the city?"

"We can't go there."

"Why?"

"We can't."

I looked over my shoulder at Rob. The rifle was still alternating between the entrance to the store and the third man, but the third man looked dead.

"What happened to the men in that car?"

"I don't know." He wouldn't meet my eyes.

"How can you not know?"

"They escaped! The two escaped—"

"Just two?" The gun was starting to feel heavy, and my shoulder ached.

He didn't reply.

I asked, "Which two?"

He babbled, "I don't know where they went. The city, maybe."

"But you said you couldn't go into the city!"

He didn't elaborate.

"What happened to the one who didn't escape?" I asked.

Shutting his eyes again, he whispered something in French.

"Why is their car still here?" I shouted.

"Because we knew you would come! We knew you would stop if you saw the car. Please, we just needed food. We're so hungry and we can't hunt; we don't have guns." His lower lip trembled and a few tears worked their way down his cheeks, cutting through the grime.

The blood had reached my shoes and I stepped back. As I did so, I connected with the car, which nudged my rifle off its mark. The man grabbed the blade from the ground and scrambled for me. I panicked, falling backward as another shot rang out from behind me, making everyone duck.

Unable to hear anything, I found my feet and regained control of my rifle, firing at the man with the knife until he stopped moving.

It wasn't until after I stopped shooting that I realized I had shot him four times before the rifle jammed. I shook the lodged bullet onto the ground.

Someone was saying something. I couldn't make it out.

I looked over my shoulder and saw Rob, whose skin seemed almost gray. He shook the gun at me and said, as if from behind a pane of glass, "Just point it in the vague direction and pray." Then he ducked behind the car and threw up.

Taking a deep breath and holding it in my chest, I put my rifle down, stepped into the blood, and went through both men's pockets. I was finding it hard to use my hands.

"What are you looking for?" Rob asked, slumping over the hood of the car.

"This," I said, holding up Dylan's car key.

We both supported ourselves against the car, unable to move for a while.

"Jon, are you okay?"

Oxygen came back to me. I had stopped breathing. "Yes! Yes, I'm fine. I'm okay. Are you okay?"

"Yeah. I think. I really don't know, actually."

I looked at the two bodies, at the blade on the ground, and then back at the flat tires of our car. Without replacements, there was nothing we could do. We'd have to leave it here and at least be grateful that we had Dylan's Land Rover.

I retrieved my backpack and ran my hands around the interior of our car in case we had forgotten anything, and we pulled away in Dylan's Land Rover.

"What happened?" Rob asked. "I couldn't hear what you were saying. I kept thinking more of them were going to appear from the store."

"They must have been desperate. They ambushed us, but they had no weapons."

"I heard you talking to them."

"Can you just drive?"

He took a deep breath, and I saw his eyes fill with tears.

"*Can* you drive?" I asked, softening my tone.

"Yeah, in a minute. I just need a minute."

"Let me." I indicated for him to get out.

"You don't need to."

"I'm fine, don't worry."

We swapped places and set off again. I was glad for the distraction. Focusing on driving meant that I didn't have to think too hard about what had just happened.

"You did a real good job under pressure back there," I said as I pulled off the road to skirt around the nails at the exit.

He laughed a little hysterically, throwing back his head. "I've never been more scared in my life!"

"Me neither. Really."

"You shot those men, though. It was . . . I was surprised."

"I knew we couldn't leave any of them there. They might have come after us. After all of us." I considered taking us back to the hotel at the next fork, but I knew we had to push on toward the city. "I don't know if it was the right call."

"Did they say anything about the others?"

"No," I said, and immediately regretted it. "No, that's a lie. I'm sorry, I don't know why I said that. He mentioned the others, he said there were two still alive who escaped and that maybe they ran toward the city. I don't know what . . . He wasn't clear about what happened. He could have been lying."

"What? They said they saw them?"

"Yeah, they said—"

"What did they say?"

"They said they ran toward the city . . . He said they escaped. He didn't say who they were."

A short silence.

Rob sighed and said, "They could have told us more if we hadn't panicked."

"I know! I just thought . . ." A stress headache, urgent and loud, was pounding on the front of my skull, and I pulled the car over onto the side of the road. "Sorry, I need a minute."

"Did they say if they'd killed one of them?"

I grappled for the handle, unlocked the car and managed to stagger out of it before vomiting onto the dying grass. Gasping for air again, I shut the door and leaned against the car, wanting to escape Rob's accusing voice.

But it wasn't accusing, not really. It was just a question.

I heard Rob open the door and his feet hit the road. He came and stood next to me in front of the wall of trees.

"I didn't mean to make it sound like you did something wrong," he said.

"No, it's my fault. I freaked out." I let out a nervous peal of laughter. "I just . . . I didn't know what to do. I was fucking terrified."

"Me too."

"You've never shot a gun before and you hit the mark the first time!"

He smiled a little. "Yes, I did, didn't I? You can tell everyone about that bit."

"I will."

He raised his hand and I awkwardly high-fived it, laughing. The high five turned into one of those awkward male hugs that would have involved backslapping if either of us had been macho enough to pull it off. I couldn't remember the last time I'd hugged someone who wasn't Tomi. I hadn't realized how much I had missed it, how much it had been missing from my life, even before the bombs. Did I hug anyone aside from Nadia and the kids? Women I was sleeping with? I couldn't remember. I didn't think so.

We swapped seats, and Rob drove for the rest of the trip.

We hit the outer suburbs, the large country houses and corner stores, and didn't see much at first. I was struck by how normal everything looked, save for the abandoned cars all over the road, making it difficult to navigate. I stared at the houses we passed and was shocked to see faces in the windows.

"This is weird," Rob said.

"I expected there to be . . ." I couldn't find the words.

"A war zone?"

"Yeah."

Rob slowed, maneuvering his way around a couple of cars that had been awkwardly left lengthways across the road. I noticed the men with guns before he did. They appeared to be wearing dark blue uniforms, but with no insignia. They motioned for us to stop and roll down the windows.

I nudged Rob, and he went white.

"Christ."

A man walked up to the window. Across his chest he held a rifle. He had flecked mahogany eyes, dark skin, and he addressed us in French.

"I'm American," I said, feeling like an asshole and hoping he wouldn't shoot me for it.

"Where have you come from?" he asked.

"Hotel Sixième," Rob replied. "It's back there."

"I know it." His eyes narrowed and he looked past us, back into the car. "There are people there?"

"Just under twenty of us," I said.

"This whole time?"

We nodded.

"What are you doing here?"

We exchanged a look. "We lost some of our group. They went out looking for food and never came back. We were afraid some . . . other people had attacked them."

"You're right. There are bad people out there, in the forest." He looked beyond our car, gestured at someone as if to say, *It's okay, these guys are okay.* "So are you here looking for food? Or your friends?"

I swallowed, unsure as to whether there was a wrong answer. "Both. We're not going to be able to survive at the hotel through the winter with what we have. What's your situation here? Are you accepting people? Are you police?"

He looked surprised. "We're all police. Follow me. I'll take you to the town hall."

"Should we leave our car here?"

"Yes. No one will steal it."

We both exited the vehicle slowly, and the man in the dark uniform shook his head at our weapons. "You can't bring those. You can leave them in the car, but you can't walk around with them."

I was happy to comply. There were about a dozen of these men guarding the roadblock, and I wouldn't have bet on my chances with any of them.

The man held out a hand to me and said, "My name's Felix."

I shook it, and relaxed a little. I couldn't imagine a man introducing himself so politely to people he was planning on shooting.

"I'm Jon. This is Rob."

"You're British?" Felix said to Rob.

"We're American, British, German, and French back at the hotel," Rob said, nodding. "A Japanese couple as well, with young children."

"About twenty, you said?"

"Fewer now."

Felix led us around the roadblock, and beyond it I could see the city, looking—for the most part—exactly like we had left it so many months ago, when we took our taxis from the station to the hotel. It was still clean. The buildings weren't crumbling. The only major difference was the flags and signs. They were everywhere, some in French and some not. They were hanging from windows and flying in gardens.

LONG LIVE SAINT-SION. PEACE.

"It wasn't called Saint-Sion before, was it?" I said, unsure.

Felix shook his head. "We renamed it. It's a different city now."

"What's at the town hall?" Rob asked as we started walking.

"Our mayor," Felix said. "And council."

"Your what?" I stopped walking.

He glanced back at me as if I were stupid. "Our mayor, and council. Our mayor is Stephanie Morges."

Rob was looking at me strangely too, but I didn't care. It was as if I'd lost control of my body, and my eyes filled with tears. I took off my glasses and hid the top half of my face, but I couldn't stop the tears from coming. A wave of the most painful relief and nostalgia knocked the wind out of me, and for a while all I could do was stand there in the middle of the street and resist the overwhelming urge to cry. I felt a hand on my shoulder. Rob.

Felix didn't say anything.

It was easy to detach yourself from the images of your former life in the hotel. I think that was why I was so scared to leave. At the hotel we could focus on survival and one another. We didn't have to think about the rest of the world, or what we had lost. Now I felt it, the crushing existential weight of the loss. Commutes, calling your representatives over something you saw on TV, reading news articles online, all of them getting progressively worse, going to march after march amid the creeping sensation that nothing was changing, that governments weren't scared and people were nowhere near as scared as they should be, spending day after day at work talking about politicians we hated and battles we were losing, worrying about your future and whether your children would have one, and then it was all gone. Your family and your TV and your worries about the future and the future as you envisioned it, and your children; all gone in the space of a day, or maybe longer, but no one could know that because the Internet, that big window, was gone too.

I missed it all so much, even though I hadn't been happy. None of us had been happy. Any image of our former lives hurt like trauma from an old wound. It was never happy, but it had been familiar. You knew every day that it wasn't sustainable, that the violence wasn't sustainable, but we'd all had to live in it, somehow. It wasn't happiness. It wasn't peace. But sometimes, for us, it had been quiet.

I uncovered my eyes, said, "Sorry," and we continued walking.

Rob was silent.

Felix didn't ask us any more questions.

I wasn't embarrassed. Who the hell cared anymore? Don't we all have enough to cry over?

We began passing stores, some of which even looked open. I wondered what everyone was doing with their money, with all this stuff. There were people walking around in normal clothes. A woman and three children crossed the street in front of us. They looked clean, happy, like normal kids.

Rob walked up to the window of a store and peered in. "So what happened here after . . . well . . ."

We still hadn't found a term for it that we were all comfortable with. Felix had, though.

"The final war?" he said. "There was panic, lots of riots and looting. It was very bad for a while, especially after the electricity stopped. People wanted the Internet. They thought we were all going to die. Fanatics were convincing people to commit suicide in the street. It was very bad."

"It doesn't look very bad now," I remarked.

"After we established order, we organized a cleanup. We fixed our buildings and our roads, we buried the dead, we exiled any who encouraged violence or fanaticism."

"Where to?"

"Just out of the city. That is why we have these patrols on the roads. We have some on the edges of the forest also, but a lot of the people moved into the middle, where we can keep everyone safe. Those that we exiled, we know they are still out there. Not all of them died. We know they stay alive by eating one another."

A shiver went up my spine. "We're worried that's what's happened to our friends."

Rob asked, "Has anyone new arrived in the last week? Do you get many new people?"

"I do not keep track of all new arrivals. They would not all pass me. The council keeps a census of all citizens, so if your friends came here, they would be on it."

I dared to smile. "So you do accept newcomers?"

Felix shrugged. "We have to make sure you can be useful, and that you are not dangerous. If you are not, I see no problem."

We carried on walking. A lot of the taller office buildings had been boarded up, completely black at the windows and guarded by men in navy blue uniforms.

"What goes on in there?" I asked, gesturing.

"Food production. We had to devise new ways of farming, because . . ." Felix gestured at the empty, sunless sky with his rifle. "Also, the rain is no good for water. Full of radiation. We organized the collection of nearby water before it was infected with rain, from our streams and lakes. We have been using that, and rationing the stocks of bottled water, while we have other people constructing wells."

I hesitated. "The rain is radioactive?"

He looked at me like I was slow. "Yes. Luckily, it has only rained once here. So the levels of radiation in our lakes will still be very low."

I couldn't believe that none of us at the hotel had considered that. It shut me up for a while.

I also wondered what "useful" meant, but kept the question to myself.

In the center of Saint-Sion, there was an old square, where the buildings were made of stone and the surrounding houses were redbrick. The road became uneven and aged. Some of the navy-uniformed officers were on horseback. To our left was a large stone building with a spire on its front; I assumed this was the town hall, as it was heavily guarded.

I paused and took a look around the square. There were market stalls out.

"What are they paying with?" I asked.

"Nothing. If anyone wants something extra, like a luxury item, they swap things. Money has no use anymore. We make sure everyone is provided for. That is it." Felix indicated for us to precede him inside, and nodded at the guards on either side of the door.

There was a steep flight of stairs in front of us, a red carpet, rooms branching off to left and right, high ceilings. Conversation echoed.

"Wait here," Felix said, motioning us toward some couches before he disappeared upstairs.

We sat down. I felt light-headed.

"This is surreal," Rob said, sounding a little breathless. "I feel like this isn't really happening."

"Yeah, like a dream sequence."

We both laughed nervously.

I said, "I hadn't thought about how weird it would be to be around other people again. I didn't think we would be."

"Which was unlikely, when you think about it."

"I just got used to the group."

He took a breath. "But we could come and live here. In a city again. Think about everyone back at the hotel; they couldn't imagine this."

"I want to know what he meant by 'useful.'"

He smiled. "You picked up on that too."

"Sounded like some *Handmaid's Tale* thing. I didn't like it."

"Yeah, I thought that too."

We exchanged a glance, and I felt a rush of affection.

"Glad I'm here with you and not Peter," I said.

"*I'm* glad you're here with me and not Peter. You might not have come back."

"Or these guys would have shot us already."

Felix came back. A woman was with him. She was in her fifties, wearing dark jeans and a smart gray coat. She shook my hand firmly, and I saw that she had strong, very direct features. But her smile was warm.

"Hello, my name is Louise Zammit. I'm deputy mayor. Felix said you arrived by car just now."

"Yeah, I'm Jon Keller, this is Rob Carmier. We come from—"

"The hotel, Felix said. We had no idea there were still people there."
She looked at Felix. "You may go, thank you."

Felix nodded in our direction and walked out.

Louise Zammit took us upstairs, and we followed until we were in
one of the offices overlooking the square. She took a seat behind a large
desk and invited us to sit. She pulled a huge ledger toward her and tried
the pen, but it had run out of ink. She had to leave the office to find
another, then came back and took our full names.

She asked about the hotel, about how many survivors there were,
who was who, who did what, what languages we spoke, what supplies
we had, and whether we'd had any violent incidents over the last few
months. She also asked how old we all were, which I thought was odd
but nothing to be concerned about, yet.

I didn't mention the girl, but we did mention what had happened
with Nicholas van Schaik. She seemed unbothered by it.

"That is understandable," she said. "Felix said you were asking about
some friends of yours who went missing three days ago."

We nodded.

"Three of them. Nathan, Dylan, and Adam. They're all fairly conspicuous guys, hard to miss," I said, sitting forward in my seat.

"That sounds familiar, yes," she said, turning a page of the ledger.
"One of our patrols found a young Englishman named Adam last week.
He was with a man named Dylan, I believe. Yes, it's right here. We have
a list of all the arrivals from your hotel."

Rob reached out and grabbed my arm. My breath caught in my throat.

"They're alive!" he exclaimed.

Louise Zammit nodded. "Yes; unharmed mostly, but quite shaken.
Neither of them spoke to us much. We moved Adam into a room near
where you left your car. Of course you can see him if you want."

Felix, who had been waiting outside the town hall, helped us find the address, and waited outside the building again as someone buzzed us into a small block of apartments, three stories high. It was clear that he had been given orders not to leave us on our own until we were on our way out of the city again.

It looked like any other residential building in Europe. The front yard was well tended, even though the grass was browning. There was a hanging basket of dead flowers, but it looked jaunty and optimistic rather than sad. Inside the entrance, a red carpet led us up a wide staircase. The front doors were white, and everything was remarkably clean.

"They still have electricity," Rob said.

"Yeah, if they have buzzers."

Rob and I went up to the third floor, and the white door opened. Adam, pale and thinner but indisputably alive, gave us a weak smile. He was wearing a white robe. It took everything I had not to bound up to him like a child and embrace him. Rob did that instead, careful not to knock him down.

"God, you're a sight," Adam said, gripping his waist like he was in pain but smiling through it. "What happened to you?"

"What happened to *you*?" I said.

"Well. What *didn't*?" He made a face and walked back inside.

We followed him into a sparse but cozy apartment. It reminded me of the first place Nadia and I had lived together. There was pale green-and-white patterned wallpaper, like in a retro candy store, and dark wood furniture.

"There's tea in the kitchen," Adam said, like it was nothing.

"Tea," Rob repeated.

"Yeah, actual tea. Kettle works and everything, though we're advised not to guzzle the electricity; otherwise they'll have to start putting curfews on it." Adam sat in one of the armchairs by the window.

Sounding a bit choked up, Rob said, "I'm going to . . . I'm just going to make a cup of tea."

"Make me one," I said.

"You like tea?" Adam snorted.

I sat in the other chair, still feeling totally out of place. "I hate it."

"There's coffee too."

"Coffee?" I yelled.

"On it," Rob replied.

Adam looked out the window and shut his eyes for a moment, as if the fatigue made his bones heavy. He was devoid of color.

"Can you tell us what happened?" I asked. "Where's Dylan?"

"Uh." He played with his beard, avoiding my eyes and looking at the window instead. "He left this morning. They gave him a car; he was heading back to the hotel. I'd have gone with him, but . . . I'm not going back into that forest again."

I didn't want to ask.

I had to.

"Where's Nathan?"

Even over the sound of the kettle, I heard Rob go still in the kitchen. It was an astonishing sound, the boiling of a kettle. It filled me with warmth and almost drowned out my question.

Adam caught his breath. "He didn't make it."

There was a long period of quiet when neither of us looked at each other. The kettle came to a boil and the roar subsided. I couldn't hear Rob moving. Everything became still. It had been a while since death had burst into the room. The last people to die whom I had known properly had been Patrick and Coralie, and that seemed like years ago now. I can't remember how I said good-bye to Nathan three days ago, and I can't keep trying to because it's going to drive me crazy. I can't remember if I hugged him or not. I don't think I did. I think I went to the front steps of the hotel to wave them off, but I can't remember what my last words to him had been.

Adam stared at the window. I stared at my hands. Rob didn't come through from the kitchen. I don't know how long we all stayed like that.

I couldn't cry. I'd already fought this battle once. If I started, I didn't think I would be able to stop.

"I'm not sure I wanna talk about it," Adam said finally.

"That's fine. You don't need to."

He got up, went into the kitchen, and started making himself a tuna sandwich. I got the impression that he was doing his best to keep himself busy, though it was obviously still painful for him to walk. I didn't ask why.

I noticed that he had defensive wounds on his hands, burst knuckles, and scratches and bruises down his arms, but I tried not to stare.

When he had returned and sat down again, he said, "They got us by grabbing me. Dylan could have just shot them, but he didn't because they got me."

"It's not your fault."

"It's . . . maybe." He scratched at the arms of the chair. "I was telling Dylan to just shoot them, but he wouldn't with me in the way, so they put their guns down and that was it. We couldn't do anything. There were only three of them."

"Three?"

"Well, three who picked us up. There were about twelve in the group, maybe ten, hard to tell. Dylan killed two getting us out of there, and then we just didn't stop running until we ran into the guards here."

"Is Dylan okay?"

"Shaken up, but he had to get back, make sure everyone was all right. I know they were planning to use one of us to get to you guys, blackmail you for food and guns and stuff."

"We hadn't noticed anything wrong."

Rob brought a couple of mugs through from the kitchen and handed me one and Adam the other.

"I didn't know how you wanted it," he said, distracted. "There's some sugar but no milk, obviously."

"Can I have sugar?"

He brought the whole bag through and put it down beside my chair. He leaned against the far wall and stirred his tea, staring into it with red eyes and a stunned expression.

"Are you guys okay?" Adam asked.

I stirred a disgusting amount of sugar into my coffee. Sugar was so scarce now that it was like a drug to me. "We had some trouble on the way here. Rob saved me."

"No way." Adam brightened up. "Big ups, mate."

"It was just luck, I'm sure."

"Three men jumped us at the store. We found Dylan's car and they were waiting for us, but they're all dead."

"Good riddance," Adam muttered. "You're okay, though?"

"Yeah, we're fine. Can you believe this place?"

Adam shook his head. "I still can't. I woke up this morning and forgot where I was and had this whole panic attack. I literally fell over, like an old person."

"I've gotten so used to the hotel," I said, glancing at Rob, who nodded.

"Can't believe we never thought of leaving before. Like, this was here the whole time. If we'd been less wimpy about it, then . . ."

Silence again.

If we'd been braver, then maybe everyone who had killed themselves, Nathan, everyone, would all be still alive now. We would have had a bit more hope.

"Is there anything weird going on here, do you think?"

Adam frowned at me. "What do you mean?"

"We spoke to one of the guards. He said everyone had to be useful. And the deputy mayor asked us about the group, about what skills everyone had, how old we are. That doesn't mean anything weird, does it?"

A shrug. "I don't know. I was asked what sort of work I could do once I felt more up to it, but that was it. They've got these indoor farms here with these red and blue LED lights. Apparently they make seeds grow faster. I'm not really good at anything, but . . . well, I asked Dylan to bring me back my guitar. Maybe I can be the town . . . what do you call it?"

"Troubadour," Rob said.

"Yeah, that."

"More like town asshole," I said.

"That too, to be honest."

"No one likes the person who brings a guitar to a party," Rob added.

"But I can play 'Wonderwall' and everything!"

"Why do you have to ruin a nice thing for everyone, Adam?" I sighed.

"You don't like . . . what, you guys don't like 'Wonderwall'?" He shook his head. "Shocking."

Rob snorted into his tea.

I had an idea. "Rob, why don't you stay here and I'll drive back?"

"Alone?"

"There's no point putting multiple people in danger now. You're here; I can deal with everything else."

He scoffed at me. "Absolutely not. Not after what happened on the way here."

"Come on, that's why I want you to stay! It doesn't make sense to put us both in danger."

"No, I'm coming back." He sipped tea and eyed me irately. "That's final."

Adam rearranged his robe. "Fair, really. Didn't wanna stay here with some twat who doesn't like 'Wonderwall' anyway."

We laughed again.

For the briefest of moments, I wondered whether Adam's ghost boy had followed him here too.

"Shit, I almost forgot!" Adam gestured at Rob with urgency. "We have a signal here—look at the Internet! I've got another phone too. People have spares here."

"You've checked the news?" I said, suddenly finding it hard to breathe.

"Yeah, and dude, it is off the fucking hook."

I was about to demand to look at Rob's phone when there was a firm knock at the door.

Adam went to answer it.

It was Felix.

"I have a message from Louise Zammit. She said you left in a rush and did not look at the full list of arrivals we have had from L'Hôtel Sixième. She thought you would be interested to look at it."

"Have you had anyone new turn up today?" Adam glanced back toward us, his features wide with hope.

"Was he named Nathan?" Rob asked.

"No, the last person to arrive came weeks ago," Felix said, making my heart drop. "Most of them arrived within the first one or two days, and we had to identify them much later. Some came in the weeks after, when it was easier to keep track of arrivals. We haven't had many since."

He handed me the list, and I was surprised to see so many names on there that I knew. A lot of the conference attendees had made it, but the majority of them were on a separate list. I asked why.

"That list," Felix explained, "is of people who arrived but left for the airport later, following the train tracks. We kept their names recorded, in case others came looking for them. Unfortunately, these records are quite recent, with a lot of entries made after. A lot of people may have gone unrecorded, so they won't be completely accurate. The only accurate list we now have is of the people who stayed."

I looked at the lists for a long time, and one name didn't make sense to me. I pointed at it.

"Uh . . . Albert Polor arrived here?"

"Yes, he is one of the people who remained."

Neither Adam nor Rob reacted, but the name came as such a shock to me that I had to make him repeat it.

"And this is Albert Polor?" I asked.

"Yes," he said. "The names with the check mark next to them are those with verified names. They showed some form of ID."

Rob frowned at me. "Do you know him?"

I made a split-second decision and decided to downplay it. "He's just someone from the conference. I didn't think he'd made it."

Felix asked if he could escort us back to our car, and I asked if we could say our good-byes.

As soon as Adam's front door was shut I turned to him and said, "You need to find out where this guy Albert Polor lives, and keep a watch on him until we all get back."

He seemed confused by my tone. "Why?"

Rob lowered his voice to match mine. "I thought you reacted strangely when you saw his name. Who is he?"

My heart was beating unnaturally fast. "I know him. He's one of the professors who pulled guns on us when we were in the store the first time around. Tomi shot him. The real Al Polor couldn't have arrived here, because he's dead."

We were given back our guns and returned to our car. Most importantly, Felix managed to find me a spare phone before we left. Rob and I pulled over as soon as we were out of sight of the roadblocks and spent the next hour poring over our screens in virtual silence.

"They nationalized Wi-Fi," Rob exclaimed. "Only takes the end of the world for people to do the obvious things."

My new phone connected to the city Wi-Fi, and I headed straight to my Facebook messages.

> "Jon, omg, I can't believe you're alive! We're doing okay here. I sent some messages out to your family but haven't heard anything yet. Will let you know if I do. I don't imagine you'll be able to get back to the US. Stay safe. It's so good to know you're still out there."

Sent by Millie Santiago

> "Thank God, there are still people alive! We r moving south, no food here anymore and the weather is so much colder than ever before. I don't know when we'll have Internet again but I sent a FB message to the Nadia in your friends list, just in case. It's so good to hear from u. Good luck!"

Sent by Alice Reader

Nothing from Nadia or Dad.

My Facebook timeline was still showing stories from nearly three months ago, in the absence of any new content.

I went to Twitter and noticed—before I looked at the news feed—that I had a direct message.

I didn't dare hope. For a long time, I just looked at the notification;

the little "1." I didn't think I could handle it not being Nadia. Twitter had always been her social media go-to. I glanced at Rob, who was gazing intently at his own phone and didn't notice. My heart was loud.

"Come on," I whispered to myself, and tapped it.

It said: "Kids scared but fine! Internet patchy. Getting to my parents too risky so trying for Canada. ily, N."

"Are you okay?" Rob asked, having noticed my face.

I didn't fight off the urge to cry then. I couldn't. It felt like blacking out. It was like . . . I don't know. I can't describe what it felt like. It was less a feeling and more like a seismic shift, like the world had moved below me, and I didn't care about anything other than that message. Nothing. Nothing mattered but my kids being alive. I was vaguely aware of Rob asking what had happened, and all I could say, and keep saying, was "My kids are okay," over and over again. Nothing else mattered for a while, because my kids are okay.

I replied immediately, and all the message said was: "I'm coming back."

We drove out of the city in silence. Eventually, hurdle after hurdle of abandoned cars was replaced by deserted forest road. I felt sick, so I tried to focus on driving. It felt wrong not having Adam with us, but he deserved to stay behind after everything he had been through. I couldn't focus on driving, though, because all that mattered now was somehow getting back to America.

Twenty-four hours ago all of this had seemed impossible. Having access to the Internet again had blown my previous theories about what was no longer possible wide open. Rob's immediate family and friends had lived on the outskirts of London, so he hadn't been expecting messages. He had been reading the news, and there was news. All over the world, in the spaces between major cities and the spaces that had been upwind of the blast zones, people had survived and were reaching out to one another, trying to organize travel to safer areas. Of course, not everywhere still had Internet. I didn't know what determined where did and where didn't. But we weren't the last people. The world was bigger than our hotel once again.

"You know he came to the hotel looking for his father," I said, having chewed my lips to shreds worrying about Dylan, navigating the roads, and not knowing what to say about Nathan.

"Adam?"

"Nathan."

"Oh?"

"His father abandoned the family after . . . Nathan told me a story once, that his parents lost all their money. His father came to this hotel and had a hallucination. He disappeared shortly after. Before he left, he told Nathan he'd found God. Nathan ended up working here when he left home. He came here intentionally. Not because he thought he'd find his father but because . . . he might find *something*."

I took my eyes off the road, and Rob was staring. "Really? He told you that?"

"Yeah, we were doing a few manual labor projects together. We were so bad at it." I checked the gas, but we were doing fine. "That story about his father made me think we were all led here somehow."

"What do you mean?"

"Like . . . we all survived the end of the world by being at this particular place at a particular time. You ever wonder why?"

Rob was picking at his nails. "I don't think there is a why."

"I feel like there is. I want to believe there was something more than luck at work."

"That girl on the roof didn't survive, though, did she?"

"No." I totally dropped the train of thought. "No, you're right. She didn't."

It occurred to me, with some sadness, that Dylan, Nathan, and I were never going to finish the rooftop project. Less than halfway through, and not only were we leaving but the whole project had been pointless to begin with. Yuka and I never got to clean the lobby, make it look proud again. I wondered whether we would live close together in the city, whether I would even be in the city long enough to settle now that I knew my kids were out there.

I'd expected to feel pure happiness, and I did . . . I suppose I just haven't seriously considered getting back to the US before now. Without planes, I have no idea what to do. I could attempt to travel west across Europe, through unknown devastation, deadly amounts of radiation, and likely die before I reach the coast of Portugal. And even if I did make it there, against all odds, then what?

But they're alive. That was already against all odds.

"Jon?"

"Sorry." I almost stalled the car and concentrated on the road again. "Sorry, I was . . . Sorry."

Rob put a hand on my shoulder. "Can we stop for a second?"

"What for?"

"Just for a second. You need to pull over."

I did so, not too close to the trees, and made sure every door was locked. I lay my rifle across my lap and turned to him. "What? Why did we have to stop?"

"You were driving . . . badly."

I took off my glasses, blinking hard as if that would shift the permanent headache and the permanent toothache. "My kids are alive. I can't think about anything else."

"You're thinking about leaving?"

"How could I not try?"

"Try to fly to the States?"

I rubbed my eyes and my head throbbed, and I couldn't tell if it was my usual headache or pain stemming from my jaw. "I was so happy to see the city, everyone still living and having normal lives—well, kinda normal . . . and now I can't even stay."

"You don't have to leave straightaway."

I looked at him. "They're alive."

He inhaled deeply. "Well, before you overthink it, let's just get through today. Then you can think about tomorrow and worry all you want."

"I know. I get it." I gripped the steering wheel and made as if to start the car, but stopped. "I need to tell you something about Dylan first. It's been hanging over me, and, honestly, I don't know if I'm going crazy or if I'm paranoid, or if it's just this damn toothache—"

"You have a toothache?"

"This is about Dylan." I sighed, and tried to stop compulsively touching my face.

"What is it, though?"

"You know the girl in the water tank?"

"I didn't ask much about it. I didn't want to know, to be honest. But yes."

"I don't know what her name was. I thought it was a girl named Harriet Luffman, but I found out that she escaped with her parents on the day everyone left. I've been investigating it for a while. I think it was more about keeping myself occupied, but I wanted to do what felt like the right thing. You know?" I glanced at him, and he nodded. "Anyway, it started to look like some of the staff might have been involved. I don't know who, but Dylan and Sophia have been acting weird, and more and more . . . guilty."

"You think they had something to do with it?"

I tried not to sound too paranoid. "It's hard to know for sure. But even though the girl wasn't who I thought she was, that doesn't change the fact that Dylan and Sophia have been trying to cover something up."

He looked out the windows, but we were fine. "What sort of evidence do you have?"

"Mostly they seemed very invested in my not finding anything. My room was broken into, the family's possessions—well, the ones they left without—were stolen, and Dylan's the only person who has those master keys."

"What did he say about it?"

"He said I must have left my room unlocked."

He shook his head. "No one ever leaves their room unlocked."

"I've never been more certain of anything: I did *not* leave my room unlocked. And when I searched Dylan's room, I swear one of those cases was there, but it had been emptied out. I swear it was the same case!"

He took a while to think, and then said, "But you said that the girl wasn't who you thought she was. Harriet. So why would Dylan steal the Luffmans' suitcases if the murdered girl wasn't even their daughter?"

"I don't know—to throw me off? I know they were stolen, and that's all I know."

"And you searched Dylan's room while they were away?"

"Please don't guilt-trip me. I had to know."

I hesitated before I mentioned the body I had found buried on the edge of the woods, but in the end I told him about that too. Afterward he went quiet for so long that it made me uncomfortable, and I thought, *He thinks I'm crazy.*

Then he said slowly, "I don't understand why Dylan and Sophia and . . . why anyone here would murder a girl and leave her up there. It makes no sense." He rubbed his arms, as if he was shivering. "They could have buried her in the forest. Why leave her up there?"

"Why murder her at all?"

"Well, why murder? Why does anyone do anything?" He shrugged. "Why is there a body in the woods? We don't know. It could have been someone else who committed suicide or—"

"If it was another resident killing themselves, why hide it?"

I went to start the car again, but he asked me another question.

"Does anyone else know about this? Or at least about you investigating?"

"Yuka knows a little. But Tomi knows almost everything I know."

A hesitation, before a concerned expression came over his face. "Does anyone else know that she knows?"

I stared at him, and then started the engine.

Dylan wouldn't, I thought. *He wouldn't hurt her.*

You have no idea what he would or wouldn't do, I thought a moment later.

Nothing ever came over the radio when we were driving. We had tried turning it on and off a few times. Sometimes we drove with some white noise, the dim crackle. But no voices, no music came through, ever. The airwaves were dead. We let the white noise take us the rest of the way home, and then left the Land Rover in the parking lot to the side of the building.

Selfishly, I was glad that Dylan had beaten us back, and it wasn't on us to deliver the news about Nathan or to try to explain the inexplicable normality of life in the city.

It was late afternoon, not yet dark, but the light was dimmer than usual. The cloud cover was low, rolling over the tops of the trees.

I wish I could say that I had a premonition that something was wrong, but I was too distracted. All I could think about was my kids, leaving, and how much I didn't want to leave. I was thinking about Nathan, and his father disappearing the way he did. Adam's theory that we were all already dead. There had to be some meaning in it all.

An absence of meaning: that would be the scariest of all things.

Rifles in hand, exhausted and not talking much, Rob and I walked around the hotel and up to the entrance. That's when something first felt off. Before we reached the door several people came out: Dylan, Sasha, Tania, and Peter.

I stopped and instinctively moved closer to Rob, who didn't notice anything strange about the tableau until he clocked Dylan's gun, and that Peter and Sasha were also carrying.

"Um . . . hi?" He raised his hands, forgetting that he was also holding a rifle.

I looked between Tania and Dylan and knew immediately what had happened. She stood a little behind Dylan but didn't directly meet my eyes.

Dylan said, "Jon, give me back my keys, now."

Peter had a hunting rifle pointed at my head. I wondered if he would shoot me regardless, no matter what I did. He could probably pass it off as an accident.

"Why?" I said.

"Um, can someone explain what's going on?" Rob said so quietly that I almost couldn't hear him.

"Don't worry, this has nothing to do with you." Dylan indicated for him to get out of the way. "I just need Jon's keys."

"Why?" I repeated.

"You know why."

"No, I don't." I took a step back and slipped my finger around the trigger of the rifle.

At any moment, I thought I'd feel the impact, a sensation like the back of my head smacking against concrete and my body being impacted by death, and then everything would go black. That's what Adam had said. He died and saw nothing, only black. No time, no sense of self, no elsewhere. No afterlife. Just black.

I thought, *I don't want to die. Please. I don't want to die.*

"Jon, give me the keys, and nothing else happens here."

"Like you wanted nothing else to happen when you had those cases stolen out of my room?"

"I didn't steal those cases, you know I didn't. I was with you when they went missing!"

"I know *you* didn't. But I know that one of them is in your room and the other one is still missing."

He sighed. "Jon, you're confused. You've gone too far with this, and it's not healthy. You're scaring people."

"I'm not confused."

"I let this go on far enough."

"Oh, you *let* me? You *let* me try to find out what happened to that girl? That's heroic, Dylan. A child was murdered, and you let me give a damn."

He looked at me with a pained expression. "You've created a conspiracy."

"Then what were you and Sophia talking about? You didn't want me getting too close, right? Well, too close to what? Why is there a body buried out there?" I gestured violently toward the rear of the building. "I found a body out there. I dug it up with my own fucking hands!"

Everyone exchanged glances.

Tania pushed her way to the front of the group. "Jon, please, you're a good guy, but you're not well. I had to say something."

Rob was shifting back and forth, unsure whether to remain in front of me or not.

Something about what Tania said made me angrier.

I snapped, "And I'm supposed to be so shocked you've taken his side? That girl was on your table, you saw her, but by all means, protect your boyfriend—"

"Fuck you." She glowered.

"Fuck *you*."

"Come on, come on, let's not just insult one another. Jon." Dylan was so calm, no tremor in his voice. "Give me the keys."

"You and Sophia know something. I'm not stupid. I'm not giving you the keys until you tell me what happened to her."

Peter tensed, and I braced myself.

Rob moved to fully shield me, his hands still raised. "Why don't we just go inside and talk?"

"We're trying to make it safe to do that, Rob. Move aside."

Rob put his rifle down on the ground but didn't move. "With all due respect, Jon saved our lives a few times today. You'll have to forgive me for not believing he's a dangerous lunatic."

"Rob, please, can you not make this even more difficult—"

"Can *I* make it even more difficult?"

Sasha, Peter, and Tania turned at the sound of Tomi's voice. I couldn't quite see her at first, but she had appeared just outside the entrance, with her handgun pointed at Dylan. It made my heart leap, and in the second that everyone reeled with surprise I raised my own gun to point it at Peter. He was the only one I had a clear shot at.

He eyeballed me, like, *Don't do this, you idiot.*

Sasha dithered, and then pointed his gun at Tomi.

It crossed my mind that the reason they hadn't waited until we were in the hotel to confront me might have been because it was easier to kill me without witnesses. I also realized, maybe too late, that if Dylan and Sophia really did have something to do with the girl's murder, they would have no problem killing me to keep that secret.

Even when I found the case in Dylan's room, it had never seriously occurred to me that my life might be in danger. I hadn't believed that Dylan would kill me before. I did now. Now all I could see was a future in which all of us, or most of us, ended up dead on the ground in a volley of fatal shots.

I looked away from Peter and addressed Dylan. "Are you really going to shoot me if I don't give you the keys? Like you probably killed whoever is buried over there?"

I saw Tania look at Dylan, to see if he would deny it, and regret flashed across his expression, like he realized he had gone about this the wrong way. Now that guns were out, everyone was in a corner.

I met Tomi's eyes. She didn't look scared.

Peter was looking at Dylan, and I saw the doubt cloud his face. "Is what he is saying true?"

Tomi raised her eyebrows and said, "Well?"

Dylan shook his head, because he wasn't going to explain the body or the cases. "This doesn't have to end badly."

"You're going to kill me over a set of keys, and you think *I'm* crazy!"

"No one's going to get killed!" Tania snapped. "For fuck's sake, Jon, just give him the keys!"

"And then what, forget about it?"

Then, unbelievably, Peter lowered his rifle and said, "I don't think this man is crazy."

Tania pleaded with me. "Please, Jon. Please, just do as he says!"

"Actually, he doesn't have to do anything you say." Tomi cleared her throat and scornfully looked Sasha up and down. "I bet I could take two of you out before this baby even notices his safety catch is on."

Sasha looked down at his gun and Tomi spun and shot him in the foot.

Everyone jumped and Sasha hit the ground, screaming, as Tomi kicked his gun away and turned her aim toward Dylan.

Dylan shouted something but was drowned out by Sasha's cries. My ears were ringing.

Someone, I'm not sure if it was me, shouted, "Fuck! Fuck, everyone calm down!"

"Wait! Everyone, wait!" Dylan was yelling, gun still pointed at Rob.

Tomi said, "There is no safety, moron."

I have no idea how everyone else didn't panic and start shooting, including me. Maybe it was shock. But I was looking at Dylan and—

This is it, I thought. *This is how it ends.*

I remember thinking that maybe Adam was right. Maybe we were all already dead. Maybe I would feel the impact, everything would go black, and I'd wake back up in the hotel as if nothing had happened. For a second, I wanted to know. I really wanted to know if I could die.

But I didn't get to die, or not die, that day.

"Stop! Stop, please stop!" The doors of the hotel slammed open and Sophia came running out with both hands in the air. "Please, put the guns down!"

Sasha was swearing in French and clutching his foot, which was leaking blood everywhere.

Sophia: "Please stop, I don't want anyone hurt! Please! Dylan!"

"Sophia . . ." He said something in French that made Tania look at him sharply.

Peter said something in German that sounded like an exclamation. Dylan lowered his gun but continued addressing Sophia, who was gesticulating wildly at the hotel, at the trees, at me . . .

Tania said something to Dylan that sounded accusing.

Tomi hadn't lowered her weapon. It was still trained on Dylan's skull. She gave me a brisk nod as if to say *I got you*, and I felt a wave of gratitude.

Dylan had clearly said something that Tania didn't like. He reached out to touch her arm and she recoiled, glaring, and went to help Sasha off the ground. She lifted one of his arms over her shoulders and carefully led him, hopping on one leg, back into the hotel.

"What's going on?" I asked.

Dylan stared at Sophia, and I saw tears running down her face.

She turned to face me and spoke in English. "Jon, I am so sorry."

My breath caught in my chest, and I didn't so much lower my gun as let it fall to my side as I leaned against Rob's shoulder. It's quite something, being told you're not crazy.

Dylan was looking at the ground, at the trail of blood Sasha had left, leading the way back inside.

"I want to stay," Peter said haughtily as we followed a distraught Sophia into the bar.

"No!" Dylan snapped.

"How is this fair?"

"I'm staying," Tomi said, taking my arm, as if that would help.

Dylan looked at Sophia, who took her hands away from her face just long enough to say, "I don't care, I don't care."

"You, out. I'll explain later." Dylan swatted Peter toward the door and shut it behind him, turning to Tomi and Rob. "You can stay. I don't want anyone spreading gossip about this until we're all on the same page."

"So what happened?" I asked, addressing Sophia.

"Jon, I'm sorry." She sat down, pressing her fingertips to her temples. "I knew, when I saw you coming back from the forest the day before yesterday. I knew it was over. I knew I was going to have to tell you."

Everyone had put their weapons on the floor.

My heart was still beating dizzyingly fast. It had been the third time that day I'd been convinced I was about to die.

I sat in one of the armchairs, and Tomi sat next to me. Rob and Dylan remained standing. Dylan wouldn't meet my eyes, and seemed perplexed. I sank back into the chair and thought of all the times I'd sat talking with Nathan in here. The bar had always been his domain.

I didn't want to know how he died. It was one of the few things I would be okay with not knowing.

"Baloche and I were getting divorced," Sophia said, still rubbing her temples, eyes half closed. "Because he was insane. He was one of those men who . . . everything was perfect, he was perfect, and then we married and he changed, almost in one night. I thought it was my fault; I didn't understand what was happening. Anyway, this is not about that. Jon, Dylan wasn't helping me hide the murder of this girl, he was helping me because on the day everything happened Baloche attacked me . . . and I killed him. It happened in the kitchen, while everyone was running around, panicking. Dylan only found out because he came to see if I had left."

I tasted the memory first. I hadn't tasted it at the time. Sugar and chocolate. I thought of eating those free cookies from my room, and I felt the wind on my face as I stood in the empty parking spaces, wondering what I was going to do, and I looked to the right and—

"I saw you," I said.

Dylan: "What?"

"I was outside and I saw you, both of you, carrying something through the grounds. It was a little while after . . . it was when most people had gone. That was how I found the body."

"You didn't think that was weird at the time?" Tomi said, frowning.

"No. It was all weird that day."

Rob was biting his fingernails, but stopped to say, "He attacked you?"

"I . . . He, well, I don't—"

"He tried to rape her." Dylan crossed his arms.

"Why?" Rob asked.

Everyone stared at him.

Rob backtracked. "No, I only meant that . . . it's the end of the world, but he decides to spend his last moments attacking his ex-wife. That's a little strange."

"Disaster rape is a documented phenomenon," I said. "Being in the vicinity of an abusive ex-husband at the time would actually make it very likely, as people exploit the chaotic situation. It's common for rape rates to increase during hurricanes and wartime—any time when societies become unstable."

"Well, thanks, *professor*," Tomi said.

"Nadia is a journalist," I added. "She talked about things like that a lot."

"It was not just that," Sophia said, like that wasn't justification enough. "Well, it was. I fought back. I didn't even realize what I had done until . . ."

"She stuck his hand in a deep fryer and got him in the neck," Dylan clarified. "Got him a few times, actually."

"Wow," I said almost inaudibly.

"So you helped her hide the body?" Tomi asked.

Dylan nodded. "It was the only decent thing to do."

"Dylan helped me hide Baloche and clean the kitchen. I threw the knife away. Then I went up to Baloche's room to . . . I don't know, take anything I needed."

Tomi and I exchanged a look.

"And you didn't find anything out of the ordinary?" I asked.

Dylan went to the door, opened it, checked that no one was out there listening, and shut it again.

Sophia paused for a long time. "No. I went to his room and found his computer, so I took that. I was using it to keep track of the news until the Internet stopped. I didn't notice anything strange apart from some emails he had sent about selling the hotel. I didn't know he had been planning to sell it, but . . . it didn't seem out of the ordinary."

There was a brief silence and then Sophia started crying, a gutting, desolate sound.

"I'm so sorry, Jon," she said again. "I thought if everyone found out I did that, I'd be forced to leave, or worse. And you trying to find out what happened to that girl . . . I was so scared you were going to find something."

I said, "I understand," and I wasn't lying.

"Do you think he had anything to do with the girl?" Rob asked. "Your, um . . . the owner?"

Sophia shook her head. "I don't know."

Tomi: "There was nothing else in his emails that seemed suspicious?"

"I didn't even know there was a dead girl until the same day as everyone else," Sophia snapped. "So no, I didn't notice anything."

"Well, could Jon and I take a look?"

"Okay, okay, everyone, just cool it." Dylan stood up straight and cleared his throat. "I don't think anyone here will have a problem keeping this to themselves?"

It took us all a beat to realize he was asking a question, and we all nodded. A pact.

"Jon, I owe you an apology," Dylan said.

I waited.

"You should know, I did let Sophia take the suitcases out of your room. And I took the CDs of that first day out of the camera room."

My chest thumped, as if with a palpitation. "Why?"

"We thought it might scare you off. You seemed so possessed by it, fixating on every little thing. It was scary for those of us with something to hide." He looked at Sophia and took a deep breath. "Instead it made things worse. It was a bad idea, and we never should have done it."

"But where are they?"

"They were both in the back of my car for a while. The one you just arrived in. After a few days, I drove them out in the middle of the night and dumped them in the trees." He grimaced. "Like I said, I don't feel good about it, breaking your trust like that. I'm sorry."

I nodded and said, "No problem. I should never have gone into your room either. Turns out I was fixating on all the wrong things anyway. The girl wasn't even who I thought she was."

None of us knew what to say for a while.

"If I were superstitious, I'd say this place was cursed," Tomi remarked.

"If I were superstitious, I'd say to the casual observer it might seem like the opposite," Rob said. "Though, of course, that's ridiculous."

I frowned at him. "What do you mean?"

He shrugged and smiled awkwardly. "You had a point earlier. The world did end, but we're all alive, aren't we?"

"Oh God . . ." I murmured, as my heart dropped. "Nathan."

And Dylan cut me off. "Jon, Nathan's here."

Rob met my eyes, and then we were both standing.

"Nathan's here?"

"Yeah." He smiled. "He's not in a great way, but he made it back yesterday. Looked like a corpse, staggering out of the forest. But he made it back. I thought he was dead for sure, after Adam and I lost him. He's been sleeping for almost twenty-four hours. You can talk to him as soon as he wakes up."

"Christ." I almost fell back into my chair. "Thank God."

Tomi put a hand on my shoulder. "First thing he did was ask for some vodka. Not water, vodka. Good to know a near-death experience hasn't changed him."

"God definitely had a hand in this one," Dylan said. "Or that crazy kid outmaneuvered death in those woods. Said he twisted his ankle and ended up hallucinating from cold one night, was sure he was going to die of hypothermia. But he woke up. And that was when he knew he was going to make it, whether he could walk or not."

A shudder went down my spine, but I didn't say anything about Adam's theory. It wasn't the time to cast my sanity back into question.

I went upstairs and slept for a long time. I didn't want to do anything else, or speak to anyone else. I didn't want to think about the city, or think about the girl on the roof, or go through Baloche's emails with Tomi. I didn't want to move to the city or to embark on a trip back to the US. I wanted to sleep forever and not wake up in this timeline ever again.

But I did wake up, as it seemed we're all destined to keep doing.

I ended up standing outside Tania's new office for a little while before working up the courage to knock. I don't know why, but I felt that I was the one who owed her an apology.

There was a movement from inside, and Tania came out and shut the door behind her, presumably to avoid disturbing Sasha.

"How is he?" I asked, having to take a step back into the corridor. "How's Nathan?"

"Sasha's going to have trouble walking. She didn't get him in the foot; it was to the left of the shinbone. It's not going to kill him, but, between him and Nath, they'll need most of our painkiller supply to get through recovery. I've given them both sleeping pills, but I can't keep them knocked out forever."

"She was only looking out for me."

"You don't have to defend her. I know." She leaned against the door, folding her arms. "So? You were right?"

"No. I was wrong about a lot."

"It's okay, I don't want to know right now. Later."

"Okay."

"Do you want to come in anyway?"

I hesitated. "Are you sure?"

"You know, I never actually get company. Everyone thinks I don't want the distraction, but all anyone comes to see me about is stomach-aches, headaches, colds." She sighed. "It's grating."

"Then yeah, okay."

She glanced over her shoulder and then let me into the room, where Sasha was sleeping. His wounded leg was propped up on a pile of books from the bar downstairs, wrapped in bandages. He was flat on his back and breathing loudly through his mouth.

"We won't disturb him?" I asked.

She shook her head. "He's going to be out for a while. Nath is next door. No major injuries, but starving, really shaken up. Needs fluids more than anything."

I considered telling her that the rain was full of radiation, but it wouldn't make a difference now. It was too depressing, and we were leaving anyway.

Sitting in one of the chairs next to the bed, she picked up a shot of some white liquid in a white cardboard cup and offered it to me.

I sat in the chair next to hers and sniffed it. "What is this?"

"Calpol. It's a children's medicine, mostly sugar and a mild pain-killer. I don't think there's an American equivalent."

"I don't think I need it."

"Trust me, you do." She smiled, poured some of the white mixture into a plastic spoon, and swallowed it. "There's a pink one for younger kids that's way nicer. But I finished that."

I took the shot. It was thick and one of the most sickly sweet things I had ever tasted. It was also, relative to everything I had eaten in the last few months, delicious.

"Okay, I take it back. This is excellent."

"I've been drinking it like orange juice, every morning. The Yobaris don't like their kids taking it, so more for me."

"Is that why you're always so calm?"

"Yeah, actually." She spread her hands. "What is even the point in being the only doctor if you can't be high most of the time?"

"Atrocious behavior. Can I have another?"

"Have it." She handed me the bottle and the plastic spoon.

"How much am I allowed before I OD?"

It delighted me, hearing her laugh. Things had been tense between us for a while.

"It's hard to think of a more uncool way to die than overdosing on Calpol, but I bet you could do it." She took a sip of water from the bottle next to the bed. "I'm sorry we didn't tell you immediately about Nathan. We shouldn't have piled onto you guys like that. And I know you're close with Nath; you deserved to know."

"Yeah, I guess we are close. Truth be told, I'm not used to having so many friends in their early twenties."

"It's a young crowd here. It feels young. Sometimes *too* young, like I miss speaking to an adult." She made a show of gritting her teeth. "I know I owe you an apology, by the way."

I took another dose of Calpol. "No, you don't. You acted rationally. In your position, I'd have done the same."

"I was in the same position. We had the same information, and I could have gotten you killed. I'm sorry about that."

"It's okay. I was starting to think I was going crazy too."

"I shouldn't have called you psychotic, though." She raised her eyebrows. "In my defense, white men being crazy is a recurring theme."

"I probably was crazy."

"You think?"

"I was woken up by the voice of a girl saying, 'Help me.' For a while, I really thought a ghost might be talking to me. Part of me is still kinda convinced that we're all dead already and this is some kind of purgatory."

She snorted. "Maybe keep the hearing-voices thing to yourself."

"You should know that your diagnosis might have been correct."

"Maybe not. Stranger things have happened than people seeing ghosts or feeling like they're already dead." Another sip of water, and a smile. "Lucky you had Thomas to fight in your corner."

"Stop calling her Thomas. It's unfair."

"I'll stop calling her Thomas when you stop laughing." She reached out and touched Sasha's forehead with the back of her hand. "His temperature is up; I'll have to keep an eye on it. Maybe I can pass him along to another doctor when we reach the city. They probably have more there. They probably have a functioning practice."

"You could take a break."

"A day. I'd take a day. But what else would I do? This is it." She indicated my face. "How are your teeth, by the way?"

Self-consciously, I covered my mouth. "Um, fine."

"I can spot toothache across a crowded room. Also, when you're stressed you grind it, I don't know if you've noticed. Can I take a look?"

"Maybe later. I'll come see you."

A stern look. "Don't be stupid, Jon. Don't leave it. We can't keep losing people. Especially not to avoidable things. No one is going to thank you for putting on a brave face when you're two-thirds through our antibiotics."

"I know."

"I mean it. I'm sick of losing people. I didn't think any of those three were coming back, and then you and Rob . . . That's it. I can't handle us losing more people." She twisted one of her braids around her hands, watching Sasha. Then she bent down and picked her MP3 player off the floor. "Do you want to listen to something?"

"Can I choose?"

"No."

"Well . . . yes, obviously."

She grinned as she scrolled through her songs and handed me one of the earphones. "What do you think you'll do in the city? Town scribe?"

"We're still going to need people like me and Tomi, to record things. We need to preserve knowledge more carefully than before. We can't just rely on the Internet for everything."

"Is that why you've been writing by hand, even though you have a laptop?"

"If we lose electricity altogether, it would be gone. No use to anyone." I shrugged. "Well, it might not be of any use to anyone, period."

A song came on.

I said, "I don't know this one either."

"Of course you don't; it's Run the Jewels." She flipped her hair away from her face just enough to give me an unimpressed look. "I never got the sense that angry rap was your thing."

The hairs on my arms and the back of my neck stood on end, and it occurred to me that our generation would probably never hear an original song produced like this again. We'd have to create our own art, something totally new. I'm sure it will happen, if we all find a way to survive. That's the biggest if, the one I hadn't wanted to consider yet; we were just over two months into the end of the world. The worst—when the loss of the sun killed everything that wasn't being kept alive in greenhouses and the radiation poisoning had reached every corner of the planet—was yet to come.

"My kids are alive," I said suddenly. "I got a message from Nadia."

"Oh my God, Jon!" She gripped my arm. "That's amazing!"

"Yeah, they drove up toward Canada." My heart hurt; it was a physical pain. "They didn't have Internet. Still don't, I think."

"What are you going to do?"

I didn't know what to say.

She gave my arm a gentle squeeze, like she got it. "You think she'll go with you?"

I exhaled for a long time. "I don't know if anyone will. It would be stupid. Especially with the city right there. We could actually have a life."

"But you have to try." Her hand was still on my arm, then she took my hand and interlinked her fingers with mine decisively. "I had a niece. She was four. I would do the same if she'd made it."

There was a brief silence, and the song finished. She started scrolling with her left hand, searching for another.

"Stay for a while, though," she said.

The tips of her fingers were cold, but her palm was warm and her grasp was strong, like someone whose hands knew work.

She added, "You're not going anywhere until I've looked at your teeth."

My whole body ached, but I was able to relax for a while.

I said, "I didn't know you had a niece."

"There's a lot you don't know about me." She smiled.

"I'd like to."

"You seem to be under the impression that that's an accident, and not how I want it."

I said, "Whatever you want."

Sasha twitched in his sleep, and Tania leaned forward to feel his forehead again, taking her hand out of mine.

There was a knock at the door, and Tomi let herself in.

"Hey, loser," she said to me. "Sophia gave me Baloche's laptop and passwords. Wanna get back on it?"

Dylan had switched the hot water and electricity and gas back on, see-ing as it didn't matter how much of the backup supply we used now. Everyone frantically recharged phones and laptops and walked around with headphones on, listening to music. As far as I could tell, everyone in the hotel was packed and ready to go. The atmosphere was hopeful. Dylan and Peter had spent the day drawing up a plan for who and what were leaving in the cars, and when. It was going to take at least half a dozen trips just to transport the people. Over a dozen depending on the amount of possessions and food we took with us. For once, I steered clear of the organization and instead waited to be told what to do.

Tomi and I had spent three hours going through Baloche's laptop, but we weren't able to find anything incriminating. The emails that were in English were solely about the sale of the hotel, and the emails in French we couldn't even read. Tomi took some printed copies to Dylan for translation, and I took the printed copies of the emails written in En-glish back to my room, where I planned to give them a more thorough reading for any leads.

I don't know why, but I had a feeling that we had managed to miss something.

On the way back to my room I stopped in to see Nathan, who was awake now, sitting up, and ravenous.

"I thought I was gonna starve to death," he said, eating his way through a third can of mangoes and a fourth packaged croissant. "Like, that's the most tragic end, isn't it? Apart from being actually eaten. Starving to death; I thought that would be so sad."

He was extremely pale, with dark circles under his eyes. But he was all right. He was here. I'm so happy he's still here.

I asked how he had managed to escape, and he seemed unable to eat for a moment.

"I mean . . . I almost made it out with Dylan and Adam, but one of them grabbed me, like, wrestled me to the ground. I thought I was a goner."

"What happened?"

"I, uh . . . I went for his eyes, and he got off me. Then I ran, but I couldn't find the others. I couldn't even call out for them, because then they would find me again. So I just ran. Then I fucked my ankle and . . . like, hopped."

I almost didn't want to ask. "So, were they? Eating people?"

He sniffed. "I don't think they were gonna eat us. I think they were gonna use us as bait to get you to hand over our guns and food and stuff. But . . . I didn't get the impression they definitely *weren't* gonna eat us. I mean, they had meat; they were eating something. We just hoped it was deer."

We both looked at the window, and I considered how much I was going to miss this place.

"So, what's been up with you?" Nathan asked.

I laughed. "Oh, nothing much. You know, went out to the city, came back, tried not to die a bunch of times."

"Trying not to die is pretty much our full-time job now." He offered me some canned mango, but I waved it away. "What have you got there?"

"Oh." I flipped through the printed emails. "Nothing. Some emails from the owner that Tomi and I are going through. He was selling the hotel to someone, who was apparently staying in Saint-Sion while they negotiated. We were trying to work out if he had anything to do with that girl on the roof, but I don't think he does. I think I might have been on the wrong track this whole time. We don't know anything—not her real name, not her real time of death. Nothing."

Nathan looked around the room. "I didn't know the hotel was being sold. Who would want to buy this place?"

"Some British guy—well, I assume he's British—named . . ." I scanned the pages. "Harold Adler."

In hindsight, I should have made the connection as soon as I saw the name.

He looked at me with inexplicable hurt, an expression that choked me.

He said, "Is that meant to be a joke, mate?"

"Um . . . no." I could barely speak with him looking at me like that. "No, it's . . . here, it's written here in his emails."

Nathan snatched them from my hands, and I saw that he was shaking.

He looked up at me and said, "That's my stepdad. That's his name, and he's not British, he's Australian, because that's Dad."

I sat in my room alone for a long time. Nathan has forbidden me to tell anyone what we've discovered until he decides what he wants to do. It's understandable, I guess. It should be up to him how we proceed with the information.

Peter and Rob are traveling to and from the city with people and supplies. Tomi, Dylan, and I are scheduled to be the last three to leave, after all the food has been taken. The Yobaris and their children were the first to go.

I don't know what's going to happen. I'm not sure I even want to go.

Dylan came to my room at some point in the afternoon and asked if we could talk. He brought the last of his pot, and we shared a joint by my window. It made my tooth hurt a little less, and eased the tension in the air between us.

I asked, "You've worked here a long time. What do you think of what Tomi said? You think this place is cursed?"

He seemed amused by the question, but, to my surprise, he shrugged. "I don't know. Maybe it is. I don't believe in curses, but I believe in . . . you know, what goes around comes around. Maybe too much has gone around in this place. There's only so much one building can hold."

"Karma?"

"Yeah. If anything is cursed, it's just the people who have stayed here. Maybe this is where we start having to try to do things better."

I memorized every part of my room. I read back through every scribbled note, every Post-it I'd ever written to myself as a reminder to "Keep it together." There must have been two dozen of them. I thought about reaching the city, where I would have a house, or an apartment, where I'd be able to use my laptop all the time, listen to music, respond to messages, maybe even stream movies. I couldn't believe how much wider the world felt with Internet access, with all the knowledge.

"Look, speaking of doing things better, I'm sorry I thought you were involved with this girl in the water tank," I said, taking the plunge first after a particularly long drag. "I can't believe I thought you would have done something like . . . that."

"No. I'm sorry for thinking you were crazy. You're not that guy. I was just trying to protect Sophia's privacy. It was her business. She was afraid." He took the joint from me, inhaled, and folded his arms. "I only destroyed the security footage because I thought the police might go through it and arrest her. Or you'd go through it and react badly. I know—stupid, that I was worrying about the police. Back then, I still thought they might be coming, eventually."

"I understand. I shouldn't have gone into your room."

"I shouldn't have let Sophia go into yours." He frowned. "We're a small group. We need to trust one another. I should have led by example, not pointed a gun at you."

"We won't be a small group anymore. There are plenty of people in the city."

"We'll still be a small group."

Maybe he was being optimistic—we didn't exactly all get along—but I like to think that he might be right, that we'll stick together.

He said, "Rob said you had a message from your wife saying your kids are okay. I'm happy for you, man."

"Thanks."

He held out a hand and gripped mine firmly.

"Got me thinking. It seemed so unlikely that your kids had made it. You said they were in a city. Maybe my daughter is still alive."

"Have you sent her any messages?"

"I did, a couple of times when we were out of the hotel. I haven't heard anything back yet, but it took your family this long to contact you. We don't know where the Internet is working. She might be okay." He shook his head. "The idea of leaving, trying to get to Munich, it doesn't make me feel good. But the idea of staying here and never trying to find her makes me feel worse."

I was relieved that he had voiced the same worries, and smiled. "I've been thinking about it. I don't know how I would get to the States. I'd probably die trying to get there, but . . . I don't know."

"You need them to know you tried?" he said.

"Yeah. Exactly that. I don't really matter, in the scheme of things, but I don't want my kids to think I just kicked back and made peace with never seeing them again."

"What would you do, if you were me?" he asked, meeting my eyes. "Would you go?"

"I don't even know if *I'm* going."

"But if you were me?"

I was grinding my teeth again, and a severe spasm flew along my jaw, up to my ear, and toward the base of my neck.

"Are you okay?" Dylan asked.

"Yeah, I'm fine, I'm fine. It's just this tooth." I circled my fingers around the spot, and it felt tender and angry. "In your position, I don't think I'd do anything without a message."

"You really wouldn't?"

"I wouldn't be thinking about trying to get back to the States if I hadn't gotten that message from Nadia. Why would I? I could carry on living here. There's so much we could do in the city. We can start over, be normal. We don't know what's going on out there. And I'm not sure I want to know."

"I'd be sorry to see you leave, Jon. We all would."

"I don't want to go." I couldn't believe how much I meant it. Even as I said it out loud I was hoping he would give me a fail-safe argument for staying. I wanted to be forced to stay so much. "I just feel like I have to. I need to find my family."

"Maybe sit on it. For a week or two. Think it over. Message with your wife. Maybe she'd prefer knowing you were alive here rather than dead trying to reach them."

"Fuck," I said, and I felt like hugging him. "You're right."

He smiled. "And I promise I'm not saying that for selfish reasons. Just because I want you to stay."

Outside, it started to rain. It wasn't falling so much as floating, a weak, discolored mist.

I said, "You know, one of the guards in the city mentioned that the rain is radioactive. We can't drink it."

Dylan stubbed the last of the joint out directly onto my bedside table. "It occurred to me a little while ago, when we were still cutting those tanks open. I just didn't want to admit that the project was useless and that I hadn't thought of it before. The rain is radioactive. Seems so obvious. Made me feel sad, you know."

"I know," I said, and saw a couple of slow tears roll down his cheeks.

LONG LIVE SAINT-SION.

PEACE.

It's a city, but not like any I remember. It's like a myth I heard once, about a word like "community," but I never saw it realized in any part of the society we'd built before.

The first day was devoted to allocating housing. There were a lot of empty properties, left by all the exiles and also the people who had simply fled the area in search of . . . a plane, a boat, somewhere safer? Who knows. It struck me that, in percentage terms, the largest-ever mass migration of humans must have been taking place over the last few months.

We were asked if we were okay with sharing apartments or houses and, if so, with whom.

"People have the right to live on their own," the housing officer had said. "If the space is there."

I said I was okay with sharing, and started to write down various people from the hotel. I wrote down Rob as my first choice, then Nathan, who I haven't had a chance to speak to since the revelation about his father. I considered Adam but hesitated because of his haunting. I also hesitated putting down Dylan, because logic would dictate that he'd share with Tania, and even if he wasn't sharing with Tania, I wasn't sure I wanted to be in their space. I thought about Tomi for a long time, and then put her name down because I felt guilty for the deliberation.

After filling out my form I ran into Tomi outside the building. The waiting area was becoming crowded, with all of us awaiting processing.

"Did you put my name down?" she asked, leaning against the wall.

"Of course." I noticed that the building across the road was a repurposed food store and that it had six armed guards outside. More than the town hall. "Did you put me down?"

"No. No offense. I like living alone."

And I felt stupid for thinking she gave a damn about who I wanted to live with.

She looked up at the orange cloud, which seemed so much lower and more menacing without the shelter of surrounding trees. "Did they give you the pep talk?"

"About what?"

"Not being a troublemaking American about their rules?"

"No. They told me a few times that I couldn't keep a gun, but that was it. Maybe I don't strike them as a *troublemaking* American."

She laughed. Since Tomi got over her illness, she's a lot thinner, and paler. She's taken to wearing her hair in a long braid, and it suits her. When I asked her about it she said it was because she didn't want her hair to get nappy, and also because having your hair loose wasn't conducive for keeping your lines of sight clear in an emergency.

My tooth was hurting again something fierce. For a while I had dared to think it was getting better, but the pain had gotten so much worse in the last couple of days. I suspected that maybe the stress had been staving off some of the effects. The human body is weird like that. When you relax for a moment, that's when the physical burnout catches up with you.

The longer we stood out there, the more I got the sense that there was something she wanted to say.

I waited for it.

"Are you leaving?" she asked finally, fiddling with her braid. "Dylan said you got a message from your wife."

She said "wife" quietly, like it was a curse word.

"I don't know," I replied truthfully.

"You know, to even get close to the Portuguese coast we'll have to travel through blast zones."

"Maybe I can get a plane from somewhere closer."

"What, and fly it?"

"I . . . What do you mean, '*we'll* have to travel'?"

"If you really are deranged enough to try to get back to America, you bet I'm coming with you."

"That's . . . Why?"

She shrugged. "It's my home too. And besides, what would you do without me?"

"You raise a good point." I smiled a little, and even that small flex of muscles felt painful. "Really, you'd come with me? Even with moving into the city and . . . well, you could have a life again?"

"Existing isn't everything."

I was shocked that the most pragmatic person here would do something so obviously stupid on my account, but, as ever, the knowledge that she was on my side made me feel safer.

"I'm not even sure I'm going to go," I said, to make everything feel less finalized. "You're right, it is a crazy idea."

"But if you even think of going by boat, I'm definitely not coming, because I'm scared of the sea."

"Why are you scared of the sea?"

"Well, not the sea. I can swim and stuff. I'm scared of the depth, the . . . There's a word for it, megalohydrothalassophobia. Specifically, it means a fear of large things in water. So it's not really a fear of the sea, it's a fear of not knowing what's out there. It's the idea of floating somewhere where you can't see land or anything you can grab on to, in an environment you can't navigate, and where you don't know what's below you. But it could be anything, and it could be so massive, so huge, that it could swallow you whole and you wouldn't even have the perspective to see it coming. All of a sudden, the space below you would get dark, maybe for miles, and you can't see it because you're floating there, no control; you can't swim away and you're struggling for air, just trying to stay afloat and keep your head up, and then, just like that, something the size of a road, or a city, has swallowed you up."

I shuddered and surreptitiously checked my new phone, but I had no new messages.

"Hey, I'm sorry you never got to find out what happened to that girl," Tomi said.

I looked at her for a long time, glancing sideways once at the entrance doors to make sure they were shut. Maybe it wasn't my secret to tell, but she deserved to know. She had helped me from the start. If anyone was going to carry on helping me, it was Tomi.

She shifted awkwardly. "Why are you looking at me like that?"

I took a breath. "I've got a really weird story to tell you about Nathan."

Whoever you are, I feel like I haven't told you everything, or at least—by omission—I haven't been entirely truthful about the kind of man I am. I think I owe it to Nadia to talk about what happened before I left, because I shouldn't have been here, and I feel like a hypocrite agonizing about finding my way back to my family when I remember being so desperate to leave them.

The night before I left, I came downstairs at about nine, after making sure both girls were still in bed, and Nadia was sitting half staring at the TV and half staring at her laptop screen. There had been another day of marches—in New York, San Francisco, DC, Austin, St. Louis; all over—but we hadn't gone to this one because there were only so many marches you could go to.

The banners being shown on TV were all the same:

STOP DOOMSDAY

END THE NUCLEAR ARMS RACE

That kind of thing.

I had poured myself a glass of wine while bitching about one of Marion's teachers, who was a fucking fascist, and I noticed that Nadia was sitting silently on the couch. I didn't realize how silently until I glanced at her laptop and saw that she was logged in to my email.

"What are you looking at?"

"Oh, I was just . . ." She couldn't be bothered to think of an excuse, so she stood up and turned the TV off. "You have a few emails that seem really urgent. You should reply to them."

It felt like there hadn't been enough air in the room for a while. Speaking to her was like navigating turbulence. A lot of what I tried to say was caught in dead air and plummeted, didn't even make it across the space.

I think I said something like, "Look, just wait . . ."

She walked into the kitchen, leaving me there.

I followed her in order to finish my sentence, but her gaze was set firmly on the wine pouring from bottle to glass.

"Look, I've told her to stop, I've told her it's inappropriate—"

She raised a hand to stop me and took a gulp of wine. But she didn't say anything.

"Nadia, come on, you can't just—"

"Can't just *what*?" Another gulp of wine, pouring more. "You know, the funny thing is I'd actually convinced myself that you wouldn't do this again, which was pretty stupid of me, wasn't it, because you're just this black hole of ego, and if one woman looks away from you for a second, you have to find two more. I'm sure it makes you feel really smart, only sleeping with twenty-year-olds, *really* important. You know, I'm amazed you still have a job—"

"I can't talk to you like this, when you're turning it into something it's not."

"What is it, Jon?" She put her hand on her hip. "Why is your compulsive need to fuck any student who smiles your way so much more special than any other man's?"

"I'm not saying I'm special, I'm saying . . ." And I thought an end to that sentence would become apparent to me, but it didn't, and she caught her breath.

The week before, I had accompanied her to one of the antinuclear marches. We had stopped taking the kids after the last one, when we realized the cops were arriving in riot gear. Nadia was reporting live, posting footage to her Twitter feed. I wanted to back away from the front of the march, but Nadia had wanted to get close enough to hear the speeches. She promised we'd leave soon after. She weaved her way out of the middle of the road to the outskirts, where it was slightly less crowded. I followed her, worrying, like I always did. When I caught up with her again, she had her phone raised and was filming a cop in a shouting match with a couple of protestors. They were young black kids, obviously college students, and Nadia had started filming without a word, and then suddenly the cop turned away from the kids and he was shouting at her, "You can't film, ma'am," and then he snatched her phone, holding her at arm's length with his other hand, in which he was holding a baton. His pale face was taut with threat. I hurried to catch up and saw the students yelling at the cop to leave her alone, and Nadia was yelling at the cop to give her phone back because she was a journalist. Then I reached them and put myself between the cop and my wife and said something like, "Hey, don't touch my wife!" and he punched me in the side of the head. I lost a pair of glasses as the crowd started to scatter and break.

When the footage made it onto Nadia's social media, one of Marion's teachers had remarked that maybe I had deserved to get hit by a cop, if we were going to be protesting against the government in public like that.

That was the last time, before I left, I was able to remember how much I loved Nadia. If you don't make the decision to love, every day, it's an easy thing to forget. But that cop could have shot me, and my instincts would still have been the same. Obviously, it didn't matter if I was punched in the side of the head, or shot. She was my wife.

Nadia said, "Wow. You can't even be bothered to think of anything."

Taking the bottle of red with her, she sidestepped me and walked back into the living room, and as I turned to go after her I saw Ruth standing in the doorway, and the expression on her face was exactly the same as Nadia's, but it hurt so much more. She had already been let down by one father. Now she had been let down by another.

"Wait. Wait!"

She bolted upstairs.

I almost threw my glass down and reached the landing just in time for her bedroom door to slam shut.

"Ruth, that wasn't what it sounded like!"

"Go away!"

I could tell that she was sitting on the floor with her back against the door.

Not wanting to barge in, or too afraid to, I stood outside as if the door were locked and said, "Come on, open the door, that wasn't what you thought you heard."

"You're such a liar!" she yelled. "Leave me alone. You're always lying!"

I couldn't go into the room and I couldn't go back downstairs, so I stood on the landing for a long time, terrified of moving in either direction.

The following day, Nadia left a cup of coffee on the sideboard for me, and I noticed that I'd spilled red wine onto the wooden countertop and it had stained.

She said, as I put my suitcase in the hallway and busied myself with searching for my passport and my boarding passes, "Do you really think leaving right now is the best thing for us?"

I honestly don't remember what I said, but I certainly remember thinking, *We'll talk when I get back. I can deal with this when I get back.*

I might have even believed that at the time, when I'd been certain that I had time.

It was quiet this morning when we crossed the city on foot, save for the uneven clack of Nathan's crutch on the pavement and my own footsteps vanishing over the low bungalows of suburbia. I had a hunch about what we were going to find.

Yesterday, as we were being processed, I had asked after Albert Polor and was told that the reclusive man was something of a town preacher. They had verified his name using a boarding pass. If you made an appointment and had something to barter, he offered to tell your future. *A curious occupation now*, I thought. *Aren't all our futures inextricably linked?* Apparently, they had always been.

Tomi had asked to come, but I told her to stay in bed. Partly because I hadn't wanted Nathan to know that I'd told her anything, and partly for plausible deniability.

We found Albert Polor's house, next door to a two-story cottage whose front had been almost entirely boarded up. Something was spray-painted across the wood in white, and I asked Nathan what it said.

He stopped and rubbed his underarm, which was becoming sore. "Coming back."

We observed the house we had come to find. The lawn was remarkably well maintained. There were plant pots outside, painted various colors, but of course nothing was growing in them. No lights were on.

"He probably ran," Nathan said, leaning a little against me. "If he heard a load of people from the hotel had arrived . . . Then what?"

"Then we go home."

He nodded, like that made a lot of sense, and we both approached the front door. Nathan put his hand upon it, then knocked firmly four times.

Nothing happened.

I thought that he probably had run.

Nathan had just let out the breath that he had been holding when we heard locks turning and the door opened.

This man stood there, in loose-fitting formal pants and a white shirt with the sleeves rolled up, with bare feet and a watery-eyed smile. He had liberal amounts of gray hair and the loose jowls of a man in his late fifties who had once had a strong, angular jawline.

Nathan didn't say anything, and for a second I was worried that it wasn't him.

But then the man calling himself Albert Polor smiled even wider, opened his door even wider, and said, "I knew it would take you a while, but I knew you'd be coming."

It looked like he had been collecting lamps, though only one or two of them were switched on, I suppose to conserve electricity. It had the appearance of a house that had once belonged to an elderly person, and it smelled like one. It also smelled like dog, and baking. There was a fluffy white Samoyed in the kitchen behind a childproof gate.

The man calling himself Albert Polor—who was really Harold Adler—invited us to sit at his narrow dining table while he made us a pot of tea. Neither of us had said anything since he opened the door to us. We waited in silence. I watched the cross on the wall and tried to acclimatize to my altered expectations of how this encounter was going to go. I had envisioned chasing a fugitive back into the woods, catching up with him, and beating him to death with my bare fists, or maybe drowning him, which would have been some poetic justice.

But we waited until he returned with green tea, and I started drinking it while it was still scalding hot because I needed something to occupy my hands.

Harold said, "I imagine you have a lot of questions."

"You think, *Dad*? How long have you been here?"

"In this house, just over two months."

"No, here!" Nathan made a more expansive, more violent gesture.

"I was staying for a while in a guesthouse, a place overlooking the square. I must have been there about two weeks while negotiating the sale of the hotel with Baloche." A troubled expression came over his face as he blew steam from the top of his mug. "I heard he didn't make it."

"Why would you want to buy it?" I asked.

"You felt that it's special," he replied. "It was where I woke up. If I needed an incentive to rebuild my life, it was to return there."

"It's not special," Nathan muttered. "You had a hallucination and went crazy. That's how I remember it."

Putting his tea down, he reached across the table and Nathan recoiled, but it didn't seem to faze Harold as his arm remained, palm upward, on the tabletop. "I knew you were going to find your way. You knew it was time to make the journey."

"We *had* to make the journey, Dad; we didn't have enough food to last the winter."

"I mean to the hotel. You got here in time."

"In time for what?"

"The end."

I thought Nathan was going to throw the tea in his face.

"Just stop this insane crap. I'm not gonna just sit here and listen to it like I did when I was thirteen. You need to tell me what the fuck actually happened."

"You know what happened."

"To the girl we found in the water tank! That's why you're still hiding out here, right? Why you're using some dead professor's name and pretending to be, what, a *priest* now?"

"Oh." A sip of tea, and he retracted his hand. "Well, what would you like to know?"

"Christ," Nathan exclaimed, exactly like a son.

"Did you kill her?" I asked in a much calmer tone than I'd anticipated.

"If you want to look at it in the most simplistic way, then yes, I did kill her. But this wasn't a sacrifice made lightly. At the end, even she knew I was only doing what needed to be done."

"Who was she?" Nathan asked.

"I don't know her name, if that's what you're asking. She had separated herself from her parents and was waiting at the side of the road, barely three streets from here. I saw that, even in the commotion, the panic, she was totally calm. She was waiting for me, so I stopped and picked her up."

And I tasted the memory, the free cookies, and looking left and seeing the arrival of a car at the front of the hotel. The only car arriving, going against the tide.

"What do you mean, you did what needed to be done?"

Harold looked at me, and I felt the assessment like the cold hands of a medical examination. Only holy men can look at a person like that, with an expression gilded with serenity and understanding while the depths are searched for your weakness, your purpose, the reason you've ended up at their altar, and how they might keep you there, kneeling.

"Jon," he said, as if he were taking great care to remember my name. "You're a man of God, I can feel it. You know the only thing that has ever saved us, the only thing that will continue to save us, is the sacrifice of the innocent. You pretend you don't understand, but you do. You listened to the voice telling you that it was time to make the trip."

I coughed and said, "I was attending a conference."

"You killed that girl, Dad? Is this where all the crazy went? You vanish for ten years after having a bad acid trip and then sacrifice a girl to save the world?" Nathan spread his hands.

"How did you kill her?" I interjected, unable to contain myself, even though this wasn't about me.

"I didn't want her to suffer, you must understand that. I gave her an overdose of sleeping pills before she went into the water. Nothing ceremonial; there wasn't time for that. It wasn't the perfect sacrifice, but I wasn't going to throw her into the tank to drown. I'm not a monster."

"What do you mean, there wasn't time?" I had started scratching the arms of my chair. "Time for what?"

"To save us."

"Where did you get the pills?"

"Shut *up!*" Nathan yelled at me. "Sorry, mate, but shut the fuck up! Just stop talking *for once!* And *wow.*" He laughed, turning back to Harold. "Save us? Really? How'd that work out for you? How saved do you feel right now?"

"We are."

"No! No, you can't just say we survived because you went full mental, you can't just look at the sun rising in the morning and be like, 'I did that.' That's not how anything works!"

"The people who were ready to be saved were saved. The pure of heart and soul were saved. Those who drank the holy water were saved. Every piece of Scripture pertaining to the great judgment foretold the same thing."

"Then why are *you* still here?" Nathan snarled across the table. "If *Thou shalt not murder* and all that crap, why are you still here?"

Harold smiled, but he smiled at me first. "I've seen my own death, just like I saw my own journey. This sacrifice, it wasn't just hers. It was mine too. I didn't say I'd dwell here long."

"That why you're using a fake name? Hope death gets the wrong house?" Nathan snapped, as a few tears ran from his eyes.

A pause. "Maybe. Maybe I did think that."

I felt trapped in my chair by conversation, with absolutely no idea how to proceed. There he was, the man I'd been searching for. Now that he was in front of me, I didn't know what to do. I put my mug of tea down, now empty.

The silence went on long enough that I dared to speak again.

"You've seen your own death. So you can see the future?" I asked.

He replied, "What do you have? I take donations."

As if he were snapping out of a trance, Nathan rubbed his eyes and exclaimed, "Jon, this is fucked."

"No, I'll do it. Tell me." I took the last pieces of Sophia's candy out of my pocket, still wrapped in paper, and slid them across the table. There were only about three left. "Tell me my future."

He accepted them and promptly took them into the kitchen, where the white dog started yapping at the sight of its owner.

In the time he was gone, Nathan and I exchanged a look. We hadn't spoken about what we were going to do. Report him to the town authorities and hope he made the same confession to them? Hope it was taken seriously without evidence, a name, or even a body? The only other alternative was murdering a man in his own house, without the impersonal ease of a firearm, and facing almost certain exile.

Maybe the reason Harold was so calm was because he knew that there was nothing we could do.

Harold brought a large empty fish tank back into the dining room and proceeded to fill it with a hosepipe attached to one of the kitchen faucets.

I was afraid to ask, so Nathan did.

"What's that for?"

"Look into the water used to baptize a man, and his sins will be revealed to you. And his future." He ate one of the candies, and then went to turn the faucet off. "Son, did you want to go first?"

"No, thanks."

"I'll do it," I said, taking my glasses off.

"You've been baptized before." Harold held out an arm. "Come."

Looking back, I don't know why I wanted it. I knew that he could have been about to drown me, but I was now no longer entirely convinced that I was going to die. *Fuck it*, I thought. *Tell me my future. Convince me there is one. Please, convince me there is one.*

I placed both hands on the table and looked down into the fish tank.

Nathan pushed his seat away from us, watching with inert horror.

Harold said, rolling his sleeves up even farther, "Remember, you'll only be allowed to see what you're prepared to see. Whatever you want to see, you have to be prepared to release it into the water."

"How do I do that?"

"You made it here because what you saw in the water showed you your path. I'm sure you'll be fine."

I stared at him. He stared back.

"Are you ready?" he asked.

I nodded, and he placed both hands on my shoulders, sending a shudder down my back.

"I now baptize you, in the name of the Father, the S—"

Everything else was lost, as my head was plunged into the freezing water. I attempted to brace myself against the edges of the tank, but it was as if an elbow was on my neck. I was leaning too far forward. I had no leverage, and suddenly no breath. I exhaled all the oxygen in my lungs, and then it was as if I were being throttled by my own organs. My chest was compressing, my throat full of water. I opened my eyes, and it was so much darker than I'd expected.

I saw the last time I'd been totally submerged in water, feeling around for the girl's yellow dress, the girl who no longer had a name but who had led me here. I wondered if I was experiencing her last moments, frame for frame. I opened my mouth to yell, inhaled water, and lurched upward as the pressure on my shoulders ceased.

The weak light of the one or two lamps was blinding in that moment, as I exploded out of the water and caught my breath, sinking forward against the table and sending water cascading over it onto the floor.

Harold had my right arm and shoulder in a vise grip as I gasped and spat water, both hunkered down over the table like we were wrestling, or simply embracing.

"I had my moments of doubt, like any man," Harold said, raising his voice over my struggle for breath, our faces inches apart. "But only God would send such a worthy adversary to my door. To show my gratitude, I will tell you what you need to know."

I tried to pull away, but he dragged me in even closer and said right into my ear, "You're conflicted, but you know your place is here now. Your destiny isn't to go backward. Listen to me, Jon: thank you for helping my son find my door. You need to know that they're free. They don't *want* you to come back!"

There was a dull smack, like a car hitting a child, and I recoiled out of his grasp and onto the floor. I reached out but couldn't find my glasses. The dog was barking, a shrill din that filled the whole room. It was all I could hear. I rubbed my eyes and continued to snatch oxygen out of the air, inhaling and exhaling raggedly, while across the table I saw Nathan raising the metal crutch above his head and bringing it down, over and over.

I was still coughing, my chest aching as it fought for life, to keep inhaling and exhaling, and all I could hear was the dog as I watched Nathan beat his father to death in the pool of water.

I took the Samoyed with us, and we walked back slowly with his leash wrapped around my left wrist. He seemed extremely unbothered by the murder of his owner. Either Harold wasn't this dog's original owner, or our dogs have always been more fickle than we liked to believe.

Nathan used me for support, having left the crutch on the floor in the dining room.

We both left a trail of water behind us, and, unsurprisingly, we made it only about two blocks before a patrol car picked us up. Because we looked like a man who had almost been drowned and a man who had just committed a murder and two men who had stolen a dog.

Nathan didn't let me take the fall for anything. He confessed and wrote a statement, and I was released, but he wasn't. When they let me go they asked why I had taken the dog, and I said I hadn't wanted the dog to start eating the body, so they let me take the Samoyed back to the house that I was now sharing with Rob. They also said that I have to return tomorrow to make my own statement but should go to the hospital first to have my tooth looked at, as the woman who picked us up noticed that I couldn't stop rubbing my jaw.

I let myself into the house, and Tomi—who had been waiting in the living room—asked me what the hell had happened, and "What's with the dog?"

I waved her away, handed her the leash, and said I needed to wash and change my clothes. I then locked myself in the bathroom upstairs with the water running and wondered what had just happened. I struggled to look at my reflection for long, as I could see that my jaw looked slightly inflamed and the visual symptom was somehow more worrying than the daily pain I've been dealing with. Instead, I sat down in the bath with the hot water running and put my phone on the side of the tub.

They don't want you to come back!

I ducked under the surface of the water and held my breath, hoping I'd be shown something, or that the pain in my jaw would lessen, at the very least. But all I heard was the roar of the faucets and the rattle of bolts.

I broke the surface and looked toward the door, but there were no bolts here. Just a single twistable lock.

Obviously, this insane man hadn't saved the world by sacrificing an innocent girl on the roof of the place where he had hallucinated pure evil crawling out of his chest. Obviously. Perhaps the thing we do have to consider, which he has caused me to think about, is that the world didn't end. If the world had ended, we wouldn't still be here, surviving, grieving, and writing about it day by day. The end of the world is a fairly comforting concept, because—in theory—we wouldn't have to survive it. Maybe what's been fucking us up, more than anything, hasn't been finding a way to cope with the world ending but finding a way to cope with the fact that it didn't.

An ending is easy. This terminal waking up, morning after morning, isn't easy. Repairing and rebuilding isn't easy either. I think that's why I've been so angry, so desperate to believe Adam's paranoid theory about purgatory, why I wanted to believe that the girl in the water tank had died for a more important reason than men's continued violence.

Instead of a conclusion, we've been offered nothing but more life.

I don't know how to come to terms with that.

A message arrived in my Twitter inbox, and I sat up to read it, wiping mist off my screen.

Nadia had replied to my message, and it said: "Please don't try to come back."

Jon Keller has not added to this record for a few days due to a severe infection in his jaw, caused by an untreated problem with his tooth, which has since been removed. It is unclear at this time if he will recover.

For the most part, the author's account is accurate, if at times flawed. Any issues with particular sections of this text have been reflected in my account, where, occasionally, our versions of events differ. However, regardless of whether he continues to add to these records or not, I've decided to submit the entire document as evidence for the defense of Nathan Chapman-Adler.

When they release the account back to me, I will attach it here, labeled Appendix A, for accuracy and completeness.

Tomisen Harkaway

ABOUT THE AUTHOR

Hanna Jameson is the author of the London Underground mystery series, the first of which—*Something You Are*—was nominated for a Crime Writers' Association Dagger Award. She lives in London.